ABOUT THE AUTHOR

From an early age, Martin was enchanted with old movies from Hollywood's golden era—from the dawn of the talkies in the late 1920s to the close of the studio system in the late 1950s—and has spent many a happy hour watching the likes of Garland, Gable, Crawford, Garbo, Grant, Miller, Kelly, Astaire, Rogers, Turner, and Welles go through their paces.

It felt inevitable that he would someday end up writing about them.

Originally from Melbourne, Australia, Martin moved to Los Angeles in the mid-90s where he now works as a writer, blogger, webmaster, and tour guide.

This book is dedicated to

Robert Collier

because when old friends meet for the first time
this is how it's supposed to feel.

ISBN-13: 978-1480044777

ISBN-10: 1480044776

DISCLAIMER

This is a work of fiction. Names, characters, places and incidents are either the product of the author's imagination or are used fictitiously. Any resemblance to actual persons, places and incidents, events or locales is purely coincidental. The sole exception are those dead people who are depicted as fictional characters, and dead people should be forever grateful that someone cares enough to spell their names correctly.

THE TROUBLE WITH SCARLETT

a novel

by

Martin Turnbull

Book Two of the *Garden of Allah* novels

Also by Martin Turnbull

Book One of the *Garden of Allah* novels

The Garden on Sunset

Right before talking pictures slug Tinsel Town in the jaw, a luminous silent screen star converts her private estate into the Garden of Allah Hotel. The lush grounds soon become a haven for Hollywood hopefuls to meet, drink, and revel through the night. George Cukor is in the pool, Tallulah Bankhead is at the bar, and Scott Fitzgerald is sneaking off to a bungalow with Sheilah Graham while Madame Alla Nazimova keeps watch behind her lace curtains.

But the real story of the Garden of Allah begins with its first few residents, three kids on the brink of something big. Nobody gets a free pass in Hollywood, but a room at the Garden on Sunset can get your foot in the door.

CHAPTER 1

Kathryn Massey let the cardboard box slide out of her arms and onto the mottled linoleum, where it landed with a thud. She turned around and addressed her apple-cheeked pal standing in the doorway. "What the hell was in this?" she asked him. "Bowling balls?"

The guy dropped his suitcases, walked over to the box, and lifted out a shiny Remington typewriter. "It's a villa-warming present from Robert Benchley and Dorothy Parker." He broke out into a giddy grin she hadn't seen in ages. "I can't believe either of them are my neighbors now, let alone both of them. Benchley's in the villa next door, and Dottie's right below me!"

Kathryn smiled back at her friend and gazed around the villa. The afternoon sun filtered through the elm tree outside the open window, filling the living room with warmth and the scent of jasmine from across the pool.

"Well then, Mr. Marcus Adler," she said, planting her hands on her hips, "let me be the first to officially welcome you to your new home at the Garden of Allah's villa number twenty-three. I trust you and Mr. Remington will be very happy."

"It's so bright in here!" Marcus said, setting the typewriter on his new dining table. He took a look around. "I can scarcely believe all this space is mine."

"No more dark little rooms for you, mister."

"Quite frankly, I can scarcely believe anything about my life these days."

Kathryn had heard that one hit movie could change a person's life, but she'd never witnessed it firsthand before now. She'd been sitting next to Marcus at Grauman's Chinese holding his hand when the credit for *Return to Sender*, a Marion Davies vehicle, flashed up on the screen: *WRITTEN BY ROBERT MCNULTY.* He'd let out a raw groan and clamped her hand in his fist hard enough to just about pop her knuckle. It didn't take Kathryn long to figure out what had happened. McNulty was Marcus' boss, and the fink had pilfered his credit when he saw what a socko screenplay Marcus had turned in. But to her credit, Marion Davies had squared things off with W.R. Hearst, and Marcus' salary jumped from seventy-five dollars a month to a hundred and fifty a week. Goodbye, horrible dark little room, hello, sun-drenched villa.

The place had exactly the same layout as the one Kathryn shared with her roommate Gwendolyn, but the girls' was painted pale coral and dotted with vases of flowers. Here, the stark white walls, shelves filled with books like *Drums Along the Mohawk* and *Northwest Passage*, and that sturdy typewriter already made it feel like Marcus' place. Kathryn hugged her friend. "I never doubted for a second that you'd succeed."

"I got my first new paycheck yesterday," he said. "Wouldn't you know it? I start making decent money the same month they introduce the income tax. Maybe Hearst is right. Income tax is a Commie plot and we should all refuse to pay it."

"At least y'all earn enough to have to pay income tax." Gwendolyn Brick appeared in the doorway with a bottle of 7-Up in each hand. The sun shone through her honey-blonde hair and onto her lightly tanned shoulders. How a movie studio hadn't snapped her up was a mystery to Kathryn. "It ain't champagne, but it's all we got."

"As long as there are bubbles." Marcus waved her into his sunny, tiny kitchen. They were clinking tumblers when a theatrical voice filled the place.

"Vive la villa twenty-three, bébé!"

The three of them turned to find George Cukor standing in the doorway holding an enormous bottle of Dom Perignon. When he saw Marcus was not alone, he apologized with an endearing blush.

It had been months since that crazy night Kathryn and Marcus ran all over Los Angeles trying to bail out poor George before the city's sleazebag journalists started their nightly trawl through the lockups in search of juicy stories. Marcus had never mentioned it again, so Kathryn had decided to behave as though nothing had happened.

"A housewarming gift!" she exclaimed. "How thoughtful!"

George looked around at the boxes. "That's today?"

"So if the bubbly isn't a housewarming present . . . ?"

George's eyes smiled through his wire-framed spectacles but he said nothing more until Marcus had conjured four champagne flutes. George filled them all and asked everyone to raise their glasses. "At the risk of sounding revoltingly self-serving," he said with a smile so wide it threatened to split his face in two, "here's to me!"

"What's the occasion?" Gwendolyn asked. She peered at her champagne but didn't take a sip. Her history with booze wasn't pretty. Kathryn wondered for a moment if Gwendolyn was going to offend MGM's best director by not partaking of his deliciously expensive champagne.

George drew in a deep breath. "Mr. David O. Selznick has just bought the film rights to *Gone with the Wind*, and he's asked me to direct."

"Holy crapoly!" Marcus exclaimed, clapping a hand on his friend's shoulder.

"That's huge!" Gwendolyn said, and took her first sip. "I read the other day that book will have sold half a million copies by the end of the year."

Kathryn leaned toward George and hinted a smile. "So, Mr. Cukor . . . ?"

George returned her grin. "Yes, Miss Massey . . . ?"

"Excuse me for being nosy, but, you know, professional curiosity and all that. Care to share with us who you see as Scarlett O'Hara?"

"You might want to tell your former boss that she's a front runner."

Kathryn bit into her top lip. Anything connected to *Gone with the Wind* was big news these days, but she could use none of this information in her column. Only one woman in Hollywood could do that: Louella Parsons.

Louella Parsons ruled the world of Hollywood gossip like a barely-literate Borgia and had managed to engineer for herself an unimaginable coup: forty-eight hours of exclusivity on all scoops. The fact that she wrote for the all-powerful William Randolph Hearst probably had something to do with that. So why then, Kathryn wondered, was George Cukor throwing around this precious information like yesterday's confetti?

"Oh!" George snapped his head around to face Kathryn's doe-eyed roommate. "I've just put two and two together. You must be Gwendolyn. The girl with the brooch."

Without pawning Gwendolyn's diamond brooch, a gift from one of her admirers, Marcus and Kathryn would never have made George's bail that night.

George blanched. "I never properly thanked you—either of you—for what you did that night. I've been terribly remiss."

Kathryn gave a discreet shrug. "Some sleeping dogs are better left alone," she said.

But she was already mentally writing her headline. "So," she asked him, "when are you sharing your news with Louella?"

George's face soured. "Miss Louella Parsons and I are not currently on speaking terms. This week, she barged onto the set of *Camille* uninvited and ruined one of Garbo's most difficult scenes. The whole thing upset Garbo so much that she flung her script at Louella, but it hit an antique lamp and shattered the damn thing. Then Garbo stormed out and went home. A complete waste of an afternoon. I was absolutely furious!"

Kathryn tried to picture the reserved, composed Greta Garbo erupting like an opera diva. Then George gave her a sly smile and laid a gentle hand on her arm. "My dear, this onc is all yours."

Kathryn heard her friends softly gasp as she held the director's unblinking gaze. You can't possibly mean what I think you mean, she thought. That would be inconceivable.

She laid her hand on top of his and squeezed it gently. "This one?"

"Selznick has acquired the rights and signed me on as director. It's all yours for the next twenty-four hours."

Kathryn's throat went dry. She looked down at her empty glass. "Louella always gets the scoops first."

The director's eyes gleamed. "Apparently not always."

* * *

It was well after eleven by the time Kathryn got the night guard to let her into the *Hollywood Reporter*. The newsroom was deserted; rows of empty desks were lined up in the shadows like tombstones, and she had only the faint glow of the streetlights to guide her. She felt her way to her desk and flicked on her lamp. It lit her silent typewriter in a solitary circle.

She had until midnight for the morning edition to be put to bed. Everything was supposed to go through the paper's owner, but Billy Wilkerson hadn't answered when she called him at home and at the club. The course of history, she decided, would have to change without his approval.

She slid a fresh sheet of paper into her typewriter.

Selznick Nabs GWTW Screen Rights, Taps Cukor As Director

Considering Tallulah Bankhead as Scarlett

by Kathryn Massey

Her fingers recoiled from the keys. You can't do this, she told herself. It was idiotic to think she could get away with breaking the unbreakable rule; Louella would have her guts for garters. And the most powerful man in the world was the last person she wanted as an enemy.

She reread what she had written, then pulled the sheet of paper out of the typewriter. "You were a nice dream while you lasted," she told it.

A crash of glass splintered the silence and Kathryn poked her head into the corridor. The light was now on at the far end.

"Hello? Anyone there?"

Wilkerson's office door was slightly ajar and a slice of light etched the parquet floor. As she drew closer, she could hear heavy breathing. The last thing she wanted to do was walk in on her boss making out with someone—especially if that someone wasn't his wife. But when she heard Wilkerson yell "JESUS CHRIST!" she decided he was in pain.

She pushed his office door open and peeked inside. Her elegant boss was sitting cross-legged on the floor with one hand bunched around the other. Blood was seeping out between his fingers.

"Mr. Wilkerson! Are you all right?"

He didn't register surprise that anyone was there. "You got a handkerchief?"

"In my purse. I'll go get— "

"Breast pocket." He jutted his head toward the suit jacket slung over the back of his chair. Kathryn rounded her boss' desk and pulled out a linen handkerchief. It wasn't until she knelt down to tie it around his finger that she smelled the pall of whiskey hanging over him.

"Careful," he said. "Broken glass."

Thick shards of what had been a bottle of Royal Crest lay scattered around him.

"Had a bit of an accident?" Kathryn asked, winding Wilkerson's handkerchief around his index finger, which had a long, nasty gash. "I think this might need stitches."

"Forget it," he mumbled. "I deserve to bleed to death."

She helped him stand up. "Bleed to death?" she asked, fashioning the ends of the handkerchief into a knot. "Now you're just being melodramatic."

Wilkerson parked his backside against the edge of his desk and slumped over his bloody finger, nursing it with his other hand. He was stony with silence for a moment or two, then mumbled something that sounded like "Sananee . . ."

"Sana . . . what?"

"Say, what are you doing here, anyway?"

"I came across a big scoop. Or at least I thought so, but it didn't check out."

He raised his head slowly and looked at her for the first time. His eyes were bloodshot and she could tell he hadn't been listening.

"Santa Anita," he said, low and hoarse.

It took a moment for the meaning of those two words to sink in. "You lost a stack of dough at the racetrack? Can't have been the first time. If you don't mind me saying, Mr. Wilkerson, you smell like a whiskey factory. Perhaps you ought to think about going ho—"

"It wasn't just a stack o' dough." Wilkerson's eyes shifted away from her. "It was the whole goddamned payroll."

Kathryn felt her jaw drop as a volley of questions pelted her mind.

Gambled the payroll away—*the whole thing?* Am I the only one who knows? Will he remember this when he sobers up? Should I tell someone? Why is he telling me?

The urge to slap her boss consumed Kathryn like a brushfire. She crossed her arms and anchored them there. "All of it?"

Wilkerson's head hung low. "There's nothing you can say to me that I ain't already said a hundred times tonight. I'm a bastard and deserve to be shot. My staff's gonna walk out on me, and they should. They deserve a boss who'll look after them. Everything I've worked so hard for, everything the *Hollywood Reporter* stands for will be *pfffft*." He looked up at her, creasing his sweaty brow. "What did you say about a scoop?"

"It's not important."

"It was important enough for you to come into the office at midnight."

"I *thought* it was," she corrected him. "But on reflection, it'll cause more complication than it's worth. So don't worry about it. You should think about getting to a hospital. That cut—"

"Tell me."

"Really, Mr. Wilkerson, I don't—"

"Come on, out with it and let me be the judge."

She shifted her weight from one foot to the other as she related the *Gone with the Wind* news. Wilkerson's eyes grew to saucers and his smile stretched from ear to ear. "How's your source?"

"The horse's mouth."

"Selznick himself?"

"One of the horses in the stall next door," she conceded.

"Oh boy, is that old nag going to be pissed when she reads the morning edition!"

"We can't publish this," Kathryn told him. "You know the rule. We break it at our mortal peril."

Wilkerson's dark eyes narrowed and a crafty smirk played on his face. "You telling me you don't have the gumption to play with the big boys? Kathryn Massey, I'm surprised at you. I thought you were made of sterner stuff."

"Me and my sterner stuff are just fine, thank you very much, but somebody in this room has to be sensible. Let us not forget, you're down an entire payroll."

"William Randolph Hearst can go screw himself. This is what we've been waiting for. Why wouldn't we print this?"

He started to bunch his hands into fists but it loosened Kathryn's handiwork and he started to bleed again. When she went to retie the makeshift bandage, he brushed her away. She grabbed his hand anyway and pulled it toward her, tightening the handkerchief while she kept him firmly in her gaze.

"We'll be crossing a line here, Mr. Wilkerson. Outscooping Parsons will unleash the four horsemen of the apocalypse, followed by the seven plagues, the hounds of the Baskervilles, and the entire contents of Pandora's box. There'll be no going back."

Wilkerson drew in a deep breath. "GO!" He pushed her toward the door. "I'll get the print room to hold the front page. I promised it to DeMille, but he can bite my ass."

Kathryn stood at his office door and stared at her boss, willing him to change his mind. He stared back at her. "What now?" he demanded.

"This is insane. You're drunk. This cannot possibly end well."

He leaned over his desk and jutted out his chin. "I've got the guts if you want the glory."

It was quite possibly the only thing Billy Wilkerson could have said to make her change her mind. Oh my God, Kathryn thought, he's actually going to let me do this. He trusts me. *He trusts me.* She looked at her watch; it was twelve minutes to midnight. "Is there even going to be a *Hollywood Reporter* tomorrow?"

He nodded.

"What are you going to do about the payroll?"

"If you can dig up a scoop like that, I can dig up three hundred grand."

CHAPTER 2

Gwendolyn stepped inside the marble foyer of the Guarantee Building on Hollywood Boulevard and clicked her purse open for a handkerchief. As she breathed in the cool air and dabbed the July sheen from her forehead, she read the name on the business card in her hand again.

ELDON LAIRD. Now there was a movie star name. Lord knows, the guy had movie star looks. His thick hair was the color of maple syrup and had just started to grey at the temples. His teeth were white as bread, and he had a jawline you could sharpen scissors on. As the cigarette girl at the Cocoanut Grove nightclub in the Ambassador Hotel, Gwendolyn Brick was used to being around dashing men with movie star looks, but Eldon Laird was far more valuable to an aspiring actress than a movie star would be—he was a talent agent.

Attracting the guy's interest, however, had been a challenge. He'd been coming to the Cocoanut Grove for months, usually alone and always casting a cool eye over the rambunctious crowd. He'd never once beckoned her over.

When Gwendolyn arrived in Hollywood nearly ten years earlier, she came up with a cockamamie scheme to get the whole town talking about her. She traveled the length and breadth of Hollywood stamping every menu, coaster, and cocktail napkin that crossed her path with *Gwendolyn Was Here.* Nothing ever came of it, and she'd all but forgotten about it until the Grove's hat check girl pulled a *Gwendolyn Was Here* coaster out of the pocket of Eldon Laird's cashmere coat. It gave Gwendolyn the courage to sass him, and he'd responded by handing her his card and asking her to bring his favorite hard-to-find cigarettes to his office.

Gwendolyn hadn't counted on his office being on the top floor of a building that had no elevator. If she'd known, she wouldn't have worn three-inch heels. But they went so well with the new dress she'd made, a white polished cotton dotted with pale yellow sunflowers that matched her hair. Any other pair wouldn't have looked half as good, and she needed to look good. A guy like Eldon Laird was the ultimate prize for a pretty girl in Hollywood.

The talent agent's front office was like nothing she'd ever seen before. The entire place was done out in a glossy white—not just the walls, but the secretary's desk, the linoleum floor, the filing cabinet, even the ceramic bowl that held a potted fern. The only exceptions were bright emerald-green drapes that framed the window over Hollywood Boulevard and the crimson lamp atop the filing cabinet. Amid the sea of white-on-white, their brash hues packed a wallop.

The door to the inner office was open. Gwendolyn called out, "Hello?"

"You can just leave it on the desk, thanks." The talent agent's voice was smooth like Italian leather.

"I don't think I can do that, Mr. Laird."

"For crying out loud, it's just—oh! It's you."

Eldon Laird had appeared at the door of his office. His shirtsleeves were rolled up to his elbows, and his tie, a dark orange fleur-de-lis pattern stenciled onto a midnight-blue background, was tucked inside his shirt.

"Your secretary doesn't appear to be in."

"It's delightful to see you," he said, gliding toward her. "To what do I owe this inestimable and unexpected pleasure? Gwendolyn, isn't it?"

Play this right, Gwendolyn told herself. Girls like you don't get many chances to impress guys like him.

She pulled out six packs of cork-tipped Viceroys. "The last time I saw you at the Cocoanut Grove, you asked me to stop by your office with as many as I could get my hands on."

A slow-burn smile. "You remembered."

"Ask a cigarette girl about cigarettes . . ."

Who knew these would be so darned hard to locate? Even Bobo couldn't get them, and he'd been running the Ambassador Hotel's tobacco stand for years. Eventually she'd tracked them down through a neighbor at the Garden of Allah who worked for Technicolor whose brother-in-law drove a forklift down at the Port of Los Angeles.

"In New York they're all but impossible," Eldon said.

"There are some things you can only get in L.A." She let that hint of a smile she'd been practicing in the mirror slip between her lips.

He smiled, too. "How much do I owe you?"

"Three fifty-five."

"Come on in."

She followed Eldon into a much bigger space, also done out in white but for a huge painting behind his desk. Thick daubs of cobalt blue, vermilion, and persimmon filled the canvas, but it didn't appear to be anything in particular.

"You like it?" Eldon asked.

"This?" Gwendolyn pointed to the painting. "What is it?"

"Do you need to know what something is before you can decide whether or not you like it?"

Gwendolyn had dealt with her fair share of smooth customers at the Cocoanut Grove, but this cake-eater was the pip. "Not always."

"It's abstract art. You're free to read into it whatever you wish."

"Does it at least have a name?"

"*Doubt. Dread. Desire.* It's a new local artist I like very much. Alistair Dunne. Heard of him?"

Gwendolyn said that no, she hadn't, but she rather liked his work—which wasn't the case at all. She preferred her paintings to be about something a person could actually recognize. As far as she was concerned, artists like this were simply people who couldn't paint faces or seascapes or castles. She did like the bold colors, though.

That cobalt blue is divine, she thought. I wonder where I could find that shade in shot silk.

Eldon Laird pulled a black wallet from a desk drawer and handed her a ten-dollar bill.

"I don't know that I can make change for that."

"The rest is for your trouble. It's gotten so that I can't smoke anything else, so I deeply appreciate the favor." He stacked the six packs into a neat pile. "I would love to be able to return it," he added, his eyes still on the stack.

"You're an agent, aren't you?" she asked him.

"Oh, so you are an actress?"

Gwendolyn was impressed by the way he attempted to sound genuinely surprised. "Yeah," she scoffed. "A cigarette girl from a Hollywood nightclub wants to get into the movies. Who ever heard of such a thing?"

He laughed the laugh of an indulgent parent, but his eyes studied her carefully. "I have to say, I'm surprised Benny Thau over at MGM didn't hire you on the spot."

"Nope."

"Minna Wells at Warner Brothers?"

"Nope."

"You registered at Central Casting?"

"Sure, but nothing ever comes up for me."

He let out a long, wolfy whistle. "You telling me that nobody in this town has offered you their casting couch?"

"I wish."

Gwendolyn felt herself blush. Everything had been going exactly as she'd rehearsed all week: playful banter, witty exchanges, sly smiles. But now she'd made herself out to be a whore. "What I mean is that I'd be flattered if they thought me good enough to offer the casting couch."

He nodded towards the far wall, where an extra-long sofa in pristine white damask sat under a window. "What do you think of *my* couch?"

Her shoulders began to wilt. This is the closest thing to a foot in the door you've gotten since you came to Hollywood, she told herself, and you'll kick yourself if you let this one slip by. If this was what it took, then this was what it took.

Carefully, deliberately, she crossed the floor and sat down on the edge of the couch. He followed her and sat next to her. Not close enough to touch, but close enough. "You don't look too comfortable, Miss Gwendolyn Brick."

Hearing her full name made Gwendolyn flinch. Her name tag at the Cocoanut Grove only said *Miss Gwendolyn*. "How do you know my last name?"

"I've been asking around. The guy behind the bar is awfully protective of you."

"Chuck? He's a good guy."

"He your boyfriend?"

"No, just a good pal. The big brother type."

"You still don't look too comfortable." It struck Gwendolyn how odd it was that he could maintain his smooth, slightly aloof tone, and yet soften the light in his eyes.

She went to slide back into the couch, but the faces of her friends swam into view. Kathryn had wanted so badly to write for the *Hollywood Reporter*, and look at her now. Her scoop had let her outmaneuver Louella Parsons. And dear Marcus caught the Red Car to MGM every morning now. Had either of them resorted to sleeping with someone to realize *their* dreams?

Gwendolyn stood up abruptly.

"Go to hell," she spat out, and started for the door.

"What's wrong?" Eldon raised his hands in the air as though she were Ma Baker and this had turned into stick-up.

She turned back to face him more squarely. He sure was handsome, with his tennis tan and his come-to-bed eyes. If this was a social call, she'd be more than happy to sit back on that white damask sofa and lap up whatever whipped cream he dished out. But this was a business call: ambitious actress and influential talent agent, not pretty little canary and roving Lothario.

"You!" she said, poking a finger at his face, "and every bottom-feeding heel in this town—you can all go to blazes."

She made a dramatic turn on her heels and was halfway into the outer office when he called out, "Hold on, hold on, you got me all wrong."

"I really don't think so." She was still committed to her dramatic exit, but she slowed her pace.

"If I'm going to represent someone, I need to know her very well."

Gwendolyn hated herself for hesitating, but felt her resistance erode. She faced him again. "What are you saying?"

"That you're going to be the guest of honor at a party I'm throwing." Eldon Laird's voice was now tender, almost sweet, like the smile in his eyes.

She counted slowly to five. "When?"

"When is your day off?"

"Mondays."

"Then it'll be on a Monday night."

Gwendolyn froze while she examined his face for any sign of insincerity. She didn't see any. "Which Monday night?"

"I'll let you know."

Gwendolyn thanked him—although she really wasn't sure why—and walked out of his office. She was almost at the front door when he called her name. He crossed the space between them in six strides and leaned in close enough for her to smell his cologne. It was heavy and smoky, like the inside of a men's club, she imagined.

"I can't let you leave without telling you that I think you're breathtakingly beautiful. And I want you to know that the talent agent businessman in me is telling the bachelor in me to back off—that this is purely business, and that rules are rules."

Gwendolyn knew she shouldn't—*This is business!*—but the question popped out anyway.

"And what does the bachelor have to say?"

"This."

Eldon bent forward and kissed Gwendolyn on the lips more tenderly than anyone had ever kissed her before.

CHAPTER 3

"What are you so goddamned tense about?" Alice Moore demanded as Marcus gazed out the train window.

It was almost midnight; there was nothing to see but night. He kept his eyes on the passing shadows and cursed the gods of fortune. Of all people to be in debt to, did it have to be this five-and-dime chorine?

"We're going to the Hearst castle with a lot of important and famous people," Marcus said. "This is a very big deal."

William Randolph Hearst's sprawling ranch lay near the small coastal town of San Simeon, an evening's train ride north of Los Angeles. Officially, it was called The Enchanted Hill, but unofficially—and always outside of the owner's earshot—it was known as Hearst's Castle. The newspaper magnate had been building it since 1919, and over those seventeen years its luxury had begun to border on the preposterous.

It boasted over fifty bedrooms, some of them decorated with ceilings lifted whole from sixteenth-century European chapels. A movie theater, an airfield, and a private zoo were set among a hundred acres of gardens. There was no other chunk of real estate to rival it anywhere in the country, and an invitation to spend the weekend up there was the pinnacle of all social invitations.

"Nah!" Alice stayed slumped against the butter-soft upholstery like a barfly at the end of a long night. "They may be important and they may be famous, but they're still just people, ain't they?"

"I hope you don't say *ain't* in front of Winston Churchill," Marcus responded.

"The fat Brit you pointed out to me on the platform?" She nudged his knee with her foot, probably leaving a dirty smudge on his best navy-blue suit, but he didn't want to look any prissier than he probably already did so he resisted the urge to look.

"Remind me who he is again," Alice said.

"He's a bigwig in British politics. Some say he's got his eye on becoming prime minister. Alice, I really need you to be on your best behavior this weekend. Please remember that everything you do and say reflects on me."

Alice flicked her home-peroxided hair. "You're taking it all too seriously, if you ask me."

"I've been invited up here to meet Hearst for the first time," Marcus insisted. "I need to make a good impression."

"You always make a good impression. You're that kind of guy. So relax already." Alice pulled out her nail file and started in on her pinkie.

It was still sinking in that he was the head writer of anything, let alone of the motion picture company set up by the richest man in America. The day *Return to Sender* became Cosmopolitan Pictures' biggest-ever success, Marcus was made head of the writing department and his thieving boss was out on his tush. Heady stuff.

For the hundredth time, he relived the one-two-three punch to the chest that walloped him when his name wasn't up on the screen. It was bad enough to realize his boss had pulled a fast one on him, but it meant that when *Return to Sender* played back home in McKeesport, Pennsylvania, nobody would know that Marcus Adler had written it.

He hadn't been home since his father threw him onto the midnight train to Chicago and told him never to come back. That was nine years ago, he thought. *So why should I still care?*

Marcus watched the passing blackness on the other side of the glass. He'd spent weeks picturing the look on his father's face as he stared up with his mouth slightly agape as the screen filled with the words *SCREENPLAY BY MARCUS ADLER.*

You threw me out of town like I was a bag of garbage, Marcus thought, and look at me now.

He was on his way to spend the weekend with Hollywood movie stars, the man poised to become Britain's next prime minister, and the biggest tycoon in America, but his father would never know it until his name was on a motion picture.

Meeting the likes of William Randolph Hearst was nerve-racking enough, but Marcus had to wonder: Did Hearst know about his link to Kathryn Massey, who'd out-scooped his prized columnist?

All Marcus could do was hope that nobody up at the Castle had made the connection. It was bad enough that he had to go with Alice, but he still owed her a favor from the night George was arrested. Two days after the announcement in Kathryn's column about his promotion, Marcus had received a card from Alice informing him that as soon as he got an invite to San Simeon, there would be hell to pay if she wasn't his "plus one." It killed him that amid the most sparkling gathering on the California coast, he was going to be seen with a cheap conniver like Alice.

The train pulled into the station at San Luis Obispo and everybody—Myrna Loy, Gloria Swanson, even Mr. Churchill himself—grabbed their own luggage and took separate limousines up the five-mile driveway to La Casa Grande, the largest structure on the ranch. Its elaborate twin bell towers loomed ahead in the moonlight.

A line of stiff-backed men in green and gold uniforms waited at the front door. Someone assigned Marcus and Alice a valet and he led them through a maze of corridors lined with portraits of long-forgotten dukes and marchionesses from pockets of European turf that had probably been fought over since the day they invented swords.

They came to a door made of wood so dark it was almost black. On it hung a plaque engraved with the words *DELLA*

ROBIA. It opened onto a suite; two bedrooms divided by a living area, with a private bathroom at the rear.

Marcus and Alice looked into the bedroom on the left. Its square bed had four heavy posts, each topped with a copper globe. Over the headboard hung a five-foot-tall statue of a pious-looking monk in robes. Alice read out the name carved into its base.

"St. Anthony of Padua. Bleech! Catholic saints give me the heebie-jeebies. I'll take my chances with the other bedroom, thank you very much."

When Marcus shut the door behind her, it closed with a loud click. The reality of having to meet the richest man in America—possibly even the world—had started to weigh on him like an anvil strapped to his back, and he felt his bravado deserting him. Watching McNulty get the shaft had been gratifying, but now all eyes were on Marcus. What if *Return to Sender* was just beginner's luck? What if the next picture he wrote for Marion Davies was a flop? Would he be out on his behind just as quickly as McNulty had been?

Marcus peered up at the face of the gloomy Franciscan monk hovering over his bed. No, no, no, Marcus thought. He couldn't live like this. If he was really going to show his bully of a father what a mistake he'd made kicking him out of town, he was going to have to find more stable employment. He had to find a way to get out of Cosmopolitan Pictures and into MGM. In the meantime, he just had to survive this weekend.

* * *

"He's an invert, you know."

Katharine Hepburn was standing beside Marcus at the edge of the lawn where Hearst was playing croquet with Charles Laughton, Harpo Marx, Myrna Loy, and Alice. Behind them was the most enormous rose bush Marcus had ever seen; at least eight feet tall. The rosebuds, a gentle shade of pink, were starting to pop open. Their delicate scent reminded him of his Grandma Adler's prize rose garden.

He was surprised Hepburn was there at all; she had been on the outs with Hollywood since *Sylvia Scarlett*, the disastrous picture in which she'd dressed up as a boy. Usually only people at the top of their game got invited up to the Enchanted Hill.

She was one of the few stars Marcus had met who looked exactly like she did in the movies: firm chin, intelligent eyes, un-fussed-with hair. She was standing like a man, with her feet apart and her clenched hands on her hips. She was dressed in a loose pair of brown linen trousers and an unstarched white Oxford shirt.

"Who's an invert?" Marcus asked.

"Laughton. Queer as a plaid rabbit. I don't care one way or the other, of course, but that blonde tarty-looking one obviously has no idea. Look at how she's flirting with him like he's Gable. Someone really ought to tell her she's wasting her time."

Alice wasn't playing croquet so much as standing around with a mallet in her hand cooing, "And what is it I'm supposed to do now?" like Betty Boop's stand-in.

"She's with you, isn't she?" Hepburn asked.

"Call it repayment of a favor."

Katharine kept her eye on the game. "Must have been one hell of a favor. Whatever she does, she'd better keep clear of these bushes. The last thing she needs to do is say the word *rosebud*."

Marcus looked at the actress quizzically and a smirk slid onto Hepburn's lips.

"You know what *rosebud* means around here, don't you?" she said.

"I don't think so."

"It's Hearst's nickname for Marion's own little Garden of Eden. I thought everyone knew that." She thrust out her hand. "We haven't met formally. I'm Katharine Hepburn." Marcus introduced himself and they shook hands. She had a firm grip, like a man's. "George told me to keep an eye out for you," she said.

George Cukor had directed Hepburn in *Sylvia Scarlett*. They were shocked when it bombed; they thought they'd made a pretty good movie. But the experience, George told

Marcus, bonded him and Hepburn together. They were determined to make another picture together, a super-successful one to eclipse the sting of their failure.

"Your first time here can be overwhelming," Hepburn said. "All this ridiculous opulence is enough to intimidate even the hardiest of souls. The ceiling of my bedroom is from some Basque monastery, mahogany inlaid with silver. The carving is exquisite; it must have taken some poor old sod half his lifetime to sculpt it. And yet, as I'm lying there looking up at it, all I can think is I'd much rather have a plain ceiling painted in some soothing color like a light grey or baby blue than all this blasted tomfoolery."

Just then, Harpo Marx thwacked the croquet ball through a difficult hoop and took the lead. Marcus questioned the wisdom of beating the host at his favorite game. Hearst, a horse-faced man in his seventies, didn't strike Marcus as the type who would lose to a vaudeville comedian very cheerfully.

"Hear, hear, Marxie! Well played!" a Shakespearean voice boomed down the entire length of the lawn. Marcus followed it to Constance Collier, the British grande dame, who was sitting on the sidelines with Winston Churchill. Marcus wondered if even that was perhaps pushing it.

"You're not nervous, then?" Hepburn asked him.

"Nervous about what?"

"Sitting next to W.R. at dinner tonight."

Marcus' head snapped around. "I'm what?"

"Haven't you seen the seating chart? They leave it on the table in the Assembly Room after lunch."

"Which one is that?"

"The one with the four enormous Belgian tapestries that would feed China for a month if he sold them."

Marcus felt the hairs on his arms spring up. Surely Mr. Churchill would be awarded the seat of honor tonight. Or Stan Laurel or Myrna Loy, both of whom Marcus had seen at the breakfast buffet that morning. "Are you sure?"

"May I make a suggestion?"

"Make as many as you want."

"The man may be richer than King Solomon, but he's not the world's greatest conversationalist. If the chitchat lags, find a way to bring up dachshunds. The old bugger adores them and we had one growing up, so once we discovered we had that in common, it was all rainbows."

Marcus nodded slowly. "Anything else?"

"Yes. Hearst is a teetotaler, but enough of a realist to appreciate that others are not. So he allows one – and only one – glass of wine with dinner. But if you need more than that for some Dutch courage, may I suggest a glass or two in your room beforehand?"

* * *

After an unusually long and hot shower, Marcus pulled on a fresh white undershirt and stared at St. Anthony of Padua. Keep breathing, he reminded himself. He knew that the whole purpose of his trip was to meet Mr. Hearst. But he'd figured it might be at pre-dinner cocktails, when Hearst would meet everyone who was up for the weekend. Ten minutes of cocktail conversation about the weather and the Botticelli above the fireplace, and Hearst would move on to someone he'd really want to meet. But the hot seat? This was not something Marcus had counted on.

"You lost something?" Alice asked. She'd changed into a frayed chenille bathrobe to set her hair for dinner.

"No, why?"

"Harpo Marx and me got chatting after the game. He really is a bit of a culture vulture. Did you know he plays the harp? Who knew? Anyway, we were doing the whole 'Which room are you staying in?' bit and he told me that St. Anthony here is the patron saint of lost things, and you were staring at him, so I just figured – "

There was a knock on the door. Marcus opened it to find Marion Davies standing in the doorway in the same lilac sundress she'd worn earlier while Myrna Loy and Rosalind Russell slugged it out on the tennis court. Marion was a petite little thing with a slim waist, a mop of curly blonde hair, and kind, lively blue eyes. Like most people in

Hollywood, Marcus couldn't figure out what she saw in an old fuddy-duddy like Hearst, but he liked her nonetheless.

Marcus pulled the door open wide. "Please, Miss Davies, won't you come in?"

She crossed through the doorway and looked around. "You're comfy here, I take it? The Della Robia is one of my favorite rooms. Some of them are so cluttered!" She rolled her eyes. "Hello there! Alice, isn't it?"

Marcus was impressed; Marion had met Alice only briefly, late the night before. She asked Alice if she was enjoying her stay and Alice assured her that she was having the most *mahvelous* time.

Marion turned to Marcus. "You got my note?"

"Your note? I don't think so."

"I popped it under the door early this aftern—oh! There it is." Marion scooped up a sheet of folded notepaper near the door. It was light puce, almost exactly the color of the carpet. "Never mind. I'm here now. It was just a reminder to have your picture ideas ready when W.R. brings it up at dinner."

"Picture ideas?" Marcus said. He rubbed the hairs along his forearm in an attempt to smooth them down.

"W.R. loved *Return to Sender*. We all did! Especially the accountants. So W.R. wants to hear your five best story ideas over dinner."

Marcus glanced at the gothic-faced grandfather clock next to the stained glass window. It was six thirty-five, which meant fifty-five minutes until dinner. *DAMN*.

"That's why I finagled you into the hot seat. Winston was most relieved and told me to tell you he owes you one. Anyway, I just stopped by to tell you not to write them out on a piece of paper or anything. W.R. won't like that. He detests anyone with a dull mind. So find some way to remember them. I use word association, myself. I'll leave you two to continue dressing. See you in the Refectory!"

Marcus fell into a chair. Five stories in less than an hour?

"You're looking a little bit pale," Alice said.

"I was expecting a brief hello-how-are-you moment, not a pitch session."

"But surely you have a ton of story ideas floating around that noggin of yours."

The truth was that ordinarily, Marcus did have a snowstorm of ideas swirling around his head, but the lava ball of panic rising in his chest had evaporated them.

"What about *Return to Sender*?" Alice said. "How did you come up with that one?"

"There was this letter opener sitting on Marion's table when she asked me to pitch her an idea."

"In other words, you did it on the fly and pulled it off like a pro. You've seen what the rooms in this joint are like. They're filled with doohickeys from all over. Use them as your inspiration."

"Thanks, Alice, but you don't know how hard that is."

"Ah, baloney. You just need a confidence booster. I've got just the thing."

* * *

The great dining hall at San Simeon was Hearst's favorite room, and Marcus could see why. It was a long, cavernous space whose ceiling came from a four-hundred-year-old Italian cathedral and featured life-sized carvings of saints. Palio banners from Sienna hung along one wall above a pair of enormous Flemish tapestries depicting King Nebuchadnezzar of Babylon. The table running down the middle of the room sat thirty people.

Marcus had been reluctant to drink anything Alice Moore had in her hip flask, but she'd assured him, "Whenever I take a slug of this before an audition, I nearly always get the job." She claimed the recipe was from her grandmother, a vaudevillian who'd juggled swords for thirty years and only lost one knuckle—which she blamed on the San Francisco earthquake in '06, so it didn't count. There was certainly booze in it, but what sort, Marcus couldn't discern. He could taste a hint of mint and perhaps some rose water, and anything beyond that was a mystery.

But it seemed to work all right. By the time Marcus entered the Refectory, he was feeling as confident as a tattooist when the fleet's in. Boy, it sure was toasty in there. A white marble fireplace—Marcus guessed it was at least a dozen feet across—blazed with a fire hot enough to heat a room twice this size. He'd heard that W.R. liked a well-heated room, but wasn't this a tad ridiculous?

They found Alice's place card—she was wedged between an MGM executive in charge of something-or-other and Miss Loy's new husband, Arthur Hornblow, Jr., a producer at Paramount—and then Marcus took his seat beside Hearst himself.

"Pleased to meet you," Marcus said.

Hearst nodded. "Not half as much as I am pleased to meet the man behind *Return to Sender*. The bean counters are still hunched over their adding machines. Terrific job, Adler. Just terrific."

America's most powerful media mogul inexplicably possessed the voice of a kewpie doll. It was an odd counterpoint to the man's serious, horsey face, his ponderously deep-set eyes, and the clump of grey hair sprouting from the top of his head.

Marcus dabbed at his forehead with a paper napkin, thinking, The man can decorate a warehouse like a cathedral but insists on paper napkins? It wasn't even very good quality paper. Marcus looked at his napkin and wondered what sort of story he could get from it. The heiress of a paper baron gets involved with the son of a . . . of a guy who . . . who is against paper because . . . because his family—damn it. Who could possibly have anything against paper?

The soup was served. Marcus hoped it was one of those new chilled soups they'd started serving in Hollywood lately, but no, it was cream of mushroom served steaming hot. Another server appeared with a bottle of chilled white wine. Oh God, yes, Marcus thought, give me anything cold.

The mushroom soup was tasty, but it was the chilled wine that hit the spot. He longed to remove his jacket, but Winston Churchill and Lionel Barrymore were keeping theirs on, so he did, too. He could feel the sweat collecting under his arms.

Marion was nattering on about a story one of the makeup artists had told her—something about Bing Crosby's recent hands-in-cement ceremony outside Grauman's Chinese—when Hepburn's suggestion about Hearst and dachshunds popped into his head. Maybe the paper heiress loses her dachshund when she stops to watch a ceremony at Grauman's, and the dog runs across the wet cement and ruins the moment. That could be quite funny. Marcus reached for his glass and drained it, wondering just how strict the one glass rule was, then thought about how the dog could run through the cement just as the newspaper photographer snaps the picture, and that's what ends up on the front page of the newspaper. The movie star would be livid. There would be yelling and screaming—

Suddenly Marcus was aware that Marion had stopped talking. He looked up to find everyone—Hearst to his right, Marion opposite him, Harpo next to Marion, and Clementine Churchill to Marcus' immediate left—staring at him. Marcus felt sickeningly lightheaded. His father's face appeared in front of him.

See, father? See who's sitting next to me? Mrs. Winston Churchill.

"I'm sorry, Mr. Adler." Mrs. Churchill's voice was ripe with generations of good breeding. "But did you say somebody was yelling and screaming?"

Marcus took a deep breath and looked across to Harpo for support. Harpo had lived at the Garden of Allah a couple of years ago, so they knew each other in a hi-how-you-doin' sort of way. Harpo mimed wiping his paper napkin across his own forehead and pointed to Marcus'. Marcus took his napkin and wiped it across his forehead. It came away soaked. He looked at Marion.

"I'm so sorry, Miss Davies. I've got this idea for a picture that's been kicking around my head all morning. You know us writers, once we're on to an idea it's hard for us to let it go."

"By all means, let's hear it," Hearst said in his kewpie-doll voice. This time, Marcus couldn't suppress the incongruity of this pipsqueak of a voice coming out of such a gargantuan man. He burst out laughing.

"So it's a comedy, then?" Hearst smiled hopefully.

"It sure is," Marcus said. Like that voice of yours.

Mrs. Churchill gasped.

"WHAT DID YOU SAY?" Hearst thundered.

Everyone at the long table fell into stony silence.

Marcus looked at Marion Davies. Her face was contorted with disbelief, then his vision blurred as though someone had dropped a pane of frosted glass in front of his face, and just as suddenly pulled it away. For God's sake, say something, he told himself. He wanted to wipe his forehead again but his napkin had disintegrated.

"Dachshund!" he exclaimed. "It's about a dachshund. We could change the breed of dog, I suppose, but, well, I don't know about you, Mr. Hearst, but I think they're the cutest darned things I've ever seen."

The most powerful man in America had awful teeth. They were yellow, stained with brown, and crooked and jagged like crumbling bricks. But when W.R. Hearst smiled, it was a genuine smile, full of all the warmth and humanity that his yellow presses completely lacked. "You've got me there, Adler. Damned cute critters."

Marion laid a gentle hand on Hearst's forearm. "What does this dachshund do?"

"She's the pet of a paper heiress, and she ruins a ceremony outside Grauman's by running across the wet cement at the worst possible time."

"Oh, that sounds funny, doesn't it, W.R.?" Marion said, giving Hearst's arm a squeeze.

Cute name cute name cute name, quick, think of a cute name.

Marion's face disappeared behind the frosted glass again. Marcus gripped the edge of the dining table and took a deep breath as his father's face reappeared, frowning and pinch-lipped. Marcus mentally wiped it away. Marion wobbled back into focus and the perfect name popped into his mind.

"It does have a name," Marcus said. "In fact, the dog's name is the name of the picture."

"Which is . . . ?" Hearst asked.

"Rosebud."

CHAPTER 4

Kathryn Massey now knew what it was like to be famous. Or infamous. She couldn't decide which. She knew what it was like to enter a restaurant and watch half the heads turn to look at her while the other half leaned in toward each other to whisper. She knew how it felt to see people raise their eyebrows and mouth, *That's Kathryn Massey?* as though they were a thousand yards away and she was blind.

Her *Gone with the Wind* scoop was big news everywhere, but the bigger news in Tinseltown was that it hadn't come from Louella Parsons. Tongues had been wagging for weeks. Kudos to Kathryn Massey of the *Hollywood Reporter*, they said—sometimes even to her face—for not serving up the story to Parsons like Hollywood's handmaiden. It was time somebody broke the unbreakable rule. But they had to wonder if Kathryn had a death wish; Louella wasn't going to take this one lying down.

"To Louella's simple mind, what we've done amounts to high treason," Wilkerson told Kathryn the day they broke the news. "Blood, shrapnel, and gin bottles will be flung from one end of Hollywood Boulevard to the other, so we'd better batten down our hatches."

But nothing happened.

Parsons simply announced the news in her column as though she were the first person in the world to know. No recriminations, no outrages, no phone calls, threats, or screaming. And absolutely no sign of flying gin bottles. Kathryn felt like she was standing in the middle of a twister, in the one sweet spot where all was at peace.

For several weeks, she braced herself for the moment the twister would move on and leave her gripping the handrails. That particular moment arrived in the form of an item in Louella's column.

Which dark-haired Tinseltowner is guilty of maternal neglect? According to my source (who is as close to the font of mother's milk as one can get), she leaves her mother virtually destitute while she hops from parties to nightclubs in pursuit of a high-profile career. Naturally, I'm all for females taking up careers. But at the expense of the loving woman who brought me into the world? To me, no career is worth it, but that sentiment may soon be cast out the window and gone with the wind.

Kathryn had just read it a second time when Wilkerson buzzed her on the intercom. "My office. Now."

None of the usual newspapers—*The L.A. Times, The New York Times, Variety, The Wall Street Journal*—were strewn across his desk. There was just one: *The Examiner.*

"You've read this morning's Parsons, I assume?" he asked. His eyes ached with the possibility that Louella's accusations were true. "This whisper campaign? Not good." He grunted. "You need to fix it."

"Me?"

Kathryn could scarcely believe that for all his talk and swagger, Wilkerson was ducking the first pygmy dart Louella blew their way.

"This isn't *The Examiner versus the Reporter*. She's seen to it that this is *Parsons versus Massey*. I know I'm asking you to unpop a balloon, but Louella Parsons is not someone you want offside for very long."

"But we knew that before we stopped the presses!"

"All it'd take is a few phone calls, and you'll find yourself banned from every movie studio in town. And that would be the end of your column. And your job."

Kathryn's hands started to tremble; she clasped them together. "Then why the hell did you agree to run the story?"

"To give her a scare. To get us some publicity. To get you some credibility. And we've done all that, so now it's time to clean up after ourselves. I don't care how you do it, as long as it gets done."

Her boss' gruff, clipped tone told her they'd reached the end of the conversation, but she found herself cemented to the carpet. He looked up at her, frowning. She had to say something. "I just wanted to let you know," she improvised, "that . . . I never got around to thanking you for meeting payroll."

Wilkerson dropped his eyes to the large diary laid out in front of him. "It was my impression that we were pretending that part of the night never happened."

"I just—"

"No," he said, looking up at her now. His tone softened. "I'm the one who owes you a vote of thanks. I never would've gone to Howard Hughes for a loan if not for your suggestion. We play cards, we give each other Cubans at Christmas. I only ever saw him as a friend."

"Who do you go to when you're in trouble, if not your friends?"

"That's what I'm thanking you for. Making me see that. When you came back to me later and suggested I ask him for a loan, I thought you were nuts. But his only question was 'How much?' So . . . thank you." He straightened up a stack of papers that didn't need straightening. "Now please go and fix your problem."

Wilkerson's gaze returned to his appointment calendar, to the line he'd written at the bottom of the next day's page. It wasn't hard for Kathryn to read, even upside down.

Hepburn 7.30pm p/u her place.

* * *

Kathryn's mother lived a brisk fifteen-minute walk up Sunset Boulevard from the Garden of Allah to the staff's quarters of the Chateau Marmont hotel, where she was now head telephone operator. Francine's hours were long—sometimes twelve hours a day—and like everyone else, she worked six days a week.

It irked Kathryn to admit (if only to herself) that it had been months since she'd seen her mother. They'd spoken on the telephone of course, but she'd been busy attending all those parties and nightclubs Louella had scoffed at. And anyway, Kathryn told herself as she entered the manicured forecourt of the Chateau Marmont, it's me who always does the calling. A girl could die of old age waiting for Francine Massey to pick up the telephone. Ironic, really, considering her mom's job.

Francine had always been the type of woman who preferred to color and perm her hair at home, thinking that the results looked perfectly fine. But the woman who appeared in the hotel foyer that day was not the same woman Kathryn had grown up with. Her hair was a warm hazelnut brown and set in a semi-permanent wave that framed her face and flattered her positives – decent cheekbones, firm jawline – and veiled her negatives – a very high forehead and ears that stuck out too far. Gone were the strands of grey and hint of a moustache.

"Mother!" Kathryn exclaimed. "Don't you look marvelous?"

Francine stopped short. "I do?"

"You've started going to the beauty parlor, haven't you?"

Francine started to fuss with the back of her hair. "Well, I am the head telephone operator here now. I need to set an example."

Since when did her mother cut such a striking figure? Was she wearing a girdle now, too? "It's time and money well spent," Kathryn declared.

Kathryn sat with her mother in the tiny garden she shared with the head of housekeeping next door. The woman wasn't much for sitting outside, so Francine had the garden to herself. Kathryn looked around at the baby pink petunias, the snowy white chrysanthemums, the warm mauve irises and Francine's favorite: dahlias. "You planted all of these yourself?"

"I don't have a lot of spare time, but what I do have, I enjoy spending out here. It's a tonic after being cooped up in the booth all week." Francine kept her eyes on the flowers around them. "Are you in trouble?"

Kathryn braced herself. "Trouble, no, but I am in a difficult position and I'd like to know if you had a hand in it."

"Me? What have I done?" Francine's eyes were wide.

"Did you read Louella's column today?"

"I might have glanced through it on my coffee break."

"Did you catch the part where she all but accused me of leaving you destitute while I hopped around nightclubs and parties to further my career?"

Francine crossed her arms. "Destitute? What an imagination! I said nothing of the sort."

The realization that her mother had said *something* to Louella Parsons hit Kathryn like a backhand. She struggled to keep her voice on an even keel. "What word *did* you use, Mother?"

"My goodness, Kathryn. How do you expect me to remember every word of every conversation I've ever had with Louella?"

"I wasn't aware you'd *ever* had a conversation with Louella."

"I didn't know her until her invitation arrived in the mail."

"Her invitation to what?"

"She wrote and asked me if I wanted to join a new club she was starting."

"What sort of club?"

"The Association of Hollywood Mothers."

What Kathryn really wanted to ask was why this was the first she'd heard of it. "And what do you all do together?"

"We usually meet at someone's house or another. Usually it's just tea and cake, a proper luncheon sometimes, and we just natter away. Hollywood gossip, mainly." Francine tsked. "It's a whole group of people, not just Louella and me, if that's what you're thinking, and I can see that you are. We have tons of members. Ginger Rogers' mother, Judy Garland's, Maureen O'Hara's. We all get together once a month."

It was conversations like this that made Kathryn feel better when Sunset Boulevard separated them. "So when you first met Louella, what did you talk about?"

"Honestly, Kathryn, it was a year ago. How can you expect me—"

"Mother! This is important."

Francine let out a heavy sigh and pretended to try and recall her first conversation with the most influential woman in Hollywood. "It was a meeting of mothers, so we talked about our daughters. She was hopeful that her daughter, Harriet, would become an actress, but it seems she's more comfortable behind the scenes. I told her I knew exactly how she felt." She rolled her eyes. "Well, I did! I had high hopes for you, Kathryn, and I worked so hard to get you auditions and to get you noticed."

Francine had only wanted Kathryn to become an actress because her own bid at movie stardom had failed. She'd never even bothered to ask her daughter if it was something she wanted to do with her life.

Is it any wonder I ran away to the Garden of Allah? Kathryn thought.

"Here's what I think happened," Kathryn said. "Louella invites you to join her coffee klatch, you both get to talking about your ungrateful daughters, and you start to play 'My daughter is even worse than *that* and here's the reason why.'"

"Oh, Kathryn."

"Can I assume that you left out the bit about your moving away and not even telling me? And that after the Long Beach earthquake you were homeless and I took you in and found you a job here at the Marmont? Oh, but saying that your daughter left you destitute makes for a far more dramatic story, doesn't it?"

Francine tensed her lips. "I never used the word *destitute*."

Kathryn closed her eyes just long enough to stop herself from snarling the words she needed to say. She opened them again and took a breath. "It's not the words we use, Mother, it's the impression we give people. It's bad enough you're giving *anyone* the impression that I kicked you out of my life, but did you have to give it to the woman with the most widely-read newspaper column in the country?"

* * *

Two things prevented Kathryn from sleeping much that night.

One was the churning undercurrent of emotions stirred up by her mother's determination to cast herself in the role of victim. But by three a.m. she'd replayed that scene among the flowers enough to burn through the anger, and she found her mind turning to her boss. She lay in bed mumbling in the dark like a crazy person.

What a hypocrite, she thought. The first time—the very first time!—they take Louella on and he backs down . . . what a weasely old coward . . . what a disappointment . . . what an unforgivable betrayal.

Somewhere around four in the morning it occurred to her why she felt so wrenchingly betrayed. She adored her boss. Sophisticated Mr. Wilkerson of the *Hollywood Reporter,* with his bespoke suits, Cuban cigars, and barbershop shaves. He took no guff from anyone, he played the big game with the big boys, and—most important of all—he gave her a chance when nobody else would. How hadn't she noticed before that she'd come to see him as a father figure?

In her eyes, he was brave, intelligent, and perceptive. She needed his public support now, but he'd chosen to kowtow to the fat golden statue of Miss Louella Parsons instead. Message received loud and clear, Mr. Wilkerson, she decided. I'm on my own.

At some point in the hour before dawn, Kathryn's thoughts turned toward what she'd seen written on her boss' calendar: *Hepburn 7.30pm p/u her place.*

Why would Wilkerson be picking Katharine Hepburn up? The woman was perfectly capable of driving herself.

Was she his date for something? Usually, the studio paired her with leading-man types. Or were they having an affair? If they were, surely he wouldn't write something like that on his calendar for all the world to see. He was a coward, not a knucklehead.

As the light started to seep in through her bedroom curtains, Kathryn came to the conclusion that something fishier was going on.

Later that morning, she waited until Wilkerson had left for a meeting at the bank, then she approached his secretary.

"Vera, I've been trying to get Katharine Hepburn on the phone for a full twenty-four hours and I've got nothing to show for it. It seems old Louella Parsons has put the word out: Send Kathryn Massey to Coventry until further notice."

"You underestimated her, didn't you?" Vera said.

Kathryn gave a noncommittal shrug. "I hear tell Selznick's got his eye on Hepburn for Scarlett O'Hara, and I want to ask her about it." Kathryn cocked her head in the direction of Wilkerson's door. "What do you think my chances are the boss would be okay with me tagging along tonight?"

"So you know about that, huh?" Vera let out a throaty laugh. "There's not a chance in Hades. He may be Mister Hollywood Reporter, but tonight he's just the delivery boy."

Delivery boy?

"Oh, Vera, isn't that being a bit harsh?"

Vera pulled a mirror out of her handbag and checked her lipstick. "He's dropping her off at Moneybags' new place. He's not going to be asked inside, or even to introduce them. Just drop her off at the front door of the Cedarhurst place and drive away. Obviously he's doing Moneybags a huge favor." Vera's eyes narrowed. "You don't happen to know what for, do you?"

Kathryn casually shook her head. "Cedarhurst? The one in Beverly Hills?"

"No, over in Los Feliz. Norma Talmadge's old place. Anyway, he's gone all gooey over Hepburn and when he found out she and the boss were friends, then it was Pow!

Favor time! You've heard how that one is. Never enough pretty girls. When you've got that much money, I guess it makes you real magnetic. Do you think he's attractive?"

"He's okay," Kathryn replied evenly.

"I kinda like 'em tall. I like 'em ambitious, too. I read the other day that he has plans to cut Lindbergh's Atlantic record in half. That's pretty ballsy."

Bingo!

Back at her desk Kathryn laid her hand on the telephone in front of her. "Sorry, boss," she muttered, "I need this white flag more than you do."

CHAPTER 5

Even weeks later, Gwendolyn could still feel Eldon Laird's full lips on hers. She could feel the urgency in his body as he pressed it against hers, his strong hands exploring her back.

She looked up at Eldon's home, a surprisingly delightful Spanish Mission crossed with a fairytale castle. It stood in the heart of the tony Hancock Park area just south of RKO, surrounded by similarly huge homes with immaculately landscaped front yards double the size of the Garden of Allah's pool. She told herself, "Remember, Gwennie, this is business. Real business, not monkey business. You've finally got someone interested in your career. Don't screw this up. That kiss was just . . ."

It was like swimming in Swiss chocolate.

She shook her head. Business. *Business!*

She checked her wristwatch. Seven thirty on the button. When Eldon opened his front door, Gwendolyn realized there was no hubbub of conversation filling the place. No laughter, no music. "Good evening, Mr. Laird," she said. "I do hope you weren't counting on me being fashionably late." She stepped into the foyer, where a glass-topped Louis Quatorze table held a tall vase filled with dark blue irises.

"They almost match your wrap," Eldon observed. "May I take it?"

Gwendolyn let Eldon slip the midnight-blue cashmere wrap from her shoulders. Dorothy Parker, recently returned to the Garden for a well-paid stint at Paramount, had insisted she borrow it for the night, calling it her "lucky un-wrap."

Gwendolyn looked around. "Am I the first to arrive? I was hoping to finally make my big Hollywood entrance."

"Oh, you will, Gwendolyn dear. You will."

He hung Dorothy's wrap in the closet under the staircase and guided Gwendolyn into the living room. In front of them was the largest sofa she had ever seen. She imagined it could easily accommodate four or five people, or two lying down. The upholstery had huge deep pink roses set against the palest of pale cherry blossom. Beyond the sofa was a large picture window framed with drapes in the exact same color.

"What is it?" Eldon asked.

"Mr. Laird!" Gwendolyn exclaimed. "Your home is nothing like your office."

"Should it be?"

"This room looks like it's been decorated by a woman."

"My mother was a professional interior decorator," he replied. "You wouldn't be the first person to accuse me of having my mother's taste."

"But your office, it's so white-white-COLOR-white-white-COLOR. But this . . ." She swept a hand in front of the graceful living room.

"One's office is for business; one's home is for other pursuits. And I think it's time you started calling me Eldon."

He guided Gwendolyn toward the sofa. At the center of a cherry wood coffee table sat a cluster of four different-sized candles and a chrome ice bucket with a bottle of champagne. Next to the bucket were two champagne flutes shaped in the old French style—a tall hollow stem opening to a wide mouth, like a martini glass—that the Cocoanut Grove hadn't used in years.

The smell of monkey business lingered in the air like ripe bananas. She thought of the coaster stamped with *Gwendolyn Was Here* in Eldon's pocket. She couldn't ask him about it or he'd know she'd gone through his jacket, but she wondered now for the first time if it was just a coincidence. He pulled the tinfoil from the top of the bottle.

"Just so you know," she said, "you'll be drinking that alone."

"Oh?"

"I'm not a drinker."

He looked at her uncomprehendingly. She was used to that look; she got it often enough from the boozers at the Garden of Allah. It'd been three years since Gwendolyn threw up on Errol Flynn's shoes at that End of Prohibition party, but the memory still made her cringe.

"Ah, but I bet you haven't tried the really good stuff. This is imported from France."

Gwendolyn recognized the label. It was Dom Perignon, the same brand George Cukor brought to celebrate his *Gone with the Wind* news. She'd sipped just enough to keep from offending him that day, and it was delicious, but she just didn't trust herself. "I'll take a glass of Coca-Cola, thanks all the same."

He hesitated, then popped the cork and filled both flutes. "Just in case you change your mind." He excused himself and disappeared into the kitchen. A huge eighteen-inch cathedral radio played softly in the far corner. Fred Astaire began to sing "The Way You Look Tonight" and the lush strings of the RKO orchestra filled the air.

Gwendolyn stood up and wandered around the room. Never in a thousand years had she suspected a smooth-talker like Eldon Laird would live in such a tasteful, elegant home. A framed certificate next to the fireplace caught her eye and she crossed the room to read it. It was from the Boys and Girls Club of America, awarding Eldon for his fundraising efforts over the past twenty years. And it was dated less than a year ago.

Eldon reappeared with a glass of Coca-Cola, a plate of soda crackers, and a small dish of tiny black eggs.

"You're a fundraiser for the Boys and Girls Club?" Gwendolyn asked.

He deposited the refreshments on the coffee table and joined her at the wall. "Is that so hard to believe?"

"Quite frankly, sir, yes it is. You don't seem the charitable type."

"When my father died he left us with nothing, so my mother went back to work. She couldn't afford a sitter, so she threw me in with the Club. Best thing that ever happened to me. It made me the man I am today. I come from the poor side of Cincinnati; without the Club, I probably would have ended up in some street gang a hop, skip, and a robbery away from the slammer. The Club helped me avoid all that, so I like to give back."

She peered into his deep blue eyes. They were clear and lacked any of the signs of deceit she'd learned to pick out at a hundred paces at the Cocoanut Grove. "This is a pleasant surprise, I must say."

She let him lead her back to the sofa where he handed her the glass of Coke. They clinked glasses and he waited for her to sit down.

For God's sake, Gwennie, be careful, she thought. This one even does charity work and is distractingly handsome to boot.

She found herself betting he looked even better out of his expensive clothes than he did in them—

STOP IT. See? He's working his charms even without the champagne. "You, Mr. Eldon Laird, are playing dirty pool."

"How do you figure that?"

"Champagne, caviar, soft music, candles. It makes a girl wonder if the business she has on her mind is the same business you have on yours."

Eldon gave her a smile; probably rehearsed in front of a mirror, but effective nonetheless. "This *is* how I do business. This is how mature adults behave. A little drink, a nice dinner, adult conversation."

Gwendolyn held her smile while she wondered how best to proceed. If he did make a move, she'd find it almost impossible to resist. His tan was a healthy bronze but not overly so. His gold tie clip with the diamond chip was in impeccable taste and it matched his gold Tiffany watch. His hair, nutty brown and slightly bleached by the California sun, was thick and styled perfectly into place. God, what she wouldn't give to rake her fingers through it.

"You think we're sitting on a casting couch, don't you?" he asked.

"You did kiss me back at your office."

"And you kissed me back." A frown flashed across his handsome face. "I'm sorry. I owe you an apology. I should not have kissed you that day. It was unprofessional and inappropriate, and gave you an inaccurate impression of how I do business." His eyes crinkled and a toothy smile, far more genuine than the previous one, surfaced. "There are plenty of agents in this town happy to represent pretty girls willing to screw their way into a Hollywood contract. Despite my behavior back at the office, may I reiterate that I am not one of them. If you'd feel better, I'll move over there." He waved his champagne flute toward one of the chairs on the other side of the table.

Gwendolyn placed her Coca-Cola on the table. She straightened her back and placed her clasped hands on her lap. "So let's talk business," she said.

"Let's."

"If you represent me, how would it work?"

Eldon hesitated for a fraction of a second, sat up as straight as she had, and placed his flute next to hers. "We'd sign a contract together. All legal and above board, but it'd be exclusive. This would mean that I, and only I, would represent you in negotiations with the studios. It also means that if I tell you to lose five pounds, or dye your hair black, or dress like Norma Shearer, or learn how to ride a horse, then that's what you do, because I believe it'll increase your chances of getting hired. The more you work, the more I earn. That's why they call it show *business*."

Eldon delivered this speech without any of the gelatinous charm he'd been pouring on since the moment Gwendolyn arrived. She spied the glass of champagne on the cherry wood coffee table and watched a rope of bubbles push its way to the top.

At long last, a talent agent sees my potential, she thought. If any moment deserves to be celebrated, surely this is it, right?

She picked up the flute.

"I thought you said you don't drink."

"Are you telling me not to?"

"Not at all. Beluga caviar and Coca-Cola do not belong in the same room, let alone the same beautifully shaped mouth."

"A toast, then." She held out her flute toward Eldon and he clinked his with hers. "To my hair," Gwendolyn said.

He frowned, not comprehending. "Your hair?"

"May you never ask me to dye it black."

CHAPTER 6

Marcus didn't know what time it was, but he didn't need to. He'd let his clock wind down because its relentless tick-tick-ticking annoyed him. There had been an inspirational symphony of sounds in his villa: the clink of martini glasses down by the pool, the clack of typewriters from screenwriting neighbors, the chirping of birds in the elms and weeping willows. But now he was back in the same dark, cramped room in the main house, the one he thought he'd escaped when he got the job at Cosmopolitan Pictures, the room he thought he'd never see again.

In this room he could hear nothing. No martini glasses, no laughter, no birdsong. He had nothing to keep him company but the lingering stink of bourbon and regret.

The disastrous dinner up at San Simeon had been followed by a hellish fourteen-hour bus ride back to L.A. with Alice and her accursed "confidence booster." The stupid broad might have mentioned it contained a mixture of cocaine, codeine, and blackberry schnapps. "What kinda lightweight are you?" she'd screeched beside him on the bus.

Marcus took another slug from the near-empty bottle of Four Roses bourbon on the pillow next to him. He rolled over and buried his face in the pillows and asked himself for the umpteenth time, "Why did you let yourself get talked into drinking that crap? Nothing good ever comes from that cheap Harlow knockoff."

Flashes of last night's party came at him like cheap fireworks. What had started out as a gathering to remember

Irving Thalberg—MGM's wonder boy, whose death threw all of Hollywood into shock and mourning—soon went the way of all Garden parties. He had vague recollections of Tallulah Bankhead and Marlene Dietrich laughing over something about a trapeze artist. He could recall balancing a full glass of bourbon on his head while someone—either Clara Bow or that production designer from Paramount who'd just moved in, the one with the Clara Bow eyes—counted to a hundred. Alexander Woollcott puffing cigar smoke in his face while Dorothy Parker threatened to squirt him with Chypre. Didn't someone fall into the pool? Was it him? He couldn't remember getting back to his room. Wasn't the first time.

"Rosebud," he whispered into the duck-down pillow. "Of all the names."

A knock on his door pulled his head up.

"Mr. Adler, are you there? It's me, Ben."

Ben was the Garden's resident bellboy, although calling a portly guy well into his forties a bellboy was perhaps pushing it. "I got a message for you."

Marcus yanked open his door and shot Ben a *Well, what is it?* look through what he assumed were bloodshot eyes.

"You have a visitor," Ben said. "Downstairs. In the bar."

"Who is it?" It was an effort to get the words out. Marcus' tongue felt like it had been ripped out of his head and dragged along the bottom of the pool. Twice.

"She's in the bar, last booth in the far corner."

Marcus looked down at what he was wearing. His dark-brown corduroy pants were reasonably presentable but his shirt was crumpled beyond repair. If he donned his burgundy sports coat he could probably get away with it, especially in the low light of the bar. Even during the day it was hard to make out the edges of tabletops, and whether your glass was empty or full.

* * *

Marcus walked into the Sahara Room and peered into the gloom. With its well-spaced rows of intimate cocktail tables and wall of deeply curved booths smothered in murky light, the bar was a perfect place for a furtive assignation . . . or meeting someone when you're still shedding the dregs of last night's fitful sleep.

In the far corner he could make out the silhouette of a woman's hat. He picked his way through the tables and drew alongside the final booth, then turned to face his caller. Her face was veiled behind a curtain of netting. "I believe you've been asking for me?"

"Won't you please take a seat?"

She had a foreign accent, familiar, but Marcus couldn't place it. He slid into the other side of the booth as she lifted the veil and folded it back over her brown satin pillbox hat. Greta Garbo pulled a cigarette from a dark-blue packet of Gitanes.

He picked up the cut crystal votive holder between them and held it for a long, lingering moment as she lit her cigarette. Although it was more than five years since he'd given up his seat for her the night the *Montfalcone* sank into the Pacific, he hoped she'd remember him. But there was no flicker of recognition. He lit a cigarette of his own.

By now his eyes had started to adjust to the muddy light. He could see her studying him with a hint of that notoriously enigmatic smile. He was wishing he'd taken the time to brush his furry teeth when she began to speak.

"I believe we have a mutual friend. Mr. George Cukor. He directed me in *Camille*. I was very wary of him at first. I don't know why; it is my nature to be wary of everyone, I suppose. But he and I, we came to be very close. He is now one of my most dear and treasured friends. I grew to trust him, and look at the result."

Marcus nodded. His head was starting to pound in a way that only a hair of the dog could help.

"Usually I do not indulge in gossip," Garbo continued. "I have no time and no interest. However, I have just been told of an incident which happened during the filming of *Camille*. You came to George's rescue. Is this true?"

Marcus nodded slowly and looked around for the bartender. The darkness seemed to have swallowed him whole.

Garbo reached out and held his hands between hers. They were soft and gentle, so pale and delicate, but they squeezed his firmly. "Thank you, Mr. Adler," she said. "Thank you so very much. If the press had learned of such an event . . ." Her voice was slightly deeper than in the movies, her accent more pronounced. She let go of his hand and shook her head sadly. "My George would have been devastated, his career over, and that is too great a loss for Hollywood to bear. I asked you here so that I could thank you."

"That's very nice of you, Miss Garbo, but not necessary."

Marcus went to take another drag of his cigarette, but it had gone out. He took the candle again and relit it. Greta Garbo broke out into a smile. It was a wide, natural smile that struck Marcus as being unconcerned with lighting and camera angles. "The *Montfalcone*!" she exclaimed. "That is where I know your face."

He smiled. "I didn't think you would remember. It was a long time ago."

"How could I forget? You were brave, gallant."

"I couldn't take the last seat on that lifeboat from a lady. Especially you, Miss Garbo."

She pushed aside his reply with a wave. "Was it a terrible ordeal to reach the shore? You must have been terrified. I thought of you for weeks, but there were no deaths reported so I assumed you were all right."

Marcus told her all he'd had to do was keep his eyes glued on the Santa Monica pier's Ferris wheel and keep swimming until he made it to shore. He didn't mention how the thought of newspaper headlines proclaiming him the lifesaver of MGM's biggest star was what really kept him going.

She made a tsking sound. "Twice you have been a savior. Once to me and once to my dear George. I am very much in your debt. How may I repay it?"

Marcus gazed at Garbo's face and thought of the screenplay outline sitting in his cramped room upstairs.

A movie about the life of a nineteenth-century journalist had been flailing around the backwaters of Marcus' imagination ever since Kathryn told him how inspired she was by Nellie Bly. Before the age of twenty-five, Bly had written investigative articles on female factory workers, lived in Mexico as a foreign correspondent, and feigned insanity to get into a woman's lunatic asylum to investigate reports of abuse. And then she duplicated Jules Verne's round-the-world trip in fewer than Phileas Fogg's eighty days. She was a strong, exciting woman whose story begged to be put on-screen. So he'd worked on it off and on during his spare time with the thought that it could be his escape from the bottom-feeding dregs of the MGM food chain.

He also quietly hoped it would extinguish the image of his father that had come to haunt him. Always staring, always frowning, always silently announcing that Marcus was the screw-up he'd always known him to be. And now that MGM had let him go, he wasn't even hanging off the nethermost ring.

"As a matter of fact," Marcus said, "there is something I'd like to run by you."

CHAPTER 7

Wilkerson never asked Kathryn how she'd managed to square things with Louella, and Kathryn wasn't about to volunteer the information. Not that her white-hot tip of the Katharine Hepburn-Howard Hughes romance completely restored balance, but it appeared to be enough to melt the ice. Louella now regarded Kathryn coolly at meetings of the Hollywood Women's Press Club, but she hadn't banned her outright.

The Ice Age with her mother had started to thaw, too. Kathryn hoped she'd managed to put her point across that while Francine liked to think of Louella Parsons as a friend, perhaps she ought to choose her words more carefully when speaking near her finely tuned ears. When Kathryn sent her mother a peace offering – a breathtaking Anatole dahlia whose vivid crimson leaves were striped with gold – Francine invited her to tea in her garden. They were tentative with each other at first, but it turned out to be a pleasant afternoon.

All in all, life had begun to settle down comfortably, so the telephone call she received at work that first week of November came as a surprise. A deep, cultured voice introduced himself as Earl Hubbings, the West Coast editor of *Life* magazine.

"Now that *Life* has just been bought by Henry Luce, we're re-jigging the whole thing," he said. "We think you have a fine style and would fit into our new format. We would very much like you to join our team and are prepared to offer you double your present salary."

After the Louella Parsons contretemps had abated, Wilkerson gave Kathryn a raise. It wasn't huge but she'd been happy enough with it. In her mind, it helped compensate for her shattered illusions about Wilkerson and the flaws she'd never suspected. Even so, her toes curled at the thought of doubling her pay. "But you don't know what my present salary is," she told him.

"You and I both know, Miss Massey, that Hollywood can be a very porous town."

Kathryn jotted the word *porous* onto her desk blotter. For all his faults, Wilkerson was a realist and she knew he wouldn't blame her for jumping at an opportunity like this. But she couldn't do it. Wilkerson took a chance when he hired her. She liked to think she'd justified his instinct that she was the right girl for the job, even if a shallow gossip column wasn't the job she'd originally wanted.

"Thank you, Mr. Hubbings, I very much appreciate the offer—"

"I want you to think it through," he told her, and ended the call before Kathryn could say no.

She stared at the word *porous* on her blotter and weighed up the pros and cons of telling Wilkerson about this herself. It wouldn't hurt to let him know, she decided. That way, she could be sure he heard something that remotely resembled the truth.

She headed to his office but the boss wasn't in. The telephone rang and Vera let out a groan. "I've been busting to go to the ladies' room for the past forty minutes, but this thing won't drop dead no matter how many times I tell it." Kathryn told her to go; she'd take the message. She picked up the phone.

"This is Mr. Chadwick of the First National Bank of Hollywood," said the voice at the other end. That was the bank her paychecks drew from. "Yes, Mr. Chadwick, what can I do for you?"

"I need to speak with Mr. Wilkerson."

Kathryn fidgeted with the telephone cord. "Mr. Wilkerson is not in this afternoon. This is Kathryn Massey. Can I help you in any way?"

"I really must speak with Wilkerson immediately."

"He's not near a telephone right now," Kathryn said. She peered into the corridor; Vera was nowhere in sight. "We expect him back right after his luncheon appoint—"

"This cannot wait."

Kathryn hesitated, then said, "The payroll account is empty again, isn't it, Mr. Chadwick?"

There was a long, empty pause on the other end of the line before Chadwick said, "Five dollars and fifty-seven cents is all that's left."

"And it's payday in two days," Kathryn added.

There was another achingly long pause. "Today, Miss Massey. He knows the number." Chadwick hung up.

When Kathryn told Vera about the phone call and asked where Wilkerson was, she didn't like the way Vera replied, "He's at Anita's."

"Who is Anita?"

Vera looked stricken. Kathryn closed the door that led into the corridor and turned back to the secretary. "Vera, I know what happened in June. And I know it was Howard Hughes who bailed him out. Is he down at Santa Anita gambling the payroll?"

Vera pressed her lips together. Her eyes darted back and forth. Kathryn laid a gentle hand on her trembling arm.

"Vera, I know you're privy to sensitive information. But payroll is due in two days. The boss needs to do something about this *today*."

Vera let out a groan and her shoulders dropped a full inch. "He spent the payroll down in Mexico at Agua Caliente a couple of weeks ago. He was up sixty grand but then lost it all on the blackjack table. He's at Santa Anita right now trying to win it back."

"What sort of plan is that?"

"The plan of a madman."

* * *

Even in a crowd, her boss wasn't hard to find. Vera had told Kathryn about his favorite box at the racetrack, and there he was in his pristine cream linen suit and matching Panama hat, hunched over a crumpled fistful of betting tickets. His knuckles were almost as white as his sleeve.

Kathryn gingerly approached this box, planted herself at the waist-high gate and crossed her arms.

"Why, you dirty, lowdown, rotten, stinking little bastard!"

"Kathryn!" At least he had enough decency to go pale. "How did you—? What are you—?"

Kathryn swung open the gate and stepped into the box. There were chairs for four, but it was just him and a magnum of champagne in an ice bucket. She poked her boss in the chest. "Everyone at the *Reporter* works so very hard. They put in long hours. They give their all, and they deserve a paycheck at the end of the week."

"Will you please pipe down?" He pulled a handkerchief from the inside pocket of his suit and mopped the sweat off his forehead.

She was aware that people were starting to look and that they knew who he was. Satisfied, she took the seat next to him. She looked out across the field and watched the trainers lead thoroughbreds toward the starting gate. A skittish black filly with a tightly braided tail reared up and yanked against her bridle. Kathryn lowered her voice. "Chadwick called. There's five whole bucks left in the payroll account. I know about Agua Caliente, the two hundred grand, and I know about the blackjack table."

"Did Vera—?"

Kathryn turned to her boss. His professionally shaved face was still pale. "Vera wasn't at her desk when the call came in."

"Look," he said, "I'm having a good day here. I've parlayed five grand into twelve. At the rate I'm going, I'll be at twenty by the end of the day. That's more than enough to cover the payroll. A couple of hours is all I need. It's as close to a sure thing as you can get."

She hoped her disgust showed on her face. "I'm sure the folks at *Life* magazine don't worry about whether or not Henry Luce will cover the payroll."

"How does that figure into anything?"

Kathryn faced the track again; a new race had just started. "They offered me a job today. *Life*'s Hollywood correspondent. Double my present salary."

"Oh Jesus no, you didn't."

She let him stew on that while the crowd around them roared. As the sleek black horse called Revere's Revenge passed the finishing post, Kathryn wondered if she'd backed the right horse herself.

CHAPTER 8

Gwendolyn sat at one of the bamboo cocktail tables in the Zamboanga South Seas Club and tried not to look like a streetwalker on the make. She squirmed in her tall chair but it was hard to sit down in the dress she'd made especially for this date. It flattered her bust and waist, but it dug into her hips and under her arms and if she didn't watch it, she was going to bust her butt seam. She decided it was more comfortable to stand—which would make her look better when Eldon walked in, anyway.

She looked at her watch again. It was well past six o'clock. Where could he be? It wasn't like him to be two minutes late, let alone nearly twenty.

Go on, admit it, Gwendolyn. You've given the goods away and now he takes you for granted.

Damn that Dom Perignon. Damn the way it slid down her throat like liquid velvet and tasted the way she expected the water in heaven to taste. It may not have made her throw up all over Eldon Laird's imported shoes, but it did take her tongue captive when Eldon declared that he was sorry but he couldn't stop himself, and took her in his arms and kissed her deeply. And it was entirely responsible for rendering her helpless when he gently led her upstairs. But she knew she couldn't blame the Dom Perignon for the fact that here she was, weeks later, still sleeping with Eldon Laird.

Gwendolyn had had her fair share of discreet affairs and clandestine encounters—she did live at the Garden of Allah, after all—so she knew enough to be able to spot a good lover. Mr. Eldon Laird had turned out to be everything she'd thought he would be: passionate, skillful, considerate, and in no rush to get out of bed afterward. She'd declared to Kathryn and Marcus that he was the best lover she'd ever had. The man regularly took her breath away. But his bedroom skills were not the problem. The problem was that she hadn't yet received any evidence that he was now her agent.

Harry Carpenter's Drive-In Restaurant, one of the few places that stayed open all night, became their usual haunt. It was an octagonal building on the corner of Sunset and Vine that customers could drive right on up to. You didn't even need to get out of your car—the waitresses came to you! A couple of times a week, Eldon would pick her up after work around two in the morning and they'd head down there for Harryburgers, then invariably back to his place to spend what was left of the night together.

They'd talk about anything and everything. The Olympic Games in Berlin and that German leader everyone was getting nervous over, William Powell and Myrna Loy getting their footprints in cement outside Grauman's Chinese, the effect Irving Thalberg's death would have on MGM. Eldon was never short of an opinion on the rumors that the FBI had made a secret report on the Communist influence on the Screen Actors Guild.

Oh, yes, Gwendolyn told Kathryn and Marcus, we talk about everything except what he can do for *me*.

It was Marcus who suggested meeting him someplace new. "Dress up to knock him out," he'd said. "Get him so bug-eyed he can't refuse you, then slug him with a *What about me?* speech."

Kathryn suggested the Zamboanga. The Polynesian thing was catching on fast, and by all accounts the Zamboanga was the best place in town.

The front door swung open and a volley of machine-gun laughter ricocheted off the Tongan happy masks. Three men stumbled in, snorting over something too riotous to hold in. They were all in their forties, wearing tailored suits. As they moved toward the bar she could see that they were virtually carbon copies of each other: well-groomed, well dressed, well tanned.

Eldon spotted Gwendolyn and waved. He said something to his pals and they wound their way around the packed cocktail tables toward her.

"Gwendolyn!" Eldon exclaimed, "I want you to meet a couple of my esteemed colleagues and competitors."

He punched the shoulder of a rake-thin guy with a Clark Gable pencil moustache and suspiciously black pomaded hair, but otherwise was decently presentable and quietly attractive in his own way. "This here's Dewey DeWitt."

Gwendolyn offered her hand and noticed that Dewey's fingernails shined with the care of an expert manicurist. She turned to the third guy, tall and fair and tanned like Eldon, wearing a snug suit tailored to his athletic frame.

"And this is Timothy Holt." The guy's handshake was firm and masculine.

"Pleased to meet you both," Gwendolyn said, and then peered at Eldon as if to say, *And you brought them on our date?* Eldon either missed or ignored it. "And how do y'all know each other?" she asked.

"We're all agents," Eldon replied.

"Yep," said Dewey, "we all started out as Broadway talent scouts, but eventually the sweet siren of Hollywood could be ignored no longer."

When a waiter in a white shirt, black bowtie, and grass skirt appeared, Eldon ordered Zamboanga Zoom-Zooms for the men and a Virgin Voom-Voom for Gwendolyn. Eldon was used to Gwendolyn's abstinence by now, but his pals fell all over themselves with shock. A drink? Without *booze*? Unfathomable.

"Hey, come on, fellas, the lady doesn't drink. That's what makes her a lady." He gave her one of his playful winks. "At least that's one of the reasons."

Gwendolyn could feel Eldon's friends' eyes on her chest. She had chosen this particular pattern because of the low neckline that placed her generous cleavage on display. Tonight was supposed to be about seducing Eldon Laird into agreeing to anything—and it could have worked. Had he sensed what she was up to and brought these guys along as a buffer?

Eldon was good like that, Gwendolyn had learned. He always seemed to know when she was hankering for a Harryburger and when she just wanted to go home. He never introduced a topic that was beyond her depth, and he had never pressed the booze issue. It had already done the trick, after all—one glass of the good stuff and she was between his sheets before she could say "Dom Peri-who?"

The Zoom-Zooms arrived in cups made of hollowed-out bamboo, and as far as Gwendolyn could tell it was some sort of rum punch, heavy on the banana and grenadine. They each had a tropical flower garnish with long tongue-like petals the color of Chinese firecrackers. It was Timothy who noticed they were the same flower as the ones on Gwendolyn's dress. They weren't, she knew—the flowers on her dress had shorter petals and were wider at the base—but they were close, so she pretended to agree.

However, by the second round of drinks she was discovering how whiskey sours and Zamboanga Zoom-Zooms didn't mix too well. The guys slid from a trio of suave bachelors holding forth on silk ties and Park Avenue restaurants to a bunch of loud drunks that made people wish they'd gone to the Seven Seas Saloon instead.

By the end of the third round, Gwendolyn had given up any hope of getting Eldon to herself in a sober enough state to talk business. If she'd known she was going to sit for hours, she wouldn't have worked all week on this tight dress.

By the time the fourth round arrived, she was fighting to swallow the ganglion of resentment pushing its way up her throat. She slipped off the bar stool and announced, "If you will excuse me, the time has come to powder my nose."

Eldon had to remind his friends that it was customary for a gentleman to rise to his feet when a lady left the table.

"My 'pol'gies m'lady," Dewey exclaimed. He raised his right hand to lift a hat no longer on his head—and knocked over a fresh cocktail. The bamboo cup fell over with a thump and dumped its contents all over Timothy's coat sleeve.

Timothy Holt leapt to his feet. "MOTHER OF PEARL!"

Great gobs of Zamboanga Zoom-Zoom soaked into the sleek material. Gwendolyn grabbed up a handful of paper napkins and started to blot at the stain, but there weren't enough napkins on the table to soak up all that sticky red crap. If she wasn't careful she was going to get it all over her dress.

The waiter appeared holding a white hand towel and a tall glass filled with soda water. "You can probably save your jacket," he said to Holt, " if you take it into the men's room and start blotting it up with this." But Timothy just stood there. Clearly, the man had never done his own laundry in his life.

"Do you think you could give it a go for him?" Eldon asked Gwendolyn quietly.

* * *

The walls of the ladies' room were painted in a California muralist's version of the African jungle: broadleaved ferns and vines like pythons covered the cinderblock wall from corner to corner. She laid the jacket across one of the basins and splashed soda water on it. As she picked it up to dab red gunk from the pocket, she felt something inside. It was hard and round, about the size of the palm of her hand. She wasn't going to peek inside to see what it was, but a crushing feeling got the better of her.

Her hand pulled out a stack of cardboard drink coasters. There were two from the Vine Street Brown Derby, one from the Hi-Hat down on Wilshire, and two from the Long Ship Café on Santa Monica pier. She didn't want to, but she knew she had to turn them over. On the back of each of them, stamped in red ink, were the same three words:

Gwendolyn Was Here

CHAPTER 9

There were many people who said that Louella Parsons was the most powerful woman in Hollywood. But those in the know argued that the most powerful woman in Hollywood might actually be someone most Americans had never heard of.

Ida Koverman had been Louis B. Mayer's secretary for longer than most people could remember. It was straight-backed, no-nonsense, poker-faced Ida who was the gatekeeper to Mayer's office. Nobody – but *nobody* – got to see Mayer without going through her first. Miss Koverman was the only person Mayer trusted completely, and without her to guide him through each long and busy day, he would have been lost to the dusty scrolls of Hollywood history. Without Louis B. Mayer, there would have been no MGM; without Ida Koverman, there would have been no Louis B. Mayer.

So when Marcus appeared at Ida Koverman's desk, he dug his hands in his pockets to hide his nerves and mustered up a big-boy voice.

"Good morning," he said. "I have an eleven o'clock appointment with Mr. Mayer."

"Marcus Adler?" she said without lifting her eyes from her Corona Sterling.

"That's right."

The woman nodded curtly and left Marcus to hover around the periphery of her desk like a Roman kitchen slave summoned by Julius Caesar himself.

"The rules are simple," she stated, her eyes still on her typewriter. "You take a seat over there until I give you the go-ahead. When you get to Mr. Mayer's desk, you stand until he points to a seat. Refer to him as Mr. Mayer at all times. And when he waves like this—" Ida made a fluttering wave with her left hand, "that's your signal to exit his office immediately."

* * *

The walk to Louis B. Mayer's desk felt like the end of a Jimmy Cagney picture—a slow walk down an elongated office toward a desk built up like a judge's platform. A hanging judge. Dead screenwriter walking, Marcus thought. Rumor had it that Mayer had seen a picture of Benito Mussolini sitting in an all-white office and decided he wanted one too. The result was stunning, but the irony that Prime Minister Mussolini was starting to look increasingly despotic seemed to have been lost on Mayer.

Marcus arrived at Mayer's elevated desk and watched the movie czar sign a stack of papers. The guy gave no indication that he even knew Marcus was standing ten feet in front of him. More than a minute ticked by before Mayer slid the papers into a tray to one side. "Take a seat," he said, then broke out into a smile. "Adler, isn't it?"

Mayer's unexpected smile threw Marcus off guard. Charlie Butterworth, an actor living at the Garden of Allah, had warned Marcus that Mayer never smiled unless he wanted to screw someone down to a smaller salary.

Marcus nodded as he sank into a seat in front of the huge white desk.

"Truly, I regret that it's taken me this long to meet the man who came to the rescue of such a highly valued member of the MGM team."

Marcus stared blankly at Mayer. "Which one?" he asked, then wished he hadn't.

Mayer's eyes widened behind his round wire-rimmed glasses. "Exactly how many valued members of the MGM team have you rescued?"

Kathryn's voice piped up in his head: *If Mayer asks you a question you don't want to answer, answer him with another question.* "Who are we talking about?"

"George Cukor, of course. I very much appreciate the help you gave George in that delicate matter some months back." Mayer leaned back into his chair. "Tell me, Adler, who else have you rescued?"

Marcus hesitated.

"Don't lie to me. I'll find out anyway."

Marcus crossed his legs and pulled at the cuffs of his shirt, but realized he was only delaying the inevitable. He gave in and told Mayer about the night the *Montfalcone* sank, and how he gave up his seat on the last lifeboat to Greta Garbo.

Mayer's eyes went beady and ratlike. "Things are starting to add up. But son, did you really save the life of the biggest goddamned star in Hollywood and then didn't tell anyone?"

"Miss Garbo is a very private person. I figured it wasn't up to me to go around town bragging and whatnot."

"I appreciate people who can keep their traps shut."

Marcus pushed out a "Thank you, sir."

"At any rate, I asked you in here for two reasons. To thank you for what you did for Cukor. I understand you really jumped through the hoops for him that night. Good job."

"Thank you, sir."

"And I hear that you've got a good idea for a picture."

Marcus wanted to blink but didn't dare. Garbo had responded with her usual Scandinavian coolness to Marcus' Nellie Bly idea. She made very little comment about it, gave no indication that she liked the idea, hated it, or didn't care one way or the other. And then she'd left Marcus sitting in a dark and empty bar.

"I believe it is," he replied.

Mayer glanced at his watch. "Can you tell me about it in less than three minutes?"

Thank God Kathryn had made Marcus rehearse a synopsis of the life of Nellie Bly and why it would make a good biopic. As he launched into the short version of the spiel they'd prepared, part of him wished he was still standing so he could shake loose the tremors that had turned his hands into spiders.

When he got to the end, Mayer said, "Fine, fine, that all sounds good. You go back to work and tell Taggert you're being switched to Garbo's next project."

Marcus held his breath. He was back. *He was back!* At MGM this time, not Cosmopolitan Pictures. But who was Taggert?

Mayer peered at Marcus through his glasses. "Is there a problem?"

"It's just that . . ."

Mayer snapped his fingers. "Wait just one goddamned minute. Adler, you said? F'chrissakes, you're not the one who went up to the Castle, are you? The one who ran around saying *rosebud* right to Hearst's face?"

"I only said it the one time—"

Mayer broke out into a honking donkey laugh and punctuated it by thumping the desk with his pudgy fist. "When I first heard about that I laughed so hard I nearly had a bowel movement. That crusty old bastard must have had a conniption fit!"

"He got so red in the face I thought I'd given him a heart attack."

"Shame you didn't, Adler. You shoulda run around that whole joint yelling *Rosebud!* until he keeled over. Jesus Christ, I'm surprised he didn't fire you."

"He did."

Mayer's jaw dropped open. "So much for me knowing every damned thing that goes on around here. You got the bum's rush, huh?" Mayer shrugged. "I guess I woulda done the same. Suits me, though." He stood up. "Let me shake the hand of the man who nearly put Hearst in the boneyard." Marcus stood and shook Mayer's doughy hand. "That will be all, Adler." He gave the little wave just as Ida said he would.

Marcus about-faced. He went to take a step but he could almost feel the heat of his father's breath on his cheek. He'd been hearing that voice a lot since his dramatic slide down the career pole. *You know what you should do, but you don't have the balls,* his father said.

Marcus pictured his parents and his four siblings lined up in the tenth row of the Bijou Theater on Walnut Street. He could see his parents—his father's handlebar moustache and his mother's homemade dress—staring up at the credit: *SCREENPLAY BY MARCUS ADLER*. His father's mouth would gape open while his mother muttered, "So that's what happened to my Marcus."

He turned around again and stayed glued to the white carpet until Mayer returned his stare.

"Is there something else, Adler?"

Marcus didn't move. Nor did Mayer. They both stood their ground like billy goats in breeding season. Finally, Marcus said, "I'm going to be writing the screenplay for your biggest star's next movie."

Don't break his stare, Marcus told himself. You saved his best director from public ridicule and his biggest star from a sinking ship.

"That's right," Mayer said coolly. "You will be."

"I'd like to come out of this meeting knowing where I stand."

"Where would you like to stand?"

"In the line marked two hundred dollars a week."

"Tell me, Adler, what line were you standing in before you singlehandedly nearly ruined the highly profitable relationship between Cosmopolitan Pictures and MGM?"

Marcus forced himself not to swallow. "The hundred and fifty a week line."

"Well now, that's extraordinarily fucking funny because I thought you were standing in the Complete Fiasco At Hearst Castle line." Mayer's eyes bored into Marcus'.

What was I thinking playing chicken like this, Marcus thought. He broke the staring contest. "Yes, Mr. Mayer."

He turned around. The march back down the length of Mayer's white-on-white office looked twice as long as it had coming in. He'd only taken his first couple of steps before he heard Mayer clear his throat. "Do you know why my desk is on this raised platform?"

Mayer's face was a frozen mask.

"I assume it's to intimidate people," Marcus replied.

"Does it work?"

"Yes, sir, it's quite effective."

"Apparently it's not effective enough," Mayer put his glasses back on. "Three hundred a week."

CHAPTER 10

The Los Angeles station for the Atchison, Topeka and Santa Fe Railway was an imposing building of sandy brownstone topped with four domes and dotted with Juliet balconies on all sides. It was a thoroughly charming building that Gwendolyn would normally have stopped to admire, but not this time. Not today. Not now.

She silently cursed the loose heel on her right shoe. She'd caught it between broken floorboards on the streetcar into downtown. It hadn't broken off completely but it was halfway there, threatening to snap away with every hurried step.

By the time Gwendolyn finally hobbled onto platform number one, the Super Chief locomotive had already pulled in and the last of its passengers, wearied by the three-day haul from Chicago, were trailing their porters. Gwendolyn looked around for Eldon Laird but it was clear she'd missed him.

She knew Eldon well enough to know he wasn't the type who enjoyed surprises, but she was past the point of caring. She was there to corner him once and for all: Did he or did he not intend to represent her? She'd made a fine plan, except she hadn't counted on being handicapped by a cheap shoe. She ignored the bead of sweat trickling down her spine and scanned the platform. Maybe he'd returned to his stateroom at the last minute to retrieve a forgotten briefcase or that homburg with the fiery red hatband. Somebody had to be the last one off the train.

Not long after that night at the Zamboanga, he took off for Chicago to check out a couple of performers in the touring production of *Anything Goes*, then went on to New York and Broadway. In the weeks he'd been back East, she hadn't heard from him at all. And now it was New Year's Eve, and she needed to start 1937 knowing where she stood. He had the power to open doors she couldn't begin to open for herself.

Eldon was big with the promises. They'd started out as "Of course I'm talking you up to the studios." Then it was "Naturally, they're showing interest. But these things take time, my darling. These people are too smart to be bamboozled." This eventually, almost predictably, gave way to "We need to do this the right way." Oh yes, Gwendolyn told herself, that sort of thing makes for great pillow talk, but sooner or later a girl needs to see results.

And then there was that other matter that nagged at her: all those *Gwendolyn Was Here* coasters. When she found Eldon's, she was intrigued and flattered, but the five she came across in his pal's jacket? That just didn't seem right.

She waited until the very last of the passengers cleared the platform, then tottered back up the ramp and onto the station's main concourse. The place had suffered significant damage some years back in the Long Beach earthquake and the railway company hadn't done much to spruce up the place. It was dim and musty, more shadow than light, and in desperate need of a vigorous mopping.

She looked around, hoping to spot a shoe repair. When she spotted a small key cutter's booth next to Topeka Tommy's Saloon, the station's bar, she headed toward it. With any luck, the guy behind the counter might at least give her a drop of glue.

It wasn't until she was almost alongside the booth that a flash of red inside Topeka Tommy's caught her eye. She stepped toward the broad glass doors that opened into the bar and peered inside. It was Eldon all right—she'd know that scarlet ribbon on his felt homburg anywhere. It wasn't until she'd stepped inside the bustling bar that she saw he wasn't alone. He sat with his back against a pillar, talking with the two sleek agents he'd dragged along to their date.

Gwendolyn sighed. Them? *Again?*

She shifted her weight onto the foot with the unbroken shoe and watched the three men talk while she decided what to do. She couldn't very well have it out with Eldon while those two slickers sneered and smiled. On the other hand, they'd eventually have to head home, and if she stuck around she could speak her mind when they got back to his place. But as she was juggling her options, a growing awareness began to dawn over her. Something wasn't right.

DeWitt and Holt were scowling at Eldon with a ferocity that made Gwendolyn blink. Holt jumped off his bar stool and leaned his bulky frame over Eldon. He started jabbing the air in front of Eldon's face.

Gwendolyn raised the collar of her overcoat to cover as much of her face as possible and stole over to the bar, sitting down on the far side of the pillar.

"That's the magic goddamned number!" one of them said. "Thirty! You remember that? Huh? Do ya?"

"Sure." Eldon's voice remained unruffled. "I came up with it."

"What'll it be, ma'am?"

Gwendolyn jumped. She hadn't seen the bartender approach.

"Oh, nothing for me, thank you. I just—"

"Ma'am, this here is a bar. If you don't want to order anything, I'm going to have to ask you to leave."

"Why do you think we're so damned pissed with you?" DeWitt's voice was raw and ragged. "With that last menu from the Brown Derby, I've now got thirty Gwendolyns. And that means I get first crack at her."

"Oh!" Gwendolyn squeezed her eyes shut and clapped her hand over her mouth.

"Ma'am, are you all right?"

"I know, Dewey," Eldon said. "I know what thirty means."

Gwendolyn opened her eyes again. "Whatever those guys are having, I'll have one too, but make it a double."

The bartender nodded. "Double whiskey, coming right up."

There was a long pause on the other side of the pillar before Eldon continued. "Well, fellas, I guess the time has come for me to make my confession. I know we had this pact and I know we had rules, but there's really no way I can sugarcoat this for you both, so I won't. I've been screwing her since September."

"You've been *what?*"

"That wasn't the agreement!"

"I know." Eldon's voice had become as nauseating as an oil slick.

The bartender placed a large shot glass in front of Gwendolyn; it was filled with amber liquid that looked cool and refreshing. She lifted the glass and slammed its contents into her mouth. It burned like acid as she forced it down her throat. "Gimme another one."

"The bet was to see who could get to thirty first," Holt said. "Ain't you forgetting that I'm the one who found her? I did the asking around. I'm the one who sent you to the Cocoanut Grove to check her out."

"Of course I know all that." Eldon's voice sounded placatingly jokey. "And I'm the one who came up with the bet."

Gwendolyn felt the color drain from her cheeks. She pressed her hands against them as the realization of what had been going on bore down on her like a trunk full of marbles.

"And we all know why," one of them scoffed. Gwendolyn had started to lose track of which one was which. "Because at the time, you already had four coasters and three menus. With a head start like that, it looked like a pretty sure thing you were going to win. And now you're telling me you've been plowing that babe since—you're a goddamned shithead, Laird."

"Yeah," the other agreed. "The dirtiest o' lowlife, double-cr—"

"Fellas!" Eldon let loose with one of his charming laughs. "Come on. You know how the game works."

Gwendolyn's second double appeared in front of her. She squeezed her eyes shut so tight she could see geometric patterns swirling in front of her like snowflakes. She wrapped her fingers around the glass and drained it in one gulp.

One of Eldon's chums yelled, "GET OFF ME! You don't want to touch me right now. I oughta slug you clear through to next Christmas."

"You saw her," Eldon countered. "How was I supposed to resist that?"

"Self-control."

"Come on! Look me in the eye and tell me you would've done anything different."

"Screw you, buddy!"

"Look," Eldon said, "what do you want me to say? I shouldn't have done it? You're right. A bet's a bet? Right again. But I can't *unsleep* with her, boys, so what do you want from me? Hey, at least I came clean."

Gwendolyn felt as though her head was a buoy in a squall. She lurched between the four emotional compass points of furious, embarrassed, demoralized, and wounded. She tried to gather herself. Right now was a perfect time to step out from behind these suitcases and lash these bastards with a stream of insults and abuse before storming away into a fade to black. But she was too crushed, too humiliated, too outraged and too drunk to gather the right words together and deliver them in a way anything close to what they deserved.

"You want a third?" the guy behind the bar asked.

"No." Gwendolyn opened her purse and pulled out a dollar bill. "I've got somewhere to be."

* * *

The first time Gwendolyn laid eyes on Eldon's Spanish Mission-fairytale castle home, she had thought it utterly delightful. Now it just seemed ridiculous. This whole affair of theirs—the wooing, the champagne, the kisses, the promises—it had all been a fairy tale. She thought about Eldon's hands as they glided over her skin while he told her how much he admired her for her depth and intelligence even more than for her stunning looks. Oh yes, Mr. Eldon Laird was indeed the well-seasoned teller of fairy tales.

She looked at the small bottle of Four Roses whiskey in her hand. She'd made the taxi driver stop at a liquor store on Wilshire and buy it for her. One more mouthful and it'd be empty. She drained it and dropped it on the grass as she headed around the right-hand side of the house towards the bathroom window. The fool always kept it unlocked. She found a stick in the petunia bed and used it to pry the window open. She gripped the windowsill to pull herself through. It kept on slipping but she somehow managed to get a strong enough grip to hoist herself in. On the way, she tore her sleeve on a nail and grazed her knee on a weathered patch of wood. "You're plastered," she told herself. "Good for you."

She tumbled headfirst into the laundry sink and heard a dull *thump* as her skull connected with the metal. It hurt but she didn't care. She extricated herself from it like a long-limbed puppet and wobbled her way down the hallway to Eldon's bedroom.

She found his collection of *Gwendolyn Was Here* in an old Toll House chocolate chip cookie tin under his bed. They were all there—the coasters, menus, and matchbooks from every joint she'd visited that year: the Brown Derby, the Alexandria Hotel, the Hollywood Grill, the Ship Café, Brewer's Café next to Columbia.

"How bold you felt!" she exclaimed out loud. "So innovative! Soon you'll get the whole town talking about this mysterious Gwendolyn." She let out a long wet raspberry. "What a cotton-pickin' joke."

She emptied the cookie tin onto Eldon's silk bedspread and tried not to think of the number of times he'd brought her to ecstasy there. "You just wanted to be the first to thirty," she told the pile. She reached into her purse and pulled out a book of matches from the Sardi's on Hollywood Boulevard – ironically, one of the places she'd never gone with her little rubber stamp. She struck a match, watched the head burst into flame, and held it over the pile.

"So that *was* you at the bar."

Gwendolyn looked up to see Eldon leaning against the doorway, casual as a summer afternoon and quite unconcerned that she was holding a lit match above a highly flammable pile on his bed.

"I assume you overheard my conversation with DeWitt and Holt?"

She nodded. The flame ate the length of the match and bit her finger. She let the ashes fall onto the bed.

"I'm very sorry you had to hear that." His words were carefully measured, glass-smooth, his eyes on her, steady and unblinking.

"I just bet you are."

She thought back to a particularly spectacular lovemaking marathon after which she'd lain in his arms and told him about her loopy *Gwendolyn Was Here* scheme. No wonder he hadn't said anything when she was through. She struck another match and watched it burst to life.

Eldon stepped inside his bedroom and removed his jacket, folded it in half, and laid it on the edge of the bed. Don't come any nearer, she thought. He said, "The whole thing was inexcusably callous of us – of me, especially – and I can only ask – no, *beg* your forgiveness."

If she didn't know any better, Gwendolyn would have sworn the guy actually meant what he said. But she did know better, and that hurt even more. She could feel heat rising from her skin. Her brain felt thick and fuzzy, like someone had stuffed it full of cotton wool. But she felt brave and reckless, too. "You can beg all you like," she told him.

"I confessed to my buddies because guilt was starting to eat me up. You're a wonderful, kind, and gorgeous girl who didn't deserve such treatment. I fully intended to put a stop to the contest – "

He took another step toward her. It wasn't large; if she hadn't been looking, she mightn't have even noticed. She told herself, I'm not so drunk that I don't know I shouldn't take my eyes off you.

Enough of his smooth talk, she decided.

"People's lives and hopes and dreams, they're not a game." The second match had burned all the way through so she dropped it. "What you and your pals did is the most despicable thing I've ever heard."

"It's the most despicable thing I've ever done."

"For crying out loud, aren't there enough rats in this town?" She made a big show of pulling three matches from the book. "Like I can ever trust anything you say to me again." She wanted to add *I thought you were one of the good guys,* but forced it down in a painful gulp.

He took an abrupt step closer to her. Only a corner of the bed separated them now. He frowned. "Are you—are you drunk, Gwendolyn?"

"So what if I am? Do you blame me? Would any decent-thinking American blame me?" She tried to close the matchbook but couldn't get it to catch.

"I want to make it up to you," he said.

"HA!" she exploded. It came out louder than she intended, but she liked the way it made him jump. "I'd rather take my chances with Leopold and Loeb."

He leaned over and reached out to take her hand but she yanked it away. The last thing I need, she thought, is to feel his skin on mine. She fumbled with the matchbook again, finally getting it to close. She held it up to him, matchbook in one hand, matches in the other.

"Chasen's," he said. "Every Tuesday night."

Chasen's Southern Barbecue Pit was a restaurant on Beverly Boulevard famous for its sensational chili and its top-drawer steaks. "What of it?" Gwendolyn asked.

"That's where Bill Grady and Fred Schussler go every Tuesday night for dinner."

Gwendolyn narrowed her eyes and wondered what the bespoke bastard was up to. Bill Grady and Fred Schussler.

She felt like they were names she should know, but she couldn't place them. She could feel a blush coming on and tried hard to stop it, but it was like trying stop a grease fire with a slab of bacon.

Eldon pointed to something behind her. "They're casting that."

She looked over at his bedside table and saw a copy of *Gone with the Wind*. When she turned back to face him again, he'd taken another step closer. He was within slugging distance; she bunched her hand into a fist.

"Bill and Fred are head of casting for Selznick," Eldon said. "They dine together at Chasen's every Tuesday night."

"That's your way of making up to me? You and your buddies made me a prize in some heartless bet and the best way you say you're sorry is to—"

"Oh, come on," Eldon cut in. "You've read the book, haven't you?"

Gwendolyn shook her head. "I grew up in the South. I sat on my mama's knee and heard all the stories about the Civil War and Sherman's march and the damned Yankees over and over. I figured I didn't need to sit through a thousand pages of the same thing."

"Oh, but yes you do," Eldon persisted. "My dear Gwendolyn, you were born to play Scarlett O'Hara."

CHAPTER 11

Arriving at MGM's scenario department from a rinky-dink outfit like Cosmopolitan Pictures felt like graduating from elementary school, then skipping junior high and high school altogether, and being thrown directly into college. Marcus would have been intimidated if he wasn't quite so excited. He could barely believe it when the freckle-faced receptionist presented him with his own office. And—luxury of luxuries—his own telephone! It seemed too good to be true, and as it turned out, it wasn't.

The first time Marcus had an inkling that he was about to run aground on the rocky shores of the writers' department was when he arrived at work a little early one morning a week or so after he started. Dozens and dozens of small squares of paper were taped onto every surface of his office.

He pulled the closest one at hand and read the single word written on it: *strawberry*. The next one he pulled off read *chocolate*, the next one *vanilla*, then *tutti frutti* and *hazelnut*. One by one, he yanked them off his chipped filing cabinet and his repainted desk: *licorice*, *peanut butter*, *raspberry*. He was carefully stacking them into a pile and examining their half dozen different handwriting styles when Hugo Marr, a screenwriter Marcus had known for years, burst into his office.

"Oh," Hugo said. His eyes flicked around. He let out a little "hmm" but didn't seem surprised. "You got here early today."

"I had a good idea last night, so I wanted to get a jump on it." Marcus pulled *pineapple* from his telephone and held it up. "Know anything about all these?"

Hugo took the note from Marcus and studied it for several long moments. "Pineapples can be sweet, but if you don't watch out, they can be bitter."

"I'm not following you."

Hugo crushed the note into a ball. "The guys around here are like pineapples. They're sweet, but they can be bitter, too. They're trying to make a point. You've got to understand, Marcus, this is a literary bunch. They've given you a nickname: Flavor."

"Flavor?"

Hugo began pulling notes from Marcus' desk, wall, and typewriter. He let out another "hmm" and tossed the paper into Marcus' metal trash can. "They watched you rise from Hearst Castle screw-up to A-list writer virtually overnight."

Resentment squeezed Marcus' throat. "And yet if the same opportunity was handed to them, they would've grabbed it just as tightly as I did."

"Yeah, probably."

Marcus could understand that nobody wanted to look too friendly with the guy who'd made William Randolph Hearst apoplectic, lest they be tainted with the same stench. But he hadn't counted on schoolyard jealousy.

Hugo clenched his teeth together and sucked in a lungful of air.

"What is it?" Marcus asked.

"I don't like being the one to tell you, but somebody's going to have to. You see, there's a perception among the guys that you broke one of the commandments."

"There are commandments?"

"Thou shalt not, under any circumstances, approach a star about your pet project."

"I didn't! Garbo approached me!"

"But did she approach you to talk about making Nellie Bly?"

Marcus sighed and pulled *banana* off his door. "Not exactly."

"Taggert's especially ropeable about that one."

Jim Taggert ran the writers' department with all the delicacy and finesse of the drill sergeant he'd probably been in some other life.

"I just thought he was the gruff, silent type," Marcus said.

"He is, but let me give you some buddy-buddy advice: Don't make the mistake of thinking that's all there is to him. He's a good guy, it's just that his preferred method of communication is the written word. Mr. Chatterbox he ain't."

Hugo shifted from the doorframe into Marcus' office and sat against the edge of the desk. He leaned in, bringing his chubby face close to Marcus, and lowered his voice. "There's something else you should know. Rumor has it Garbo's getting more and more demanding. So to dupe her into thinking she's getting her way, Mayer promised to let her have a say on her next project. His hope was that she'd bring him something completely unsuitable so he could turn around and say, 'That's a bad choice for this, that, and the other reason, which is why you should let us pick your movies.'"

"You think that's why Mayer said yes to my idea so quickly?"

Hugo gave a well-sort-of-yeah shrug.

"So I'm just a pawn in Louis B. Mayer's game of movie star chess?"

Hugo gave a weary smile. "Aren't we all?"

Marcus pulled off the last of the paper squares. He ripped them into shreds and dropped them into the trash.

Not if I can help it.

* * *

George Cukor offered Marcus a Cuban cigar from a humidor on his sideboard. Marcus took it and they lit up in silence. After Tallulah's screen test, she was deemed too old, too well-known, and quite frankly too slutty to play Scarlett

O'Hara, and Selznick announced he wanted an unknown to play the role. An avalanche of headshots had come crashing in and now covered every horizontal inch of George's corner office. Marcus wondered if Gwendolyn's was among them. He had never seen her so fired up.

"It's a hard sell," George said. "Garbo is great at playing Europeans—queens, courtesans, countesses—but Nellie Bly? You don't get much more American than that. Back in the silent days it wouldn't have mattered, but are modern audiences going to buy Garbo as an ace girl reporter from Pittsburgh? Carole Lombard, sure. Joan Crawford, even. But Garbo?" George unbuttoned his collar and loosened his sky-blue necktie. "Only Garbo has the power to make sure Mayer doesn't give you the big brush-off."

"But Mayer would have realized that as soon as I said it."

"Remember, we're talking about Garbo here. Who's more precious to MGM than Garbo? He'd say anything to keep her happy."

"So if it's all just a game of Parcheesi, why would Mayer double my salary?"

George started disappearing behind a cloud of cigar smoke. "Garbo's on six thousand a week now. It's not a game of Parcheesi; it's a game of numbers."

"I don't want this to go down the drain." Marcus thinned out the smoke cloud with a sweep of his hand. "It has all the makings of a terrific picture."

"I'm telling you, Marcus, it's Garbo you want in your court. You might want to visit the men's room on the third floor of the admin building at about three o'clock."

* * *

The administration building at MGM was a fairly nondescript five-story structure, painted tan like all the others, located at the top end of the studio. The third-floor men's room was at the end of a highly polished corridor nobody seemed to use. The place was absent the clacking typewriters and insistent telephones Marcus had become used to.

He pushed open the wooden door marked *MEN* and stepped inside. Down at the far end of the room, past the urinals and stalls, Greta Garbo leaned against the edge of a large window. She was dressed in a loose suit of billowing black satin with sleeves that hung like drapes past her hands. Marcus was halfway across the room to her when she turned to look at him.

"Hello," she said simply, almost as though she were expecting him.

"George told me you like to take your afternoon break here," Marcus said, joining her at the window.

"The view is unparalleled." They gazed across the bungalows and oak trees of Culver City, the palm trees that punctured the last of the afternoon haze and nodded along Wilshire Boulevard like nuns walking to vespers. Finally Garbo said, "I shall go so that you can conduct your men's business in private."

"I came to see you," Marcus said.

He launched into what happened during his meeting with Mayer, then what Hugo told him, and then lastly what George said. He worded his speech so she'd get all riled up enough to march into Mayer's office and throw her weight around. But instead she just shrugged and stared out the window.

"I suspect George is right," she said. The late afternoon sun slanted in through the window and her face filled with resignation. "Maybe this role is not for me."

Marcus' stomach lurched. Nellie Bly was going down in flames over Culver City right before his eyes. "It's a tremendous role!"

"Indeed," she agreed, "but the American people, would they accept me as one of their women? I suspect they would scoff at Greta Garbo with her Swedish accent playing such a go-get-'em American woman." She kept her eyes on the view. "I had high hopes for this picture. I thought that if I can convince the American public that I can be a Yankee doodle dandy, then maybe I'd have earned all . . . this." She dragged a hand over the skies above Los Angeles.

“I’m not giving up on it,” Marcus told her.

“And neither should you,” Garbo responded with a stern smile. “It deserves to be made, but not with me.”

CHAPTER 12

The chrome frames of the Cocoanut Grove's solid glass front doors had five-foot silhouettes of palm trees etched on them in acid. The maître d' pulled open one of the doors and smiled as Kathryn walked into the nightclub. The buzz of what she called "post-premiere passions" enveloped her like a swarm of butterflies. It was a familiar heat, the sort generated by an overly enthusiastic crowd who'd hit the bar right after a flamboyant Hollywood opening.

"So pleased to see you here tonight, Miss Massey," the maître d' said. "I've seated you with the Hacketts, if that's all right."

"Perfectly," Kathryn said. Francis and Albert Hackett were a savvy screenwriting couple who'd had back-to-back successes at MGM with a pair of *Thin Man* pictures. They were also her neighbors at the Garden of Allah.

The Grove looked exceptionally spiffy tonight. Gwendolyn had confided to Kathryn that management had spent a small fortune carefully cleaning each of the papier-mâché trees that loomed over the tables like observant giraffes. They'd even replaced the dusty stuffed monkeys who clung from the fronds ten feet above the swirl of tiaras, cashmere, and silk lapels.

"Table twelve, Antoine?" Gwendolyn said, hooking her arm through Kathryn's. "That's okay, I'll take her to her seat."

Kathryn smiled at her friend, who was dressed in her usual light green and dark purple satin uniform with the drum-majorette gold braid crisscrossing her chest. "The royal treatment, huh? Gwennie, I—are you all right?"

Gwendolyn's angelic face was carved with worry. Kathryn took her by the hand. It was clammy and cold. "Whatever's the matter?"

Gwendolyn said nothing as she guided Kathryn to a quiet area at the rear of the club. She pulled off her cigarette tray and placed it on the end of the bar, then turned to face Kathryn squarely. Her eyes shined with tears.

"You remember Broochie?" Gwendolyn's voice was hoarse.

"Broochie" was the nickname the pair of them had given to a former Cocoanut Grove regular who'd given Gwendolyn a glorious diamond brooch. The last time Gwendolyn saw him he was lying in a pool of his own blood after she conked him on the noggin for forcing himself on her.

Kathryn gasped silently, unblinking. She squeezed Gwendolyn's pale hand. "Of course I do. Why?"

"He's back," Gwendolyn whispered. "Here. Tonight!"

"Are you sure it's him?"

"Positive."

"That clears up one thing: you didn't kill him."

"I'm starting to wish I had."

"Don't talk like that, honey."

Words tumbled out of Gwendolyn. "My stomach's a pretzel. I can barely think straight. He's drunk as ever, and you know what he's like when he's drunk. He could have me up for attempted manslaughter. What's the statute of limitations for this sort of thing?"

Kathryn took Gwendolyn's hands in hers and gripped them as strongly as she could muster. "Gwennie, honey. It's been what, five years? If that baboon was going to have you arrested, he'd have done it by now. Can you have him thrown out?"

"Not unless he does something unsavory. And even then, his brother is the assistant head of production at Paramount. He's too well connected."

"So all you have to do is keep out of his way. Keep him in your sights as much as possible. I'll keep an eye on you and if I see him heading toward you, I'll do what I can to head him off at the pass." Gwendolyn's shoulders sank a full inch and she breathed again. Kathryn asked, "Has he seen you?"

"Not yet."

"Then try and lay low. A bit hard to do with your job, but do the best you can. You're not alone; remember that. Now, tell me what he looks like."

* * *

Kathryn didn't see Broochie on her way to where Francis and Albert were waiting for her at the edge of the dance floor. As Kathryn sat down at their ringside table, Francis crushed her cigarette into a palm-tree-shaped ashtray with the gusto of a sumo wrestler. "Kathryn dear!" she exclaimed, and leaned in conspiratorially. "Aren't you the brave one?"

The huge bash at the Grove that night was for the premiere of Janet Gaynor's new Technicolor movie, *A Star is Born*. Dorothy Parker and her husband, Alan Campbell, had written the screenplay, so half of Kathryn's neighbors were there. And a good thing they were, too: *A Star is Born* had been produced by Selznick International. Kathryn hadn't heard from the Selznick camp since her Cukor scoop, so she wasn't sure how Mr. Selznick felt about it—and more specifically, how he felt about her. She doubted he'd cause a stink on a night like this, but Hollywood was filled with dramatic people so she knew she had to keep a cautious eye out. One for her and one for Gwendolyn, because if anybody else got into trouble, she'd be all out of eyes.

"Listen up," Kathryn said. "Gwendolyn has a problem and we need to be watchful."

"Whatever's the matter?"

"She has a—well, let's call him an overly enthusiastic admirer. She can handle him when he's sober, but he's a lousy drunk. Big time trouble." She repeated Gwendolyn's description—tall, Mediterranean complexion, bulky frame with hairy knuckles. "If we see him stagger toward her, we need to signal her or distract him somehow."

"Leave it to us," said Albert. "We adore Gwendolyn! But in the meanwhile, look lively. The big kahuna approaches at seven o'clock."

"Oh, Christ," Francis muttered without breaking her smile. "He's probably going to ask us what we've got cooked up for the next *Thin Man*. I wish he'd just—Mr. Mayer!" She extended her hand. "What a delight to see you tonight."

Louis B. Mayer nodded curtly. "Francis. Albert." Then, much to Kathryn's amazement, he turned to her. "Dance, Miss Massey?"

Thoughts of Gwendolyn, Broochie, and David O. Selznick flew from Kathryn's mind as she took Mayer's hand. She let him guide her onto the dance floor and launch her into a moderately fast foxtrot.

"You look a little stunned," he observed after a minute.

Kathryn looked at the stout gentleman and nodded. "I am."

"And why is that?"

"Two reasons," she said. "We've never met, and yet you asked me to dance as though we have."

He nodded and spun her into a series of sharp turns that might have caught Ginger Rogers by surprise. It was a small miracle she didn't stumble into him. "I saw you at the Trocadero last week and admired the way you danced with Louis Calhern. And the other reason?"

"You're head of MGM, Mr. Mayer, and this is a Selznick party."

"We're rival Hollywood studios, not the Hatfields and the McCoys. I can guarantee you that by midnight I'll be roped into a poker game with Zukor and Zanuck. Warner and Cohn will probably want in as well."

Kathryn gazed around the periphery of the Cocoanut Grove's dance floor. Tables for four and six with red and green chairs crowded the edge. Every one of them was filled with sleek women in huge jewels and handsome men in expensive tuxedoes. She couldn't see Broochie or Selznick, but she could see Gwendolyn standing to the far left corner of the orchestra, her eyes wide open. *Oh, my God! That's Louis B. Mayer!* she mouthed.

Kathryn mouthed back, *I know! Can you believe it?*

Kathryn felt rather silly now. When Mayer asked her to dance, a part of her—the part that had spent her entire childhood taking endless dance classes—had leapt to the conclusion that Mayer was thinking of offering her a contract. She blushed when she realized he was just asking if she knew how to waltz, foxtrot, and quickstep.

But now that she was actually on the dance floor with Mr. Louis B. Mayer himself, foxtrotting past George Burns and Gracie Allen, Gary Cooper and Ann Sothern, she wondered if she was going to have to fend him off later.

"How's Margaret?" she asked.

She felt Mayer's chest lurch slightly away from her in surprise. "Margaret Hamilton or Margaret Sullavan?"

"Margaret, your wife."

"Oh." Mayer shrugged and pulled her close enough for her to smell his coconut oil pomade. "She's fine. Not one much for social outings. More of a homebody, really."

"She doesn't resent you going out all the time, surrounded by all these beautiful women?"

He looked at her with a piercing gaze. "What's with all the Margaret questions?"

"Just wanting to keep her front and center."

Mayer's eyebrows shot up as he cottoned onto the fact that she was thinking he was road-testing her for an onramp into his pants. It made him laugh so loud that dancers near them turned around. She took a moment to scan the nightclub again. She couldn't see Gwendolyn or Broochie, but she spotted Harpo Marx.

"You can relax," he told her. "I love to dance, but I can rarely find anyone to go ten rounds with."

"How am I doing?"

"Very well. I'm quite impressed."

Just then, the music came to an end and the Paul Whiting orchestra started up with "It's De-Lovely."

"Another round?" Mayer suggested.

"Love to."

They danced for a few bars while Kathryn summoned up a bucketful of courage. "Mr. Mayer, you do know who I am, don't you?"

"I didn't get to where I am today by being an imbecile, Miss Massey."

"Of course not," Kathryn replied quickly. "It's just— "

"If you have anything you want to ask me, now would be the time. You have my undivided attention."

Are you kidding? she thought. I have a thousand things I want to ask you. Is this just a one-question deal you're handing me?

In case it was, Kathryn knew she'd better make the most of it.

"Are you going to loan Clark Gable to Selznick to play Rhett Butler?"

"For someone who seems to be an expert on *Gone with the Wind*, I'm surprised you need to ask me anything about it."

Kathryn chose her words carefully. "One scoop does not an expert make."

"I'll tell you about Clark Gable if you tell me your source."

Ah. "Like that, is it?"

"We both know Hollywood is a mutual back-scratching society, and a small one at that." Mayer plowed them through the crowd like a racehorse in the Kentucky Derby. He leaned into her ear. "I could count on my fingers the number of people who had that information. And I'm sure George Cukor is chummy with at least one or two of your Garden of Allah queers."

Kathryn shot him a startled look. He was peering at her from the side now, his eyes hard black beads. She tried to think of a quick retort, but her mind was blank. All she could see was Marcus' face and how he'd be smiling at her if he knew she was dancing with the most powerful man in Hollywood. Oh, God, she realized, Mayer has probably already put two and two together.

It was Mayer who broke the silence. "Have you read the book?"

"*Gone with the Wind*? Who hasn't?"

"Can *you* imagine anyone else playing Rhett Butler?"

"Are you telling me he will be playing Rhett?"

"I never said any such thing."

"So then what are you saying?"

The song came to an end and Mayer sank her into the smoothest, surest dip of her life. He held her there for a moment. "You're very good," he told her. "There aren't many women who can follow a subtle lead." As the crowd around them broke into applause for the orchestra, he lifted her upright and escorted her to her deserted table.

She thanked him for the dance and watched him blend back into the crowd.

"Making new friends, I see?"

Kathryn turned to find Harpo Marx grinning at her.

Kathryn greeted him with a hug. "Yes, it appears I've attracted somebody's attention."

"You attracted everyone's with that scoop of yours. Well done, by the way."

"Have you seen Gwendolyn?"

"Yes, she's floating around as usual. Hard to miss in that uniform."

Kathryn grabbed Harpo by the elbow. "She's in a bit of a fix tonight. We need to look out for her."

Harpo frowned. "I'd do anything for that living doll. Say, does it have anything to do with a baboon in a monkey suit?"

"Hairy knuckles?"

"Scary hairy."

"Yes!"

"I bumped into him in the men's room. Talk about lit. Mumbling something about uppity cigarette girls."

"Oh God, that's him. Do you know where he is now?"

"If you need me to go looking, I will. Maybe Benchley and Dottie have seen him. They were up at the bar a minute ago with her husband."

Kathryn turned to grab her handbag from the table. "Let's go see."

"No, no, I'll go." Harpo's eyes were on something over Kathryn's shoulder. "I think you're about to make a new friend."

Jack Warner ran Warner Bros. like Mayer ran MGM: with Genghis Khan-like authority that was never questioned and never contravened. Dissention meant dismissal and hundreds of employees cowered in his wake. It was surprising to Kathryn, then, that Jack Warner was such a slightly built man with a slim, pale face and an insignificant moustache.

He bent at the waist slightly. "May I?" She nodded and he launched them into a waltz. He was a more leisurely dancer than Mayer, less focused on finishing first. He was smoother, too. No, not smoother, Kathryn decided. Oilier.

He said nothing for the first two laps around the dance floor. Kathryn kept her eyes on the growing crowd. At one point she thought she saw Broochie duck behind one of the palm trees. The guy fit Gwendolyn's description, but she couldn't be sure.

Warner pulled her closer. "It's very nice to meet you finally," he said. "That was an impressive way to make a name for yourself, young lady."

Kathryn wondered if, at twenty-eight, she still qualified as a young lady. Perhaps in the eyes of men like Jack Warner, younger women were all young ladies.

"I like your column," he said.

She could smell his hair pomade: coconut, like Mayer's. "So you read it, then?"

"It's smart. Perceptive. Literate. I respect ladies like that."

"Ladies like Bette Davis?"

Bette Davis, Warner Bros.' leading actress, had recently refused what she considered yet another bad role and had accepted a two-picture deal with a British producer. Warner had been forced to sue her for breach of contract.

"I would respect Bette Davis if she'd lived up to the contract she signed, and if she'd thought twice before skipping across the pond because she believes U.S. law doesn't apply to her."

For the first time, Kathryn looked directly into Jack Warner's face. To her surprise she saw a fatherly look staring back at her. Almost wounded, in a way. "Are you really going to force one of your biggest stars to come back to work like a kid who skipped school?" she asked.

They continued around the dance floor for a full lap before he said, "Nobody wins if I send Bette to the corner in a dunce's cap."

"What will you do?"

"There are all sorts of things I can do. Pay her legal fees. Get her better scripts."

"In other words, give her everything she asked for all along?"

Jack Warner rolled his jaw around like he was licking food out of his teeth. He said nothing more until the end of the song. He walked her back to her table, where Frances and Albert were sipping cocktails, and bid her "a fine good evening."

"Connolly was looking for you," Albert said.

Marc Connolly was an Algonquin Round Table chum of Benchley and Dottie's who had recently arrived at the Garden to write a Spencer Tracy movie for MGM. He and Kathryn had recently fallen in the pool together during an especially raucous birthday party for Lillian Hellman and stayed there most of the night.

"Apparently he's seen the gorilla," Frances said. "Almost knocked over one of these paper palm trees."

"Where is he now?"

"He headed thataway." Albert pointed in the general direction of the restrooms.

Kathryn was threading her way around the packed tables toward the rear wall of the nightclub when she saw a six-foot hulk of a man staggering a wobbly path toward the far wall. At first she thought it was Selznick, but the guy was too disheveled. She looked ahead of him and saw Gwendolyn selling cigarettes to Errol Flynn's table. Errol wore his usual good-natured grin, probably giving Gwendolyn a hard time about throwing up on his shoes a few years back. Gwendolyn had no idea how close Broochie was.

Kathryn hurried ahead. "Hey, mister!" she called out.

The guy turned around, barely a dozen feet away from Gwendolyn. He had a round face that was bloated from too much booze. His eyes were bloodshot and unfocused.

"You got a light?" Kathryn asked.

Broochie looked down at Kathryn's hand. "You got a cigarette?"

Caught out, Kathryn shrugged in her best helpless-damsel way. She went to ask him for one of his when he let out a "Puh!" and made a dismissive swipe of his hand through the air. He turned his back on her.

"HEY!" He pointed a wobbly finger at Gwendolyn. "You! Cigarette girl! We needa talk."

Gwendolyn turned around and reared back as Kathryn stepped to one side. She caught Errol's eye and mouthed the word *help* at him, then pointed at Gwendolyn.

Errol was on his feet in a moment. He rounded the table and planted himself between Gwendolyn and Broochie. "Listen, fella, you needa take a step back." His words were as slurry as Broochie's, his eyes just as glassy.

Without saying another word, and faster than Kathryn would ever have suspected possible, Broochie shot a right hook that connected with Errol's jaw. The punch caught Errol unaware and sent him hurling into the papier mâché palm tree. The pair dropped to the floor like a bag of rocks.

Broochie raised the hairiest finger Kathryn had ever seen and pointed it at Gwendolyn.

"You and I, we're gonna talk, and I mean now."

Kathryn only had time to take in Gwendolyn's deathly pale face before a giant of a guy, easily six and a half feet and dressed in a tux a size too small for him, swooped in from the right and grabbed Broochie by the shoulders.

"Okay, Hank," he growled, "we're going to take this circus outside." He shoved Broochie toward the door. Broochie grunted his resistance, but he was out-muscled.

The cigarette packs in Gwendolyn's tray wobbled around like Mexican jumping beans. Kathryn took a step toward her but a hand on her arm stopped her.

It belonged to a short guy, barely five five, a little rough around the edges and dressed in a white suit with a splotch on its sleeve that could have been ketchup . . . or blood.

"Now that we've got all that drama sorted out," he said, "I'd like this dance."

Kathryn glanced at Gwendolyn, who mouthed, *I'm fine. That's Harry Cohn. Go!*

Kathryn allowed the head of Columbia Studios to guide her to the dance floor, where the Paul Whiteman orchestra was playing "The Music Goes Round and Round." Almost straightaway, Cohn got all elbowy and started pushing their fellow dancers out of his way.

The guy had a squarish sort of face, crammed with determination, no sign of bullshit. He was thinning on top but wasn't trying to delude himself with a comb-over. His mean eyes darted around the dance floor like killer bees.

"Is that ketchup on your sleeve?" Kathryn asked him.

"Goddamned chili sauce," he replied. "I got so mad I pounded the table with my fist, only I clipped the edge of the dish and it went flying ass over tit, s'kuse my French. Claudette Colbert copped some of it. She wasn't happy, and she wasn't even sitting at my table!" He found that last part hilarious and started laughing.

She let the laughter pass before she said, "Mr. Cohn, we've never been formally introduced. I'm Kathryn Massey."

"I know."

Some silence passed between them before he piped up again. "You like sculpture?"

"When I know what I'm looking at."

"Same here. This abstract shit—s'kuse my French—I don't get. But some book-learning type back at my table just said something to me that's got me thinking."

"What did he say?"

"He said that the view taken by Michelangelo—you know that Eye-talian guy? He said that sculpture was about whittling away the bits you don't need. Starts out as a big block of marble, right? But you bang away at it, knock off all the bits you don't need until you got something. Same applies to us."

"It does?"

Cohn didn't smell sweetly of coconut like the other two. This guy smelled like cheap clams and expensive cigars. He stepped on her foot but didn't seem to notice. "Take screenplays, f'instance. Those writers, they come up with all them words. Yabba, yabba, yabba. Jesus, these writers and their fucking words—s'kuse my French. So you start chipping away and then you chip away some more, and then some more and bingo, you got a script that you can actually film. You know what I'm saying, sweetheart?"

"Yes, I think I do."

"Take our next big picture, f'instance. Costing me a bundle. Two mill by the time we're done. *Lost Horizon* it's called, the new Frank Capra picture. Not a long book, but Jesus! Packed with words I ain't never heard of. Talk about chipping away."

But Kathryn barely heard him. What the hell's going on here? she wondered. First Mayer, then Warner, and now Cohn? She felt like a bundle of brown paper in a game of Pass the Parcel. Who was next? She scanned the Cocoanut Grove for Selznick. Then she realized what Cohn had just told her.

Columbia, the king of cheapie filler pictures, was spending two million dollars on one picture.

She looked at him with her eyebrows raised as high as they could go. "Did you say two million?"

"Damn it," Cohn said under his breath. "I wasn't supposed to tell no one about that yet. Something about stockholder meetings. I dunno." He looked at her with a cocked eyebrow. "Oh well, it's out now."

Cohn couldn't seem to hear the beat of the music. They charged around the dance floor at more or less his own pace. It seemed to absorb most of his attention because he didn't say anything after that, which suited Kathryn just fine. Thankfully, the song came to an end and he dumped her at the side of the dance floor like she was a trash can. She didn't even mind that he hadn't taken her back to her table. Gwendolyn appeared at her side.

"Are you okay, sweetie?" Kathryn asked.

"Yeah, I'm fine. That was one of Cohn's goons. He came back to tell me that Broochie won't be bothering me anymore. But what about you, little Miss Popularity 1937?"

"So you saw that?" Kathryn exclaimed. "First Mayer, then Warner and Cohn! What the hell was that?"

"Seemed pretty obvious to me." Gwendolyn could barely keep from breaking out into a laugh.

"What am I missing?"

"When you were dancing with them, was it just meaningless chitchat, or was it all business?"

"We talked about—"

Kathryn thought about Mayer and his Gable for Butler, Warner and his Bette Davis, and Cohn and his *Lost Horizon*.

"Oh!"

Gwendolyn pulled out a pack of Chesterfields and handed it to her. "Honey, you've just been drafted into the scoop business."

CHAPTER 13

It was cramped in the back seat of the taxicab. If Gwendolyn had been wearing anything else it might have been fine, but her floor-length gown – white linen, tight at the waist, generous at the bust, and layered with broad frills – took up more space than she'd anticipated. It was nice of Robert Benchley and Dottie Parker to press themselves against the doors so it didn't get crushed.

"Gwendolyn, darling," Benchley said, "this outfit of yours, it really is most becoming."

Gwendolyn looked at him earnestly. "Not too frilly and flouncy?"

"Not at all," Dorothy cut in. "Your flounce per ounce ratio is just right."

Gwendolyn looked at Dorothy with a nervous squint. In all the years Dorothy Parker had been drifting in and out of the Garden of Allah, Gwendolyn had never acquired the knack of knowing when she was being sincere or just being a bitch. It was usually safer to assume the latter, but for some reason she was never as brutal with Gwendolyn as she was with everyone else, which made it all the more disconcerting.

"I never would have taken you as the frilly and flouncy type," Dottie continued. "But this looks good on you. I suppose you made it yourself?"

Gwendolyn nodded. "I modeled it on the dress Scarlett wears to the barbeque in the beginning of the book. It's not hooped, of course, but it comes close, so I think it was worth all the needles and thread."

"Give me a needle and thread and you can guarantee that it'd end up in my left eyeball," Dottie commented. "If only out of boredom." She patted Gwendolyn on the knee. "It's perfect for its purpose. And how lucky for you that the flat-chested flapper look is dead and buried these days."

Gwendolyn had never really been one for reading novels—she was more of a magazine girl—but after what Eldon Laird said about her being born to play Scarlett O'Hara, she'd had to read this *Gone with the Wind* thing that everyone was so obsessed over.

She whipped through it like a plague of boll weevils and by the time she finished the final page, she knew she had to play that role. Oh, how she loved Scarlett! How she admired her, how she understood her, how she longed for things to work out for her.

So Gwendolyn made a plan.

She laid it out to Marcus and Kathryn in the Sahara Room. They had originally met there to commiserate with poor old Marcus, whose contract had turned out to be valid only while he was writing Nellie Bly. When Garbo bowed out, he was given the ol' heave-ho. He tried to make out like he wasn't disappointed, but his third bourbon inside half an hour suggested otherwise, so Gwendolyn changed the subject and unveiled her plan.

She wasn't aware, though, that Benchley and Dorothy were sitting two booths up and listening to every word. Gwendolyn was thankful they'd invited themselves along; this was the big time, and she needed all the support she could get.

When their taxi pulled up outside Chasen's, Dorothy helped Gwendolyn and her dress get out of the car while Benchley paid the driver. Kathryn appeared from inside the restaurant. "Grady and Schussler are here," she announced, and then took in Gwendolyn's dress. "Oh, Gwennie!"

Now that she was about to get the casting directors in her crosshairs, Gwendolyn could feel her confidence slipping away like soap bubbles. She pulled at her ruffles. "Not too costumey? Be honest."

"Not at all." Kathryn took Gwendolyn by the hand. "The bar is to your left. Grady and Schussler are in grey suits at a booth near the far end, downing martinis. Sit at the second stool from the end. I've got us the booth next to them."

Chasen's had opened the year before with six homemade tables, a wooden bar that looked like something out of a Saturday-matinee Western, and an eight-stool counter at which chili was dispensed for twenty-five cents a bowl. Word quickly got out that it was the best chili in town, and the place became the new in spot.

Gwendolyn crossed over to the bar, took the second to last seat, and cast a casual glance around the room. She spotted the two grey suits, then realized that they were the only men in the place who were wearing suits. Most of the diners weren't even wearing neckties. Oh God, she thought, and here I am in a frilly white ball gown. And it's not even summer.

But it was too late to worry about that now. And besides, Scarlett wouldn't chicken out, so neither would Gwendolyn. If she could survive that horrible scene at work with Broochie, then this should be a walk in the park.

She stole another glance at the casting directors; neither of them appeared to be paying the slightest bit of attention.

The bartender approached her. "What'll it be?"

Gwendolyn hesitated, wondering what Scarlett would drink. Or should she order what casting guys would think an actress who wants to play Scarlett thinks Scarlett would drink? Or should she order a martini like they were drinking? Oh, God no—then she'd have to drink it right in front of them, and look what happened last time she drank. She'd nearly set fire to Eldon's house.

The bartender was looking at her expectantly. "You need some time to decide?"

Gwendolyn ordered the only thing she could think of. "I'll have a mint julep, thank you, barkeep." She turned to give Grady and Schussler a side view, took a compact from her handbag, and pretended to check her makeup. By now, Kathryn, Benchley, and Dorothy were seated at the neighboring booth. Kathryn was talking about the sensation a young Judy Garland had caused at Clark Gable's thirty-sixth birthday party by singing a song called "Dear Mr. Gable." She was relaying the story in a loud-but-not-too-loud voice that Gwendolyn hoped wasn't too transparent.

The bartender placed the mint julep in front of her. It smelled sweet and minty and looked like iced tea.

"Oh, my goodness!" It was Kathryn. "That's the one I've been talking about in my column!"

"Which one what where?" Benchley said.

"The gorgeous one in the lovely white dress."

"Who *is* she?" Dottie asked a tad too theatrically.

"Her name is Gwendolyn Brick. It seems like everywhere I turn, her name comes up for Scarlett O'Hara."

"What do you know about her?"

"Not a lot," Kathryn said. "Did she just order a mint julep? She must be from the South."

Gwendolyn could see both tables in the mirror behind the bar; the two men were looking at her now. She picked up the mint julep, held it to her lips and took a sip. It took a moment for the taste to register, then it hit her tongue like a lion's claw. What in tarnation did they put in this ghastly concoction? Her face contorted like a wad of paper on its way to the trash.

The two casting guys started to laugh. "Guess they make 'em sweeter back home."

By the time she worked up enough courage to look in the mirror again, she saw that they were now paying her no attention at all. One of them – the one in darker grey – was talking to Kathryn. Their voices had dropped and Gwendolyn could no longer hear them. Kathryn did a lot of nodding, then extended her hand for the guy in the darker suit to shake.

They chatted some more. Kathryn pointed toward her and nodded some more. Then Gwendolyn heard Kathryn say, "Everywhere I turn it's Gwendolyn Brick, Gwendolyn Brick, Gwendolyn Brick."

Kathryn pulled a small handkerchief out of her purse and dabbed at the corner of her mouth. That was their signal to meet in the ladies' room. Gwendolyn told the bartender she'd be right back and slid off the stool. She made a point of taking the long way past their tables.

The ladies' room was paneled in dark wood. Four vanity mirrors edged in plain gilded frames hung along the right-hand wall behind chairs upholstered in deep cranberry-red leather. An enormous bouquet of roses fought against the pervasive aroma of chili. She sat down and looked at herself in the mirror.

Back home she'd looked like a radiant Southern belle, but now she looked more like a desperate scheming amateur. She'd spent an hour selecting the right shade of lipstick, but now it looked too bright, too gaudy. Her cleavage looked inviting and her waist was Scarlett-slim, but her honey-blonde hair looked lifeless and flat. Or was it just the light in there? "You're second-guessing yourself," she said into the mirror. "And anyway, what does it matter? You lost them the moment you screwed your face up." Damn that disgusting drink. How was a lady supposed to pour that witch's brew down her throat?

Gwendolyn had just stood up to check her dress again when the door burst open with a convulsion of giggles and a couple of teenage girls flew into the room.

"The look on the waiter's face!" the one in tight red pigtails said. "Did you ever see such a thing?"

"Never!" Her friend burst into a squall of giggles. She had freckles splattered across her face and down her arms. "I thought he was going to pop a blood vessel right—oh!" The girl stopped when she saw Gwendolyn. "You're the girl at the bar," she said. "We were looking at you."

"Admiring your dress," her friend said. "It's very lovely."

Gwendolyn looked down at the ceramic bowls of chili in their hands.

"We're stealing the chili," Pigtails whispered.

"Why?" Gwendolyn asked.

"Have you tasted it yet? It's beyond *beyond*! My mother's from Texas and she likes to think she makes the best chili in the world. It's super, but this stuff pips it at the post, so we're swiping it. I'm taking it home so Ma can figure out what's in it and make it for us any time we want!"

Gwendolyn looked toward the door. Where was Kathryn? What was she telling the suits? Had she managed to regain the ground Gwendolyn had lost with that mint julep face?

Freckles walked past Gwendolyn and over to the window, which slid up easily enough. "Could you hold my chili?" she asked. She gave the heavy bowl to Gwendolyn and hoisted herself through the window without much effort.

Pigtails was a good deal heavier than her friend, and heaving herself through the opening proved more of a challenge. "I need a leg up." She stuck her foot out. "Would you mind terribly much? I promise not to get anything on your lovely white dress."

Gwendolyn set the bowl down on a vanity table and helped the girl through the window. True to her word, she managed to squeeze herself through without putting her foot on Gwendolyn's dress. Gwendolyn passed the bowl over.

As though on cue, the two girls launched into another fit of giggles. "You know what?" said the heavy girl. "We don't need two bowls. Have this one." She raised her bowl above her head. "CATCH!"

The bowl catapulted toward Gwendolyn. She raised her hand to defend herself but the edge of the bowl caught her fingertip and thick slop sloshed all down her side. The girls took off, spasming with laughter. All Gwendolyn could catch was one of them saying, "That God-awful white frilly mess . . ."

"Gwendolyn!" Kathryn stood in the doorway, her hands pressed to her mouth. "What the hell's happened?

"Chili . . ." was all Gwendolyn could say.

Large splashes of brown-red goop oozed from her thigh down to her ankle. Gobs of meat and pellets of pinto beans dripped off the frills into a thick puddle on the floor. The smell was now sickening and pungent. "It's not going to come out, is it?"

Kathryn soaked her handkerchief under the faucet and started to dab at the stains, but only succeeded in spreading them.

"Forget it," Gwendolyn said. "Sitting there in a frilly white barbeque dress drinking mint juleps. Who did I think I was fooling?"

Kathryn gave up. "Schussler's never even read the book," she said, standing up.

"He's casting *Gone with the Wind* and he hasn't even read it?"

"As far as those two are concerned, it's just a women's book."

Gwendolyn fought the tears stinging her eyes. "I want to go home."

Kathryn shook her head. "Perhaps if I explained—"

"No, really, thanks for everything. And thank Benchley and Dottie for me, too. But I'm going out the way those two little ratbags did. Maybe a long walk in the night air will clear the smell a bit."

The window was wider than the one she'd had to climb through at Eldon's, but she struggled in her tight, full dress, and she hit her knee on the brickwork as her feet found the top of the dumpster below the window.

She climbed down from the dumpster and leaned against it for a moment. She'd have happily tossed her dress inside if she had something to change into but this wasn't how she'd planned leaving Chasen's tonight. She started heading west. For a January night, it wasn't so chilly, and the walk back to the Garden of Allah wasn't terribly far.

She'd only gone a few blocks when a burgundy Packard pulled up beside her and a man's voice called out, "Can I offer you a lift?"

It wasn't a voice Gwendolyn recognized. "No, thank you," she said firmly, and kept her eyes on the sidewalk ahead.

"You look like you could use a lift, Miss Brick." Gwendolyn glanced at the driver. He wore a grey suit; it was either Grady or Schussler, she didn't know which. "I'm sure the chili doesn't stink too badly."

"I can assure you it does."

The man pulled the car to the curb a few yards ahead of her, got out, and walked around to the passenger side. He gallantly opened the door. "Wherever you need to go, Miss Brick."

Gwendolyn hesitated.

"You remember me from Chasen's, don't you?"

She nodded.

He raised his eyebrows.

"I live at the Garden of Allah," she said.

It wasn't until they were heading east on the Sunset Strip that Gwendolyn found the courage to ask how he knew her name. "Are you really from the South?" he asked.

"Mama's family is from Augusta, Georgia, but I myself am from Hollywood, Florida."

He let out a "Ha!" of a laugh. "From Hollywood, Florida, to Hollywood, California. Cute." The large Garden of Allah sign loomed ahead of them on Sunset. "I don't know if you believe in fate, Miss Brick, but I have to wonder if fate played her hand tonight."

"You do?"

"My name is Schussler. I'm in charge of casting for *Gone with the Wind*."

"Uh-huh," Gwendolyn said, trying for glacier cool.

"I doubt that I ever would have noticed you, had it not been for something I overheard your friends say back at Chasen's."

"My friends?"

"The ones at the table next to ours."

"I was there to meet an actor pal of mine, but he never showed up."

"We both know that's not entirely true."

"We do?"

"Kathryn Massey was at that table. She works at the *Hollywood Reporter*. The *Hollywood Reporter* is owned by Billy Wilkerson. Wilkerson often plays at our poker games. Wilkerson talks about her a lot, really respects her. He's mentioned once or twice how she lives at the Garden of Allah. So do Robert Benchley and Dorothy Parker. It's been a long time since I've had to use my fingers to put two and two together."

The jig was up. The pathetic, transparent jig that she'd never had any hope of pulling off in the first place and should be slapped for thinking that she could. She offered Schussler her sweetest smile. "It was worth a try. Thank you for your diplomacy, Mr. Schussler. It was more than I deserved." Schussler stopped his Packard outside the main entrance to the Garden of Allah. She held her hand out toward him, hoping that it would convey no hard feelings.

But he didn't take it.

"This dress you're wearing, can I assume it's supposed to be Scarlett's barbecue dress? The one from the opening of the book?"

"I heard you've never read the book."

"We're not making the book," he replied. "We're making the movie. I read the synopsis Selznick's people typed up for me. It's very good—the dress, I mean. I can see you put a lot of effort into it."

"Yes, and someone put a lot of chili *onto* it. I really must be getting out of your lovely Packard, Mr. Schussler. I fear I'm starting to stink it up." She pushed open the heavy door, bunched up her dress and got out of the car. She looked down to see a goopy stain the size of her hand on the passenger seat. It was oozing its way to the edge of the leather. Horrified, she looked up at him. "I'm so—"

"Good night, Miss Brick."

"Again, thank you for the ride home. Thank you so much." She closed the door and headed toward the main house.

She was no further than the start of the gravel path when she heard him say, "It worked, you know."

She held her breath and turned around. Schussler was leaning across the width of his car and smiling.

"You looked like Scarlett O'Hara," he said. "Not perfectly, but enough." He threw his car into gear and roared away from the curb.

Gwendolyn watched him merge into the traffic heading east along Sunset.

"Enough for what?"

CHAPTER 14

Marcus' dear friend Alla Nazimova had once been the biggest movie star in the world, with a huge mansion on Sunset Boulevard. But like so many of her contemporaries, she'd fallen on hard times. So she converted her estate into a hotel and called it the Garden of Allah.

In recent years, Madame had found significant but spasmodic success by touring the country in *Hedda Gabler* or *Zaza*. Whenever she was in town, she and Marcus resumed their ritual of taking tea together on weekend afternoons. Alla prepared her own blend with orange peel and violet petals and perfected the baking of German butter cookies called Buttergebäck. She was one of the first people he told about Nellie Bly being dumped. Goodbye, dream job, hello cramped, dark little hotel room.

He hadn't been at MGM long, but oh, how he missed it. There was something stimulating about hearing the clattering of typewriters around him, knowing that in a few months, all those words would be heard in theaters from Seattle to Miami. And more specifically, the ones *he* was typing would be heard from the mouth of the great Garbo. Even that business with the flavor notes was soon forgotten. He was glad he'd followed Hugo's advice to be the first to laugh it off. The boys had put their point across, and that's all they were looking to do. When the word came down that his project had been nixed, a few of them stopped by his office and encouraged him to keep at it. The Depression was abating, they told him. Things would pick up again soon.

When Alla appeared at his door one day with a spare ticket to an MGM premiere, he hesitated. The release of a new Jeanette MacDonald-Nelson Eddy picture was cause for celebration. *Naughty Marietta* and *Rose-Marie* had done so well that the two stars were rushed into a third pairing, *Maytime,* a concoction about opera singers in love. Marcus felt awkward about going to an MGM event, so he nearly said no, but he quickly came to his senses. When was the last time he'd scored an invite to a big Hollywood premiere with all the trimmings – Grauman's Chinese, radio broadcasts, klieg lights? He'd even have a movie star date for the night.

The crowd stayed seated until the final credit rolled up the screen. When the lights came up, they jumped to their feet and filled the ornate auditorium with spirited chatter. Marcus and Alla allowed themselves to be moved by the river of diamonds and shoulder pads as it flowed up the aisles toward the bar in the foyer. The pair moved over to one side near an enormous Chinese vase and stargazed over the likes of John Barrymore, Norma Shearer, and Tyrone Power.

Grauman's foyer was anchored by the vases in its four corners and its ceiling was a series of ornately carved dragons set against an Art Deco patina of geometric shapes. In the center, a tall wrought iron chandelier with panels of red, yellow, and orange glass hung over the boisterous gathering.

"Is it just me," Madame asked, "or was that picture a bit hokey?"

"It's operetta," Marcus replied. He scanned the room for the bar. He could really do with a drink; it'd been hours since his last one. He pulled at the sleeves of the tuxedo he'd borrowed from his new neighbor, a down-and-out type who called himself a tango dancer but who Marcus suspected was probably more like a taxi dancer. They wore the same size suit, although the neighbor's arms were a tad shorter.

"I don't like this hokey-hokey." When Madame frowned, Marcus thought she looked extra Russian. Her flawlessly oval face was still luminous but had given way to more interesting lines now that she was deep into her fifties. "Give me proper opera with big-breasted sopranos singing Wagner, or musicals, like this new girl Judy Garland and her swingtime jazz. Wonderful, she is! But this in-between stuff?" She gave a scoffing sound. "This operetta—" Alla broke off when she spotted something across the foyer. "Oh! Isn't that Ramon Novarro?"

Slim, with glossy black hair and smooth, tight skin that still glowed with health, Ramon Novarro was the one Marcus always thought of as the One That Got Away. They hadn't seen each other since the Long Beach earthquake of 1933 had interrupted them mid-*flagrante*. Their timing had always been so off that Marcus had tried to put the screen lover out of his mind. It was a double-edged sword to see that handsome face again. His knee-buckling Latino good looks only reminded Marcus of opportunities lost. Damn him to hell and back—he still sucked the air out of Marcus' lungs.

"I know that gentleman with whom Ramon is speaking," Nazimova said. She grabbed Marcus by the wrist. "Come. We say hello."

Navarro was chatting with Franklyn Pangborn, a middle-aged queen meticulously dressed in a dark-blue suit of fine gabardine. He'd made a career of playing prissy butlers and sissified hotel clerks. As Marcus and Nazimova approached, he and Ramon shared a joke that made them both howl like a pair of Catholic schoolgirls.

"Madame!" Ramon said as they approached. He saw Marcus trailing behind her and his face lit up even brighter. "Marcusito! This is a *muy* pleasant surprise."

When Nazimova and Pangborn fell into a conversation about a mutual friend who now worked for Selznick, Ramon turned to Marcus. "You are looking very well and healthy."

"You too, Ramon. Whatever you're doing, it agrees with you."

Ramon's smile was so blindingly white, his teeth so even and his lips so sensuously full that it made Marcus feel a little light-headed. Look at you, he told himself, four years later and you're still all watery knees over this guy. What made you think swallowing half the bourbon on the West Coast was going to help you forget about him?

Ramon said, "I returned recently from four months in Britain touring music halls. It was a very successful tour, I am happy to say."

"The British air must agree with you."

Ramon's hair was thick and shiny, and his skin toned and tanned. Damn it, Marcus thought, I preferred it when I thought I'd gotten you out of my system.

"But what about you, my Marcusito? Tell me about your life."

Marcus obliged, delivering a mostly fabricated account of the last four years, playing up *Return to Sender* and skipping over the Hearst Castle fiasco. But he couldn't take his eyes off Ramon the whole time he was talking. He could still remember how Ramon's lips felt pressed against his own. He cleared his throat and asked, "Are you looking to get back into pictures?"

"Republic have offered me something called *The Sheik Steps Out*, but I do not know what to tell them."

Marcus groaned inwardly. It was a tacky title. Obviously, Republic—a cheapie studio which churned out program fillers and second-rate serials—was looking to cash in on Ramon's Latin-lover image. Marcus ached to tell Ramon he deserved better. "It doesn't sound like your style."

Ramon sighed. "I have a large family who depend on me. The money must come from somewhere."

Nazimova and Pangborn burst into laughter. Marcus was used to Nazimova smiling, but she rarely laughed. It was a rather high-pitched bubbly sort of laughter, the type that Marcus wouldn't have expected. It was nice to see her having a good time.

"Oh, Pang, you are *terrible*," she said, pulling at his burgundy silk necktie.

"Which is why you must come lunch with me at the Cock'n Bull and you can see for yourself. It's called a

Moscow Mule—vodka, ginger beer, and something sharp, lime juice, I think. Deee-*licious*."

"It's a date." Nazimova turned to Marcus. "My dear, would you mind if we went home now? Anything past eleven o'clock is too late for me these days."

Nazimova took Marcus' arm as they said their goodbyes and dodged the footprints and handprints enshrined in the concrete forecourt of Grauman's Chinese. They turned left and headed up Hollywood Boulevard to where Alla's new Pierce-Arrow was parked. She'd bought it after selling a book of poems Rudolf Valentino wrote for her. It had seemed a ridiculous extravagance to Marcus at the time, considering she'd been reduced to living in a bungalow at the rear of what used to be her own backyard, but it wasn't his call.

Madame was taciturn as they wandered along the sidewalk. Marcus knew her well enough to know that when she had something interesting to say, she first said nothing.

"All right," he said. "Out with it. You've got something on your mind."

They continued up Hollywood Boulevard for half a block before Nazimova answered his question. "Stardom is like a yoke of the heaviest lead slung around your shoulders. They tell you to dance the polka for fourteen hours and they scream, 'Do not sweat, otherwise you must to start over.' That is a heavy load to carry when you are just a little boy from south of the border."

"Why are we talking about Ramon Novarro?"

"I crossed a different border, but I wore the same yoke. He was MGM's top male star. He was Ben-Hur! Ramon has been gone from MGM since two years. Enough time to work it all out of his system."

Marcus forced a swallow. His throat felt clamped in a vice. "Two years is a long time," he said evenly. "You're probably right."

Madame was a foot shorter than Marcus, so when she stopped to take his face in her hands, she had to reach up high. But when she did, she locked it in place so he couldn't shake free.

"My darling boy," she said tenderly. "You have a pure heart. And so your eyes are naked; they cannot hide your feelings. That is a good, *good* thing. I shall be sixty soon, and filled with regrets. Do not live your life as I have."

He covered her hands with his. Her skin felt desiccated, like winter leaves. "You've had an extraordinary life. The heights you've reached in your career—"

"They mean nothing without someone to share it with."

A groan escaped from Marcus' lips before he had a chance to catch it. His eyes began to burn. "But he . . . he doesn't think of me . . ."

Madame smiled. "Are you sure?"

Marcus stared for a moment into the violet eyes of his friend. Those eyes, once so clear and bright, were paler now and starting to cloud over. He shrugged and pulled her hands away from his face. He took her arm and led her up Hollywood Boulevard toward her car.

As they passed the front portico of the Hollywood Hotel, he watched a taxi pull up and an elderly gentleman get out. With a small suitcase in his hand, the man climbed the steps with some effort. He walked with a limp and had nobody to help him. He pulled open the front door and disappeared inside. A sudden wind blew up and the door slammed behind him. The thwack of wood against wood shot through the still evening and landed on Marcus' cheek like a slap.

CHAPTER 15

Kathryn looked over at her friend, who was sobbing into her black gloves in the back of George Cukor's limousine. "Do you need my handkerchief?"

Gwendolyn nodded. "I can't believe I forgot one. I can't believe she's gone."

Jean Harlow was, by all accounts, one of the most decent stars in Hollywood. She treated everybody the same—from the studio heads to the guy who swept the soundstage floors. When she fell ill just a week ago, it was just one of many items for Hollywood's gossip columns. Word got out a little while later that Louis B. Mayer had overruled Jean's mother and rushed her to the Good Samaritan Hospital, but nobody was prepared for the news that broke on Monday: Jean Harlow had died of kidney failure.

Gwendolyn had been more upset by Harlow's death than anybody Kathryn knew. The poor thing had been crying off and on since the moment she heard the news. Kathryn never knew her friend looked up to Jean Harlow as a role model in an *If she can make it, I can make it* way. She thought Gwendolyn was just as attractive as Harlow; it seemed right that if Harlow could make it, then why not Gwennie?

The window between George's chauffeur and the back seat wound down. "Mr. Cukor," the driver said, "we're coming up to Forest Lawn now. Were there instructions about where to park?"

George pulled out a stiff white cardboard invitation. "No, Redmond, it just mentions the Wee Kirk o' the Heather chapel. No doubt the MGM police will be out in force today, so just follow their directions."

Hundreds of folks lined the street. As George's car moved past them, many people leaned over looking for a famous face. Disappointed, they shook their heads at their neighbors. An MGM cop in a blue uniform was stationed at the park's elaborate black wrought iron gates. He stopped each car to check that the occupants possessed the same white invitation George held.

When they got out of the car, Kathryn saw David O. Selznick and his wife Irene emerge from their black DeSoto, and behind them three of the Marx brothers—Groucho, Chico, and Harpo—climbed out of a deep crimson Buick.

"You've got to get into that funeral," Wilkerson had told her. It didn't matter that Kathryn had never met Harlow. Nor did it faze him that she'd not received one of those printed invitations that MGM were handing out like éclairs at a hunger strike. "Cukor's going, isn't he?" was his response. "You know him. That's your in right there, and Parsons won't be able to say a thing."

That was the moment when Kathryn realized that one-upping Louella Parsons was more important to her boss than the dignity of Jean Harlow's funeral. Kathryn had been too caught up in making amends to think about how much Wilkerson hated having to force her do it, and he'd been on an anti-Louella tirade ever since.

The rumor mill had been working double-time to decide whether it was MGM or Harlow's mother that kept Louella Parsons away from the funeral. Either way, it was clear that gossipmongers were personae non grata. So when Wilkerson got it into his head that Kathryn must talk her way into the service, Kathryn was horrified. She argued with him for the best part of half an hour, but he was insistent. He gave her no choice but to ask George Cukor if she could go with him.

The Wee Kirk o' the Heather chapel was a quaint little building of pale brick with a steep roof and a simple bell tower. Members of MGM's security force stood ten feet apart, holding lengths of rope to keep uninvited onlookers a hundred feet from the chapel. Kathryn and George left Gwendolyn to merge with the teary masses and walked toward the chapel's front door.

George took out his invitation again. "It's got only my name on it." He glanced at another MGM cop checking the invites as people filed in. "But I know this guy; I think I can get you in."

"Oh, George," Kathryn sighed. "This doesn't feel right. I think I'm going to stay outside with Gwendolyn."

"Your boss said there'd be hell to pay if you didn't get inside."

"He did, but—oh, look."

A rustling murmur swept through the crowd. Jean Bello—Harlow's mother—got out of a taxi with her Negro maid. Mayer rushed up to Mama Jean and enveloped her in a showy hug.

George took Kathryn by the elbow and led her to the gate in front of the chapel. He went to present his white card to the MGM cop, but she stopped him, feigning a crying jag. They stepped aside and let Clark Gable and Carole Lombard through. "This isn't kosher," she whispered to George.

"But Wilkerson is right. It'll kill Parsons to know that you're inside."

"Jean doesn't deserve her funeral to be turned into a game of point scoring. It's so disrespectful, George. I can't do it."

"If Louella were in your shoes, she would."

Of course she would, Kathryn thought. And that's the whole problem with Louella Parsons.

* * *

Kathryn sat in the sixth row of the chapel for the biggest celebrity funeral since Rudolph Valentino feeling cleaved in two: guilty for allowing herself to be talked into coming inside, and pleased that she'd out-Parsoned Louella. She jumped when she felt a tap on her shoulder.

"Miss Massey?"

She turned around to see Harry Cohn with a knowing smile plastered on his bulldog face. He stank of cigars. "The way I heard it, no press was allowed."

Kathryn stared at him, almost relieved that she'd been caught out. She was on the verge of getting to her feet when she felt George's invitation being pushed into her hand. "I'm here as a mourner, not a reporter." She waved it at Cohn, careful not to let him see the name written in exquisite calligraphy.

Cohn leaned in and whispered, "Are you kiddin' me? Everybody in this room is workin'. They're desperate to get their picture took so they can say, 'See how much of a rat's ass I give? I even went to the funeral.' If a bomb went off in the next ten minutes, there would be nobody left to make pictures."

The church organ started and Nelson Eddy, a man with an elongated face, high forehead, and ramrod posture, began singing "Sweet Mystery of Life." As he crooned his way through the song, Kathryn took in as much as she could and tried to memorize names as discreetly as she dared. Spencer Tracy was in front of her, Robert Montgomery beside him. Wallace Beery was at the end of their pew and across the aisle was Howard Hughes, who'd given Jean her big break in *Hell's Angels*.

It struck Kathryn that despite its renown, Hollywood was really just a small company town where everybody knew everybody. A tragedy like this brought everyone together, and when brought together like this, "everyone" didn't seem like many people.

Her eyes wandered down the pew until it landed on a woman sitting at the far left. She wore a dress of heavy black lace and a hat with a broad brim and matching veil.

When Eddy finished his song, the priest returned to the podium and started the eulogy, but Kathryn's eyes kept returning to the woman. Even when Jeanette MacDonald got up to sing "Indian Love Call," the woman remained focused on her lap.

As MacDonald's song came to an end, the woman in the black lace dove into her handbag and pulled out a handkerchief. As she raised it toward the black lace veil, Kathryn saw a silver ring with a chunk of violet glass cut like a robin's egg. It was an unusual ring, and Kathryn had only seen one like it.

The service came to a dignified end and the crowd waited until Mama Jean was helped down the aisle by her maid. Then everyone except Louella Parsons started filing out of the cramped chapel.

Kathryn let herself fall behind George Cukor and saw her opportunity when they drew alongside an enormous vase of lavender rhododendrons. She stopped to pretend to search for something in her purse, keeping Louella in her peripheral vision. The crafty old bat slipped out an emergency exit at the far end of the chapel. Kathryn stole away from the somber crowd and followed her outside to a small side yard. She caught the door before it closed.

"Louella, this was a funeral. How could you?"

Louella grabbed her black lace veil and threw it over the top of her hat. Her bleary eyes looked even more mottled in the shadows of the large pine tree looming over them. "Jean Harlow was a close and precious friend of mine."

Nobody is a close and precious friend of Louella Parsons unless they've got a good story to tell, Kathryn thought. She raised an eyebrow.

"How would you know who my close friends are?" Louella said, and turned away.

"And you're drunk."

"What? How dare—"

"I can smell the brandy on your breath, Louella."

"You're being ridiculous. Not to mention libelous."

"Something is only libelous if it's written down. I saw you take a n—" Kathryn stopped herself.

"Saw me take a what? A nip? Where?" Louella cocked her head toward the chapel. "In there? During the service?"

Kathryn realized that she'd let herself be pulled into the Hollywood mud. She could have said no, but she was too deep into the murk to backtrack now. She waved George's invitation in front of Louella's face. "I was invited," she said, and shoved it back into her purse.

Louella's only reply was a fiery glare.

"Louella, it's not just that you gate-crashed Jean Harlow's funeral, but you were drinking all the way through it. Oh, Louella . . ." Kathryn thought of her mother and wondered why anyone would want to associate with this woman.

They eyed each other for a moment or two until Kathryn watched Louella's face implode in a burst of tears. A loud wail. "I've been through hell since Jean died," Louella cried. "It's been such a shock. It puts all this . . ." she made a flittering motion with her hand, "this stuff and nonsense we do, puts it into perspective. It's really been very difficult and I wanted to say goodbye to her. Mayer wouldn't let me in but I couldn't not say my final farewell. That's all I wanted."

"Louella," Kathryn said gently, "we haven't really spoken since that incident." Louella peered at Kathryn expectantly, her eyes wet with tears. "You know what I mean. And you countered with those veiled accusations about me neglecting my mother's welfare. You and I both know that's not the case at all, don't we?" Louella pressed her lips together and didn't look like she planned to say anything. "I know you're used to getting the scoops first, but come on, Louella, you have to know that sometimes I, or someone like me, will come across something first. Of course we're going to publish it. There's more than enough news to go around, don't you think?"

Louella Parsons drew her head back and her eyes flared. "Kathryn, this is a *funeral*. I'm standing here before you in mourning. I'm utterly distraught about what's happened to Jean and you stand here talking to me about business. Really, Kathryn, if your mother were here right now, she'd be so disappointed in you."

Louella opened her purse and pulled out a handkerchief. Something fell onto the cropped lawn. Kathryn bent down to retrieve a sheet of paper folded up in a tight square.

"I'll have that, thank you very much."

Kathryn would have handed the paper right back to Louella, but there was something in the way Louella's eyes dimmed as she stared at Kathryn's hand. Without taking her gaze from Louella, Kathryn unfolded the paper and began to read the names listed on it: *Mayer, Benny Thau, Joseph Schenck, Rbt Montgomery, S. Tracy, N. Eddy, G. C. + H. Marx, Gable, Victor Fleming, Zukor, Laemmle, Cohn, L. Barrymore, Beery, DeMille, Zanuck, J. Warner, Selznick+wife, Ronald Colman, H. Hughes, Hal Roach.*

Louella snatched the list from her, glaring at her with eyes that had turned beady and hard. "There's only room for one seat at my table," she said. Kathryn stared at her.

And here I was, she thought, thinking you were just some silly middle-aged woman who had somehow managed to muddle your way into a powerful position.

Louella jabbed a gnarled finger in Kathryn's direction. "Now listen here, you little Jilly-Come-Lately. Everyone knows of my agreement with the studios. I get *all* the scoops before anyone else. And that includes *you*." Her bloodshot eyes turned to shriveled peas. "I don't know who you're sleeping with to get your information, but I shall not rest until I find out who it is."

"Louella!" Kathryn's eyes cast about to see if anybody was close enough to hear. Nobody had noticed them. She turned back to see a withering smile plastered across the battle-ax's face that begged to be slapped off.

"And when I do," Louella continued, "I shall expose you for the tramp you are."

Kathryn took another step; she was close enough to see the rotting edges around Parsons' teeth. "You've had it real good for a real long while," Kathryn told her. "And what have you done during that whole time? Earned everybody's respect? Won their admiration? Their genuine friendship? No. You've worked very, very hard to make sure that everybody is running very, very scared of you. Well, maybe we're all sick of running."

CHAPTER 16

"I've got it!"

Gwendolyn stared at her new friend, Countess Dorothy di Frasso. "What have you got?"

The countess pushed a dark lock of her softly marcelled hair away from her face. Gwendolyn guessed the countess hovered around fifty, but she had the eager face of a teenager. Her cornflower blue eyes always twinkled, her irises seasoned with a life fully lived. She tapped her pointed chin a couple of times, then pointed a finger at Gwendolyn. "From the moment I saw you standing next to me at Jean Harlow's funeral, I've been wondering how I knew your face."

"From the Cocoanut Grove?" That was how this conversation usually went, and Lord knows, Gwendolyn had had it plenty of times.

"You live at the Garden of Allah, don't you?"

"Yes, I do. You too?"

A tentative smile bloomed across the face of Gwendolyn's funeral friend, as they'd started to refer to each other. "Oh, God!" Dorothy slapped a hand in front of her mouth. "I should never have brought it up."

"Why not?"

"I was told not to."

This sounded intriguing. "Told by whom?"

Dorothy sniffed at the bottle of perfume in her hand and put it back onto the counter. They were in the makeup department at Bullock's Wilshire—a store far beyond Gwendolyn's budget, but certainly not Dorothy's. She fixed

Gwendolyn with a serious stare. "I'm in the midst of an affair right now. Positively *rampant*!"

Since the moment they met outside the Wee Kirk o' the Heather, Dorothy di Frasso had struck Gwendolyn as the worldly type of woman for whom rampant affairs were de rigueur. The woman's hair was always styled so chicly, her makeup impeccably applied, and her clothes tailor-made from some of the most expensive material Gwendolyn had ever seen.

"Sounds fun," Gwendolyn said. She picked up a bottle of Chanel No. 5. She'd been longing to smell it for months, ever since Olivia de Havilland mentioned it in an interview on the set of *Anthony Adverse*, saying it made her feel like a complete woman. She took a sniff. The floral notes made her think of the early summer roses her mother would sometimes pick up on the rare days when Mama was sober enough to get off the sofa. Mmmm . . . divine. She dabbed a drop behind each ear.

"We've been meeting at the Garden of Allah," Dorothy continued. "In the main house."

"Oh, but it's so dark in there."

"Exactly! I've never had an affair this *deliciously* naughty. He's from the East Coast so he doesn't know a soul here. Some sort of businessman." She waved a hand so heavy with rings—sapphires mainly, to match her eyes—that Gwendolyn had to wonder how she signed her checks. "I can't remember what type of business. He's devilishly good-looking, in a dark and slightly swarthy way. Italian, I presume, but he could be Arabic for all I care. All I know for sure is that he's terrific in bed and to never call him Bugsy. He hates being called that."

"So what do you call him?"

"I play it safe," the countess declared, "I call him Ben. Sometimes Benji when we're, you know, afterglowing."

"What does he call you?"

She let out a high, tinkling laugh. "Usually it's 'my captivating countess.'"

"I thought you didn't use that title out here."

Dorothy drifted over to the Max Factor counter. "You know those East Coast types, they're all terribly impressed by stuff like that. That's why I prefer it here, nobody gives a hoot one way or the other. I'm terribly grateful to Coop for that."

Dorothy had had an affair in Italy with Gary Cooper a dozen years ago and followed him to Los Angeles when he decided to try for a career in the movies. They'd long since parted but were still on good terms. That was another quality Gwendolyn liked in her new friend – she seemed to be on good terms with all her ex-lovers. And there seemed to be quite a few.

They arrived at a large Coty display that featured a huge reproduction of the *Gone with the Wind* book that stood taller than Gwendolyn. The title took up the top two-thirds, each letter the size of Gwendolyn's hand. She gazed at the display and thought yet again about her encounter with Fred Schussler at Chasen's when he'd told her she looked enough like Scarlett O'Hara for him to order a screen test. She picked up the tester bottle of Scarlett and sniffed it. Roses and lavender, perhaps orange. It was a gentle smell, soft and girlish.

"Why are you so glum today?" Dorothy asked.

"Have you ever heard of someone called Fred Schussler?" Gwendolyn asked, although it wasn't a necessary question. Dorothy di Frasso knew everyone in Hollywood. She even knew Marino Bello, Jean Harlow's stepfather, but got to Forest Lawn too late to be let inside the chapel that day. The service had already started and the place was packed, so she'd stayed outside the gate, next to Gwendolyn as it turned out.

"Schussler? Isn't he in casting for Selznick?"

Gwendolyn nodded. "A few months ago he promised me a screen test for Scarlett O'Hara."

"How exciting! You know what? I can see you as Scarlett."

Gwendolyn harrumphed. "I'm still waiting for his call. It's been months. I've left messages, of course, but I don't know what else I can do."

Dorothy took the bottle of Scarlett perfume from Gwendolyn and deposited it onto the glass counter. "My best advice to you, my lovely little miss, is to take matters into your own hands."

"I thought that's what I've been doing, but all I seem to get is ignored."

"Oh, my sweet. It's time you learned that the men of this town think they're all in charge—but heavens! If they only knew! They believe they come up with all these wonderful ideas, all this creativity and innovation they blather on and on about. And yet none of them seem to catch on that half the time it's their wives who have planted the idea inside their pea brains in the first place!"

"The wives?"

"Or girlfriends. Or mistresses. Tick where applicable." Dorothy took Gwendolyn's hand and gave it an encouraging squeeze. "All you have to do is ask your funeral friend to see if she can arrange for you and a certain studio wife to be together in the same room."

* * *

With its perfectly manicured gardens and its three-car garage, 913 Bedford Drive in Beverly Hills was every bit as palatial a home as Gwendolyn imagined a countess would have. She may have downplayed the title her Italian ex-husband had given her during a brief marriage in the early twenties, but she never downplayed the millions she'd inherited from her father.

The doorbell chimes were answered by a British butler dressed in full livery that included a haughty expression that could get him lots of work at Central Casting. "Madame and Mrs. Selznick are in the front parlor," he informed her.

Gwendolyn clasped and unclasped her gloved hands and tried to steady her breath. It wasn't enough that Irene Selznick was the wife of the producer of *Gone with the Wind;* she was also the daughter of the head of MGM. As far as

Gwendolyn was concerned, this was as close to meeting royalty as she was ever going to get.

Dorothy and Mrs. Selznick sat in a light-filled parlor on love seats upholstered in a striking floral. They looked up expectedly at Gwendolyn and smiled as they rose to their feet. Gwendolyn smoothed down the ruffles of her dress. It was the same one she'd worn to Chasen's; after a long soak in bleach and half a dozen washes, it was as good as new. She'd spent a week unpicking the bits that were too frilly-frilly-frou-frou and replaced the bodice with panels of plain white rayon, shortened it to knee-length, and dressed it up with an emerald-green sash around her waist. That morning, she'd attached a gold horseshoe pin Kathryn gave her for good luck.

Dorothy made the introductions and commented on how lovely Gwendolyn looked in her dress. The Central Casting butler wheeled in a tea cart and poured tea while Dorothy launched into a wandering discourse on the effect *Gone with the Wind* was going to have on fashion. It was Dorothy's theory that hoop skirts might come into vogue, but she hoped that wasn't the case. "Lord in heaven above, can any of us imagine running around in those things?" She rambled on for a while about corsets and hair ribbons and embroidered slippers, and then abruptly ended with ". . . and that's why I think it would be glorious if you could recommend to your husband that the lovely Gwendolyn here be screen-tested for the role of Scarlett."

It was so sudden that it even took Gwendolyn by surprise. She paused for a moment to let the notion sink into Mrs. Selznick's consciousness, holding her breath, and then hazarded a glance. Irene had the sharply etched lines of the no-nonsense type of woman that Gwendolyn generally liked. Her dark brown hair was pulled back in an easy-to-manage ponytail, her eyes, clear and astute, belied none of the indulgence that she surely must have experienced as the child of America's highest-paid individual.

Irene Selznick's slim face blanched. "You thought . . . what?"

"Don't you think Gwendolyn would make the most marvelous Scarlett O'Hara?"

Irene kept her eyes trained on Dorothy as her mouth drooped open just slightly. "Dorothy," she said quietly, "you really should have told me what you were up to."

Silence filled the room so profoundly that Gwendolyn could hear "Ebb Tide" playing on the radio in the kitchen all the way in the back of the house.

Irene turned to Gwendolyn. "I'm sorry, my dear, please don't take this as a reflection upon you in any way. As it happens, I agree with Dorothy; I can see you as Scarlett. But David would be simply horrified if I were to interfere in any of the casting. *Especially* Scarlett. This is completely out of my league."

"Oh, Irene. Don't you remember?" the countess cried. "We were talking at Joan Fontaine's party about how the men in this town think their best ideas are their own, when we womenfolk really know who put them there in the first place. And you were saying how much you would love it if David could include you in some way in the making of *Gone with the Wind*, because it's taking up so much of his time and energy. You said that if you could be involved—even in a small way—it would help bridge the gap. His *A Star is Born* picture was originally your idea, so clearly you know what you're doing. So I thought if, and only if, you thought Gwendolyn here has potential, then you could find a way to make it known to David that you've—"

"Excuse me, please, ladies," Gwendolyn broke in. "Where is the powder room?"

"First door past the stairs, dear."

Gwendolyn shot to her feet and beelined out of the living room. She closed the powder room door behind her and turned the key until she heard a click. The mirror over the basin was framed in ornately carved mahogany leaves, angels, and flowers. Gwendolyn stared at her reflection. She had gone pale; her eye shadow now looked far too bold. She watched her forehead crinkle up and she looked away.

"Oh, how could you, Dorothy?" It was Irene's voice. "Get that poor girl's hopes up like that. And to put me in such a spot. Really, you might have warned me."

Dorothy's reply was too soft for Gwendolyn to make out; not that it mattered. The countess' heart was in the right place.

"You were foolish to think Selznick's wife could do any such thing," Gwendolyn told her reflection. "That sort of stuff happens *in* the movies, not behind them."

Her vision went misty. Don't start crying now, she thought. Not over something like this.

But it didn't work.

CHAPTER 17

One stroke. Two stroke. Three stroke. Four stroke. Breathe.

As someone born far from any significant body of water, it always struck Marcus as odd that he should feel so at home in a pool.

One stroke. Two stroke. Three stroke. Four stroke. Breathe.

At some point during his too-brief stint at MGM, he'd discovered that he did his best thinking in the Garden of Allah's pool. There was something about the rhythmic swings of the arms and the way he took a breath on every fourth stroke that settled his mind and left it free to mull over any problems at hand. Doing twenty laps every other day soon became nearly every evening after work. And now that he no longer had to worry about turning up at a movie studio, nearly every evening had become every morning and every afternoon, even though the problems with plotting a picture were no longer his to mull over.

One stroke. Two stroke. Three stroke. Four stroke. Breathe.

What he needed now was a sock-it-to-'em idea to sell a studio on. Dreaming up ideas for movies had never been much of a problem for Marcus, but this time he needed one that would knock the toupees off half the scalps in the front office. But whammo-blammo ideas didn't grow on the orange tree at the end of the Garden of Allah's yard, so Marcus took to the pool in an effort to come up with something useable.

He pulled up at the end of the pool just beside the diving board and held onto the edge. While he regained his breath, he found himself staring at a stack of ten crates of Coca-Cola.

He climbed out of the pool, dried off, and was calculating the number of bottles when a dapper gent with a long, sagging face came charging around the corner.

"I'm so sorry," the man said, stepping aside just in time to avoid knocking Marcus over. He had one of those Ivy League voices, deep with casually rounded vowels, and wore his necktie a little too short. He swiped the sweat off his forehead and introduced himself.

"I'm Scott. Moving is a terrible thing, isn't it?"

Scott was moving into the villa behind the stack of Coca-Cola. When he said he only had two more loads of boxes and he'd be done, Marcus offered to help. On the way back from Scott's battered Ford coupe, Marcus discovered he was carrying a lidless box of journals covered in dark brown suede—with the monogram *F.S.F.* stenciled in gold in the bottom right-hand corner.

"These your initials?" Marcus asked when they were back in front of the villa.

Scott looked at the gold letters for a long moment. Then he raised his blue-grey eyes and studied Marcus for an even longer moment. "Yes," he said quietly.

Marcus studied the initials, then blinked slowly as though he'd seen a mirage. Scott Fitzgerald? Standing in front of him? Close enough to touch? This was like encountering Lewis Carroll.

"It's a pleasure to meet you," Marcus said, then wished he hadn't sounded teenage-girl gushy.

"That box must be getting heavy," Scott said. "Follow me."

Marcus trailed him into his villa. It was larger than the one Marcus used to have, roomy enough for a large dining table, but not as sunny. A standard lamp with a fringe of butter-yellow tassels lit the living room in a gentle, forgiving light. The walls were painted in a light green but needed a fresh coat. Scott directed Marcus to deposit his box on the dining table, where he'd already set out a number of framed photographs. Four more crates of Coca-Cola nearly took up the whole kitchen counter.

Scott shook Marcus' hand. "I've just landed a job at MGM," he said. "Only ten weeks, but one of those can't-say-no offers, and so here I am."

"Try the chicken soup in the commissary," Marcus said. "Mayer's mother's recipe. The most delicious matzo ball soup you'll ever taste."

Scott gave something between a smile and a grimace. "I plan to work from home," he said. "I've never been much for the whole working in an office routine. I can get a lot more done if I'm free to write whenever the mood takes me."

Marcus nodded appreciatively, wondering whether MGM would let him. They liked to keep their writers on-site and in sight.

"Well, cut off my legs and call me Shorty!"

Marcus and Scott turned around to find Robert Benchley and Dorothy Parker standing in the open doorway.

"Bench!"

The two men wrapped their arms around each other in an affectionate bear hug. In an odd sort of way, they were polar opposites. Benchley's nightly drinking had made him grow portly and today he wore an oversized bowling shirt, whereas his old friend had dressed in a collar and tie to move in July. Scott's clothes hung from his underfed frame looking two sizes too big for him; Benchley's attire grew ever more snug. Declarations of how long it had been since they'd seen each other quickly segued into "Do you remember that time in Paris . . .?" Marcus stood to the side, envious of their heartfelt friendship.

"Oh, God. Here we go again," Dottie muttered.

"What is it?" Marcus asked.

She jutted her head at the crates of Coca-Cola. "Scott must be back on the wagon. When he's sober, he guzzles the stuff like a foot soldier in the French Foreign Legion. Common with raging alcoholics, apparently. Something about the need for sugar in the blood or some such nonsense." She let out a melodramatic sigh. "I do hope it sticks this time."

"He plans to ask MGM if he can write at home here at the Garden."

"Oh, yes." She rolled her huge brown eyes. "The Garden of Allah—just the place you want to be when you're trying to stay dry. Why don't we just move him into the nearest whiskey distillery and be done with it?"

She spotted the photographs Scott had set out on the dining table and picked one up. It was a black and white line drawing of a tussle-haired man in his twenties wearing a white cravat pinned at the neck with a large diamond. She turned it to Marcus. "Do you know who this is?" Marcus shook his head. "It's Francis Scott Key, writer of 'The Star-Spangled Banner.' Scott here is related to him, cousins or some such. Right, Fitzy?" She held up the portrait for Scott to see.

"Second cousin twice removed, however that works," Scott replied.

"Had quite the adventurous life," Benchley said. "American War of 1812, burning of the White House and all that. Not to mention writing 'The Star-Spangled Banner.'"

"Having two famous people in one family is inexcusably greedy," Dorothy announced. "Come along, Mr. Benchley. We're already late for my manicure and you know how Helga the Austrian detests tardiness. Never piss off a Teuton with a manicure knife."

They disappeared down the path toward the parking lot at the back of the Garden. Marcus stared at the portrait of Francis Scott Key in his hand. Hmm, he thought, the burning of the White House . . .

CHAPTER 18

Kathryn slammed the *Los Angeles Examiner* onto the top of her desk so hard the telephone wobbled in its cradle.

Last night saw the glamorous premiere of MGM's Saratoga. *Everybody turned out for Jean Harlow's final screen performance. And a gem of a performance it was, too. But conspicuous in her absence was the* Hollywood Reporter's *Kathryn Massey, whose fanatic zeal for the late actress compelled her to sneak into Harlow's NO PRESS ALLOWED funeral service at Forest Lawn. No wonder Massey had so much to say the next day.*

Kathryn grabbed the paper and marched down to the end of the corridor, passing Vera without stopping to say hello. Wilkerson was hanging up the phone when she strode into his office. Louella hadn't merely crossed a line—she'd trampled it. Kathryn demanded why he wasn't frothing at the mouth.

"Close the door." His voice was thin and terse. She obeyed, but before she had a chance to open her mouth, he cut her off. "I'm going to ask you to write a mea culpa."

"A mere what?"

"It's Latin for 'my own fault.' It's when an individual recognizes her flaws before God. It's not a confession of sins, but an admission of one's flawed nature and the willingness to make amends for it." He said all this in a curtly authoritative tone she'd heard him use on other people, but never on her. "Kathryn, you are to apologize."

"To whom and for what?"

"To Hollywood for sneaking into Jean Harlow's funeral."

The *Examiner* crumpled as Kathryn's hands balled into fists. "You can*not* be serious."

"I'm dead serious. It was in bad taste—"

"*I'm* the one who said it was in bad taste. *I'm* the one who didn't want to do it. But you made me—*forced* me. And now you want me to apologize? To hell with—"

Wilkerson kept his eyes on Kathryn's crushed newspaper. "Louella has forced our hand. Now everyone thinks that all press was banned, not just her, and that you snuck into that funeral like a rat. You can't deny you were in there. People must have seen you."

"And if they did, they would have seen me waving a written invitation around."

"Did it have your name on it?"

"You know very well it didn't."

"Therefore you snuck in, and nobody in this town is going to like or respect you for it. Not at the funeral for someone as well loved as Jean Harlow."

Kathryn couldn't believe he was backpedaling. Again. "And let me repeat: YOU are the one who insisted I go." She rolled her copy of the *Examiner* into a club and hurled it at him.

Wilkerson swatted Kathryn's missile away and raised his voice a few decibels. "All right! So I didn't think this one through. It was a tacky thing to do and I don't want tackiness associated with my publication. So you will write a mea culpa and you will have it on my desk an hour before tomorrow's deadline."

"There is no chance—"

"I don't care how you have to put it," her boss thundered. He was on his feet now. "Louella has damaged the *Reporter*'s reputation, and I can't allow that. This is not a request."

"Excuse me," Kathryn retorted, "but whatever happened to 'Let's stick it to 'em'?"

"You're lucky I'm not firing you."

"And you're lucky I haven't told anyone how you gambled with the payroll."

Wilkerson's face descended three shades of red. "How *dare* you throw that into my face?"

"And how dare you threaten me with my job."

"I'm under pressure to fire you."

Kathryn slapped Wilkerson's desk so hard it made her palms tingle. "You don't have a board of directors to answer to. Who could apply any sort of pressure to you?"

"Hearst."

Wilkerson's admission sucker-punched the air out of Kathryn's lungs. She stepped back and let herself fall into the chair behind her. "What are you talking about?"

"He's threatening to buy the *Reporter*."

"He can't do that."

"He's William Randolph Hearst."

"He can't buy anything that you're not willing to sell him."

Wilkerson looked at her as though he were straining to pass gas. The red-hot anger in his face drained away. "He's talking about offering me four times what the paper is worth."

Kathryn realized that this was a whole new ballgame now. Hearst, king of the yellow rags, own the *Hollywood Reporter*? That would be a disaster, and probably the end of the paper. And if it wasn't, then it would be the end of her. She certainly couldn't stay on with Hearst in charge, not that she'd be given an option. After her encounters with his high-profile pet journalist, she'd be the first one to be shown the door.

"Four times what it's worth?" she asked. It was impossible not to see the desperate look in her boss' eye. "Which you'll lose at Santa Anita or Agua Caliente before the month is out, and then you'll have no money and no newspaper."

"He told me he'd back off, though."

Kathryn swallowed hard. "If Kathryn Massey published a mea culpa for gate-crashing Jean Harlow's funeral last month." She was cornered like a fox at the hunt. "What did you tell him?"

"Nobody likes a liar, but everybody loves a penitent."

"You said that to Hearst?"

"No, I'm saying it to you."

* * *

Kathryn glared at her typewriter. She had no idea how to say what she had to say. Damn that miserable bastard and his oceans of money, Kathryn thought. And damn that vindictive bitch who works for him. And damn Wilkerson for putting me in this situation.

She closed her eyes and thought of the person she always thought of when she was harried or blue: Roy Quinn. A guy as simple and straightforward as his name. He was just about the nicest guy Kathryn had ever met, and certainly the nicest guy she'd ever dated. The memory of having to tell him that she'd lost his baby when in fact she'd had a furtive abortion still wrenched her with guilt. But he was married to a strict Catholic, and she was about to start her job at the *Hollywood Reporter*, so what other options were there? It'd been two years since she'd last seen him and she still missed him like crazy.

If he were here, he'd wrap her in those strong arms of his, he'd press his lips to her ear, and he'd whisper something encouraging and comforting. He'd tell her that he was on her side, and together they'd come up with a blasted mea culpa that would satisfy Hollywood—

The telephone rang. "This is Kathryn Massey."

"And this is Ida Koverman."

"Yes, Miss Koverman." Louis B. Mayer's secretary wasn't the sort of person anyone would presume to call by her first name—probably not even Mayer himself. "What can I do for you?"

"I was wondering if you might be free to attend one of my cat's parties."

CHAPTER 19

The guy who answered the door wasn't wearing any shirt. Or shoes. Or pants. Just a pair of shorts. His body was lean and tanned like an Olympian's.

"Alistair Dunne?" Gwendolyn asked.

"You must be Gwendolyn," the man said. "Come in, please. Excuse my attire. The heat makes this place the devil's workshop."

Gwendolyn stepped into an enormous room with a glass ceiling and walls of exposed brick. To the right lay Dunne's portrait studio, an airy space filled with easels and a stack of blank canvases. A lounging sofa in sun-faded green velvet stood in the center by a card table littered with tubes of paint in every imaginable hue. To the left, a double bed was pushed against the far wall near a couple of shelves jumbled with books and papers. Another sofa stood against the far left wall with a coffee table in front of it.

"This is quite some place you've got here," Gwendolyn said. She started to fan herself. He was right—it was a touch warm, even for August.

"It's the glass ceiling." Dunne pointed upwards. "All that grime and soot filters the direct sunlight and diffuses it gloriously. Perfect for my needs, but it also traps in the heat, and there are only three small windows to let it all out. You won't be very comfortable, but the deadline is September first, so we can't put it off until the weather cools down."

Gwendolyn had been shocked when Irene Selznick cornered her at the Cocoanut Grove a week ago. She'd never expected to see her again, and frankly didn't want to.

Dorothy had been well-meaning, but the rest of that afternoon couldn't have been more uncomfortable if she'd spent it with a knitting needle jammed into her thigh.

"Have you ever heard of Alistair Dunne?" Irene had asked her.

It took Gwendolyn a few moments to connect the dots. Alistair Dunne was Eldon Laird's favorite artist. That abstract painting with the huge splashes of bold colors that hung in Eldon's office was a Dunne. Gwendolyn's guard shot up like a steel fence. She hadn't heard from Eldon since the night she left with his copy of *Gone with the Wind,* and that was just as well. The man might be able to kiss like Casanova's lovechild, but he was bad news. She'd told Irene she'd never heard of him.

"He's an artist," Irene explained. "An amazing one, and I'm trying to encourage his career. The longer David's production of *Gone with the Wind* goes on, the more neglected I feel. I hardly ever see him, and when I do he's too tired or preoccupied to talk. For heaven's sake, I know a thing or two about putting a movie together. I've thought and thought about this, and I've decided that I agree with the countess: you *do* look like Scarlett O'Hara. I have a plan."

Irene's plan was to have Gwendolyn sit for Dunne as he worked on an entry for the Carmichael Prize, the top prize in the country for portraiture. Just getting him into the competition was Irene's goal, as it would propel his name to the national level. Once the competition was over—Irene was positive that he wouldn't win, because although he was talented, he was still too green for something as prestigious as the Carmichael—Irene would buy the portrait, which she would then hang in the projection room in place of their George Bellows landscape. As distracted as he was, David loved the Bellows; he was sure to notice the change.

"David's a terrible art snob, so when I explain that I've replaced the Bellows with one that was short-listed for the Carmichael, he'll be happy. Then I'll be ready to draw comparisons between Margaret Mitchell's description of

Scarlett and you. If I had a hand in casting the movie role of the decade, that's something I'd be very proud of."

Alistair Dunne was all business and no chitchat. He guided Gwendolyn to the studio side of the room and sat her down on the green velvet sofa with her head resting against its high back. It smelled of other models: five-and-dime perfume, sweat and craving.

"I want you to grip the sides of the chaise lounge," he told her, "as though you're about to set yourself down after a long, hot day on your feet."

Gwendolyn did what she thought he meant but got a frown. "No, no, no," he said, and grabbed her by the elbows. His hands were soft and warm and made her skin quiver. The mat of blond hair covering his chest looked like summer hay. He arranged her the way he wanted, with her legs slightly spread apart. "Think of it like this: you've just heard the front door open and you know it is your lover come home to you."

Coming from someone else – even Eldon Laird – a suggestion like that would've come off lewd, but in Alistair's mouth it sounded sophisticated and mature. Still, she wondered, I simply can't imagine how this pose can possibly lead to a portrait that's going to make David O. Selznick say, "Find me that girl!" Especially when this guy might turn her into a chaotic hodgepodge that would blind the Carmichael committee.

She let herself smile anyway.

He said, "Ah yes, that's it. Now I need you to hold that position for me. Can you do that?"

"It is getting a mite warm in here."

"If I win the Carmichael, an electric fan will be the first thing I buy."

He picked up a blank canvas and placed it on his easel. He stared at it for the longest time then suddenly, as though he'd been kicked, he grabbed a tube of pale pink paint and squeezed some of it onto a porcelain dinner plate. He added a small drop of black paint to it and mixed it in with the focus of a safecracker.

Gwendolyn felt her shoulders relax. The summers in Florida had been worse than this, plus hair-wilting humidity. She breathed out and closed her eyes, and pictured herself as Scarlett O'Hara, sitting on the porch of Tara with the Tarleton twins, talking about the possibility of war . . .

* * *

When Gwendolyn woke up, it wasn't with a start or a gasp, but with Alistair Dunne's hand cupping her right breast. Firm yet gentle, almost reverent.

"What in the name of Robert E. Lee do you think you're doing?" she asked.

"You fell asleep."

"Did that answer my question?"

"You don't move a muscle when you're asleep, which suits my purpose. So naturally I didn't want to wake you." He showed no sign of removing his hand. Gwendolyn felt herself go a little steamy inside.

"So you thought you'd awaken me by putting your hand to my breast?"

"Do you mind?"

Gwendolyn felt herself blush. No, she didn't mind at all. She met his steady gaze. "I'm awake now, Mr. Dunne."

"Call me Alistair."

"Alistair?" she said, lowering her voice.

"Yes, Gwendolyn?"

"With the Carmichael deadline less than three weeks away, I don't know that you have the time to be distracted by . . . ," she tilted her head down toward the breast still cupped in his hand, "this sort of thing."

"I've done as much as I can. The light has gone." His eyes, Pacific Ocean blue, were almost hypnotic this close up.

Gwendolyn looked around her. The space had cooled in the gentler light of late afternoon. "What time is it?"

"Cocktail hour," Alistair replied. "Have you ever tried absinthe?"

"Cocktail hour?!" Gwendolyn pushed Alistair's hand from her breast and stood up. "I'll be so late for work!"

Alistair stayed on the sofa. He stretched his bare legs out, brushing his right with her left. "Two parts champagne mixed with one part absinthe makes a cocktail called Death in the Afternoon. It must be tasted to be believed."

Gwendolyn looked down at Alistair Dunne sprawled out on his faded velvet sofa. How easy would it have been to sink down into his arms? Don't be such a cliché, she told herself. The model who allows herself to be seduced by a bohemian artist, indeed. That's as bad as an actress allowing herself to be seduced by her agent.

She spotted her handbag across the room and started for it. "A working girl needs to pay her half of the rent," she said over her shoulder. She hoped she sounded as annoyed as she felt.

"Come Tuesday, twelve noon. It is important that you are not late."

She opened the door and turned to look at him sprawled out on the sofa like a panther on a tree branch. She closed the door behind her and stood for a moment in the humid corridor, then let out a breath she wasn't aware she'd been holding. She closed her eyes. She could still feel the warmth of his hand on her breast.

CHAPTER 20

The sound of Scott Fitzgerald's typewriter keys stopped. Marcus looked up from the page he was reading to see Scott staring at a framed photograph of his wife, Zelda.

"Something wrong?"

"I met someone recently," Scott said, keeping his eyes on Zelda. "Screen Writer's Guild dinner dance."

Marcus stifled a groan. He was loathe to stop work, but if they talked about why Scott was so preoccupied and distracted, maybe it'd get it off his chest and they could churn out a decent chunk of screenplay. "You did?"

Marcus watched Scott open another bottle of Coca-Cola. Three weeks ago, after Scott hired Marcus to help him fashion his screenplay, Robert Benchley had told Marcus, "You don't need to worry until the Coca-Cola runs out." The bottle Scott had just opened was the third to last one.

"Someone called Sheilah Graham," Scott replied. "Heard of her?"

"I know the name."

"She's British. Some sort of writer, I think. Should be a movie star. Got that poised look about her. Classy. You know how British women can be."

Marcus wasn't sure he'd ever met one, but he nodded anyway and asked something about page eighty-one of the draft in front of him. But Scott didn't answer. Marcus held his breath as Scott drained the bottle.

It had occurred to Marcus that in the midst of all the growing tensions in Europe and talk of another world war, a patriotic movie about the writing of the national anthem might be a shot in the arm for a country still crawling into the sunlight from the pit of Depression. And who better to write this movie than F. Scott Fitzgerald, who was both under contract with MGM and related to the composer who witnessed something as cinematic as the burning of the White House?

He'd pitched it to Scott, who took it to MGM, which bought it. Then Scott got cold feet and privately enlisted Marcus to help him write it. He'd already been taken off his first picture and Marcus could see why; it was a mess. The man might be a master at prose but he had no idea what went into crafting a screenplay. Once the screenplay was finished, Marcus planned to find a way to let the studio know he'd helped Scott write it, but work was progressing at a funereal pace. The thrill of working with The Voice of a Generation had worn away; now it just seemed like a hard slog through a Delaware winter.

Scott got to his feet. Marcus liked Coca-Cola as much as the next guy, but the bottle Scott just finished was his ninth for the day and it wasn't even noon yet. "This stuff goes through me like French beer."

It was the first time Scott had referenced his halcyon days. During the twenties he'd lived in France and run around with ex-pats like Ernest Hemingway and Gertrude Stein. Over the summer, Hemingway had been in Los Angeles to raise money for the Spanish Republic, but apparently their reunion didn't go well. People around the Garden were saying that Hemingway's up-coming novel, *To Have And Have Not*, promised to be yet another reminder to Scott of how Hemingway was still producing relevant literary fiction for the future, while Scott was failing to live up to his past.

Marcus eyed the two remaining Coca-Cola bottles. "This is turning out well for a first draft," he said.

Scott stood in the doorway to the bathroom and fixed Marcus with silent, untrusting eyes. He reached upwards and stretched out his body with a soft groan. "If I drink too much Coca-Cola it makes my muscles ache."

It occurred to Marcus that Benchley hadn't told him what would happen when the Coca-Cola ran out. Would Scott start drinking something else? Something stronger?

Please don't, Marcus thought. You've got too much riding on this project.

Even at the thousand dollars a week MGM was paying him, Scott would need to extend his contract to pay everything off. Marcus watched him disappear into the bathroom and thought, You're not the only one with a lot riding on this movie.

His father's face superimposed itself on top of Scott's. *You screwed up your big opportunity at Cosmopolitan Pictures, and you screwed up writing Garbo's next picture. How are you going to screw this one up?*

The telephone rang.

"Could you get that for me?" Scott called from the bathroom.

It was Benchley: "How's it going in there?"

"It's been going fine, I guess, but I don't know, something's going on. He's real withdrawn."

Benchley paused. "He's not drunk, is he?"

"I've been sitting right there in front of him pretty much the whole time except when he's in the john, which is a lot because he's putting away the Cokes like I've never seen before."

"So, the bottles—where are they exactly?"

Marcus looked about him at the bottles lined up in a lazy loop around the room. "He's got them all lined up."

"Like little glass wagons making a circle before the Injuns strike? That's not good," Benchley told him. "You know what he said to me the other day? When the vanguard overtook the rear guard, he would celebrate by jumping off. I didn't know what he meant at the time, but Dottie thinks he meant jumping off the wagon. Zelda's birthday is coming up, and it doesn't look like she's coming out of the nut house."

"Looks to me like he's on the home stretch," Marcus whispered. "He needs to convince the front office that he can complete at least one draft of a decent script."

"He's rarely lasted a whole year sober," Benchley warned. "I suspect he doubts he'll be able to see the year out. Lord knows I love and respect Fitzy, but once he takes that first drink, it's a burlap sack slide all the way down."

Marcus eyed the space between the first and last Coke bottles. "What should I do?"

"Don't let him close the gap."

He wished Marcus luck and hung up. Marcus heard the toilet flush and he started toward the kitchen. *If I can hide the last of the bottles –*

Scott opened the bathroom door and caught Marcus mid-stride. "Going somewhere?"

"No, I was just . . . I seem to think better when I'm in motion. That's why I swim so much. So, this scene when Francis is aboard the *HMS Tonnant* and he's trying to negotiate the release of the prisoners – "

"I found her quite gorgeous, really."

"Who?"

"I think she's a gossip columnist. I wonder if your friend Kathryn knows her."

Marcus eyed Scott as he walked into the kitchen and flipped the top off the second to last Coca-Cola bottle. By the time he got back to his desk it was already half empty. "So," he said, sitting down, "the scene on board the *Tonnant*?"

Marcus started pacing the room. "Okay, so he's there to negotiate the release of American prisoners from the British. The Americans know the British navy's going to attack them at Baltimore. Francis spends the night watching the bombardment. Finally, the smoke clears and he sees an American flag. The sight of it inspires him to write 'The Defense of Fort McHenry,' which eventually becomes 'The Star-Spangled Banner.' But what's in it for him? Why would he volunteer for such a dangerous assignment? The audience needs to understand his motivation. Do you know what that would have been?"

Marcus got no response. He turned around to find Scott slouched in his desk chair. "Scott?" he asked, but he got no response. He walked over to the desk and stood close enough to hear a gentle snoring sound.

He sniffed at the most recently emptied Coke bottles but couldn't smell booze. When he stepped into the bathroom, his eyes landed on the toilet. He lifted off the lid. Inside the water tank was a large unlabeled bottle of dark copper liquid. He pulled it out and held it up to the light. Whatever Scott had been doing in here, he hadn't been drinking: the bottle was filled to the brim. He pulled at the cork and it shot out of the neck with a hollow pop. Marcus didn't need to take a sip to confirm his suspicions, but he did anyway. It was filled with Four Roses.

Oh, sweet irony, he thought. We drink the same brand.

CHAPTER 21

When Ida Koverman invited Kathryn over for a cat party, Kathryn wasn't sure what to make of it. Koverman was every inch a spinster, but even if she had the requisite houseful of cats, throwing them a party seemed unthinkably frivolous. Koverman had breezed over Kathryn's request for details, which made Kathryn suspicious; Louis B. Mayer's secretary was not the breezy type.

Kathryn had said yes, she would be delighted to come, but now that she was standing outside Koverman's house, a tidy little cottage with an impressive bed of pink and purple petunias along the front, it confirmed her suspicions that she was about to walk into a trap. It wasn't completely out of the question that Mayer himself was sitting inside this trim little bungalow with the sweet flower boxes.

A burst of laughter splashed through the open window. Kathryn snuck up and peeked in. The first person she saw was Jeannette MacDonald dressed in a sky-blue sundress, her light-brown hair resting on her shoulders. She held a small crystal liqueur glass and her mouth was gaping open as if someone had just shocked her. Kathryn ducked down. Jeannette had sung at Harlow's funeral. Someone let out a high-pitched squeal and said, "Sophie Tucker, you're too much. Now stop that! She'll be here any minute."

Sophie Tucker was doing that new Judy Garland-Mickey Rooney movie at MGM, and she was at Harlow's funeral, too. No, oh no, Kathryn decided, this wasn't good at all. She hurried to the gravel path and started for the freshly painted white picket gate. She wasn't halfway there when she heard someone call out her name. She paused to draw a steadying breath and turned around.

Ida Koverman stood at her front door looking quite different from the humorless secretary Marcus had described. This version of Ida Koverman was smiling. She had her hair down and wore an orange cotton dress dotted with lilac buds. She looked like the sort of neighbor who would welcome you to the neighborhood with a pineapple upside-down cake. "Did you forget something?"

Kathryn was too panicked to answer.

"Whatever is the matter?" Ida asked.

Kathryn stared at Ida Koverman for a moment, then marched back up the path to the bottom step. "This is an ambush, isn't it?"

"Oh, good gracious. Ambush is the wrong word entirely."

"I know for a fact that Sophie Tucker and Jeannette MacDonald are in there."

"Why, yes they are."

"They were both at Jean Harlow's funeral. That's what this is about, isn't it? If this cat party is some sort of ambush and you're going to trounce me like a defenseless gazelle—"

"I don't think anyone has ever thought of you as defenseless, my dear."

Her sly smile gave Kathryn pause. She looked past Ida to see Joan Crawford hovering in the doorway. Kathryn had never met Crawford, and she hated herself for getting such a thrill out of being this close to her.

"Please come on inside," Crawford said. "We leave our fangs at the door."

When Kathryn stepped into Ida's cheery parlor, she took mental roll call and tried to discern a pattern. Norma Shearer sat next to Claudette Colbert. Colbert was a Paramount star, but she was just about to start a movie called *Tovarich* for Warners; maybe this wasn't an MGM ambush after all. Jeannette MacDonald and Madeleine Carroll stood by a mantle filled with photos of Ida with President Hoover. Janet Gaynor was on the sofa with Sophie

Tucker, who'd kicked off her shoes. The women rose to greet her warmly. This was all so far from the scenario Kathryn had built up in her mind that she found herself beyond the ability to string together a sentence.

"Tea? Sherry?" Ida offered. "Or perhaps something stronger?"

"Sherry would be lovely." Kathryn accepted a glass like the one Jeannette was holding and Ida filled it from a matching decanter. Kathryn then took a seat on the sofa.

"We were just talking about how you gate-crashed Jean's funeral," Ida said.

"Yes," Kathryn said, "about that . . ."

"My goodness, but you did it so artfully," Jeanette said. "The way you waved around George's invitation."

"At least *you* didn't go and get yourself tipsy," Sophie said with a laugh.

Kathryn took a sip of sherry. It was full and smooth, expensive. The tension began to slip off her shoulders. "So you all saw her, too?"

"We've all been trained to recognize that woman from two hundred paces." Joan Crawford rolled her enormous eyes. "One does not confront Louella Parsons over something like that and live to laugh another day."

"But *you* did!" Claudette Colbert said. "You marched right up to her and you didn't flinch."

Kathryn nodded at the women and smiled. *And to think I assumed nobody saw us.*

"Kathryn, my dear," Ida said, "let's get down to business. Nobody has ever stood up to Louella the way you did outside that chapel."

Joan let out a whoop. "I tell you, when I saw you there duking it out with her, I thought, Oh Lord, I think we've found our girl."

"Your girl?" Kathryn ventured. She took another slug of sherry.

"The girl to give Louella a run for her money," Ida continued. "Someone needs to show her she's not the only queen bee in the hive."

But hives only have one queen, Kathryn thought. She wondered what happens when a second one comes along. A fight to the death? "You think I have what it takes to knock Louella off her perch?"

"I doubt that anyone can do that," Claudette said. "She just needs to be rocked around on her throne. She and her husband just left for Europe. For the next month and a half, the field is wide open and it's all yours. We called you here to tell you that we're behind you."

"Even you, Ida?" Kathryn asked.

"To be frank, I didn't like that you crashed Jean's funeral, and I was still hesitant when the cats here told me to invite you over. Then you made your public apology. That impressed me very much."

"It was one classy move," Madeleine put in. "Everybody thought so."

Kathryn didn't know what to make of all this. She thought of the night at the Cocoanut Grove when she'd been passed around from mogul to mogul. Had she passed muster with the army generals? Was this all really Mayer's doing? Publicly, he couldn't side against Louella, so was this his way of attacking her from the flank? Kathryn decided it didn't matter. The important thing was that a door was being opened for her.

"By the time Louella gets back from Europe," Ida continued, "what happened will be yesterday's fish wrapping. What we're talking about here is a six-week campaign of goodwill. From here on in, it's all scoops, on-set interviews, tips, insider gossip, anything we can think of."

Kathryn looked around at these powerful, talented women and tried to comprehend what they were offering. Taking on Parsons alone was one thing, but to have the backing of half of Hollywood? Her heart started to pound.

"Ida!" Jeanette pointed to Kathryn's empty glass. "More sherry."

As she refilled it from the decanter, Ida asked, "So, you're on board?"

Kathryn nodded.

“Terrific!” Joan Crawford exclaimed. “Because in return for all this, we’re going to need a favor.”

CHAPTER 22

Gwendolyn studied her reflection in the mirror and wondered if she was pushing her luck by saying she was in her early twenties when she'd be twenty-seven in just a few months.

Yes, she decided, she probably could get away with it.

After all, the guy at the Republic Studios cattle call last week hadn't blinked when she'd told him she was twenty-two. She didn't get the job, but that was probably because she didn't look much like the cowgirl type he was looking to cast. But he did remember her from the last time she'd tried out, and she did make the first two rounds of cuts. Not that any of this stuff really matters, she told herself, because when she finally gets in front of Mr. Selznick—

A knock on the front door interrupted her mirror gazing.

Alistair Dunne stood on her landing in bare feet. Now that summer was starting to slip away, surely even he would have to start putting on shoes, she thought. But at least he was wearing a shirt and pants. It was nice to know he owned some; she had never seen him wear anything but paint-spotted shorts. Then again, she'd never seen him outside his studio.

"Alistair!" She swung the screen door open to him. "This is a surprise."

He nodded without smiling and walked into the villa. "Very nice," he said brusquely, looking around. He stared at the daffodils in a cut-glass vase that Joan Crawford had sent to Kathryn. "Homey."

It was September first, the deadline for the Carmichael Prize. Even for a fast worker like Alistair, three weeks to create a prize-worthy portrait was a challenge. Especially when during each sitting, Gwendolyn had to fight him off at least once. Well, perhaps not fight him off, exactly, but rebuff his gamut of hand-on-body part maneuvers. It was difficult because, quite frankly, she wanted it as much as he did.

The man was intelligent, intense, and radiated animal magnetism. Saying no to him was harder than saying no to Eldon Laird. However, it seemed to Gwendolyn that Alistair Dunne was the type who was consumed with the chase. Gwendolyn feared that once he'd netted his prey, he'd lose interest in her. Look what had happened when she gave in to Eldon. So she found ways to let Alistair know that perhaps after the portrait was finished . . .

She assumed he was here now to collect on her implied promise. Fine, she thought, because oh my goodness, who knew he could look so attractive with his clothes *on*? His sun-streaked hair gleamed like polished brass, and his teeth, so white and even, belonged on the screen.

She pointed toward the faded blue suede sofa. "So tell me all about it. What happened when you submitted the painting? Could you gauge any response?"

Alistair sat on the sofa and leaned his head back. "I decided not to submit the portrait."

"You *what*?!"

"I took it out of the car and gave it a final once-over. But when I saw it sitting there I realized how deeply infatuated with you I am, and I couldn't bear to part with it."

"Oh, Alistair," Gwendolyn sighed.

Aren't there already enough people in this town standing in my way? Part of her wanted to sock him one right in the kisser. Did she have to battle him, too?

On the other hand, what he was saying was so terribly romantic that she wanted to lean over and plant one right on his kisser instead.

"My painting doesn't give you one-tenth of the justice you deserve," he said. "So I put it back in the car and I drove here."

He made a dismissive gesture with his hand that snapped Gwendolyn out of her daydream. I'll be damned if I let one more person get between me and Selznick, she thought. I have his wife on my side, for crying out loud.

Over the past few weeks, not one but two paintings had been submitted for the Carmichael—both with controversial subjects. One of them was a portrait of Max Pruss, the commanding officer of the *Hindenburg* zeppelin, who survived a fiery disaster earlier that summer. The other was of the recently married King Edward VII and Wallis Simpson. Dinner parties around the country were still erupting in arguments over whether or not he'd given up the crown for the love of his life or a greedy, ambitious social climber. Consequently, the Carmichael Competition for Portraiture had been thrust to the forefront of the art world and was garnering coast-to-coast attention like never before. For Alistair's portrait to be in the running for this year's Carmichael would make it even more likely to attract Selznick's attention.

Gwendolyn looked at her watch. It was 2:45. "When is the deadline?"

He made a what-does-it-matter shrug.

"Close of business?" she asked. "Five o'clock?"

"Four."

"And where are the submissions lodged?"

"I'm going to destroy it."

Gwendolyn's body jolted back. "Alistair!"

He leaned forward and laid his face on his hands. "I have so miserably failed that to see what I've done is physically painful."

"I'm sure it's nowhere near that bad." She hadn't seen the finished painting; he wouldn't let her near it during any of the sittings.

"If only you'd permitted me to have you, I know I could have captured your essence. There is no other way."

"Where is the painting now?"

"Gwendolyn, let's forget about this blasted painting. Let's you and I—"

"Where is the goddamned painting, Alistair?"

Alistair wasn't used to seeing this side of Gwendolyn. Frankly, Gwendolyn wasn't used to seeing this side of Gwendolyn, but goddamnit, time was running out.

I'll be twenty-seven soon, she thought. How much time do I have left?

He stared at her as though she really had socked him. "It's in my car, parked down on Havenhurst."

"So there's still time to get it to the committee."

"It is my tradition to douse failed paintings with gasoline and then set them on fire. I'm leaving here to go—"

Over my dead body, Gwendolyn thought. She rushed down the stairs and along the path to the side entrance of the Garden of Allah on Havenhurst Drive. She started running from car to car, peering in through the windows in search of a large painting, but she couldn't see it. When she heard him run up behind her, she turned to face him. "Where is it?" she demanded.

"Gwendolyn, my darling, there will be other portraits. Other prizes."

"Not for me!" she said, thinking, Lordy, what a drama queen I must look like to you right now.

It occurred to Gwendolyn for the very first time that she and Irene were both simply using Alistair to get what they wanted: David Selznick's attention. For a moment she felt bad for him, but then she pictured her portrait over Selznick's mantelpiece and she couldn't bear for this opportunity to slip through her fingers. She'd make it up to Alistair later.

"I will paint another portrait of you," Alistair insisted. "We can start tomorrow. But only if you—"

"NO! It has to be *this* portrait."

He grabbed her by the wrists. "I had no idea it meant so much to you."

"I admire you so enormously," she told him truthfully. "I can't imagine anything you paint would be unsuccessful." She could see Alistair hesitating. She pressed further, but more sweetly. "Don't be so harsh on yourself. Go down and register for the Carmichael. Don't spend the next year wondering if maybe you could have won."

They stood on the sidewalk and stared at each other. Gwendolyn imagined her portrait lying on some deserted beach and Alistair pouring a can of gasoline on it. God no, she thought, anything but that. "Where is the Carmichael office?"

"Wilshire Boulevard," he said. "Near the corner of Fairfax."

"That's not even twenty minutes away. We could be there and back in less than an hour."

He narrowed his eyes, then sucked his upper lip into his mouth for what felt like three hours. Without warning, he took her hand and they ran toward a rusty olive-green Ford pickup. He leaned over the bed and pulled out a large object covered with a ratty blanket. "I will submit it, but only if you truly feel it's worthy."

Gwendolyn nodded.

Alistair slipped the blanket away. Gwendolyn let out a soft "Oh!"

It was like he'd alchemically transformed the most flattering photograph ever taken of her into the most wondrous portrait. How did he achieve that dewy look in her eyes simply with blobs of paint and ox-hair brushes? Was her mouth really shaped that way – puckered and pouting, so invitingly come-hither? And the dappled shadows he'd painted in across her hands, like she'd been sitting in a shady pecan grove down on some cotton plantation. Never had her hair looked so soft and full, her skin so radiant.

"Is this the way you see me?" she asked, her voice a whisper.

"I told you the painting was unsuccessful."

"UNSUCCESSFUL?!" She slapped him across the face. He stared at her, his eyes glazed with confusion. "You're an idiot! A blind idiot who should be shot if you ever take a match to anything you create. This painting . . . Alistair! It's . . . I never dreamed . . . it's so . . ." She couldn't think what else to say, so she slapped him again. "Put the blanket back on. We're going. NOW."

She rewrapped the painting, then ran around the truck and climbed into the passenger seat. She looked across to find that Alistair hadn't moved.

He leaned in through the window. "First we make love."

"No, no, no," she said. "The competition has a deadline. Lovemaking doesn't."

He shook his head. "My body cannot wait one minute longer." He reached into the pocket of his chino pants and pulled out a matchbook. She eyed it warily. It was from a place called Marcel's, a place in downtown L.A. popular with the crowd who liked to go to the boxing fights next door.

"What are you doing?" she asked.

He plucked a matchstick from the book and struck it. The head flared orangey-red. "Lovemaking first, or I throw this in the back."

CHAPTER 23

Marcus sat on the edge of his bed and held his leaden head in his hands, glad for once that his cramped room was so dark. He let out a series of husky groans and wondered what the chances were that he could locate his watch without having to open his eyes.

He reached over to his bedside table and groped around, knocking a bottle to the floor. His eyelids flashed open like a camera shutter to see if he'd spilled bourbon onto the rug. The rug was dry; the bottle was empty. It had been another one of those nights. His fingers wrapped around his watch and he brought it toward his face. It was twelve minutes past five.

That can't be right, he thought. There's too much light for five in the morning. He forced his eyes open and looked at the watch face again; it still read twelve past five. He looked around. The meager sunlight his little room received peaked in the mornings. This light was at its apex. He peered vacantly at the floor. His empty bottle of Four Roses lay at his feet next to an upside down ashtray filled with cigarette butts. The pall of hooch and ash hung in the air.

It took more effort to stand than he feared he possessed, but he made it into his bathroom to look for the cheap travel clock he kept on top of his medicine cabinet. When he saw it read ten twenty, a cold sweat broke out across his chest.

"Damnit! DAMNIT!" He turned on the cold water and thrust his head under the tap. The cold shock jolted the breath out of his lungs. He dried off as best he could inside ten seconds, pulled on the first stitches of clothing he could lay his hands on, and shot out the front door.

* * *

He knocked on Scott Fitzgerald's door a third time but knew it wasn't going to do any good. Scott wasn't home. And that meant Scott wasn't inside working on the revisions that Jim Taggert had requested on *The Star-Spangled Banner*. It was past ten thirty now. Marcus leaned his throbbing head against Scott's door. "Where the hell are you?"

He sank to the steps leading up to the doorway and scraped the top of his tongue against his upper teeth. It felt like sandpaper coated in glue; he didn't want to know what it looked like. He leaned his back against the door and lifted his face toward the sun. Maybe a few deep breaths of fresh air . . .

The sound of George Cukor's voice cranked up inside his head. He'd told him about a new movie Hunt Stromberg was developing, something that had never been done before. An entire movie with no men, just women. "Real prestige picture, lots of dialogue, sharp and fast"—and Stromberg wanted Fitzgerald. And he wasn't the only one.

"There's a Robert Taylor war picture," George had said, "*Three Comrades,* and Frank Borzage asked me what I thought about getting Fitzgerald to write the screenplay. If you want my advice, wrangle some way of sticking with Fitzgerald; he could take you all the way to the A-list."

The full bottle of Four Roses Marcus had lifted out of Scott's john filled his mind. Please don't let me find him slumped over some back-alley gutter—

"Marcus?"

He looked up to find Kathryn, who was dressed in a smart suit in black and mahogany, matching hat, shoes and handbag—the works.

And here am I looking like a hobo, he thought.

She crouched down so their faces were level. "What on earth are you doing?"

"I just woke up," he said lamely.

"Okay," she replied, but her eyes said, *Really? At ten thirty? On a weekday?*

Marcus took a moment to decide how best to explain his situation in as few words as possible. "MGM's got a long list of changes to 'Banner.' Scott should be inside working, but he's not. I'm scared he's gone off on some bender and I wasn't here to prevent it."

"Marcus, darling, that's an awful big conclusion to jump to. It's not really your—"

He could feel a cocktail of guilt, adrenaline, and apprehension pumping through his veins. "I found a bottle of booze in his bathroom so I confronted him. He swore he hadn't taken a sip, and I believed him—the bottle was full—but he confided in me that he didn't think he had it in him to resist it much longer. He asked me to help him get through this screenplay without falling off the wagon. He's got a lot riding on this."

"You both do," Kathryn observed. She took his hand. "Instead of jumping off a cliff, maybe you should look for him. Maybe he went to Schwab's for coffee. You know how he loves their Bavarian chocolate mint bars. I'd go with you, my wretched little Marckie-Moo, but I've got an interview over at Paramount so I have to skedaddle. Doing something is always better than doing nothing." She sighed. "Now you've got me talking like my mother."

* * *

Scott wasn't at Schwab's, but Marcus spotted Dottie and Benchley in one of the booths that hugged the right-hand side. They were gingerly sipping at coffee and taking mouse-sized nibbles of dry toast as though it were an after-school punishment.

"He was here a little while ago," Dorothy said, "buying a whole bunch of cigarettes. I thought about telling him to cut back, he had so many packets." She lit up a cigarette to replace the one she'd just finished. "And then I figured, who am I to advise anyone to cut back on anything?"

"Did you speak to him?" Marcus asked.

"Sort of. I called out, 'Where you off to?' and he said, 'The usual.'"

"Where do you think that might mean?"

"If we hadn't been sitting here looking like the wreck of the *Hesperas*, I'd have told you to try Schwab's. But given that we are here and he's not . . ." She wafted her cigarette around in lieu of finishing her sentence.

"He's fallen off, hasn't he?" Benchley said darkly.

Marcus nodded, but even that hurt. "I fear he has."

"May I suggest you try the Sneak Inn?"

"Is that its actual name?" Marcus asked.

"It used to be a speakeasy," Benchley said. "When Scott and I were out here a few years after the Great War, it was our favorite hangout. It's still around. Still dark and dingy. Still a barfly's idea of a fun time. He asked me about it the other day. I should've picked up the clue. I'm a terrible friend."

"Oh, Mr. Benchley." Dorothy grabbed the paw of the greying dachshund in her lap and used it to tap her friend on the wrist. "You're neither his keeper nor his mother. You're not even his mother's keeper."

Benchley turned to Marcus. "The Sneak Inn is the perfect place for tormented souls."

Marcus shifted his weight and thought of the haunted look that he sometimes saw in Scott's eyes. In his more quiet moments, Marcus had wondered if it mirrored the look in his own eyes. "Where is this place?"

"It's on Western Avenue a block or two past Pico. You going to look for him now?"

What choice did he have? The only copy of their script was the carbon inside Scott's villa. Marcus nodded.

"There's no sign," Benchley said. "Look for the burgundy door with the black trim."

* * *

It would have helped if Benchley had thought to mention that the Sneak Inn's burgundy door had faded since its halcyon days during Prohibition. When he finally found the dusty-rose door on Pico Boulevard, it reminded him of a wallflower left long after the dance was over. He pushed open the door to find a bar every bit as depressing as he'd imagined. A row of threadbare booths lined the wall to the left and a long bar with a few scattered stools faced it on the right. A barman stood at the far end fixing a clock.

"What'll it be?"

"I was looking for someone," Marcus said. He described Scott as best he could.

"Yeah," the bartender said. "He was in here earlier." Marcus' fur-lined mouth went dry. "Drank me dry of Four Roses. Tell me straight up: he used to be somebody, didn't he?"

"What makes you say that?"

"He sat at the end of the bar muttering about Paris and Hemingway. He has that look about him. Like those stars who were big in the silents."

The last thing Marcus wanted to do was contribute to the besmirching of F. Scott Fitzgerald's name. "Aren't we all somebody to somebody?"

"In this joint? Not necessarily."

"Did he tell you where he was going?"

The guy shook his head and the telephone rang.

"Thanks anyway." Marcus started to head out but the guy called him back and told him the phone call was for him.

"Marcus? Benchley here. Dottie had a good idea. Give Sheilah Graham a go. Got a pencil?"

Sheilah Graham was a gossip writer with a syndicated column; something Marcus suspected Kathryn was more than a bit envious of. He wrote down the number and went to the pay phone at the far end of the bar. A cultured British accent answered the phone.

"Miss Graham, hello," Marcus said. "We haven't met, but my name is Marcus Adler. I'm working with Scott."

"Yes of course," Sheilah replied. "Scott's mentioned you a number of times."

"I'm trying to track him down and I was hoping he might be with you."

Sheilah had assumed that Scott was hard at work in his villa; she bristled at the suggestion that he was off drinking somewhere instead. The best he got out of her was that he might be at Musso and Frank's, a grill on Hollywood Boulevard that was popular with writers, which Scott had recently discovered.

* * *

He pushed open the glass door and peered around the room through a fog of cigarette smoke. It was fairly busy, but Marcus saw nobody even close to matching Scott's haggard, pale face.

Damnit.

"You looking for someone?" the maître d' asked.

Marcus had barely begun to describe Scott when the guy interrupted him. "You mean Mr. Fitzgerald, don't you?" He sighed. "Where were you an hour ago?"

"Why?"

"He was already two and a half sheets to the wind when he came in. I tried to shoo him away nicely, but then he pulled the do-you-know-who-I-am routine. So I showed him to the far corner of the bar. It gets around that a name like that comes here, it can be good for business. He promised he'd be quiet. And he was—for the first three drinks."

Marcus braced himself. "And then?"

"He went from being Mr. F. Scott Fitzgerald to every drunk I've ever met. Loud, opinionated, impatient. Then he got weepy. Turned into a big baby. Worked himself up into a lather over I don't know what. I'm not against cursing, but not here. Not like that. We've got a nice reputation, you know? So I told him where he should go to dry out."

"Where's that?"

"You ever been to the Hollywood Athletic Club down on Sunset? Weissmuller put me onto it when he was training for his Tarzan pictures. Best steam room in L.A. It'll sweat out every drop of rotgut you pour in."

The maître d' walked off to appease a demanding table of conventioneers and left Marcus to stare out at the traffic moving along Hollywood Boulevard. This was turning into a daytime version of that night he'd had to run all over town to spring George Cukor from jail before the newspapers saw him.

"Marcus?"

Marcus turned around to see Dierdre, the receptionist for MGM's writing department, a friendly girl with a lopsided smile. She sat in one of the booths with a woman who looked just like her but with more grey, more wrinkles, and less charm.

"This is my sister Jo-Ellen." Dierdre lowered her voice to what she probably thought was a stage whisper, judging from the empty martini glasses. "She's just come from Reno, where she got a huge settlement in her divorce. We're living it up on the rat bastard's dime."

"Dierdre!" her sister admonished.

Dierdre waved away Jo-Ellen's feigned shock. "Meeting somebody?"

"Looking for someone."

Dierdre's face took on a pained smile. "It's not Scott Fitzgerald, is it?"

"What makes you say that?"

"I saw him stagger out of here a while back. I'm sorry, but I've got to ask. Are those rumors I've been hearing true?"

Marcus gripped the back of an empty seat and vacillated between asking Dierdre what she meant and hightailing it down to the Hollywood Athletic Club. Dierdre raised her thick eyebrows. Her face said, *You really need to hear this.*

He decided that if Scott was fall-down drunk right now, he'd still be fall-down drunk in five minutes. He took a seat. "Depends on what the rumors are."

"One of them is that Mr. Fitzgerald couldn't tell a screenplay from a bucket of sand, and that this picture he's writing about "The Star-Spangled Banner" was your idea in the first place *and* that the script is really all your work. Is that true?"

"What's the other rumor you've heard?"

"That Fitzgerald's paying you to ghostwrite the entire screenplay for him, but that you're secretly getting him plastered by sneaking booze into all that Coca-Cola he drinks so you can take all the credit. Is it true he drinks Coke by the boatload?"

Marcus took off his fedora and fanned himself with it. "Is that what they're really saying about me?"

Dierdre made a dismissive wave of her hand. "It ain't like he was Sober Sam when he left here an hour ago." Marcus was too taken aback to say anything. Dierdre continued. "Look, honey, I like you, I really do. I think you got shafted over that Garbo picture. Okay, so maybe she wasn't right for the part, but now they're turning it into a musical—"

"They're what?" Marcus' fingers crushed the brim of his hat.

"They're reshaping it for Eleanor Powell. By the way, I overheard Taggert telling someone he thought your Garbo version was first-rate. You know what he's like. Never one to praise a guy, but he's a fan of your work."

* * *

The Hollywood Athletic Club was a white building with a nine-story residential tower. No, the guy behind the counter didn't remember seeing anyone coming through drunk like that. No, he couldn't just come in for a look-see. No, he didn't have to be a member to use the club's facilities. No, there was nothing to stop him from paying seventy-five cents and coming on in.

Marcus had never considered himself the sporty type. Dumbbells and medicine balls were the domain of the he-man types he had always found vaguely intimidating. Making his way through the cream-tiled corridors filled him with a clammy mix of anticipation and dread.

The locker room—all polished wood and sea-foam-green tiles—was empty when he walked into it. He found his assigned locker, got undressed, and wrapped a towel around his middle. He followed a sign that pointed the way to the steam room. If Scott wasn't here, he was out of ideas and there was nothing left for him to do but head back to the Garden, sit on his doorstep and try not to get all churned up over the Nellie Bly picture. *A musical? What the hell were they thinking?* He found the steam room easily enough, hung his towel on one of the hooks, and opened the door.

A fog burst forth to envelop him and he stepped into a cocoon of menthol-infused steam. "Scott? Are you in here?"

There was no answer.

"Scott? It's me, Marcus."

He heard a low groan. It wasn't much, but it was enough to let him know that Scott lurked somewhere deep in the fragrant mist. He followed the groan until he could make out the silhouette of a figure. The banks of steam parted, and Marcus softly gasped. For an eye-blink of a moment, he thought he saw himself slumped against the tile wall. Not as he was now, but how he could look in thirty years' time—his best days far behind him, his creative peak a clouded memory, and forty years of bourbon bingeing taking their toll.

He sat down next to Scott and gave him a gentle nudge. "How you doing?"

Scott Fitzgerald managed to keep his body completely still as he raised his head just enough to look at Marcus out of the corner of his eye. "Get away from me."

"If it's any consolation, I'm feeling about as bad as—"

"You're the reason I'm in here, in this condition, in hell."

"Scott, I—"

"You weren't there. You were supposed to be there at eight thirty." The words tumbled from Scott's mouth, slurry and falling over each other. "As long as I have you during the day and Sheilah at night, I'm okay. I'm not good when I'm left alone. You know that, but you didn't care. You didn't show."

"Of course I care."

"Not enough."

Marcus leaned back against the cedar bench. He wasn't going to get anywhere with Scott on the attack like this. He let a minute slip by. The menthol was so sharp it was almost making him giddy. He was starting to feel human again.

Scott dropped his head down onto his chest. "Zelda's beyond help," he said. "The doctors all agree. So why do I feel guilty?"

Marcus looked at the man's skin, pale and sagging, glistening in the steam as sweat seeped out like magma. His heart went out to the guy, who'd achieved so much, lived fully, loved deeply, and had pretty much lost everything. "Your wife's condition isn't your fault," he said.

"I'm cheating on my wife with the most decent woman I've ever met."

Marcus tried a friendly elbow nudge. "Aren't you being a bit hard on yourself? You've got the respect of your peers, a towering talent, a good reputation, a well-paying job, and a blooming romance with a good woman. That's a lot right there, wouldn't you say?"

"PAH!" Scott scoffed. "What respect? What reputation? Not one of my four novels is in print anymore. What does that leave me with?"

"A thousand bucks a week and enough self-pity to drown yourself in."

Scott's eyes shot up with a look of *What did you just say to me?*

Before Marcus could stuff the words back in his mouth, Scott nodded. "Good point, well taken." He smiled the first smile Marcus had seen on his face all week. "This screenplay of ours, do you think it's in the trash can by now?"

"Taggert messengered back his list this morning."

"His list of what?"

"Changes, cuts, edits, suggestions. It was quite some list."

Scott pried his eyes open. "He wants us to continue?"

"Just as soon as we've sweated enough bourbon out of our system."

While Scott Fitzgerald slumped in the steam, nodding weakly, Marcus thought about Nellie Bly—*his* Nellie Bly—and how someone else was getting to put her up on the big screen. You can roll with the punches, he told himself, or you can end up sitting in a place like this, bitter and resentful, sweating booze until you're wrung limp.

Marcus heard the slap of skin against wet tile and turned around to see Ramon Novarro standing naked in the mists of menthol. Competing rivulets of sweat trickled down the man's torso, over his hipbones, and into a thicket of hair that Marcus had only dreamed of.

"Marcus? Is that you?"

CHAPTER 24

Kathryn spent four weeks waiting for the cats to pounce, bracing herself for whatever demands they would make on her. That day at Ida's cottage, the cats had been more interested in Mussolini's son, of all things.

Vittorio Mussolini was expected in Hollywood soon to hold talks about an American-Italian film production deal. The Hollywood Anti-Nazi League, headed by Fredric March and James Cagney, had gotten all steamed up over the visit. Dorothy Parker was one of the league's charter members, so the issue had been the center of some particularly heated debates around the Garden of Allah, and the cats wanted Kathryn's take on it. By the time Kathryn had finished, everyone seemed to have forgotten about this favor they'd alluded to.

The cats kept their word with tips and introductions and invitations that came in every day. They got her an interview with Barbara Stanwyck on the set of her new movie, *Stella Dallas,* over on the Samuel Goldwyn lot. Kathryn also scored a front-row seat at Tyrone Power's footprint ceremony at Grauman's, followed by a sneak preview of his new picture, *In Old Chicago.* But Kathryn knew she was really floating through Hollywood's rarified stratosphere when an invitation to Mary Pickford's wedding to Buddy Rogers at Pickfair arrived in the mail.

Then, one day late that summer, Kathryn was invited to the Warner lot. Claudette Colbert was there, working on *Tovarich* with Charles Boyer. She was her usual chatty self as she walked Kathryn to the soundstage. Oh, yes, they had been very welcoming here at Warner Bros. Oh, yes, the cast and crew could not have been more accommodating. And oh my goodness, yes, Charles Boyer was a dream to work with, and it certainly felt as though they had the sort of chemistry that would translate well to the screen.

They walked onto a set bustling with stagehands. It was grand in a way not usually seen at Warner's, whose pictures tended to be more about the working and criminal classes and used drab and dreary sets. In other words, cheap. A large staircase carpeted with a thick plum rug wound its way down from left to right and opened onto a marble foyer crowned by a crystal chandelier so elaborate it would have made Nicholas Romanov look twice.

"Why, this is wonderful!" Kathryn exclaimed.

But Claudette's face had fallen into a petulant frown. "They're setting up for a shot that I was told wouldn't be attempted until after lunch."

"Attempted?"

"It's a six-minute take filled with all sorts of stage business, cigarettes, and champagne flutes. There's even a dog. And on top of it all, I have this two-page speech right in the middle. I've been dreading it."

An assistant director in a bright orange bowtie approached Claudette with a forced smile. "They've moved up the champagne speech scene."

"So I see," Claudette replied.

"Mr. Boyer's wife has fallen ill, so he has to go right after we've finished."

"How unfortunate."

"They're waiting for you in makeup."

The assistant director hovered for a moment, waiting for Claudette's nod of acknowledgement. As soon as he got it, he scampered away.

"Darling," Claudette said, pointing to a chair, "if I had known they were going to pull this on me, I'd have invited you to drop by much later. This is going to be rather tedious. I'll understand if you want to leave."

"Not at all," Kathryn replied. "I'm not so jaded yet that the process of shooting a movie bores me."

Claudette permitted herself a smirk. "Stick around." She headed off toward the makeup station on the far left of the set.

Kathryn stood for a while watching stagehands arrange drapes and set out champagne flutes. It didn't look like anything was going to happen for a while, so she decided to get in a quick cigarette.

Outside the soundstage, she watched a line of unshaven and disheveled extras dressed in prison uniforms saunter past her. She took a long drag on her Chesterfield and wondered if perhaps the right angle for her story might be the apprehension that an actress as experienced as Claudette Colbert feels doing a six-minute take.

As she ground her cigarette butt into the asphalt, her eyes landed on a figure outside the opposite soundstage. There was something familiar about the way the guy—

It was Roy Quinn.

She knew in that moment, as he stood there looking so tanned, fit, and healthy, that he was her One Who Got Away, as Ramon Novarro was for Marcus.

They stood across the way from each other for a few elongated seconds until he started walking toward her. She wanted to head toward him, too, but something held her back. She didn't even work up a smile until he was close enough to see that those two years had treated him well. All barrel chest, chiseled jawline, and dimples: he looked even more handsome than she remembered.

"Hello, Kathryn," he said.

"Roy," she said. She dragged a fingertip along the pearl necklace coiled around her neck. "You here working?"

"Teaching Errol Flynn to fence for *Prince and the Pauper*."

"Fencing? As in dueling?"

"I was the California State Junior Champion three years running."

"I didn't know that."

Roy's jaw took on a harder edge. "There was a lot you and I never got around to sharing." His eyes locked onto hers. "Now I teach actors how to swordfight. I've even gotten to choreograph a couple. Fun way to earn a living."

She watched the sun play with his chestnut hair. "It must agree with you," she said. "You're looking very well."

Roy smiled. It deepened those dimples of his that always made her melt. "All that leaping around on stairs and banisters, off window ledges and onto horses. Keeps a guy sharp." He took a step closer to her. Roy never wore cologne like so many of the men in this town; his body manufactured its own unique scent. It made her think of horses and barns and outdoorsy pursuits that weren't part of the regular routine of city men. She couldn't always smell it on him, but when she did, it turned her knees to Jell-O, and she could smell it now.

"You're looking wonderful yourself," he said. They looked at each other some more. "You married?"

"No," she told him. "You?"

She'd meant to sound playful, but it came out brittle. His eyes darkened. "Of course I am."

They eyed each other warily for a few moments. Kathryn groped for something to say but came up empty-mouthed.

"You didn't have a run-in with no streetcar, did you," Roy said suddenly.

Her fingers let go of the pearls and her hands dropped to her side. "What?"

"I've got a cousin. Works for the city. Got him to check on all reports of accidents with streetcars around the time you said you lost our baby. He told me there was nothing that matched anything like what you described to me."

Oh. *That* streetcar. The fictitious one that fictitiously ran her down, causing her to fictitiously miscarry.

He took another step closer. He was even beefier and brawnier now, and Kathryn hated that she found it both a little bit frightening and a little bit exciting at the same time.

"I know you didn't have a miscarriage," he said.

"I lost our baby."

"You had an abortion. Didn't you?"

A voice inside her head piped up. *You don't get to make me feel bad.* Kathryn jerked her head at him. "I was an unmarried woman starting a career with a high-profile publication. What the hell was I supposed to do?" He went to say something but she cut him off. "And do *not* tell me that I could've given it up for adoption. I don't need to hear any Catholic bullshit about murdering babies— "

"I still love you."

"You *what*?" She blinked at him. *You never told me that before. Why are you telling me now? What good is that going to do either of us?*

She could hear Marcus' voice now: "He's the one that got away, and I don't know what to do."

"I've thought about you every single day since we had that awful fight," Roy said. "Every single day, Kathryn. I tried a couple of times to find someone else I could . . . see. But nothing came of them. I just felt like I was cheating on you."

Kathryn stared into his handsome, crumbling face and thought, Oh, who are you kidding? You still feel the same about him too. But what's the good—?

He said, "The truth of it is that if I had been in your shoes, I probably would have done what you did."

"But you're Catholic. You— "

Roy leaned over and put his mouth near her ear. "What a guy does when he's in church is one thing, but what he does when he gets a woman pregnant—that's a whole different blue plate special."

She was about to reply when Roy suddenly pulled back. The assistant director with the loud bowtie was standing at the door to the soundstage. "Miss Colbert is ready for you."

Kathryn nodded, wondering how long he had been standing there. "Thank you," she said. She turned back to Roy. "I have to go."

"I want to see you again," he told her. "I *need* to see you."

"I—I'll call you."

"Leave me a message at the Hollywood Academy of Fencing. It's in the book."

"I really must go."

Her head was starting to spin and she had trouble catching her breath. She needed to think. She stumbled toward the door into the soundstage and let the door close behind her.

"Who's the side of beef?" Claudette asked when Kathryn sat down in the director's chair next to her.

"The what?"

"Outside. The A.D. told me you were tête-à-tête with some beefcake."

"He's just a tipster. You know, one of those people who gives me gossip."

"Is that all he gives you?" Claudette asked.

Kathryn feigned shock and gently slapped Claudette on the wrist. "Stop that!"

Claudette's face suddenly turned serious. "I have something to tell you. Remember that favor we told you we had in mind? We're ready to call it in."

CHAPTER 25

Greek and Roman gods, winged angels, and cupids gazed down on the elite of Hollywood's left wing from the ceiling of the public corridor of the Biltmore Hotel. Marcus looked at his watch. It was well past seven and it wasn't like Kathryn to be late.

"Ladies and gentlemen!" The maître d' did his best to make himself heard over the chattering crowd. "There has been only a very slight delay. We shall be opening the doors very soon. We thank you for your patience." But hardly anyone was listening. The talk that evening was all politics, politics, politics, which was to be expected at a fundraising dinner for the Hollywood Anti-Nazi League.

As the months rolled through 1937, it became increasingly apparent that Adolph Hitler wasn't just some big-talking madman the German people hadn't gotten around to ostracizing yet. He was a man with a plan, and that plan was becoming more and more alarming.

The implications of Hitler's posturing took a dark turn when German bomb casings were found in the rubble of Guernica, a recently bombarded city in Spain. It was proof that Germany had cast its eyes well beyond its own borders. Did that mean Madrid might join the Rome-Berlin Axis? The implications were too horrific to bear.

When Dorothy Parker took it upon herself to buy up two tables of tickets for the League's fundraising dinner, she'd strong-armed both Marcus and Kathryn to attend with such insistence that they could hardly say no. Who wanted to be perceived as being on the side of the Nazis?

"Have you ever heard of someone called Melody Hope?" Kathryn slipped her arm through his and gave his hand a squeeze.

"There you are!" Marcus exclaimed. "Melody Hope? I don't think so. Why?"

"She's been given the lead in *The Pistol from Pittsburgh.*"

"Should I know what that is?"

Kathryn threw him a double take. "It's the movie MGM's making out of your Nellie Bly script. That's what they're calling it now: *The Pistol from Pittsburgh.*"

Marcus tried not to wince. Since that day at Musso and Frank's, he'd only been semi-successful in not letting himself mull over the fact that he wasn't good enough for MGM but his Nellie Bly idea was.

Kathryn gave his arm a jiggle. "Don't give me that face. I know how disappointed you are, but do try not to be bitter. Your chance will come. What's important is that your idea was sound and our Nellie Bly is getting her life story put on the screen, just like we both wanted. We've been talking about how Nellie's life would make a great picture almost since the day we met. And finally it is! At any rate, this new discovery of theirs—this Melody Hope girl—is going to star in it."

The maître d' opened the Biltmore Bowl with a flourish. The crowd surged forward; Kathryn pulled him toward the open doors. "Come on," she said, "you look like you could do with a drink."

***

The Hollywood Anti-Nazi League for the Defense of American Democracy was very serious in its intent to show Hitler and his mob that they weren't about to take any of his bullying. Speaker after speaker addressed the audience on far-ranging topics that covered Nazism, socialism, Semitism, fascism, communism, imperialism, bolshevism, and every other -ism on the list. It was important stuff, God knows, and quite possibly nothing less than world peace was at stake, but Marcus hardly heard any of it.

What a blow that they hadn't decided to use it until after they'd pushed me out the window, he thought. But a musical? Nellie Bly spent most of her life reporting hard stories on insane asylums and falsely accused murderers. What were they going to do? Set a big dance number in a women's loony bin?

He thought about his screenplay as he plowed through a couple more bourbons. The centerpiece of it was the trip around the world that she undertook in 1889 in an effort to replicate Jules Verne's *Around the World in Eighty Days*. They could have a montage of dance numbers: the can-can in Paris, whirling dervishes in Persia, Cossacks in Russia. That could work. In fact, it could be spectacular, if done right. And anyway, who said all musicals had to be light and frothy and silly? Couldn't they also have something worthwhile to say?

God, what he wouldn't give for a chance to work on that script.

As the final speaker of the night stepped down from the podium to vigorous applause, Kathryn leaned toward a table not far from them. "That's Jim Taggert, isn't it?"

Taggert's nearly bald head shone like a beacon in the light of the chandelier. He was sharing a joke with the German director Ernst Lubitsch, which seemed odd at such a decidedly anti-German event. But Taggert was smiling, which made for a pleasant change. During his time at MGM, Marcus had hardly ever seen the guy smile. Dierdre's comment came back to him: "Taggert's a fan of your work."

When Taggert got to his feet, Marcus did too. He followed his ex-boss to the men's room and loitered in the corridor. He lit a cigarette and weighed the best approach. Drunk or not, Taggert was the type who appreciated straight shooters. Getting Marcus rehired at MGM was above Taggert's pay grade, but they'd listen to him. It was worth a shot.

Somebody cleared his throat and a smooth Latin accent said, "At least you're not naked this time." Marcus spun around to find Ramon Novarro standing beside him. "I still don't understand what happened that day," Ramon added.

Oh, that day, that terrible, terrible day when Marcus had finally seen Ramon naked, his beautifully slim body dripping with sweat, shrouded in fragrant mist. It'd just about killed him that there was nothing he could do about it. He'd had to get Scott out of there before the poor bastard dissolved into a puddle on the floor, and before Ramon could catch sight of Marcus' inconveniently nudging hard-on.

"I encountered you sitting naked with another naked man."

"We were in a steam room," Marcus said.

"You seemed like you were having a very intimate moment together. I felt like I was intruding."

"He was having a very bad week. I was trying to be a friend."

This was a conversation Marcus wanted to have, but not here, and not now. For an actor, Ramon Novarro had annoyingly bad timing. Marcus glanced toward the other side of the corridor. Had Taggert left the men's room while Marcus was preoccupied with yet another of Ramon's surprise appearances? Couldn't they just agree to go out for a drink like a pair of normal people?

Ramon looked at the door to the men's room and turned back to Marcus. His dark eyes flared and his eyebrows came together in one line. He raised his right hand and jabbed at the air over Marcus' chest. "You need to know that after a while, it can get very lonely bouncing the basketball all by yourself." Ramon whipped around and took off like the walls were about to cave in.

Bouncing what basketball? Marcus thought. What the hell?

Taggert exited the men's room and bent down to retie a loose shoelace.

"Oh, hey, Adler," he said, standing up. "You got roped into this too, huh?"

Marcus opened his mouth, but Novarro's outburst had rattled his resolve.

Just then, a guy whose blond hair was battling an onslaught of grey approached them. He walked with a limp but didn't seem to be in pain. "I had to get out of there," he said to Taggert. "That Lawson fella can really chew a guy's ear off if you let him." He looked at Marcus as though trying to figure out if they knew each other.

"Marcus Adler, this is Hoppy Terrell," Taggert said. "Hoppy, this is Marcus Adler."

Marcus had heard about this guy. Originally, he'd wanted to be a movie cowboy. He'd been an extra on *The Squaw Man*, the DeMille movie that brought moviemaking to Los Angeles, but then he was drafted into the Great War, lost a leg at Verdun, and came home with a wooden replacement. It seemed to Marcus that Hoppy was a cruel nickname for someone who'd lost his leg like that, but Hugo said it came from Hopalong Cassidy, whom Hoppy had hoped to portray on the screen. Getting stuck behind a desk had unleashed his hidden talent for coming up with clever stories, and these days he was MGM's most invaluable ideas guy. He worked them up into a detailed outline and handed them over to someone who turned them into screenplays, like Marcus used to.

Hoppy had already extended his hand to shake Marcus' when his pale blue eyes popped open. "Oh!" he exclaimed. "*The* Marcus Adler?"

Marcus cocked his head to one side. "I'm famous enough to warrant a 'the'?"

"Are you kidding?" Hoppy said. "Between Hearst Castle and that bit in *The Lion's Roar*?"

The Lion's Roar was MGM's in-house staff newspaper that covered productions, casting, new hires, and the rumors that flew around the studio like ravenous pterodactyls.

Marcus felt his lips go dry. "What bit is that?"

"It was on that silly gossip page. Typical blind item. I read it, wondered if it meant you, and didn't think much about it. Then that other one appeared a month or two later. A little more . . . obvious, shall we say?"

Marcus faced Taggert and steeled himself. "I haven't read whatever it is Hoppy's talking about, but I have heard rumors of me getting Scott Fitzgerald drunk on purpose. So let me just say that Scott's been a lifelong idol of mine – it certainly wasn't my intention to steal any credit away from him. If you want to know the truth, he probably never would have finished that screenplay if it hadn't been for me."

The Star-Spangled Banner had come out the previous month and had been hailed as a solid hit, commercially and critically. Both Kathryn and Gwendolyn had told him he ought to be proud of what he'd accomplished, but the whole experience had been a frustrating one for Marcus. He was proud of it, but it was yet another picture without his name on it.

"I thought it was a terrific effort," Hoppy put in. "Really well put together. So if that was your work up on the screen, my hat's off to you. I heard Julius Caesar Mayer liked it. A lot."

"So it's true, then?" Taggert asked. "Fitzgerald brought you in to help him with the screenplay?"

"His outline was pretty good. But he was flailing about trying to turn it into a script, and he knew it."

"Smart guy," Hoppy said.

Taggert squinted at Marcus. "Was there something else you wanted?"

Marcus glanced at Hoppy, but the guy showed no signs of moving along. "I understand you're taking my Nellie Bly picture and making it into a musical."

Taggert sighed. "Wasn't my idea. That story deserves to be told, but not as a musical."

"It's just that I've been thinking. I'm real familiar with the story and I'd love another crack at it. I've already got some great ideas. Any chance of putting a good word in for me? Just another one-picture contract is all I'm asking. I never got a chance to prove myself. You know I can do it,

Jim." It was a gamble, calling Taggert by his first name. The guy wasn't the type who invited anyone to do that.

"I'm sorry, Adler, but we've already assigned it to someone else. In fact, his final draft is due on Monday. But don't feel too badly, it went to a friend of yours."

"Who?"

"Your pal Hugo."

CHAPTER 26

"I have wonderful news!" Irene Selznick exclaimed, cornering Gwendolyn underneath the huge Cuban flag John O'Hara had strung up between his villa and the one Frances Goodrich and Albert Hackett shared. Hemingway's novel about a fishing boat captain running contraband between Cuba and Florida had just been released to great acclaim, and a bunch of Garden of Allah'ers decided to throw a Cuban-themed party.

Gwendolyn was surprised to see Irene—until she saw Dorothy di Frasso ladling cups of God-only-knew-what into the huge punchbowl that Lillian Hellman conjured up from God-only-knew-where.

"Wonderful news is always welcome," Gwendolyn said.

"Alistair lost the Carmichael! Isn't that terrific?"

If Gwendolyn hadn't started sleeping with Alistair Dunne on the day of the Carmichael deadline, this news would have indeed been terrific. She'd said yes that first time purely as a matter of expediency, but the second time she'd slept with him—much like the time after that and all the times after that—had nothing to do with *Gone with the Wind*. There was really no polite way of putting it: Alistair Dunne was spectacular in bed.

It wasn't as though Gwendolyn's love life had been conducted in a convent and she brought no experience to his bed. She was an attractive girl in a town full of attractive men, many of whom had laid it on thick and heavy with her, and some of whom she had said yes to. But none of them—not even Eldon Laird—had prepared her for the relentless tidal wave of gusto with which Alistair pursued her pleasure. He was a wrecking ball of a lover, demolishing all memories of the men who preceded him, as well as any vestiges of Southern belle modesty she may have still clung to. As far as Gwendolyn was concerned, her sex life began the day of the Carmichael deadline.

Within weeks, Alistair's talk had changed from "If I win the Carmichael" to "When I win the Carmichael." When Gwendolyn pointed it out to him, he smiled that dreamy smile of his and she felt like she was the only girl in the world. He said to her, "All I needed was to watch your face when you looked at the portrait . . . I felt like Perseus, Odysseus, and Hercules rolled into one."

He started to dream of prizes, coverage in *Art Digest*, gallery openings, collections, retrospectives. If it had all been just talk, Gwendolyn probably wouldn't have paid much attention. Years of living and working around creative types at the Garden of Allah and the Cocoanut Grove had taught her that excessive volumes of yackety-yak came with the territory. But with Alistair, the talk paralleled a prolific period of work during which he produced a painting almost every week.

It was a remarkable output—two abstracts, a still life, and a painting of elephants juggling Bibles against a background of Japanese pagodas and the setting sun that he'd called surrealist, but which escaped Gwendolyn's boundaries of comprehension altogether. His most recent work, a portrait of his seventy-year-old Mexican cleaning lady, took Gwendolyn's breath away almost as much as the one he'd done of her.

Not only had Alistair convinced himself that he'd won the Carmichael, he had almost convinced her that he was going to win it. To hear that he hadn't won disappointed Gwendolyn, but it was going to crush Alistair.

Red Chinese lanterns punctuated the elms around the pool area, from which a loud shriek was followed by a huge splash. Tallulah Bankhead was touring the country in a play she herself proclaimed wretched, and she'd only been in Los Angeles three or four hours before she sniffed out the party.

Already blitzed on Lillian's punch, she'd pulled some handsome boy-next-door type into the pool with her and started singing "You're the Top" at full volume.

Gwendolyn guided Irene to a quiet spot behind a banner duplicating the cover of *To Have and Have Not*. Sweet irony, she thought.

"When did they announce it?" Gwendolyn asked.

"They haven't yet."

"How did you find out?"

Irene rolled her eyes. "Oh, it's all a bit sordid, really. Our neighbor's ex-husband is currently sleeping with the chap who heads the committee. Turns out I know them all, so I called in a favor. In case the news was bad—bad for Alistair but terrific for us—I wanted to know ahead of time. I wanted to be sure that he learned the news from someone who could protect him from all sharp objects in a six-kitchen radius."

"Perhaps you'd better let me tell him," Gwendolyn said.

Irene gasped and grabbed Gwendolyn's arm. "Are you *sleeping* with Alistair?" she whispered.

"If I said yes, would you think worse of me?"

"Are you *kidding*?" A shriek burst out of Irene so loudly that Tallulah stopped mid-song and demanded to know who was in the shadows. "The man is *electric*!" Irene said. "Good Lord, you're only human. Even I'd have trouble saying no to that man, and I'm the most married woman I know. But if you want my advice, give him the news gently and sensitively . . . and then run for the hills. And while you're at it, you might like to think how you're going to get out of the affair."

Gwendolyn felt her shoulders rear back. Get out of the affair? She felt like she'd just got into it.

"Take it from me, dear, the Alistair Dunnes of this world do not cope with losing very well. Whatever sort of man he has been until now will bear no resemblance to the man he'll become after he learns that he did not win the Carmichael."

Gwendolyn agreed that he wasn't likely to take the news well. Blind Freddy could see that Alistair Dunne was a complex person made up of gangs of conflicting angels, but Gwendolyn doubted he would change so drastically. Maybe with other people, but certainly not with her. Not after all those heartfelt sweet nothings he'd murmured into her ear.

Oh my goodness, she wondered for the first time. *Have I fallen in love with the guy?*

"The timing is perfect," Irene continued. "Last night David and I had a late supper at Chasen's and he told me he might even test Lana Turner. That's how desperate he's getting. The Carmichael announcement is being made on Friday, so you might want to remind Alistair that he promised the portrait was mine if it didn't win. And for your sanity's sake, pick a very public place."

* * *

The ladies gathered at the tables in groups of twos, threes, and fours had probably never seen anything like it. Their hair would have stood up on end had it not been starched heavier than the linen napkins on their laps. As the couple passed by each table, conversations lulled to a whisper or stopped altogether. It was quiet enough for Gwendolyn to hear the light classical music playing over the loudspeakers.

The red paint splattered down his neck was bad enough, but he could've at least combed his hair. Not that it would have done much good. Alistair's hair had a will of its own; apparently no amount of pomade had ever coaxed it to buckle under. The disconcerted looks of Los Angeles' society ladies weren't going to have the slightest effect on it.

Gwendolyn and Alistair both ordered French onion soup, crab salad, and chicken fricassee. When the waitress left them, Alistair splayed out his hands on the table. "I'm going to see my bank manager on Friday."

It occurred to Gwendolyn that he didn't look like the type of man who even had a bank account, much less a manager.

"What for?"

"I'm going to open my own gallery."

"You are?"

He nodded. "I've been doing some serious thinking. Winning the Carmichael will catapult me to national prominence. That's all well and good, but I don't want to be known as a one-painting wonder."

"That's hardly likely," Gwendolyn replied. "Look at all the work you've produced. That painting of Camilla alone is enough to show the critics that you're not a one-painting wonder."

"You are certainly my muse, darling. At this rate, I'll have enough to fill a gallery by the end of the year. But why pay out those huge commissions to some gallery owner when I can do it all myself? Of course I can't do it *all* myself, which is where the bank comes in. They've agreed to loan me forty grand—"

"FORTY THOUSAND DOLLARS?" The words flew out of Gwendolyn's mouth like startled geese. Mounds of starched hair turned to look at her, then lingered on Alistair for a moment longer.

"I'm not going to do it at all unless I can do it right," he said. "So on Friday I go in and sign the papers, and I was hoping that perhaps on Sunday we could start looking for a suitable place."

Gwendolyn looked at Alistair and mentally braced herself. "Alistair, I have something to tell you."

A frown flickered across his wide face. "Are you all right? You're not . . . in trouble, are you?"

Gwendolyn could feel her smile tremble. Stabs of guilt pricked at her heart. From the outset, her plan had been to use Alistair to catch Selznick's attention, but somewhere along the line, she now realized, it'd become so very much more than that.

Face facts, she told herself. You're not the cucumber-cool career gal you like to think you are. You've fallen for this lug and it's about time you admitted it.

"Darling, the decision has been made, and, well, it's like this: someone else has won the Carmichael."

Gwendolyn leaned back in her chair and waited for an explosion, but barely a ripple broke his surface. She released a deep breath of air. Irene was wrong; he wasn't Jekyll and Hyde. The waitress placed their onion soups in front of them. Alistair stared at the steam rising from their bowls and said nothing. It didn't even look like he was breathing.

"Alistair, darling, I'm terribly disappointed for you."

A glacier of silence rammed its way between them. She had chosen the Bullock's Wilshire Tea Room because it was no place to make a horrible scene, but the crushing silence radiating from Alistair was becoming unbearable. Maybe, she thought, I should have told him in his own home, where he could yell and scream and throw around easels and snap paintbrushes into splinters.

"So much for omens." He picked up his soup spoon but it hovered over the bowl like a hummingbird.

"You had an omen about winning the Carmichael?"

"Looks like it was just a daydream. Let's forget it."

Gwendolyn struggled to keep the conversation going through the crab salad. It staggered through the chicken fricassee, falling into absurdities of ordinary everydayness—the recipe for succotash, and how there never seemed to be a good pencil sharpener around when you needed one.

When the waitress returned, she stared at their half-finished dishes. "Something wrong with the fricassee?" she asked.

"No," Gwendolyn said, "I guess we filled up on crab salad." It was a silly thing to say. The crab salads were only four or five bites at the most. The girl nodded and took the plates away.

"I must have you." Alistair's voice was hoarse.

"What do you mean, 'have'?" Gwendolyn asked, although she had a fair idea.

"Now. In the men's room. I'm going to go in and when I see the coast is clear, I'm going to pull the door slightly ajar. I'll stopper it with a wad of paper. If you see it, come in and I'll be in the last stall."

"Alistair!" Gwendolyn whispered.

He jumped up from the table. "Give me sixty seconds and follow me."

She watched him thread his way across the dining room. A men's room was not Gwendolyn's idea of a comfortable location for sex. Why not just go back to his loft, where they could groan and moan to their hearts' content?

***

The men's room smelled different from the ladies'. It was a more pungent smell, raw, unmasked with potpourri or perfume. This was a place where men went for relief, and it made Gwendolyn's skin tingle.

Alistair was waiting for her in the final stall. His pants and shorts were already down around his ankles and his cock was fully erect. It looked different in the harsh light—more red than pink, more urgent. He grabbed her dress and pushed it up over her waist. She heard the seams of her new silk panties rip and a couple of snaps on her garter belt give way, but he gave her no time to think about them. He lifted her up, pressing her against the cold metal of the stall door, and eased her down onto him. He started to grunt as he pushed himself deeper and deeper. He didn't give her his usual *If you look away, I'll die* scowl. Instead, he buried his face in her breasts to muffle the short, breathy growls that blew from his mouth in guttural gasps. He sounded like an animal fighting for its life.

Where's the passionate lover who thought only of me? she wondered. Where's the man who takes his time and gently but firmly leads a girl to an explosive orgasm that sucks the breath from her lungs?

He'd been replaced by a panting dog whose only thought was to satisfy the sole urge that mattered to him, and if it tore some seams and bruised some legs in the process, who gave a rat's ass?

In one final, raw grunt he came inside her, then let her slide off him until her feet landed back onto the tiles. He turned away from her.

"Oh, Alistair," she whispered into his ear, "It's going to be okay. It really is."

"It will never be okay."

CHAPTER 27

Kathryn rapped on Marcus' door. When he answered, she held up two tickets. "Free tonight?" she asked.

He squinted at them. "What's playing at the Loew's State theater?"

"A preview for *The Blushing Bridesmaids*."

Marcus grimaced. "Doesn't sound like my kind of movie. Why don't you take your mom? She'd enjoy a wedding picture a whole lot more than I would."

"Ordinarily I wouldn't think of asking you to something like this," Kathryn replied. "However, in a featured role as one of the bridesmaids is a certain Melody Hope." She watched the name sink in.

"Nellie Bly?" Marcus asked.

"My contact in MGM's P.R. department tells me she's marvelous."

"In that case, you better believe I'm free."

Ten minutes later, they were on the Sunset Boulevard streetcar rattling toward downtown. Marcus pushed back the brim of his fedora. "I wonder if this movie resembles anything—"

"The cats have called in their favor," Kathryn blurted out.

Marcus' eyes widened. "Oh!" Then narrowed again. "Not good, huh?"

Kathryn shook her head. "This Melody Hope girl, they want me to drag her name through the mud. And they want to start by trashing every movie she appears in. Unless I can convince them otherwise, that includes *The Pistol from*

Pittsburgh. I can't believe Ida Koverman wants me to wreck the career of one of MGM's up-and-comers, but our Miss Koverman is a very moral woman."

Kathryn saw the light dim a little in Marcus' eyes. He nodded slowly, no longer looking at her but at the empty seat in front of them. "What have the cats got against her?" he asked.

Kathryn pictured the hard lines on Claudette Colbert's face when she'd informed her how they were calling in their IOU. "They think she's having an affair with one of their husbands."

"So what did you tell them?

"I told them that I'd need to at least see the movie first."

* * *

The screen curtains had closed, the house lights had come up, and most of the audience had cleared the theater before Kathryn looked at Marcus. It wasn't hard to read his thoughts. He stood up and stepped into the aisle. "So, what are you going to do now?" he asked.

She took his arm and they strolled up the aisle. "I am in a pickle."

"The worst."

"She stole that movie right from under Sophie Tucker and Buddy Ebsen's feet."

"She certainly did."

"And she'll make a terrific Nellie Bly."

"She's perfect."

"But they want me to do everything I can to sabotage her."

"What choice have you got? Those cats don't sound like they're the type you want as enemies. Especially if Mayer really is pulling all the strings."

"I'm starting to think he doesn't know anything about Ida and her cats. I've been out dancing with him several times now. This sort of thing isn't his style. He'd just fire Melody and shove her out the back door."

They were in the theater's foyer now surrounded by moviegoers waiting for the next show. Kathryn pressed her hands to her face. “That girl is the genuine article. How am I supposed to tear her to pieces?”

“Perhaps you should meet her,” Marcus suggested. “If you’re lucky, she’ll turn out to be a vile bitch.”

“That’s not a bad idea. I wonder if I can organize an interview without Ida or any of the cats knowing. What’s the bet those little kitties have got eyes and ears everywhere?”

“Or you could just go into the ladies’ room.”

“What, here?”

“I could be wrong,” Marcus said with a wry smile, “but there was a girl wearing a dark red headscarf and no makeup sitting two rows in front of us, and she’s just gone in there.”

* * *

The ladies’ room of the Loew’s State was better than most. It had a generous dozen stalls—why did most theater bathrooms never have enough stalls for women?—and the same number of basins. The place was done out in tiles of cream and two shades of green. A girl in a dark red headscarf peered at herself in the mirror above the final basin. As Kathryn approached, she could see telltale tracks of mopped-up mascara.

“The movie wasn’t quite that sad,” Kathryn said.

The girl looked at her with soft, brown, saucer eyes. “No, no,” she smiled. “These are good tears.”

Kathryn pretended to do a double take. “Say, didn’t I just see you in that wedding movie?”

Melody nodded, and offered her a tentative smile. She looked so different in person, barely resembling the scene-stealing firecracker she’d portrayed on-screen.

Why, Kathryn thought, you’re still in your teens.

She ventured over to the basin next to Melody’s. “May I tell you how wonderful you were?” Tears welled up in the girl’s Clara Bow eyes. “Good tears are the best kind,” Kathryn said.

Melody looked away. “These are more the bittersweet kind.”

Kathryn pretended to check her lipstick in the mirror. "I was just saying to my date as we were walking out of the preview what a marvelous picture that was, and how great you were in it. You should be very proud of your work."

"I am," Melody replied. "And that's sort of the problem."

"It is?"

Melody wiped at her eyes, ruining her mascara again. "I'm sure your date is wondering what's happened to you."

"He's a patient guy."

Melody studied Kathryn's face for a moment, then took a deep breath. "I'm the daughter of a minister. We moved out here a year ago from St. Louis when Father was transferred to run that Methodist church a block north of the Hollywood Hotel. My parents are terribly old-fashioned, you see, and they're dead set against my having anything to do with Hollywood. They still think actress is another word for . . . prostitute." She whispered the last word at Kathryn as though it were heresy to even say it.

"But that's ridiculous," Kathryn said. "I know countless actresses who aren't like that in the least."

"I should have you talk to my parents. They only agreed to let me audition for MGM because they didn't think I stood the least chance of getting anywhere. When I got this movie, they were mortified. Father said, 'You're not the one who will have to get up in front of my congregation knowing that they know that my daughter is an *actress*.'"

"But this is a Hollywood congregation, not a St. Louis one. It's quite different. People who live here know it's not always like that."

"Somehow that's escaped his notice. And Mother's, too. I keep reassuring them over and over. I still adhere to the morals they brought me up with. I'm a good girl. I'm saving myself for marriage. I'm still their little Melody. Nothing's changed just because I've made a movie. But none of it seems to register."

Kathryn smiled at Melody but her mind was ticking. Still saving herself for marriage? If this girl was still a virgin, how could she have slept with anybody's husband?

CHAPTER 28

Standing underneath the Santa Monica pier at five thirty on an October morning was not Gwendolyn's idea of a splendid time. Thank God for her friend Chuck, the barman at the Cocoanut Grove. He'd insisted on lending her his jacket and waited with her until the first Red Car of the morning arrived.

She shivered in the shade of the pier and looked around for Alistair. She was happy to meet him anywhere he wanted, but why did he have to pick Santa Monica Beach at dawn?

Alistair's face peered out from behind one of the weathered pylons. She waved but he didn't wave back.

"I was hoping maybe you'd have built us a nice fire." She spotted a whiskey bottle lying on the sand.

"Your knock-off time was three hours ago," he told her.

"You said to meet you here at dawn."

"I figured you'd come straight from work."

"The first Red Car wasn't till five."

"You couldn't have caught a taxi?"

She wanted to sit down but the sand looked cold and damp. Couldn't he at least have brought a blanket to sit on? She was cold, hungry, and tired, and could feel a grumpy attack coming on. "And you could've paid for it, I suppose?"

He pulled a handful of crumpled bills from his shirt pocket and flung them toward her. Most of them ended up near a slimy mound of seaweed.

Gwendolyn collected the scattered bank notes. There were nearly twenty dollars there. "Where did you get all this?"

"I lost the Carmichael."

"You don't get prize money for losing."

"So I sold the painting."

"You *what*?" Gwendolyn was quite awake now. She noticed several days of growth sprouting from Alistair's chin. Lines of fatigue had etched themselves around his eyes since the last time she'd seen him.

She had continued to see Alistair after that day in the men's room at Bullock's, and despite Irene's warning, their relationship hadn't changed. If anything, it'd deepened. He'd taken to holding her hands every chance he got, he often praised her appearance, and their lovemaking had taken on an intensity Gwendolyn never suspected possible. No Hollywood movie love scene came close to the way they tackled each other in every corner of his loft now. His bed, studio, kitchen, dining table, shower, sofa—no place was taboo. Good Lord, they even did it on his fire escape one particularly hot September night. She loved to feel the way his back rippled as he thrust deeper and deeper inside her, to hear the way he grunted into her ear. It was almost animalistic, and she loved it.

They'd sometimes go for a few days without seeing each other, but now it had been a week. Then he'd sent her a telegram to meet him under the pier.

"It was a worthless pile of crap." He grabbed the whiskey bottle but found it was empty and tossed it back onto the sand.

"No, it—"

"It was a failed piece of art. So when this philistine with a fat head to match his fat wallet offered me a hundred dollars for it, I took it."

Gwendolyn wanted to hit him. She understood the scene in the men's room. She understood his disappointment and frustration, especially since she had come to appreciate and admire his work so much. But this? Oh, no, no, no. This crossed a line. "You have to get it back!"

He glared at her, his eyes bleary from fatigue. "I have to . . . what?"

"You have to get my portrait back."

"The hell I do."

"You have to tell him that you made a mistake. That the painting was promised to someone else."

"Who?"

"Irene Selznick. You agreed she could have it." She stopped short of adding *When you lost the Carmichael.*

He dug the toe of his shoe into the sand and flicked a lump of it against the nearest pylon. It hit the wood and fell apart.

Gwendolyn moved closer to Alistair and laid a hand on his shoulder. "I understand your disappointment at not winning the Carmichael," she said into his ear. "Truly, I do."

He ignored her hand on his shoulder and got to his feet. The sand squelched underneath the soles of his shoes as he walked a few steps away. "Perhaps you'd like to see this," he muttered.

Alistair pulled a painting from behind one of the pylons. He turned it around—it was her portrait.

"What is this? A copy?" she asked.

"No, I only made one. Even I'm not that fast."

"So—I don't get it. There was no philistine?"

"Yeah, there was a philistine, all right. And he wanted to buy you. But I told him I had other plans, and I sold him one of my others."

Gwendolyn scrambled to her feet and joined Alistair at the seaweed. It was hard not to admire such a breathtaking work. He had made her look lovelier than she could have ever imagined. It made her wish Mama was still alive to see it. It would have made her cry.

The first rays of the dawning sun hit the canvas and she saw that it was wet. "You didn't drop it in the water, did you?"

"No."

She brought her face closer to the painting and a strong smell shot up her nostrils. Whiskey. She turned around to find Alistair with a book of matches in his hand.

She picked up the portrait and hugged it to her chest. The fumes made her woozy. She looked around for the fastest escape.

"Put the painting down."

She gripped it tighter. "You are not going to burn it."

"It is a failed piece of art."

"Because it didn't win some crummy art prize?"

"The Carmichael isn't just any prize. It's *the* prize; the only prize that matters."

"This is a gorgeous piece of work. I'm very proud to be in it and you're no longer entitled to do anything with it. When you lo – the Carmichael went to someone else, this painting became Irene Selznick's."

"Nobody can truly own a painting unless they painted it themselves. Everyone else is a mere custodian."

"This is not yours to destroy."

"Put the painting down." Alistair used the same tone of voice that he'd used to order her to meet him in the men's room. Back then, it was thrilling and dangerous; now, it just sounded dangerous.

"No."

Alistair scraped the head of the match along the strike pad and flicked the lighted match onto the wet sand. His eyes took on a heartless glare. "My painting must be destroyed." He lunged toward her. He was very quick – quicker than she expected – and he managed to hook his fingers around the wooden frame and yank it.

Gwendolyn lost her balance and stepped backward onto the mound of seaweed. It was slick, and she lost her footing. She tumbled sideways but managed to hang onto her end of the painting. "Don't, Alistair," she pleaded. The rotting seaweed was making her gag. "You don't know what this means to me."

He twisted the frame out of her hands and she grabbed a handful of seaweed that slithered out of her hands like wet licorice before she could throw it at him.

"You're a silly little twit who doesn't understand a thing."

He pulled another match out of the book and struck it. Gwendolyn ignored the barb and struggled to her feet. She threw herself at him and caught him by the elbow. "Don't do this!"

He shoved her and she slammed into the pylon, scraping her arm on the concrete as she slid down to the sand. She could see her own blood in the dim light. Her arm stung like hell.

Alistair stood over the painting and struck another match. Gwendolyn grabbed a handful of damp sand and hurled it at him. It smacked him solidly on the side of his head and he lost his balance and dropped to his knees. She scrambled to him on her hands and knees and threw herself on top of him, straddling his shoulders and pinning down his arms.

"I need you to calm down," she panted. "Maybe you think you botched it, but I don't. It's too lovely to destroy."

The anger had left Alistair's eyes now, but Gwendolyn wasn't convinced. She kept her knees planted firmly on top of his shoulders. He glanced at her crotch and smiled lasciviously. "Raise your skirt," he said. "I want to see what's underneath."

"You've seen what's underneath."

"But I want to see it again."

Gwendolyn hesitated, then gripped the hem of her dress. A flare of sudden orange light caught the corner of her left eye. She looked back and saw that Alistair had managed to light the whole book of matches singlehandedly.

"A party trick that comes in handy in no end of ways," he said, and flipped it onto the canvas.

CHAPTER 29

Kathryn and Marcus looked up at the towering spire of the Hollywood United Methodist Church and sighed at the same time.

"I haven't been inside a church since . . . I can't remember when," Marcus said. "Do you think God will strike me down?"

Kathryn felt bad about pulling Marcus out of bed so early on a Sunday, but only slightly bad. These days he seemed to spend half his nights drinking and half his days sleeping off the booze. It was about time he saw the morning light. She pulled at her gloves. "I thought you didn't believe in God."

"What if I'm wrong?" Marcus replied. "What if I'm wrong about everything?"

They ascended the steps to the church and followed the crowd inside to the cavernous nave. The vaulted ceiling rose several stories above them and a hymn drifted from the organ at the side of the altar.

"We're not going to have to sit too near the front, are we?" Marcus asked.

"Just near enough to see her."

She led him down the center aisle until they were ten rows from the altar and pushed him into the pew beside a fresh-faced young couple who smelled annoyingly of *eau de newlywed*.

"Remind me why we're here."

"The cats are starting to breathe down my neck," Kathryn whispered. "They really mean business."

"You knew that going in."

"But I don't get why they've got it in for Melody so much. She's a nice girl, sweet as can be."

"You really think she's Hollywood's last remaining virgin?"

"I do, but those cats don't want to hear it. They want blood. And if they don't get Melody's, they'll come for mine. Her father's the minister here."

"Here? This church?"

"I figured I might run into her again, or maybe somebody who knows her. Before I'm forced to drag her name through the mud, I want to be sure I'm wrong about her." Just then, Marcus' comment outside the church came back to her. "Say, what did you mean back there about being wrong about everything?" He handed her a shamefaced pout. "Oh, Marcus, please tell me you're not still giving yourself grief over what happened with Scott."

"I just . . ." Marcus' eyes looked like they'd been scraped raw. "I just can't help feeling that Scott falling off the wagon like that was my fault. If I hadn't been hungover and if I'd gotten myself to work on time—sober—he wouldn't have given up and gone searching for booze like that."

"Scott Fitz—" She forced her voice back into a whisper. "Scott's problems are not your fault. They go a lot deeper and a lot further back than these past couple of months."

"Maybe, but—"

"But nothing. The picture worked out wonderfully well, so what are you worried about? You need to let go of feeling responsible for something that was never your responsibility. And you need to focus instead on your own drinking. I'm not your mother and I'm not going to lecture you on—"

"Thank . . . you . . . Mother."

They held each other's eyes for a long moment; Kathryn could tell it was time to shut the hell up.

She looked around. The congregation was a typical gathering of meek-faced do-gooders in their Sunday best, and for a moment, she found herself almost envying them their implacable faith in the unknowable. Her heart gave a start when she thought she saw Roy a couple of pews down across the aisle. Since running into him at Warners, she'd been seeing him everywhere—or at least thought she was. It was never him, though, and it was especially unlikely to see him in a Methodist church. Like all the other times, she was half relieved, half disappointed it wasn't him.

The congregation fell silent when a man dressed in black approached the pulpit. He looked to be in his mid-forties, already greying, already balding, with a kind face perhaps overly inclined toward pinched piety.

"Good morning, all," he said. "And welcome."

Melody's father had a voice to match his face, meticulous and thoughtful. It was the voice of every father from every family movie made since the dawn of the talkies. "I want to speak to you today of the role of music in our spiritual lives. I would like to break with tradition and start today's service with a hymn. I ask you now to gather up your hymnals and turn to number three eighty."

Reverend Hope made a gesture with his hand and the choir started to make its way onto the steps in front of the altar. Kathryn picked up the hymnal resting on the ledge in front of her and opened to number three-eighty: *There's Within My Heart a Melody*.

Kathryn looked to Marcus and found him already staring at her. She'd never seen the haunted look in his eyes that she saw now.

She looked down at the hymnal.

There's within my heart a melody
Jesus whispers sweet and low:
Fear not, I am with thee, peace, be still,
In all of life's ebb and flow.

How lucky you are, Miss Melody Hope, Kathryn thought, to have a father who disagrees with what you are doing and sticks by you anyway.

She sighed and looked up at the choir; her eyes fell on Melody and she gave a little gasp. She nudged Marcus. He followed Kathryn's gaze.

"Is it just me," Marcus whispered, "or does she look like a younger version of . . .?"

"No," Kathryn whispered back. "It's not your imagination."

"But she didn't look anything like that in the movie. Did she look like that in the ladies' room?"

"She was wearing a scarf, no makeup, and had been crying. She didn't look like anybody, except maybe Little Orphan Annie."

"But the resemblance – it's uncanny."

"I know!"

Marcus threw Kathryn another glance. "Mystery solved?"

***

The house at 426 Bristol Avenue in Brentwood wasn't the mansion Kathryn had expected for one of MGM's most magnetic stars. It was unquestionably big, but it wasn't some ridiculously over-the-top recreation of a Normandy castle or Mediterranean villa. It was a two-story place in the Mexican hacienda style so popular in L.A., painted white, with roof tiles in bright red. A line of azalea bushes in full bloom along the driveway matched the roof almost exactly.

The white front door was as unadorned as the house, with a wooden doorknocker in the same shade of red as the roof. Kathryn kept her eyes trained on the knocker as she approached it, rehearsing the opening salvo she'd decided on. The door swung open before she got there.

"Why, hello!" Joan Crawford exclaimed, perhaps a little too brightly. "This *is* a pleasant surprise."

"I do hope I'm not intruding," Kathryn said, "but I wasn't near a telephone. This isn't a bad time, is it?"

"No! Not at all. Come on in. I was just doing some dusting and saw you coming up the path."

Kathryn found the concept that Joan Crawford did her own dusting a bit hard to believe. Then again, she thought, the story that Crawford scoured every hotel bathroom she walked into never seemed to go away.

Joan led Kathryn into a spacious, light-filled foyer that lead to a living room in one direction and a dining room in the other. "I was thinking of making coffee. Can I interest you in some?" Joan led her into a spotless kitchen with nary a cup, spoon, or stain in sight. "I'm sorry the place is such a mess, but after working all week at the studio, who can be bothered?" She started fussing around with the coffeepot. "To what do I owe this pleasure?"

"I've just come from church," Kathryn said.

Joan swung around to look at Kathryn, but not before her eyes landed briefly on the octagonal clock above the stove. "You're a churchgoing girl?"

"Not usually."

"Just for show, huh?" Joan shrugged. "Well, you're hardly alone there. The Good Shepherd in Beverly Hills, I suppose?"

"The Methodist one just north of the Hollywood Hotel."

"Methodist? Really?"

"It's where Melody Hope goes to sing in the choir."

Had she not been looking, Kathryn would have missed the pause as Joan ladled ground coffee beans into the percolator. "For crying out loud, she sings in a church choir, too?"

"Her father is the pastor there."

"Of course he is," Joan muttered. "What else would he be?" She threw Kathryn a classic Crawford glare. Square jaw, wide mouth, steely eyes. It struck Kathryn for the first time that Joan Crawford really only had one look. She'd made it work for her, but it was all she had. On the other hand, there was Melody Hope, whom Kathryn had seen three separate times and who looked quite different on each occasion. Crawford drew a long breath. "I thought we made it quite clear what we wanted you to do about Miss Melody."

"You did."

"And yet I turn to your column every morning and have yet to see anything resembling what we've asked for."

"I needed time to figure out your angle," Kathryn said.

"Our angle? We've told you. That God-fearing little slut has been sleeping with one of the cats' husbands."

"No, Joan, I meant *your* angle."

"What makes you think I have any angle? The men of this industry have their old boys' club, so us kitty-cats have to stick together. Cream? Sugar?"

"I've seen what she looks like, Joan. Not as a blushing bridesmaid, or as Nellie Bly, but as herself. The resemblance is remarkable." Joan Crawford kept her back to Kathryn. "That's what this hateful campaign is all about, isn't it?"

Crawford strummed her blood-red fingernails against the blue and white tiling for a few moments. "The cats have handed you your career on a platter." The Crawford voice had become low and raspy.

"Joan, I'm not against doing a favor for you or any of the cats. I'm just against doing this particular favor."

"Who said you get to choose?"

"Have the cats seen what Melody Hope looks like when she's not made up as Nellie Bly? Do they know she looks like you, but a dozen years younger?"

Joan tapped her watch. "You know what, Kathryn, this is going to sound awfully trite, but I swear it's true. I've got some people coming over for lunch and I haven't done a thing to prepare. You're going to have to excuse me, but I've barely got an hour to throw the whole thing together."

The way she'd been checking her clock every two minutes told Kathryn that Joan was expecting someone, but she doubted it was half a dozen people for lunch.

"I'm just trying to establish why—"

"OH, ALL RIGHT! Clearly, they are grooming that little minx to replace me because I've got a salary negotiation coming up. By this time next month, I could be getting five thousand a week, which pushes me into the Too Expensive bracket."

"But you're one of their biggest stars. You're too valuable—"

"They hand me a ton of money each week and I hand them back a head-to-toe, twenty-four-hours-a-day movie star who makes pictures that earn them scads of dough every time a new one leaves the gate. I think it's a fair exchange and I don't see that I've given them any reason to groom some no-talent shortstop who happens to look like me—"

"She's not short on talent."

"How would you know?"

"I went to a preview for *Blushing Bridesmaids*."

Joan rolled her eyes. "Pah!"

Kathryn decided on a different tack. "Have you met Melody yourself?"

"I wouldn't piss on her for practice."

"She's a genuinely lovely girl, daughter of a minister, sings in the choir—"

"Oh, stop it. I've made that picture a hundred times and I'll probably make a hundred more before I'm through."

"But to destroy the girl's career—"

"You listen to me." Joan raised her voice. "Your job is to do what we say. If we want to scuttle the career of some minister's whore of a daughter, that's all you need to know. Fail us and there will be repercussions, I can assure you."

Kathryn and Joan were almost toe to toe. Joan breathed in and out of her nose, her nostrils like an angry buffalo's. Suddenly she stepped back and pulled a smile onto her face. "Now really, Kathryn, I need to get ready for my guests."

The front door chimed.

"That wouldn't be Spencer Tracy at the door, would it?" Kathryn asked.

Joan flashed her enormous eyes at Kathryn. Bull's eye! Kathryn silently thanked Marcus. If Joan starts calling Melody a slut, he'd told her, bring up Spencer Tracy and see if she doesn't have a conniption fit. Hugo got drunk at the Hacketts' dinner party last week and blabbed that the word was out around the studio: those two had been having a roaring affair since the day they started work on *Mannequin*.

Joan's perfectly lacquered upper lip pulled back in a snarl. "I'll be damned if I let some trumped-up little nobody steal my career."

Kathryn looked at Crawford and thought of the Hays Code, which required every film to obtain a certificate of approval before being released. To get that approval, it had to be stripped of all references to any sort of behavior the Hays Office deemed inappropriate. Back in the rollicking 1920s, pretty much anything went—on-screen or off. But nowadays, movie stars were held by both their studios and the Hays Office to be the same paragons of virtue off-screen that they portrayed on-screen. For someone like Crawford, who was as big a star back in 1927 as she was now, this reining-in of presumed entitlement must be a terrible drag.

"Isn't there room for both your career and hers?" Kathryn asked.

"Not if she looks like me. I don't get it. Why the hell do you care about Melody Hope, anyway? Oh, God, don't tell me you're related to her. That's all I need."

The doorbell rang a second time. Joan's breath became ragged. Holy hell, thought Kathryn, that really is Spencer Tracy standing out there. "I don't suppose," Kathryn said, "that his wife is with him on your front porch?"

"What is it you want?"

"If you promise to call the cats off," Kathryn said quickly, "I'll go out the back way. He won't even see me. I won't say a thing to anyone."

Joan thought for a moment. "No deal," she said. "I'll walk you to the door. Have you ever experienced the Spencer Tracy charm firsthand? It's really quite something."

Kathryn's heart sank. She'd played her last card and Crawford had called her bluff.

Joan curled an exquisitely manicured finger, beckoning Kathryn to follow her to the front door. They were less than a dozen feet away when the chimes filled the house for the third time.

"Joan, honey, are you in there?" It was Tracy's unmistakable voice on the other side.

Joan turned on a heel. "All right. You win."

"You give me your word? You'll call off the cats?"

Joan nodded. "But I need that favor you said you weren't against doing. Quid pro quo is all I'm asking for. As long as it stays between you and me."

"Joan? JOAN! C'mon, open up! I'm giving you ten seconds, then I'm leaving."

Kathryn stretched out the moment as long as she dared. "What kind of favor?"

CHAPTER 30

Billy Wilkerson's gait took on peculiar characteristics when he was on the warpath. He leaned to the side slightly, as though his pocket was filled with bricks, and led with the opposite shoulder. He'd cock his head to one side, too, and thrust his chin forward as though he had an underbite. Kathryn watched him march his warpath walk as he strode to her desk with a pile of envelopes in his hand.

"I let the first few columns go through because I thought it was your idea of a joke. Then I thought it was some sort of joke being played on you. I give you free rein to write whatever you see fit, but this is getting out of hand."

"What is?"

"Joan Crawford for Scarlett O'Hara? You can't be serious."

"I'm quite serious," Kathryn said. The hell she was.

"This needs to stop."

"So my free rein only applies to things you agree with?"

"Come on, now, you've written plenty of copy I don't agree with. But now you're embarrassing the paper."

Kathryn made the sort of tsking sound a mother makes when her five-year-old is just being plain silly.

He raised the stack of letters in his left hand. "Your fan mail, ma'am." He dropped them on her desk. "Reel it in, ace."

* * *

She stopped reading after the fifth one. They all said the same thing: the notion of casting someone as patently unsuitable as Joan Crawford in the most important role in

Hollywood history was ludicrous, and Miss Massey's support for Crawford was turning her into a joke.

Kathryn knew from the start that she was letting Joan Crawford paint her into a corner, but she wanted to save *The Pistol from Pittsburgh,* so she had no choice but swap a smear campaign for a P.R. campaign. She hadn't reckoned it might be at the expense of her professional credibility.

Kathryn started flicking over the pages of her desk calendar and wondered if there was a way to hurry things along. She landed on Thursday's page and saw what she had written: *Dinner & Dancing date with LBM.*

She had assumed their dance at the Cocoanut Grove was a one-off, but then Mayer had approached her during a big bash NBC Radio threw at the Biltmore Bowl to publicize the *Edgar Bergen and Charlie McCarthy Show*. To her surprise, he'd asked her out—"strictly dinner and dancing, you understand." The mogul was quite serious about his dancing and had found few women with the stamina to keep up with him. In Kathryn he'd finally found a worthy partner.

Kathryn's eyes narrowed. *Hmmm . . .*

* * *

The Trocadero on Sunset Boulevard, decorated with what must have been several hundred poinsettias for the holidays, was unusually busy for a Thursday night. Kathryn shared a primo table next to the dance floor with Mayer. When she noticed a lot of head-turning, she looked toward the entrance: Charlie Chaplin in a sleek tux and Paulette Goddard in silver lamé were making their grand entrance—and unknowingly bringing with them Kathryn's opportunity.

"Do you think they're married?" Kathryn asked Mayer.

"For their sakes, I hope they are."

"I keep hearing this rumor that they got hitched on a boat back from China."

"Literally the slow boat from China?"

"You don't sound convinced."

"Is anyone?"

The maître d' approached their table with a telephone in hand. When he'd plugged it in, he surprised them both by handing it to Kathryn.

"This is Kathryn Massey."

"Hey, it's me," Gwendolyn said.

Kathryn looked at her watch. It had just gone ten o'clock—too early for Gwendolyn's cigarette break.

"I'm calling from the phone booth in the lobby so I have to be quick," Gwendolyn continued. "It's Joan Crawford. She's out for blood."

Kathryn could feel Mayer's eyes on her. She maintained a honeyed smile for his benefit. "Oh? And why is that?"

"The gal who runs the ladies' room just told me that she overheard someone telling Joan that Melody Hope's role in *The Pistol from Pittsburgh* was an unofficial screen test for Scarlett O'Hara. Joan started raising all kinds of holy hell, declaring that she'd burn Atlanta herself if Melody got the role over her. She's on the warpath to find Mayer, and someone told her he's dancing with you tonight at the Trocadero. Then she smashed something on the floor and stormed out."

"And how long ago was this?"

"Ten, maybe fifteen minutes ago."

Kathryn thanked Gwendolyn and hung up.

"Business call, I take it?" Mayer asked.

"Aren't they all, in one way or another?"

Right on cue, a new tune started up. It was a quickstep, one of Mayer's favorites, and Kathryn suggested they hit the floor. She gave it a few moments before she said, "Can I ask you a question?"

"Of course. Whether or not I answer is something else again."

"It's about Melody Hope."

"Oh?" He sounded surprised.

"Is it true that the only reason you signed Melody is to make Joan Crawford nervous?"

Mayer wasn't a tall man, so when the two of them danced together, they were eyeball to eyeball. He squinted at her. "So, you and Joan are best friends now?"

"Not particularly."

"These days your column reads like you're the chief manager of the *Joan For Scarlett* campaign. I never imagined the two of you ran in the same social circles."

That's interesting, Kathryn thought. He didn't seem to know about Ida's cats.

"Joan's never been the type to play best girlfriends," he added, "which leaves me to wonder. Maybe there's another reason she's getting so many inches in your column."

"What did you come up with?"

"I think she's got something on you."

"And I think you've been watching too many of your own B pictures."

"Whatever it is, perhaps I can fix it. I'm a pretty good fixer."

Kathryn tried a gentle, girly flutter of a laugh, something she'd never been able to pull off as effectively as Gwendolyn. "It's just that I believe Joan has a lot of qualities in common with Scarlett." Kathryn gathered up the laundry list she'd expected to trot out for Wilkerson. "She's headstrong, stubborn, knows her own mind, knows how to seduce men and how to get her own way. She's resourceful, pampered, tempestuous. Joan Crawford is all those things, too, and I think she's worth screen-testing."

"If you say so."

"I do say so."

"And I say that I'm a pretty good fixer of problems."

"I promise you that if I ever develop a leaky faucet, you'll be the first person I call." Kathryn let a few bars of music float by. "Getting back to Melody Hope. I'm asking purely out of curiosity. We're on the dance floor, so don't you worry – the rule applies."

When Mayer picked her up in his limo for their first dance date, he'd made clear the one regulation she must adhere to: this was purely a social arrangement. No business. When the subject of business did come up—and Hollywood was such a cross-breeding company town, how could it be avoided completely?—the rule was that everything they discussed was strictly off the record. The implication was that if she ever broke the rule, he'd see to it personally that her career was ruined.

Kathryn smiled at Mayer sweeter than huckleberry cobbler.

"Why don't you ask the cat where curiosity got her," Mayer said.

"Okay, look, forget I asked," Kathryn said. "It's just that when I saw Melody in church the other day—"

"You go to her church?"

"I was there with a friend of mine and it struck me how much she looks like Joan in real life. So I got to thinking . . ."

"Of course we did," Mayer said bluntly. He was looking over her shoulder, scanning the crowded floor for a break in the traffic.

Kathryn said, "Joan's going to shoot for five thousand a week, you know."

"And we might even pay it. But that makes every movie we put her in an enormous commitment, and so if she gives us trouble . . ."

"You've got Melody in the wings."

"It's hardly the first time a studio has done something like that to keep a monstrous ego in check. We gave Melody the lead in that little Nellie Bly B picture because we needed to show Crawford she ain't the only cocksucker in town."

Kathryn winced. Melody would've died to hear anyone refer to her like that. "That's not what I heard."

"Oh?"

"The word around town is that *The Pistol from Pittsburgh* was really a screen test because Melody is being very seriously considered for Scarlett O'Hara." Kathryn expected surprise or derisive laughter, but neither sprang from Mayer. Instead, he glanced at her sideways, past the rims of his glasses. But it was an intense sort of gaze that told her she had his full attention.

"Is this why Crawford is getting all that support in your column?" he asked.

"Why do you keep thinking I have some ulterior motive?

Mayer shrugged a shoulder, as if to say, "So you tell me what I'm supposed to believe."

"I still say both Joan and Scarlett are strong, determined, driven women." Kathryn pressed. "There are any number of parallels. So why not let her test?"

"Because screen tests are expensive, especially when there is no point."

"No point? Susan Heyward's been tested, and Lana Turner. So has Carole Lombard. Surely Joan deserves a shot."

"Because I'm already giving my overly ambitious son-in-law his male lead."

"Gable? He's signed?"

"Print that in your column and I'll drown you in the Pacific myself. No, he hasn't signed. He doesn't even want it, but the American public won't accept anyone else. It's just a matter of Gable getting used to the idea. Selznick is prepared to pay through the nose for him, which he'll have to do because now that Gable's fallen for Lombard, he's going to have a mighty expensive divorce on his hands. A fat bonus check is going to be waved in his face, one so big he won't be able to say no. So with all that going on, I doubt Selznick's going to be able to afford to get his female lead on loan from us, too. Giving Crawford a screen test is a waste of time and money."

"But you gave Melody a whole movie as a screen test for Scarlett."

"I never said that." Several bars of music later, he said, "You know it doesn't pay to screw me over, don't you?"

Kathryn nodded and pictured Joan Crawford stampeding through the Trocadero's front doors. Kathryn tried her honeyed smile on Mayer again. He smiled back but said nothing. When the quickstep changed to a foxtrot, Mayer said, "I heard the trip to China is very long indeed."

"Oh?"

The look in Mayer's eyes had turned impish. When a roar of laughter erupted from the Chaplin table, he jutted his head in their direction and a twenty-one gun salute fired off inside Kathryn's head. She leaned her mouth into Mayer's ear. "Paulette Goddard? For Scarlett?"

"David tells me she's the pick of the bunch."

"Selznick can't cast the biggest-ever female role with a woman who's living in sin. Even if it is with Charlie Chaplin. It'll never happen."

"You rooting for Joan Crawford is fine by me. It's more free publicity for MGM, and keeps Joan's name in front of the public. But I'm telling you—David has his eye fixed on Paulette Goddard, out of wedlock or not."

"The public won't stand for it. Not for their Scarlett."

"Maybe they will, maybe they won't, which is why you also ought to keep your eye on Vivien Leigh."

"Who's that?"

"A British actress who—"

Kathryn stumbled over Mayer's feet and almost crashed into June Allyson and Dick Powell. It took her a few beats to regain her rhythm. "A *Brit*?" she whispered. "We both know there'll be rioting in the South if Selznick casts anything but an American." Kathryn saw her chance. "Somebody needs to point out to Selznick that Joan Crawford may not be ideal, but she's better than anyone living in sin, and she's certainly better than some English rose. Not to mention the publicity for MGM when it gets out that Selznick is thinking of casting Crawford as Scarlett."

Kathryn could see the gears behind Mayer's eyes clicking over. "That's Selznick's call, not mine," he said after a few moments. "Can we change the subject now?"

"All right," Kathryn conceded. "But I hear *Pistol from Pittsburgh* is better than a B picture."

"You call that changing the subject?" When Kathryn didn't reply, Mayer said, "I'll tell you something—and, unlike the rest of this conversation, this *is* on the record—what we hadn't counted on was that Melody would be so talented, nor that the director could be capable of doing so much with so little. We shelled out the usual B-picture budget of a hundred and fifty grand, but if we promote it to the A-list, we could stand to make five, six, maybe seven times that amount."

"So you're releasing it as an A picture?"

Mayer deftly pivoted Kathryn on her right heel and bent her back into one of his famously deep dips. She dropped her head back and wished she hadn't. Upside down, she saw Joan Crawford on the edge of the dance floor in a floor-length gown of black silk with fuchsia swirls the size of dinner plates. Her hands were bunched into fists on her hips. Even from this angle, Kathryn could see the fury in her eyes.

Mayer glanced at Joan, then back at Kathryn. "What does that bitch have on you?" She eyed him evenly but said nothing. "I can hold this position for quite some time."

Just then the music stopped and the bandleader announced that the musicians would be taking a break. Mayer didn't move. Pretty soon, the dance floor had cleared and they were the only ones left. People were beginning to stare.

"That phone call I got," Kathryn said, "was about her. She's heard the Melody Hope-Scarlett O'Hara rumor and she's furious."

"So I see."

"She's not above making a public scene."

"I know."

"So you'd better have some good news for her, like maybe the promise of a Scarlett O'Hara screen test."

Mayer let out a "Hmm" and lifted her upright. "Casting Scarlett is Selznick's decision. His and Cukor's. If Selznick isn't going to listen to his director, then the whole project is in trouble. Which I think it is anyway. I don't care how many millions that book has sold, Civil War pictures don't make money. So this whole Scarlett thing? It's all a moot point." He took Kathryn by the arm and led her toward Joan. "Mark my words: this movie is going to be the biggest goddamned bomb of the nineteen thirties."

CHAPTER 31

Gwendolyn could feel they were no longer moving. She took a deep breath, but the air inside the box was getting stale and she could feel something rising in her throat. "Are we there?" she called out.

"Pretty much. You okay in there?"

Gwendolyn silently blessed Marcus for giving up his Christmas morning to do this for her. He hadn't hesitated one bit when she asked. Not even when she told him he'd have to get dressed up in the smart blue Confederate soldier uniform with the gold trim that she'd borrowed from her downstairs neighbor who worked in costuming for Republic Studios. Marcus really looked quite dashing in it. He gave passersby on Sunset a cheerful wave as the two of them loaded a life-sized reproduction of the *Gone with the Wind* book. Now that they were in front of Selznick's house, she had to wonder: Was Marcus as nervous as she was?

After watching Alistair Dunne set fire to her portrait, Gwendolyn decided she'd had enough of relying on other people to make her dream come true. So she joined a twice-weekly group of aspiring actresses who met in the basement of the Hollywood Studio Club—a chaperoned dormitory for single girls who came to Hollywood in search of fame—to practice monologues and scenes together. She hoped to find the same us-against-the-world camaraderie she felt at the Garden of Allah, but found that a you're-my-competition atmosphere pervaded the place.

Still, she'd heard there about some cattle calls at the studios, one at Warners and a couple at Twentieth Century-

Fox. The Warners one was a bust, but the casting director at Fox seemed to like her. At the first call he chose the blonde standing next to her, but at the second, he stopped to look at her for a heart-pounding moment. He didn't select her, but leaned in and rather cryptically whispered into her ear, "Fortune favors the bold."

Okay, so maybe this new scheme of hers was as cockeyed as they come, but there was no arguing that it was bold.

According to Kathryn, Selznick was starting to narrow down his choices, so this was her last chance to get his attention. She *knew* she could do this; she *knew* she could play Scarlett O'Hara, if only she could get herself in front of him. If this failed, then she had nobody else to blame. "Fortune favors the bold," Gwendolyn whispered to herself. "Fortune favors the bold."

"How close are we?" she called out.

"We're about to turn onto his driveway."

"Why did we stop?"

"Are you sure you want to go through with this?"

A tingling of mild panic mixed with slight claustrophobia gripped her throat; she could feel a film of sweat across her forehead. She gulped in huge breaths as she fumbled around for the pocket hidden in the folds of her rented crinoline. She pulled out the tiny bottle of smelling salts Kathryn gave her just before they left, uncapped it, and sucked in through her nose. The aroma hit her like a pillow-covered sledgehammer and every blood vessel north of her chest opened up in less than a second. All her doubts and fears evaporated.

"Let's get this show going!"

She gripped the box's wooden frame and braced herself as Marcus pushed the giant book up Selznick's driveway. The wheels under her came to a stop; she heard a doorbell chime. The excited screams of two young boys on Christmas morning grew louder and louder until she heard one of them exclaim, "Dad! There's a Christmas present at the door!"

"It's huge!" the other voice screamed.

Gwendolyn started to feel lightheaded again. Come on, Selznick, she thought. I can't stand inside this damned book for much longer.

"Mr. Selznick!" Marcus said in his best announcer's voice.

Somebody was clapping loudly—was it Irene?—and then she heard a deep voice groan, "Oh, good grief, no, what is this?"

Gwendolyn took as deep a breath as she could manage. She pushed open the front panel of the book and stepped out. The air was cool and fresh and it took her breath away for a moment. She forced herself to focus on her prey.

David O. Selznick was taller than she expected, more than six feet. He had a full face, a hatch of dense black hair, and thick lips. He stood before her in a jade silk dressing gown and blue-checked slippers and scowled at her through his wire-framed glasses.

She raised the white lace parasol in her right hand. When she thumbed the switch and it opened with a soft pop, she saw the first hint of a smile. "Merry Christmas, Mr. Selznick. I am so very pleased to make your charming acquaintance this fine and sunny Christmas morning. Please allow me to introduce myself. I am your Scarlett O'Hara!"

Selznick crossed one arm against his stomach and supported his chin with the other. "Oh, you are, are you?" he said.

"Oh, yes, indeed I am!" Gwendolyn struggled to maintain her bright smile as she watched the amusement fade from his face.

"Nice try," he said eventually. "I applaud your spunk."

An unspoken "but" hung in the air.

She looked across to Irene, pleading with her eyes. If Irene hadn't encouraged her, she probably wouldn't have attempted this. But Irene hadn't thought it was the craziest thing she'd ever heard of. "That guy was right," Irene had said last week. "Fortune does favor the bold." But now she had nothing to say. Instead, she stood behind her husband

and shrugged her shoulders helplessly. Gwendolyn looked across to Marcus, who mouthed the word *smile*.

"You're not what we're looking for, sweetheart," Selznick said. "However, you will make a good dinner-party story for weeks, so I thank you for that." He turned to go back inside.

Gwendolyn could feel her chin start to crinkle. The sight of Selznick's back disappearing through the doorway wobbled through the tears she wished would retreat. It had been worth a go, she told herself. They could never say Gwendolyn Brick didn't go down trying.

"David, darling, are you sure?"

Irene had her eyes on Gwendolyn and her hands on her husband's shoulders, turning him around.

"What?" he said.

"Look at her. The pointed chin, and those marvelous green eyes. And her hair, that's the exact right shade." At Irene's suggestion, Gwendolyn had dyed her hair a very dark brown. She didn't think it particularly suited her, and she'd noticed a drop in her tips at the Cocoanut Grove, but she did match Mitchell's description of Scarlett. "What's your name, dear?" Irene asked.

"Gwendolyn."

"My, but that's a pretty name. Are you from the South, Gwendolyn?"

"Yes, ma'am. As a matter of fact, I'm from Hollywood, Florida."

Irene clapped her hands together. "Oh my goodness, there's a Hollywood in Florida? How's that for a story, David? An unknown actress from the other Hollywood gets to audition for Scarlett O'Hara. I don't want to interfere, but I would be lying if I told you that I pictured Scarlett looking anything other than this."

Gwendolyn watched Selznick throw his wife an exasperated look, but he took a couple of steps closer to Gwendolyn. He towered over her. "Did Mayer put you up to this? Don't lie to me, now."

Gwendolyn shook her head and twirled the lace parasol Dorothy di Frasso had loaned her. "Why, no, Mr. Selznick, he most certainly did not."

"I bet it was Darryl. This has got Zanuck written all over it."

"Mr. Selznick, I can assure you, I undertook this all under my own initiative."

He nodded silently, still studying her. "You're standing on private property, young lady," he said. "If you'd pulled this sort of stunt on Mayer, or Warner, or Cohn, they'd probably have had you arrested by now." He gave her a final once-over and walked back into the house. The boys followed him.

Irene took her hand. "I'm sorry, Gwen darling, you gave it your best shot."

Gwendolyn could only nod. It was getting harder to breathe now – all she wanted to do was get out of that suffocating dress.

She mouthed *Thank you* at Irene and picked up the front of the skirt. "Come on, Marcus, let's get this book back into the truck." It was a display piece she'd convinced the owner of the Stanley Rose bookshop to give her. God only knew what she was going to do with it now.

"Where are you going?"

Selznick was standing at his front door waving a piece of paper in his hand. Confused, Gwendolyn looked at Marcus, who gestured for her to go back.

Selznick handed her the paper. "This is the number of my Hollywood casting office. Call in February. We're doing another sweep of the South all through January, so any earlier than that won't do you any good. And you'd better tell them you're the Christmas Scarlett. Trust me, by then they'll all know who the Christmas Scarlett is."

CHAPTER 32

Marcus turned to Robert Benchley. A passing streetlight through the window of the taxicab strafed his amiable face. "Thanks again for doing this."

Benchley's face, reddened by a lifetime of protracted boozing, broke into a smile. "Think nothing of it."

"No, really," Marcus said. "I appreciate it."

"I would love for you to think I'm sneaking you into MGM at midnight for purely the most altruistic of reasons, but alas, that's not the entire scenario."

"It's not?"

"Don't get me wrong, Adler, I'm more than happy to help out, but I also need to get inside the studio at a time when I won't bump into Ren Rowland, the producer on those short films I'm making. I'm four days overdue delivering the script for *How to Figure Income Tax,* and I just know he's about to start hounding me for it."

"Surely this isn't the first time you've been late on a script." Robert Benchley's chronic tardiness was legendary.

"No, but it is the first time I've owed Ren four thousand dollars to cover my bets at Santa Anita." Benchley belched. "That son of a bitch can pick eight out of ten winners just by the sound of their names. No word of an exaggeration. Positively uncanny."

"Why don't you just bet on the same horses?"

"That's why he's a son of a bitch; he never tells me until after they're out of the gate. I need another week before I can deliver my script and pay him back. No, no, I must avoid him at all costs. And he often works until late, so we have to come later than that. Have you ever been at a studio when it's completely deserted? I passed out at the Christmas party the first year I was here. I woke up hours later, completely alone, and walked through the back lot by moonlight. Oh! Magical!"

The taxi pulled up at an unobtrusive entrance on Overland Street that Marcus had never noticed when he worked at MGM. The guard seated inside the security booth was Hooley, who'd once chased Marcus all over the lot, but Marcus could see something had happened to him. His cheekbones hung like old curtains on a face that had once bloomed with strength and health.

"Mr. Adler," Hooley said. Even in the dim light, Marcus could see Hooley's chain of thought. It'd been many months since Marcus Adler was a full-time employee of MGM. It was Hooley's job to keep out unauthorized personnel, and he took it very seriously. "Been a while."

"Nice to see you," Marcus replied, even though it really wasn't. The man must have lost thirty pounds. "We're here to – "

Benchley kicked Marcus in the ankle. "How d'you do this fine night, Hooley?"

"Very well indeed, Mr. Benchley. Very well, I must say."

Benchley eyed the *L.A. Times* spread out on the counter inside the booth. "Crosswords still keeping you company, I see."

Hooley nodded. "How long will you be tonight?"

"Two hours at the most."

Hooley waved them through with his flashlight.

Benchley and Marcus headed down the shadowy street. "You do this often?" Marcus asked. "Come here in the middle of the night?"

"I work so much better when there's nobody around, and I can hardly do that back at the Garden. I often come here to work out my physical bits. I have all the space I need." He glanced back at the solitary figure in the security booth. "Poor guy. You heard about his bout with TB, I suppose? No? Very near fatal. He recovered, but it's left him an incurable insomniac and a bit of a hermit. Not so good for his social life, but it made him a perfect candidate for night guard."

They made their way down a curved street past a row of suburban homes. Marcus had only ever seen them by day when they looked like any neighborhood from any town in the U.S., which of course was the whole point. They were largely façades, but all America knew them as Mickey Rooney's neighborhood in the hugely popular Andy Hardy series. By moonlight they took on an enchanted quality, as though conjured by pixies for their own amusement.

Their destination was MGM's publicity department, which, among other things, produced *The Lion's Roar*. Since the night of the Anti-Nazi League dinner, Marcus had been bothered by the gossipy item Hoppy Terrell had alluded to. Marcus hadn't deliberately spiked Scott's Coca-Cola, but perception was everything in this closely knit town. If there was any chance that this rumor was keeping him from getting hired by the studios, then he needed to know what they knew. Or at least what they thought they did. And he needed to figure it out soon. His MGM money was starting to run out and he hadn't exactly been like Gwendolyn when it came to getting off his butt and getting what he wanted. If he wasn't generating an income soon, he wasn't even going to be able to stay in his dark, cheap little room at the Garden of Allah.

They approached a three-story building that was the size of a city block and had broad windows overlooking the deserted street.

"Don't they lock the doors to this place at night?" Marcus asked.

"Indeed they do."

They took a short flight of steps to the front doors, where with a theatrical flourish worthy of Douglas Fairbanks, Benchley plucked out a metallic prong that looked like a jagged tuning fork. "Ask me no questions," he said, and hunched over the lock.

It took him less than a minute and they were inside. The elevator to the second floor spat them out into a huge open office that ran the entire length of the building. Benchley and Marcus switched on their flashlights and threw out strong beams of light that caught the dust floating on the air.

"Whoever does the filing around here redefines the word *meticulous,*" Benchley said.

"So you've been here before?"

"Oh, yes." Benchley's voice turned uncharacteristically dark.

Marcus hadn't yet asked if Benchley had his own reasons for coming to this specific building. He was usually housed in the writer's building, where Marcus once worked. He could see it through the windows, sitting in the moonlight like an abandoned temple. He longed to run over there and find his old office.

"What you are looking for," Benchley said, "is a cabinet marked *Internals.*" He pointed toward the south wall, where a line of twenty filing cabinets stood. "You'll see that it's all clearly labeled," he said. "Best of luck." He headed off into the dark recesses of the long room.

Marcus had spent weeks tracking down copies of *The Lion's Roar* but failed to turn up a single one. Most staff members thought of it as something to read while slurping down Mrs. Mayer's chicken soup in the commissary or to fill in time between camera setups. Those who did bring them home to the Garden of Allah threw them out as they would any other magazine.

He'd been lamenting this fact to Benchley and Dottie at a recent Garden of Allah celebration for the opening of *Snow White and the Seven Dwarfs,* Walt Disney's first full-length movie. Several of the Garden's current residents had slaved through fourteen-hour days to get it finished on time. Now that the nightmare was done with, the natural thing to do was get ridiculously drunk. When Benchley had offered to sneak him into the studios, Marcus wasn't sure if he would remember the offer, so he was very glad when Benchley came knocking on his door the following afternoon to make their nocturnal plans.

It didn't take long for Marcus to track down the cabinet that housed the back issues of *The Lion's Roar*. He found the ones covering the time when he was working on *The Star-Spangled Banner* with Scott and took them over to a nearby desk. He switched on the lamp and came to a page called *The Shoosh File* that featured a clever drawing of MGM stars lined up in a game of Chinese Whisper—Katharine Hepburn whispering to Clark Gable whispering to Garbo whispering to Spencer Tracy whispering to Jeanette MacDonald whispering to Mickey Rooney. At the end stood John Barrymore with his index finger pressed against his lips and a wide-eyed look of surprise on his face.

Marcus read though items about budding romances between staff members, rumored changes of personnel, lots of trivial stuff, mainly. But then he came to the third to last item:

Is working from home the new trend? A Big New Name on campus – currently in the employ of the Typewriter Department – has managed to finagle himself a nice pajama assignment. Sounds delightfully cushy, says the Shoosh File, so more power to you.

Marcus read the item three times. It wasn't hard to figure out who the Big New Name on campus was, but there was nothing in it connected to Marcus. He opened the next issue—August 1937—and flipped to the *Shoosh File*. He only had to read the first item.

Those of us who actually turn up at the studio to work wouldn't know anything about this, but apparently working from home makes for real thirsty work. We all know that drinking Coca-Cola is The Refreshing Thing To Do, but oh my heavens, it can't be THAT thirst-making! Word is buzzing around the studio that a certain pencil-pushing pajama peon downs the stuff by the ever-loving bucketload. And that would be just the dandiest, but is it just soda pop in them thar bottles? Why not spike it with pineapple? They can be sweet, but if you don't watch out, they can be so, so bitter. In that case, just pass the bourbon, please – oops! It's empty? That's enough to adler anyone's brain.

Marcus groaned when he saw his name instead of *addle*. He read the piece again and stopped at the bit about pineapples. Where had he read that before?

He headed down the long room and found Benchley hunched over another line of filing cabinets.

"I found what I was looking for," Marcus said.

"Uh-huh." Benchley was focused on the stack of papers in his hand.

"How about you?"

"Indeed I did." Benchley slammed the drawer shut and fixed Marcus with an intense stare, his increasingly furry eyebrows pulled together. "At our recent Snow White party, Mrs. Parker and I found ourselves talking to a chap from Paramount. Some sort of production designer."

"Wasn't he the one who concocted the Seven Dwarfs punch? It sure—"

"Did you know I am quite the expert on Queen Anne?"

Marcus had always been struck by the dichotomy between Benchley's alcohol-drenched informality and the long-standing interest he had in a British monarch. "Yes, but what does that have to do with a production designer from Paramount?"

"After a few whiskeyfied slugs, he starts prattling on about the devil of a time he's having planning out a new picture they're doing called *The Last Stuart*. Oh, really? says I, my ears all aprickle. *The Last Stuart*? This motion picture wouldn't be, by any chance, about the final monarch from the house of Stuart—I refer, of course, to Queen Anne? Yes, he replies, it would. Well, I just about hurled up my roasted peanuts on the spot."

"Why?"

"You know that yearly screenwriting competition MGM used to hold? I submitted a screenplay for consideration one year. It was about Queen Anne and it was called *The Final Stuart*. Best thing I ever wrote, which I now believe someone has stolen and sold to Paramount. I later realized that I no longer have a copy of my submission. This is where they keep the results of all their public competitions." He held the papers aloft, his eyes flaming with outrage. "And here it is. My original submission."

"What do you plan on doing with it?"

"I plan to sue, of course."

Marcus had entered that same competition and remembered the rules. "You may have written it, but as soon as you submitted it, it became MGM's property. Removing it from MGM grounds amounts to theft and therefore is quite possibly inadmissible in court."

Benchley contemplated the script in his hand as though it were a fragile little bird. "I fear you might be right, Adler. Thank you. I might never have thought of that." His rheumy eyes gaped at Marcus in a cloudy mix of admiration and gratitude as he stood up. "Let this be a lesson to you, young Adler. The big brass ring is much too shiny for the mere mortals of this loopy burg to resist. My advice to you is befriend whomever you like, drink with whomever you choose, sleep with whomever you prefer, but *trust nobody*. Bitter advice, I know, but there it is."

Marcus nodded soberly at Robert Benchley, but saw instead a vision of Hugo Marr's face looming in front of him like a mirage. The word *bitter* pinged inside his brain and Hugo's words rushed back to him. The day he went to work and found those notes plastered all over his office, Hugo had said, *Pineapples can be sweet, but if you don't watch out, they can be bitter.*

CHAPTER 33

Gwendolyn's hand held David O. Selznick's business card. It trembled as she listened to the Garden of Allah's operator dial Hillside-4059. She'd been waiting to make this call for more than a month, and finally the day had arrived. She heard someone pick up the line at the other end.

"Casting."

Sound confident! she told herself. Sound assured! "I'd like to speak with Mr. Selznick, please."

The guy at the other end pushed out a sound that sounded like a cross between a cough and a scoff. "What is this in reference to?"

"Mr. Selznick gave me his card and told me to call this number to arrange a screen test."

"For the role of Scarlett O'Hara."

"Yes, that's right."

The guy sighed. "And your name, sugar?"

"Gwendolyn Brick."

"Please hold." He was back on the line inside three seconds. "You ain't on the list."

"I don't know about any list, but you see—"

"To stop me from hanging up on you, you have to be on the list. And there's no Gwendolyn Brick, or anything close to it."

The guy hung up with a loud click.

Gwendolyn stared at the telephone in her hand. That wasn't how it was supposed to go. This time it was supposed to go *her* way. This time the guy was supposed to say, "Why yes, Miss Brick. We've been expecting your call. Shall we say Tuesday at eleven?"

Then she heard the Garden of Allah operator call her name. "Gwendolyn? Are you still on the line?"

"Yes, Manny, I'm here."

"I think your line got cut off."

"No, I didn't get cut off." She hung up. "Except at the knees." She tossed Selznick's card onto the telephone table and stared at it for a few moments. "Oh, my goodness!" She picked up the telephone again and asked Manny to dial the same number.

"Casting."

A different voice, but just as gruff.

"Hello, my name is Gwendolyn Brick. On Christmas Day I met Mr. Selznick and he gave me his card and told me to call this number to schedule a screen test for the role of Scarlett O'Hara."

"Didn't you just call?"

"Yes, but I didn't get a chance to explain—"

"And weren't you told that your name isn't on the list?"

"Yes, but I'm the Christmas Scarlett!" Saying it out loud like that sounded odd, even to Gwendolyn.

There was a pause. "You're the what?"

"The *Christmas* Scarlett."

There was another pause, then, "Oh! You're *that* Scarlett."

Relief flooded through Gwendolyn. She sank to the sofa. "Yes, that Scarlett."

"I'm glad we've got that sorted out. I'm hanging up now."

"But I just explained—"

"Listen, honey lamb, do you know how many phone calls we've had since that story got out? We get calls every week from girls who all sound just as sweet as you, claiming to be Selznick's Christmas doorstep girl."

"But I *am* Selznick's Christmas doorstep girl. I can prove it. All he needs to do is look at me for a second—he'll recognize me straightaway."

"And you think the dozens of girls who called before you and the dozens who'll call after you have said anything different?"

"But . . . I . . . I am—"

"Look, toots, just go home, will ya? Go home and marry that nice small-town Rhett Butler you left behind and leave us alone."

Gwendolyn dropped the telephone into its cradle and stared at it for a few moments. "The hell I will."

CHAPTER 34

Kathryn had always heard how red and blotchy Wilkerson's face got when he was really, *really* angry, but she'd never seen it for herself until the dreary February morning when he dumped a mock-up on her desk for a full-page ad announcing the premiere engagement at Grauman's Chinese Theater of MGM's new feature, *The Pistol from Pittsburgh.* Her boss had broken out in blots the color of overripe tomatoes. His forehead gleamed with sweat and he'd pulled his upper lip back off his teeth. Their eyes met but his were filled with such fury that she looked back down at the mock-up. It had a thick X slashed over it in red pencil.

"What's this?" she said.

Wilkerson didn't say anything, but instead stormed back toward his office. She let a few moments pass before she picked up the ad and followed him past Vera, whose eyes were filled with *Enter if you dare*. He'd planted himself at his window.

"So what's with this fat red X?" she asked him.

He kept his back to her. "Louis B. Mayer is a rat," he announced. "From this moment on, all MGM personnel are personae non goddamned grata. That means no advertising accepted and no positive language written about anything connected with Metro-Goldwyn-*Merde*." He turned around and started counting on his manicured fingers. "Not in editorials, not in letters to the publisher, in articles, in columns or reviews. And we're certainly not accepting—" he pointed to the mock-up in Kathryn's hands, "THAT!"

Kathryn laid the ad face down and walked away from his desk.

"Where the hell do you think you're going?" Wilkerson yelled.

Kathryn said nothing until she reached the door. "I'm going to give you some time to calm down."

She didn't return to her desk. Instead, she went to the chief accountant's office and closed the door.

"Ira," she said, "what's going on with the boss?"

Ira Chalke was exactly the sort of person any well-balanced businessman would want holding his company's purse strings. He was honest, thorough, loyal and discreet: the type probably driven half mad by someone like Billy Wilkerson. Ira took off his horn-rimmed reading glasses and considered his response.

"Any information Mr. Wilkerson wishes to share with you will come from him."

"Has he blown the payroll again?" Ira involuntarily blinked three or four times in rapid succession. "I know he's done it before," Kathryn said, "and I know the signs. You can trust me, Ira. It won't go any further than this room."

"Yes, the payroll is gone."

"Damnit!"

"And next month's payroll."

"For God's sake. What's it going to take for him to – "

"And next month's office rent."

"Tell me you're kidding."

"And next month's mortgage payment on his house."

Kathryn dropped herself into the chair in front of Ira's desk. "Santa Anita?"

"Poker."

"How much?"

"Two hundred and fifty grand."

Kathryn wilted. "In one poker match?"

"Two-day poker match over the long George Washington Birthday weekend."

"Do you know if Louis B. Mayer was at that poker game?"

Ira permitted himself a thin smile. "Who do you think he owes the two hundred fifty grand to?"

Kathryn shot up out of her seat. "Thank you, Ira."

She beelined back to her boss' office and closed the door behind her. "You want to tell me what's really going on with you and Mayer?" she said. "Or shall I give you my theory?"

The blotches on Wilkerson's face had subsided somewhat, but Kathryn could still see where they'd been. He said nothing.

"George Washington's birthday was a long weekend, so you probably spent it gambling. My guess is cards, and therefore probably poker, in which case Mayer was there and you lost a fortune to him. Am I close?"

When Wilkerson didn't answer right away, she slapped her hands down on the top of his desk for dramatic effect. "How can you be so reckless with other people's money?"

"What other people's money? That was my money, and I'll spend it any damn way I see fit."

"If you lost a hundred grand and still had another hundred grand to meet your responsibilities, then yes, you're free to spend that money any damned way you please. But that money you've gambled away? You were simply holding for your staff, your landlord, and your bank. And now Mayer's got some IOU for it and he's not about to cover your nut. That's what this MGM crap is all about, isn't it?"

Kathryn maintained her glare. She watched as the blotches resurfaced and went from crabmeat pink to paprika red.

He jumped to his feet. "THERE IS A CODE!"

"What code?"

"The code among high-stakes gamblers. There's business and then there's gambling. I play poker with Mayer and Hughes and Zanuck and Selznick. From nine to five we fight, we bicker, we agree, we disagree, we compete, we hate each other, we love each other, we hate each other again. But when we sit down at a poker table, none of that matters.

We're just a bunch of guys playing a bunch of cards for a bunch of money."

"Two hundred and fifty grand is hardly a bunch."

"God damnit, Massey, where did you hear that? You and your goddamned tipsters. The point is, come the dawn, whether you've had a bad night or a good one, the IOUs are signed and accepted in good faith. It's a gentlemen's agreement; all debts will be paid in due course."

It was time to douse this situation with some calming oil. She let a couple of silent moments crawl by, then she sat down. "How's about you tell me what happened."

"He said that he'd only accept cash, or otherwise he'd be happy to take payment in the form of partial ownership of the *Hollywood Reporter*."

The value of a paper like the *Reporter* was its independence from the long arms and deep pockets of the studios. For one of the movie moguls to own a piece of the *Reporter* was as unthinkable as Hearst owning it. "How much would two hundred and fifty thousand buy him?" Kathryn asked.

"I'll be damned if I'll let that rat bastard get his greedy hands on my paper."

"Can't you get one of your other poker buddies to cover you?"

"I went to Selznick, but Mayer told him if he lent me the money, he could kiss goodbye any hopes of getting Clark Gable for Rhett Butler."

"But what about Howard Hughes? Or Zanuck?"

"Zanuck came through for me."

Kathryn let out a long breath. "So you're covered? You can make payroll this month?"

"Yes, everybody will get paid. Don't you worry your pretty little head."

Kathryn crossed her arms and cocked her head to one side. "So what's with all the amateur dramatics?"

"I told you. There is a code. And Mayer didn't just break it, he jumped on it, smashed it to bits, and then he took out his tiny Jewish dick and he pissed all over it."

Kathryn tried hard not to smile. She loved it when Wilkerson treated her like one of the boys and didn't mind his language the way he did around the more ladylike girls in the office. She forgave him his "pretty little head" jab.

"It hardly seems like a serious threat when he knew very well Hughes or Zanuck or someone would cover your losses."

"That's not the way we play, and he knows it. This poker business was just the start. He's got something else on his mind, I can just feel it. Well, I can play hardball, too."

For God's sake, Kathryn thought. Look at you all. Together you run the most high-profile industry in the country, probably in the world, and you behave like little boys measuring each other's peckers.

"I want you to pen the first salvo," he told her.

"Don't you go pulling me into your little-man schoolyard fights."

Wilkerson narrowed his eyes. The blotches started to creep up his neck again. "As long I pay your salary, you'll do what I tell you to do."

Kathryn uncrossed her arms and leaned forward. "Keep blowing the payroll on cards and horses, and I guess I won't have to worry about that much longer."

"Don't push your luck with me, Massey. Not today."

Even if Wilkerson thought of her as one of the boys, calling her by her last name gave Kathryn pause. "What is it you want me to write, exactly?"

"I want two thousand words of the most vitriolic, condescending, scathing public flaying you can muster."

"Any particularly subject?"

"Yes." The mock-up of the ad for *The Pistol from Pittsburgh* still lay face down on the edge of his desk. He flipped it over. "I want you to denounce this picture as the worst piece of time-wasting trash that's ever been foisted on an unsuspecting public."

Kathryn's head reeled. MGM had a bunch of movies coming out that month, and *this* was the one he wanted to trash? She'd only just managed to get Joan Crawford a screen test with Selznick, and was turning the corner in restoring her own reputation. Not to mention the fact that the word was out: it was a terrific picture, and Melody Hope's performance was probably going to be one of the acting triumphs of the year. No, she decided, this was too much. "I can't do it."

"Yes. You. Can."

"You're right. I can do it. But I won't. There's a reason why MGM promoted *The Pistol from Pittsburg*h to their A-list. It's a wonderful picture with a strong message, and features a star-making role. These are people's careers. You can't assassinate lives because of the latest little sandbox squabble you're having."

"I won't be. You will. Midday. Two thousand words."

Kathryn stood up and leaned over her boss' desk. "Absolutely not."

Wilkerson jumped to his feet and shoved his face close enough for her to smell the tuna salad he had for lunch. "I swear to God, if you don't do what I say and write a scathing review of that goddamned picture, I will fire you."

Kathryn felt a jolt whip through her. Her eyes fell on the credenza behind Wilkerson's desk, where he had a pile of a dozen different magazines. On the top was a copy of *Life* with a color cover from that *Snow White and the Seven Dwarfs* movie everybody was still raving about. She wondered if Earl Hubbings' job offer was still open. Probably not; that was months ago. She eyed the magazines, thinking that every one of them had a Hollywood desk.

Wilkerson took her silence as capitulation. "Go back to your desk and write that piece."

Kathryn lifted her chin.

"I quit."

CHAPTER 35

Marcus planted himself at the front door of Hugo's new place in an apartment block off Melrose Avenue called *Le Parc de Belleville* and knocked three loud raps. He heard running feet; the door swung open so quickly he felt the back draft blow against his skin.

"I thought you were going to—oh! It's you." Hugo's hazel eyes were wide with surprise.

"Can I come in?" Marcus asked.

"You—ah—sure, yeah."

Hugo's front door opened onto a large square living room with a set of sofas facing each other over a long narrow coffee table. A baby grand piano sat in the corner with sheet music piled on it. A series of British pastoral paintings hung in a line along one wall and on the other was a mirror with a series of beveled edges.

Marcus turned to Hugo, ready to launch into the speech he'd been rehearsing. What exactly did Hugo hope to gain by spreading rumors around MGM that Marcus was getting Scott Fitzgerald drunk? Admittedly, he only had that crack in the *Lion's Roar* about pineapples to go on, but it was specific.

"Hugo, I have something I need to—"

Hugo's mouth hung open as though he'd been slapped.

"Are you all right?" Marcus asked.

Hugo squeezed his eyes shut as his face seemed to collapse. A high-pitched moan squeezed out of his mouth. "My uncle just called. Mom's been taken to County Hospital. They're not sure, but they think she's got a ruptured appendix. Uncle Ray said the ambulance guy used the words *gravely ill*. She may not see the morning." He pulled a handkerchief from his jacket pocket and pressed it against his eyes.

"What are you doing standing here?"

"My uncle has his own car. He only lives a couple of blocks away—he's on his way now to pick me up. When the doorbell rang I thought it was him." He erupted in a crying jag and blubbered something into his handkerchief.

Marcus found himself patting Hugo on the back. "Is there anything I can do for you?"

Listen to me, Marcus thought, I was here to chew him out and now I'm asking him how I can help.

Hugo calmed himself with a deep breath. "I can't let Uncle Ray see me like this. He's the most emotional man I've ever met. If I start, he'll turn into a puddle and probably run us off the road. You know what? My Aunt Julia is going to be calling. That's Mom's sister—I left a message at her work. Could you stay here and wait until she calls and tell her to meet us at the hospital?" The sound of a claxon in the street cut into the room. "That'll be him now. Thanks a million, Marcus. She should be calling any minute." Hugo ran out of the apartment.

Marcus scanned the room and realized how scrupulously maintained, cleaned, and arranged it all was. Nothing was out of place or the slightest bit grubby. The eight crystal brandy snifters lined up on the mahogany sideboard sparkled like snowflakes, and the black lacquer on the baby grand looked like it hadn't seen dust since before the Great War. Even the sheet music looked as though it had been straightened with a slide rule. He crossed the living room and stood at the doorway into the kitchen. Every inch of it shined like it had never been used.

He returned to the living room and started strumming his fingers against the edge of Hugo's piano, thinking about the blind item. He wondered if perhaps he'd inaccurately recalled Hugo's remark about pineapples. Maybe that's not what he'd said at all. Maybe it wasn't even Hugo who'd said it. But now that he was standing inside Hugo's apartment, so neat, so clean, so obsessively pristine, Marcus felt simultaneously unnerved and intrigued.

The temptation to go through Hugo's things was overwhelming. But how could he get away with it when Hugo was so freakishly neat? Perhaps just a surface search? But Marcus wasn't even sure what he was looking for. A copy of *The Lion's Roar*? A pineapple? No, no, this is ridiculous, he decided. Just because he's obsessively immaculate on the surface, it doesn't mean he's hiding anything.

He spotted a desk in the corner opposite the piano. It was a dark wood, polished to a high sheen. A typewriter sat dead center and several piles of paper sat on either side, each stacked as sharply as the sheet music on the piano. They were all screenplays, one an earlier draft of *Marie Antoinette,* which Hugo had worked on before it was passed to Scott Fitzgerald for a short while. Scott hadn't asked for Marcus' assistance on it; another missed opportunity.

Although Scott no longer paid Marcus to help him, they met sometimes for coffee or lunch at Schwab's. As far as Marcus could tell, Scott had staggered back onto the wagon. His romance with Sheilah was still blooming and he seemed to have gotten the hang of this screenwriting thing. Still, Marcus had seen enough dipsomaniacs around the Garden to know that he was just one drink away from disaster, so he did his best to veer Scott away from places like Musso and Frank's.

Marcus stood at the desk and stared at the drawers. The temptation grew too great and he carefully slid open each one. He wasn't sure if he was disappointed or relieved when he found nothing incriminating. They were filled with the usual stuff—pens, pencils, ticket stubs for *Modern Times, Snow White,* and *Tovarich.* There was a stack of subscription notices for an extraordinary number of magazines—*Time, Life, National Geographic, Reader's Digest, Colliers, Fortune, American Mercury, Atlantic Monthly, The American, Ladies Home Journal, Photoplay.*

Lately, Marcus had been able to eke out a living selling short stories to magazines. They paid well enough to keep his head above water, but only just. He longed to work at a studio again and create screenplays that would come to life up on the screen. In particular, the screen of the Bijou Theater in McKeesport, where his whole family would gape when they saw his name flash in front of them in four-foot letters. But studio jobs were hard to come by if everybody thought you were a career saboteur.

He found Hugo's bedroom equally neat. Four cushions were lined up on the bed, each with green stripes that deepened from light pistachio to dark avocado. Even the stripes on the slipcovers lay exactly parallel to each other. Marcus stepped into the room. None of the horizontal surfaces—not the bureau or the matching bedside tables or the bookshelf in the corner—held a speck of dust. The windows were so clear it was hard to see if there was any glass in them at all. This place, he thought, is The Apartment That Banished Dust.

He opened the wardrobe to find Hugo's suits, shirts, and ties arranged according to color, from blacks and dark blues on the left all the way through the spectrum to pale yellows and whites at the far right. Each shirt, starched like a nun's habit, was almost but not quite touching its neighbor.

Marcus felt like he was wandering through a museum.

He opened the second set of doors in the wardrobe and found sweaters, socks, and underwear fastidiously arranged on shelves. On the right-hand side, twelve pairs of Hugo's shoes were lined up, freshly shined and smelling of boot polish.

A box at the bottom caught Marcus' eye. It was an ordinary shoe box from the May Company department store with the word *MAIL* meticulously lettered across the front. He'd picked it up to take a closer look when the telephone rang. The jarring noise gave Marcus such a fright that the box leapt from his hands and fell to the floor. A collection of letters spilled out onto the carpet.

"Damnit! Damnit! Damnit! Damnit! *Damnit!*"

Marcus dashed back into the living room and answered the phone. He introduced himself to Hugo's aunt and explained the emergency, then returned to the mess of letters scattered across the floor.

"You were probably arranged in some sort of very specific order, weren't you?" Marcus asked the letters. "Christ only knows what that may have been."

He got down on all fours and started to collect them. Had Hugo arranged them chronologically? Was the oldest at the front, or the most recent? Had Hugo grouped the letters together according to who sent them? He decided to go with the most obsessive ordering, so he started to arrange them according to sender and in chronological order.

But as he did, he came across an address that sounded familiar—5609 Valley Oak Drive. He looked around. There were more envelopes from this same address. When the realization came, it hit him in such a rush it almost hurt. Why was Hugo getting letters from Ramon Novarro?

That name, that blasted name—Ramon Novarro—never failed to pitch Marcus' insides like a butter churn. Ever since that odd encounter at the Biltmore, he'd longed to speak with Ramon again but could never figure out the right approach. What should he do? Place a telephone call? Send a telegram? Write a letter? Just turn up at his front door? It was so easy when it was a guy and a girl. Society had rules about who calls on who, and how. But a guy and another guy? There was nothing in Emily Post about that. So in the end, he fell victim to his own indecision and fears, and did nothing. And now it looked as though someone had jumped in ahead of him. And not just any someone.

He didn't begrudge Hugo for landing *The Pistol from Pittsburgh*. He was touched, flattered even, when Hugo came to him for advice with the screenplay. Sure, Hugo's request made him prickle with jealousy that later fermented into resentment, which later still had fueled an all-night bourbon marathon, but it wasn't Hugo's fault he'd been handed Marcus' pet project. The important thing, Gwendolyn reminded him, was that Nellie Bly was getting the studio treatment.

Had Hugo started seeing Ramon? The thought of it tugged painfully at Marcus' heart.

He picked through the letters and eventually found over a dozen dating back a number of years; the earliest one was postmarked Christmas 1933. Marcus sat with his back against Hugo's bed and stared at the letters in his hands. He desperately wanted to read them—so why did he suddenly want to trust Hugo?

There was no reason Ramon and Hugo couldn't be friends. But if they were just friends, why didn't Marcus even know they knew each other?

He couldn't possibly read through any of them. What a gross invasion of privacy that would be.

Then Marcus thought of the blind item in *The Lion's Roar*.

"Screw you," he muttered, and opened the first envelope.

CHAPTER 36

Wilkerson's bitter words still stung Kathryn's ears.

His call had come after midnight on the first day of torrential rain that deluged L.A. for three continuous days. People at *Life* were starting to joke about building an ark—but this time around, they'd only let the photogenic animals on board, like peacocks and swans, and not bother with aardvarks and warthogs.

When the telephone rang so late at night, she jumped out of bed and ran into the living room. Her heart pounded. Had somebody died in the floods?

"Hello?"

"You, Kathryn Massey, are an ungrateful little worm."

Wilkerson's voice was hoarse and croaky, which meant he was drunk. "I took a chance on you when you had no right to expect a job with the *Reporter*—or any publication. And this is how you repay me? You get a job with *Life* magazine? Don't ever darken my doorstep again."

And now she sat at her new teak desk in the West Coast headquarters of *Life*, with her substantial pay raise and her generous expense account and her leisurely deadlines, watching the rain pound against the windows and wishing it would rain hard enough to drown out Wilkerson's voice.

What I need, she decided, is a juicy story. Some sort of scoop that will help me make a splash.

And she needed it now, because that afternoon there was one of those bi-weekly editorial meetings they were addicted to around there. Wilkerson didn't need a committee or a show of hands.

They were a nice enough bunch at *Life,* but meeting a weekly deadline instead of a daily one, they were inclined to work at a more casual pace. Kathryn enjoyed the escape from a relentless clock . . . for the first week. But by the third week she was starting to see them as a bunch of blissfully ignorant lazybones.

She decided it was time to go fishing, and started flipping through her file of business cards. She stopped when she came to Michael van der Ploeg, her contact at the Academy. She hadn't spoken to him in ages. She dialed his number. "Hello, Michael, sweetie, it's Kathryn."

"Is it true?" Michael asked. "*Life* magazine?"

"Yes, it is, and that's quite a coincidence because that was the exact question I was going to ask you. Is it true-oo?" she said in a singsong voice. "Because I hear a ru-mor! From a very dependable sour-rce!"

"Dang it, Kathryn," Michael said, "I swear you must have ESP. I've only just read the memo myself."

Oh God, Kathryn thought, how I do love to go fishing. She grabbed a pen. "You know me, I'm a stickler for the details. Go on, read your memo to me, sweetie."

* * *

As far as Kathryn could tell, Earl Hubbings wasn't the type to show surprise. He hadn't been surprised when she'd called him twelve months late to see if the Hollywood correspondent job was still on the table. He'd acted like it was the most natural thing in the world when she called on the same day his correspondent announced her pregnancy and her resignation. And he wasn't fazed when Kathryn offered to open the editorial meeting that morning.

"I have some exciting news!" she announced to the staff. "I've just gotten off the phone with my contact at the Academy."

"Which academy is that?" Earl asked.

Kathryn blinked at him. "The Academy of Motion Picture Arts and Sciences. The ones who present the Oscars. My contact just told me they're introducing a new rule at their awards ceremony this year. You know how a week before the presentation dinner, the Academy publishes the names of the winners? Well, from now on, they won't be announcing the winners beforehand. They're not telling a soul!"

She looked around the conference table to find herself walled in by *So what?* faces. "I know I've already submitted my lead story, but I can do a quick rewrite."

Earl waved his hand dismissively. "That won't be necessary. Next week is soon enough for that sort of thing."

"But this changes everything!" Kathryn persisted. "The whole nature of the ceremony! Oscar ceremonies have gotten lifeless because the only people who show up are the ones who know they're going to win. But now, if people want to collect their Oscars, they'll have to turn up to the ceremony in person. That means every big name in Hollywood is going to attend. This is about as big as it gets."

Nobody said a word, let alone expressed any sort of excitement. Don't you silly people get it? she thought.

"You do realize, don't you," Earl said, "that we're currently in flood crisis? Did you not see this morning's *L.A. Times*? It hasn't rained this hard in Los Angeles since the 1880s. The last time it rained like this, it caused the river to *change its course*. The Army Corps of Engineers just told me that they're gathering together three million bags of concrete. Once this abominable rain stops, they're going to concrete the entire Los Angeles river. The whole thing. Covered over with concrete. But that's not the immediate issue. By eleven this morning, all three railway lines into L.A. were severed at various points around the county. There is currently no way in or out of this city. Now, weigh all this against the news that the Oscars will be kept secret until the night of a ceremony wherein a bunch of overgrown children who play dress-up for a living gather together in overpriced outfits for the sole purpose of slapping each other on the back before inserting a steak knife for sleeping with each other's wives. You tell me: Which story should lead the West Coast?"

For a few long moments, the only sound in the room was the rain pounding against the glass. Kathryn stared at the notepad in front of her until she heard her boss say her name.

"Kathryn, your focus is Hollywood," he said, then pointed a finger at her. "*Your* focus is Hollywood. But it's just one corner of a much larger, much more diverse canvas than perhaps you're used to dealing with. This isn't the *Hollywood Reporter*, Kathryn. This is *Life*."

CHAPTER 37

Gwendolyn found herself staring at the telephone. Again. Still.

She'd been doing it all summer, clinging to the last vestiges of hope that Selznick's office might call, but the day came when Kathryn told her he'd given Paulette Goddard an exclusive contract.

Paulette had been the frontrunner for Scarlett for quite a while, so it really wasn't much of a surprise, but it still took Gwendolyn a while to recover. She was sure she was right for the role. Born for it! It felt like getting slugged in the face with a shovel.

But when it dawned on her after a couple of months that there'd been no announcement of Paulette winning the role, her hopes began to rise again. Kathryn told her that some British actress was being considered for Scarlett, but Gwendolyn put no stock in that. Still, as the months skipped past, she found it harder and harder to keep her hopes from evaporating. She wasn't normally given to the blues, but this business was getting her down something awful.

Gwendolyn pulled her eyes from the telephone and got to her feet. Tonight was Halloween, and the Cocoanut Grove had a big night all planned. Every table in the place was booked; they'd all be buying up every cigarette in the place. She looked at her reflection in the bathroom mirror. Her puffy eyes stared back at her as if to say, You're really not up for this, are you?

She put on lipstick, but it just looked drab. "Are you sure you want to miss out on all those tips?" she asked herself, and found she couldn't dredge up two hoots of enthusiasm.

She went back to Kathryn's telephone and got the operator to dial a number.

"Cocoanut Grove main bar, this is Chuck."

"Chuck, it's me."

"Hi th—oh, God," said Chuck. "You're not coming in, are you?"

Good old Chuckie. That man could read her like a kid's picture book. "I'm just not up for it."

"You okay? You sound morbid."

"I'm having a real off night. Kathryn's at some big party *Life* is throwing at the Bel Air Country Club so I've got the place to myself. I'm going to write to my brother and turn in early."

Gwendolyn wished her friend a night full of big tippers and hung up.

She'd bought her brother a box of Bavarian chocolate bars at Schwab's after he complained about the terrible food on the naval base, and he wrote back that they were a huge hit. They'd turned into a form of currency over there and had made him rich. Monty always seemed so happy with his decision to join the navy; she envied him that.

She pulled out a pad and pen, sat herself down at the dining table with a cup of coffee and one of the chocolate bars—"Sorry, Monty, but my need is greater than yours right now"—and started her letter. She preferred to jump on the couch and pour out her disappointments to him face to face, but Guam was more than a streetcar ride away.

She leaned over to the edge of the table and turned on the Bakelite radio. The final verse of "Stardust" flowed out and she sang along, absently twirling the fountain pen around her fingers. Then a smooth-voiced emcee announced that she'd been listening to Señor Raquello and his orchestra, live at the Meridian Room in the Hotel Park Plaza in downtown New York. "And now here's another classic for the ages: 'With a Song in my Heart.'"

Gwendolyn was almost at the bottom of the page when her attention was pulled to the radio by a male voice, different from the silky-throated host's, deeper but more strained.

"Ladies and gentlemen, I have a grave announcement to make. Incredible as it may seem, both the observations of science and the evidence of our eyes lead to the inescapable assumption that those strange beings who landed in the Jersey farmlands tonight are the vanguard of an invading army from the planet Mars.

"The battle which took place tonight at Grover's Mill has ended in one of the most startling defeats ever suffered by an army in modern times; seven thousand men armed with rifles and machine guns pitted against a single fighting machine of the invaders from Mars. One hundred and twenty known survivors. The rest strewn over the battle area from Grover's Mill to Plainsboro, crushed and trampled to death under the metal feet of the monster, or burned to cinders by its heat ray. The monster is now in control of the middle section of New Jersey and has effectively cut the state through its center. Communication lines are down from Pennsylvania to the Atlantic Ocean."

Gwendolyn pressed her hands to her mouth and stared at the radio. What on Earth? She turned up the volume.

"Railroad tracks are torn and service from New York to Philadelphia discontinued, except routing some of the trains through Allentown and Phoenixville. Highways to the north, south, and west are clogged with frantic human traffic. Police and army reserves are unable to control the mad flight. By morning the fugitives will have swelled Philadelphia, Camden, and Trenton, it is estimated, to twice their normal population. Martial law prevails throughout New Jersey and eastern Pennsylvania. At this time we take you to Washington for a special broadcast on the National Emergency."

Gwendolyn ventured a peek out the window across the pool. Everything appeared to be quiet and still. Too quiet and still. This was Halloween night at the Garden of Allah—where was everybody? The next voice that shot out of the radio sounded so desperate it made Gwendolyn spin around in fright.

"I'm speaking from the roof of the Broadcasting Building, New York City. The bells you hear are ringing to warn the people to evacuate the city as the Martians approach. Estimated in the last two hours three million people have moved out along the roads to the north.

"Hutchison River Parkway still kept open for motor traffic. Avoid bridges to Long Island . . . hopelessly jammed. All communication with Jersey shore closed ten minutes ago. No more defenses. Our army is . . . wiped out . . . artillery, air force, everything wiped out.

"This may be the last broadcast. We'll stay here to the end."

Gwendolyn shot out the front door of her villa, down the stairs and to the pool area. It was so deserted, so deathly quiet.

She called out, "HELLO! HEL-LOOO . . .?" just as a police siren erupted on Sunset Boulevard. She got no response.

Basement! Yes, the Garden of Allah had a basement. Gwendolyn wondered if that was where everyone was hiding. But where was it? And why hadn't anybody told her?

She ran up the path into the main house. "Manny? Ben? Are you there?" But the foyer was deserted. "Anyone?"

She dashed into the reading lounge, a long, sofa-filled room that used to be Alla's living room during the peak of her career, but she found it empty, too.

She suddenly thought of Alla sitting alone in her villa, sipping her orange blossom tea with Marcus. Why hadn't Marcus come to check on her?

She flew out the back doors and threw herself down the gravel path and slammed into something. She screamed and pushed against it as hard as she could.

The figure of a man lay sprawled on the grass. The moon wasn't out so she couldn't see who it was, but she was fairly sure he wasn't an alien.

"What the hell's the matter with you?"

Gwendolyn pressed her hands against her chest. "I'm so terribly sorry!" She reached out to help him to his feet.

"Have you heard what's going on? New Jersey and New York – they've been invaded!"

"You're not talking about the Martians, are you?" the guy asked, brushing grass and leaves from his elbows.

"YES!" she croaked. "You heard it too? Have you heard anything more? It sounds like they're landing everywhere!"

"You can't be serious," the guy responded.

"I don't think it gets any more serious than – "

The complete lack of alarm in the man's voice stopped Gwendolyn cold.

"Oh, you precious thing," he said with a laugh in his voice. From what Gwendolyn could see, he looked like an older guy, in his fifties perhaps, his hair thinning. "It's a radio play."

"A what?"

"You've been listening to Mercury Theater. On CBS, right?"

"I just fiddled with the dial until I found some music I liked."

"Ever heard of Orson Welles?"

"Should I have?"

"He's one of those wunderkind actor-director-writer types. Good at everything. You've been listening to his radio play version of H.G. Wells' *The War of the Worlds*. A pretty good adaptation, too, from what I've heard."

Relief washed over Gwendolyn, quickly followed by a jug of ice-cold embarrassment. She stared at the guy and wondered open-mouthed how she could have been so gullible. Really, she scolded herself, invaded by Martians indeed. She blushed deeply. "I feel so silly now. I was at home alone . . ."

"Don't feel too bad," he said. "They're doing a very convincing job. It all sounds very, very real. You could probably do with a drink. Brandy's marvelous for calming the nerves."

"I don't drink much," Gwendolyn said, but she heard her voice shake.

He smiled and pointed down the path toward a villa on the west side of the garden. They started toward it. He went to open the front door when he stopped and offered his hand. "I'm Scott Fitzgerald."

"Oh, you are? The writer that Marcus worked with? *The Star-Spangled Banner*, right?"

He nodded and switched on a lamp. An unopened bottle of Hennessy brandy stood on top of the low bookshelf just inside the door. He poured a couple of shots into each glass and handed her one. He motioned for her to sit down on the sofa and he took the easy chair.

She watched him take a sip and wished Marcus was there to see it. He gave himself such grief over what happened that day he turned up late to Scott's villa. She took a couple of sips of brandy and let its warmth seep through her. She hated to admit it, but she did feel better. "I'm sorry," she said, "but I've never read anything of yours. Although I did try one of them. *Gentle Goes the Light* . . .?"

"*Tender is the Night*, perhaps?"

Gwendolyn blushed again. Fancy making such a faux pas in front of an author like Scott Fitzgerald. She ventured another sip. Whatever must he think of her? "You're dating Sheilah Graham, aren't you?"

He nodded.

"How's that working out?"

"The woman is a saint, as far as I'm concerned," he replied.

"And what are you working on now? Marcus did tell me." Gwendolyn remembered the disappointment in Marcus' voice when he'd read it out over Sunday coffee and bagels one morning at Schwab's. How dearly he'd loved to have worked on something like—"Oh! *Marie Antoinette,* isn't it?"

"That was earlier this year."

"And now?"

"Something very exciting," Scott said, and motioned to refill her brandy. She shook her head—this brandy stuff didn't need long to take effect.

"Last month Selznick approached me to take a swing at *Gone with the Wind*."

Gwendolyn's mouth popped open and she felt her head spin just a little. "That's . . . that's . . . Lord have mercy, what is that like?"

"I have to admit, I was surprised at being asked. *Star-Spangled Banner* worked out well, but I suspect that's largely due to your pal Marcus. Overall, though, I've not exactly set Hollywood on fire with my screen work. I was flattered to be considered."

He pointed to Gwendolyn's left, at a desk underneath a window that looked out onto the ghostly branches of a large manzanita bush. Next to the typewriter were several notepads and piles of paper, and a copy of *Gone with the Wind* with dozens of paper bookmarks sticking out of it.

Gwendolyn slid off the sofa and approached the desk. She picked up a legal pad and ran a finger down his notes. Each line had a page number and a one-sentence summary of what happened on that page. He joined her at the desk. "There's a lot to absorb," he admitted, "but it's very exciting."

"Do you know if they've cast Scarlett yet?" she asked.

Scott laughed. "They don't exactly keep me abreast of everything, but the last time I spoke to George Cukor, they'd narrowed it down to Paulette Goddard, Doris Jordan, Joan Bennett, and Katharine Hepburn."

"You heard of this Vivien Leigh girl? The one from England?"

Scott made the same scoffing sound she'd heard everybody else make when this British nobody came up. Coming from an insider like Scott, though, it made her heart beat just a little bit faster. One less contender for the role. "Selznick would be lynched if he cast someone like that as Scarlett. But if you ask me, I don't think any of those four girls should get it. It has to be an unknown."

Gwendolyn put down the notepad. "Have you heard of the Christmas Scarlett?"

Scott laughed. "Everyone at the Selznick studio has heard that story. I'm not sure I believe it, but you have to admire a girl with that much spunk."

Gwendolyn said, "You're looking at her. Christmas Scarlett. It was me!"

It was hard to read the look that descended onto Scott's face, but it looked to Gwendolyn like he was trying to think of the telephone number for the insane asylum.

"That's one story I'd love to hear," he said gently.

By the time Gwendolyn was done with her story, Scott was looking at her in a whole new way. No longer was she just a silly, gullible girl taken in by some fake radio Martian invasion.

"That's remarkable," he said when she'd finished. "So after all that, how did the screen test go?"

Gwendolyn put her brandy glass down on the coffee table with a clunk. "It didn't. I've called his office four times, and even tried to talk my way into the studio. Gracious, Mr. Fitzgerald, but you have no idea how hard it is to get in to see Mr. Selznick when you're not a world-famous writer."

Scott smiled. "But I am a world-famous writer."

"And bully for you. But for the rest of us, Selznick may as well be the king of England."

Scott placed his empty brandy glass next to hers. "I think you've missed my point. I am a world-famous writer who happens to have a script conference scheduled with your elusive Mr. Selznick later this week. I shall be with him at least three or four hours. I am positive that at some point I'll find a slot in the conversation in which I can mention the Christmas Scarlett."

CHAPTER 38

The building that fronted Washington Boulevard looked just as Kathryn pictured Tara: a huge white colonial-style home with seven tall columns guarding the front porch. Tonight, however, the front gates of Selznick International Studios resembled a prison. A squad of security men armed with rifles was patrolling the perimeter as though President Roosevelt himself were expected any minute.

Kathryn's photographer, a wiry chain-smoker called Lenny Schultz, pulled his rattling Buick into the driveway. "Christ almighty, it's just a damned movie."

Kathryn didn't normally care much for been-everywhere-seen-everything-nothing-surprises-me-anymore ex-war-photographer types like Lenny, but there was no denying that the guy had a keen eye. He'd recently taken a shot of Howard Hughes in Paris just after Hughes cut Lindbergh's time in half. He had one foot in the cabin and one on the ladder, and had thrown his long arms high into the air in a rare display of public exhilaration. Kathryn admired Schultz's work enormously.

"It's not just any old damn movie," she told him. "This is the first night of photography for *Gone with the Wind.*"

"Big whoop-de-doo."

"This could well be the movie of the year," Kathryn insisted. "Perhaps even of the decade. We're lucky we were invited. We get to see Selznick burn down Atlanta!" The fact that she got the invitation from Selznick International at all implied that the producer had forgiven Kathryn her scoop. And that's not even the half of it, she thought.

Last month, she'd been sent across the Mexican border to the Agua Caliente racetrack. She didn't particularly want to go—it wasn't out of the question that she might bump into Billy Wilkerson—but nobody else would, even though Seabiscuit himself was racing for the Agua Caliente Cup.

As the horses approached the starting line, Kathryn had surveyed the crowd in search of movie stars. She couldn't believe it when the very first person she trained her binoculars on was Roy Quinn. Her heart lurched and she couldn't pull her binoculars away from him. She never had left a message for him at that fencing academy. The mutual attraction was palpable, but their previous encounters had led to an unwanted pregnancy—not to mention an abortion—*and* he was married. No, no, she'd decided, those sleeping dogs were better left alone.

As the most famous racehorse in the Americas pounded across the finish line, her eyes hadn't been on the stallion, but on Roy. She smiled as she watched him and his buddies jump up and down like a bunch of schoolgirls who'd just seen Tyrone Power in the flesh.

When she and Lenny went down after the race to claim their winnings, Roy and his friends were in the line next to hers. He never saw her, but she drew close enough to hear that he was doing stunt work for Selznick. One of them made a joke about Roy facing the fires of Atlanta next month, and she assumed he was going there on location. But when she received an invitation to watch the crew of *Gone with the Wind* incinerate old sets from RKO productions that included *King Kong* and Marlene Dietrich's *The Garden of Allah*, the conversation back at Agua Caliente suddenly made sense.

A security officer directed Lenny to park his car in a makeshift lot at one end of an open field. About a third of the way down they passed a large viewing platform that had been constructed at a safe distance from the massive pile of discarded wooden movie sets. A trio of enormous Technicolor cameras faced what was soon going to be Atlanta aflame. Scattered around the platform were knots of people in overcoats and winter hats. The late November air was cooling and Kathryn wondered if she'd dressed warmly enough. She looked around but couldn't see Roy anywhere.

Lenny lit up a cigarette. "Who're you looking for?"

"Someone gave me the name of Roy Quinn to ask about being a stunt man with tonight's filming. You know, to get a different point of view."

Lenny cocked an eyebrow in the direction of a short figure with glasses, a prominent nose, and an overcoat, standing off by himself on the other side of the platform. "He might know."

It was George Cukor. She greeted him with a kiss and asked if he knew any of the stunt doubles working on the picture.

"No," George replied. "I've been drafted to help with prepping that *Wizard of Oz* picture. At any rate, this is all second-unit stuff so I've had nothing to do with any of it. How's *Life*?"

Kathryn hated it when people asked this question, and people asked it all the time. They all expected her to say, "It's *Life* magazine! It's wonderful! How could it not be?" But in truth, she wasn't very happy. The extra money and the national readership were terrific. And now that she was no longer in direct competition with Louella Parsons, relations with her mother had softened. Kathryn hoped they were entering a new phase in their relationship; a warmer, fuzzier one, in which they could get through an entire afternoon without turning into Tasmanian devils.

For that matter, relations between Kathryn and Louella appeared to have thawed as well. At a gathering to witness the very first coast-to-coast radio broadcast, Louella offered Kathryn a gentle nod. At the memorial concert for George Gershwin at the Hollywood Bowl, she'd even said hello.

Yes, all of this was lovely, but somehow it didn't make up for the thrill of writing for a daily paper. Goddamnit it, she missed the volcanic explosions and unpredictable feuding that went with working for someone like Billy Wilkerson.

"It's been seven months now. Enough time to feel like home," she told George. It was her standard response.

George eyed a tall gentleman climbing onto the platform, trailed by a phalanx of assistants. He muttered a quick "You'll have to excuse me, dear," and slipped away. The tall man in the thick woolen overcoat stepped into the light: it was Selznick himself. He was every bit as tall as Gwendolyn had described, and his hair was blacker than the night sky above them. He positioned himself behind one of the enormous Technicolor cameras and slowly nodded his head.

After some last-minute double checks, an assistant held up a megaphone. "And . . . ACTION!" A zigzag of personnel spread out across the field gave a series of waves, and then the mountain of old sets erupted in a wall of fire. The heat blew across them, prickling Kathryn's face. A tall chap in a white suit sat at the front of a horse and cart. He raised his whip and snapped off a crack that cut the air. The horse sprang into action and they passed the flaming sets into an area where stagehands emptied a huge tub of flaming branches on him. The horse reared up and nearly toppled the buggy. The guy leapt out and rushed to the front of the horse and grabbed the reins. He wrapped a shawl around the terrified horse's head and pulled it along toward the tower of blazing sets.

The director of photography yelled, "Cut," and Kathryn relaxed. She held a hand to her chest as she panted to get some air.

"You all right?" George asked. She hadn't noticed him rejoin her.

"Where did you get to?" Kathryn asked. "I'd have thought you'd want to witness this front and center."

"David and I had a knock-down drag-out fight this morning over scheduling and budget. I didn't want to be a distraction to him for his big moment. But don't worry, I saw it all from down there in front of the platform. Thrilling, wasn't it?"

Kathryn nodded. "I can't wait to see it on the screen. I can't imagine what must be going through that stunt double's head right now."

"He's probably thinking about his big fat danger bonus," George replied. "Your photographer tells me you were asking about Roy Quinn? He's Clark Gable's stand-in tonight. You watched him go through his paces just now."

Kathryn wanted to yelp. "That was Roy? With the flaming sets and the frightened horse?"

Before George could reply, the director of photography lifted his megaphone and yelled, "Okay and quiet, please. Get that horse into place. We're doing the big one now, people. Detonators ready?"

Detonators? "Hold my hand?" she asked George.

George grabbed her left hand and pressed it between his. They felt warm and firm.

"Detonators on the count of three," the guy boomed into his megaphone. "One . . . two . . . *THREE.*"

Four distinct explosions filled the air and the mountain of tinder-dry sets, with the village gates from *King Kong* piled in the center, exploded one after the other. Within seconds they were a flaming wall of yellow and orange. The heat smothered Kathryn's face. Roy pulled the horse and buggy along the wall of fire not more than twenty feet in front of it all. She heard a low rumbling and the sets begin to tremble.

The director barked "FIVE!" into the megaphone; another explosion tore through the air. The column of heat and smoke wobbled and lurched. Roy was only halfway past the inferno when it started to cave in on itself. The sound of the collapsing sets filled the night as they crashed to the ground. Cinders and flaming branches shot out in all directions, smoke billowed in thick clouds, and the smell of burning wood enveloped them. The left-hand side started to collapse, and the mountain of fire buckled and avalanched to the left. Roy disappeared into a cloud of smoke and embers.

Someone yelled, "CUT!" Then, "Looks good, boss."

Kathryn let out her breath and looked over toward Selznick. He stood facing a man Kathryn hadn't seen before. He was shorter than Selznick, with a rounder face and thinner hair.

"Hey! Genius!" the shorter man was saying. He was holding a woman's hand.

"Who's that guy with Selznick?" Kathryn asked George.

"That's his brother Myron, the agent. Too powerful for his own good, if you ask me. Unless he represents you, of course."

"And who's that with him?"

The bright glow of the burning sets lit up the woman facing Selznick. She had a narrow face, pointed chin, and dark hair down to her shoulders. Her eyes, piercing and intense, almost catlike, held Selznick's. She was smiling quietly, not too confidently, but not a fake, actressy sort of smile, either.

A strong wind blew up, strong enough to open the woman's mink coat and reveal a slight frame draped in beige silk. Her dress was gathered tightly at her waist, which couldn't have been much more than twenty inches around. "Good evening, Mr. Selznick," she said.

"David," said Myron Selznick. "I want you to meet your Scarlett O'Hara. This is Miss Vivien Leigh."

Good God, Kathryn thought, she's perfect. She turned to Lenny. Out of the side of her mouth, she murmured, "Get a photo of them. Quick, before—"

"Already taken six. Enough for—"

Suddenly an almighty CRACK! shot through them.

"What the hell was that?" said someone on the ground below the platform.

Another voice answered. "The King Kong gate? I don't like the way that came down. It wasn't supposed to fall to the left like that."

A second crack, this one even louder, filled the night air, then a stack of flaming sets started tumbling toward the ground.

Kathryn peered over the edge of the platform and saw a stagehand cup his hands to his mouth. "Where's the stuntman with the horse? Is he clear?"

Several men ran toward the burning sets. By the light of the flames, she could see the wagon was turned over on its side and the horse struggling to get up from its knees. It started to neigh a plaintive, high-pitched shriek. Somebody yelled, "GET BLANKETS! THIS GUY NEEDS BLANKETS!"

Stagehands started running down the slope but Kathryn could see no sign of Roy in his white Rhett Butler suit.

"Quick!" someone yelled. "Get that ambulance down here!"

Kathryn took the rear steps two at a time, rushing down the gentle slope toward the flames. She heard a voice call out, "Hey, lady, you can't go there!" but she ignored it.

A hefty brute of a guy stepped in her path and grabbed her by the shoulders. "I can't let you get any closer."

"But Roy!" she cried out. She tried to wrench herself free, but she was no match for his strength. "I need to know Roy is okay!"

CHAPTER 39

The sound of the doorknocker wedged itself into Gwendolyn's dream and transmogrified into a woodpecker the size of a beaver with a yard-long beak bashing its way into the villa while Gwendolyn tried to slip out the bathroom window. She was more than halfway out when her hand slipped and she fell with a scream.

"Miss Brick! Miss Brick!" The knocking persisted. "Are you there?"

Gwendolyn looked at her clock. It wasn't even nine o'clock; she hadn't been asleep for four hours.

"Who is it?" she called out.

"It's Manny, from the front desk."

Gwendolyn pushed back the bedcovers with her legs and pulled on her bathrobe. Bleary, she tottered over to the front door. "Are we on fire?"

"No," Manny replied. "There is a chauffeur at the front desk. Says he's here to collect you."

"Collect me for what?"

The sound of running footsteps drew Gwendolyn's attention past Manny to the sight of Scott Fitzgerald racing toward her. He dashed up the stairs. "I got it for you!" he told her breathlessly. "That screen test for Scarlett. They said yes!"

"I think it's right now," Manny said. "I've seen enough studio cars parked out front to know one when I see one."

More running footsteps. "Gwennie! Gwennie!" Alice turned the corner in the path that wound around from the parking lot and bounded up the stairs. "Look at you! The biggest break of your life and you're not even dressed. I assume that's Selznick's car out front?"

"Why does everyone know about this but me?" Gwendolyn asked.

"I just bumped into a pal of mine at Schwab's," Alice said. "He's a second assistant director at Selznick. Started telling me all about how they finally tracked down the girl who landed on Selznick's front door on Christmas Day. So I rushed right over." She turned to Manny. "Tell the driver Miss Brick will only be a couple of minutes," then pushed past Scott and shooed Gwendolyn inside.

Scott called out, "Let me know if I can help!" but Alice closed the door in his face.

"Okay," she said in a take-charge voice. "Wardrobe. Something real quick and eye-catching." She threw open the doors to Gwendolyn's closet and flung outfit after outfit onto the bed like sloughed-off snakeskins. "Too conservative . . . too starchy . . . too hooker . . . too school marm . . ."

She seized a dress Gwendolyn didn't particularly care for. It was a deep mauve with pencil-thin plum lines etched through it. It looked good when she wore her hair dark, but now that she'd returned to her natural blonde, the colors clashed in the worst way. "Got shoes to go with this?"

Gwendolyn hesitated.

Alice said, "We have one minute."

Gwendolyn yanked off her robe and pulled on the dress. If they'd had a little more time, or if she was a little less dazed, she'd have stopped to argue that there was surely a better outfit to turn up in, but she had neither option at her disposal, so she did what she was told.

Alice pulled out a pair of black leather shoes and said, "These'll have to do." In a blur, she grabbed a handbag, a hairbrush, and a hand mirror, and pushed Gwendolyn out the door before she could stop to draw breath.

* * *

When the car pulled into the Selznick lot, the driver delivered Gwendolyn and Alice to a two-story building not too far from a large open field with a wooden platform erected conspicuously in the middle. He pointed them toward a door marked *TESTING*. Inside, they found a striking brunette about Gwendolyn's age with several phones lined up in front of her. "Gwendolyn Brick?" she asked. "We were starting to get worried."

The girl led them down a short corridor and into a room with costumes, wigs, and props lined up along one wall. "I'm going to alert the technical crew. We'll be ready to start in fifteen minutes." She lifted up a hoop skirt in dark jade green that was dotted with tiny pink roses and held together at the waist with a pink satin sash. "I'd pick this one if I were you. It's the prettiest." She pointed to a cream-colored chemise and instructed Gwendolyn to put it on over her bra, as the scene involved putting on a corset.

Bra? Gwendolyn thought. Who had time to put on underwear?

A shoulder-length brown wig was on a stand to Gwendolyn's left. "We do need you to wear that," the girl said. "Oh, and here." She handed Gwendolyn two sheets of paper stapled together. "I'll be back in ten. Stay here until you're called."

Gwendolyn spun around to face Alice. "They expect me to learn all this in ten minutes and get into costume, too?"

Alice grunted. "Makes a girl wonder if they've ever had to do it themselves."

Alice picked up the hoop frame next to the dress and got to her knees. Gwendolyn stepped inside it and pulled it up to her waist. It was so enormous that a beach ball could have hidden comfortably inside it, and it reeked so badly of mothballs and cigarette smoke that Gwendolyn had to hold her breath. She pulled on the lacy chemise and picked up the script.

It was the scene where Mammy tries to get Scarlett to eat something before the barbeque. Gwendolyn started reciting the dialogue as Alice tied the sash around her waist as tightly as she could. She went over the scene again but didn't get through it before there was a knock on the door. A male voice said, "Two minutes, Miss Brick!"

Alice spun her around. "How do you feel?"

"It's so heavy. How did girls get around in these things?"

"Say it again, but say it Southern Belle style."

Gwendolyn did, and Alice looked at her with wide eyes. "Wow, that's pretty good. Now be all batting eyes and flirty mouth and read out something in the scene."

Alice pulled the wig off the stand and ran her fingers through it. She pulled it over Gwendolyn's scalp and tucked in loose hairs while Gwendolyn practiced her lines.

The door flew open and a young guy, not even twenty years old, stepped into the room. "They're ready for you. Follow me."

Gwendolyn mouthed "thank you" to Alice and followed the guy out of the dressing room and further down the corridor, through another doorway that opened onto a small soundstage. A painted backdrop of a bedroom with flowery wallpaper hung along the rear and a hat stand stood off to stage left. The lights burst to life, blindingly bright.

A square-faced guy with red hair introduced himself as the director, then led her over to the hat stand. "This is one of the posts of Scarlett's four-poster bed, which Scarlett grabs onto while Mammy pulls her corset as tight as she can. And here is your Mammy."

He beckoned a large black woman to join them. "Gwendolyn Brick, this is Hattie McDaniel. She'll be reading the part of Mammy."

"I know who you are," Hattie said. Her face was set in a disapproving frown. "You're the gal who plopped herself on Mr. Selznick's front door stop over Christmas, aintcha?" When Gwendolyn nodded, Hattie broke out a wide, white smile, and a cloud of maternal air enveloped them both. "Good for you, child!"

As the technicians around them started to prepare, Gwendolyn asked Hattie, "If you get the part, will this be your first movie?"

Hattie let out a whooping laugh. "Oh, my sweet Lord, I've lost count of the number of movies I been in. Probably fifty by now." Suddenly her face reverted to her semi-frown. "But let me tell you something. Never have I felt this way about a role. Miss Gwendolyn, honey, I'm looking you in the face and I'm telling you with all the certainty I can muster: there ain't nobody—an' I mean not one soul in this here town—who can play Mammy better'n me. I was born for it. I can feel it in my bones. And if you don't feel the same way about playing Scarlett O'Hara, then you got no business being here."

"Oh, but I do!" Gwendolyn bunched her hands together. "I've tried everything I could think of to get this screen test."

Hattie's mouth broadened into a glowing smile. "When I heard what you done last Christmas, I thought, Now there's a girl I can tip my Sunday hat off to!"

"Quiet on the set. Ladies, your places, please."

Just out of camera range, Gwendolyn found Alice waving and then pointing to her right. Standing next to her was a guy holding sheets of cardboard in his hands. In large black letters was the first line of Scarlett's dialogue.

"Do you see your cue cards okay, Miss Brick?" the director asked.

Gwendolyn felt her whole body relax as a procession of images paraded in front of her: the book on Eldon's bedside table . . . Chasen's chili dripping down her dress . . . Alistair's sun-bleached velvet sofa . . . the seaweed under the Santa Monica pier . . . the look on Selznick's face as she stepped out of that balsawood box.

It's like how they say your life flashes in front of your eyes when you're about to die, she thought. But how strange that none of this is intimidating in the least. I am here because this is where I should be.

Hattie wrapped the corset around Gwendolyn's waist and leaned in. "Child, I'm giving you my best Mammy, so you give me your best Scarlett, okay?"

Gwendolyn nodded.

"Quiet, please," the director said in a low voice. "Rolling film and . . . action."

Gwendolyn felt the spirit of something fill her and she started the scene. When she heard the Southern Belle accent come out of her mouth, even she was impressed. She flirted, she pouted, she protested. Sometimes she improvised dialogue that she couldn't see on the cue cards. And Hattie scolded and tsk-tsked and harrumphed in Gwendolyn's ear, sounding every inch as Mammy sounded in Gwendolyn's mind every time she read the book. As the scene got under way, Gwendolyn's hopes took flight. This was one of her favorite scenes and she had read it several times over for the sheer pleasure of it. So perfectly painted, so perfectly staged. She understood Scarlett so perfectly well.

But as they worked their way down the second page, a flare of light in the corner of her eye caught Gwendolyn's attention. She ignored it until she saw a strange look pass over Hattie's face. An acrid smell filled the air and she felt a strange warmth near her feet.

Hattie looked down. Her eyes bugged out.

"Oh, my! My! My oh my! Goodness! This girl is on *fire*!"

Gwendolyn looked down to see flames lapping at the bottom of her rosebud dress and she instinctively looked around for Alistair.

"Someone!" Hattie called out. "Fire! Does this place have any buckets of sand? A blanket, maybe?"

Gwendolyn heard the director yell, "CUT!" then, "Someone! Get a blanket!"

Without thinking, she backed away, trying to put some distance between herself and the flames. She stumbled backwards and fell against the painted backdrop, and the antebellum bedroom folded in with her weight.

She started to kick at the bottom of the dress, thanking God the hoop was wide enough to keep the flames away from her feet. Someone shoved her onto the floor by her shoulders and the skirt flared in an arc over her head. She screamed when suddenly she couldn't see anything, but then she felt someone pressing a blanket against her legs and another against the rim of her hoops.

Long moments crawled by before she heard someone say, "It's okay, everyone. The flames are out. You all right, Miss Brick?"

Gwendolyn told him that she didn't think so. He lifted the blanket and the dress to inspect her legs. It wasn't till then that Gwendolyn remembered she wasn't wearing any panties. In her rush to leave the Garden of Allah, there hadn't been time, and in the dressing room there'd been every sort of apparel but panties. Oh, sweet Jesus, no! She clamped her eyes shut and held her breath.

"Everything looks fine, Miss Brick," the guy told her.

She let her breath out, then heard the sound she dreaded: a male titter. Then a female titter, which was worse. Gwendolyn wanted to pull the charred edges of the hoop skirt all the way over her head, but she realized that would only serve to highlight the last thing she wanted to draw attention to.

She heard the stagehand at her feet let out a surprised "OH! Um . . . ah . . ." He pulled the dress down suddenly. "Yes," he muttered, "everything's fine."

She buried her face in her hands and mumbled a weak "Thank you very much" through her fingers. She lifted her face out of her hands and scanned the room until she found Alice. She mouthed the words, *Get me out of here. Now.*

CHAPTER 40

The crowd of tastefully dressed men in George Cukor's living room held its collective breath until the front door had closed with a distinct click.

"Lord in heaven above!" Cecil Beaton drained the last of his Manhattan. "I thought they'd never leave."

"Oh, come on," someone said. "Lillian Gish is all right."

"Lillian Gish is a delight," Cecil sniffed. "She's Hollywood royalty, but Georgie handed that hat and coat to her half an hour ago. Take a hint, please, madam. You're a filler. Be gone!"

"Filler" was code at George Cukor's parties for heterosexuals invited to make his core group of friends look not so obviously homosexual. It was nearly midnight when the last of them left his Christmas party.

Stevie, a thin chap who was the senior assistant to Gilbert Adrian, MGM's leading costumer, turned to the host. "Sometimes, my dear George," he said, "your parties are *too* much fun. The fillers want to stay too damn long."

George laughed and loosened his tie. "Next Christmas, remind me to throw a more boring party. Now, let's go into the sunroom, where I'll mix us up this new drink that Carl Standish introduced me to the last time I was down at Agua Caliente."

"Where is Carl?" Cecil asked. "I thought you said he was coming tonight."

"He said he'd be here," George said, "but I've found that when you're the general manager of Agua Caliente, there are many, many distractions."

"Such as pretty little Mexican jockeys?" someone asked.

"Among other things. Come on, you lot. You're going to love this one. It's called a Hemingway Daiquiri."

"Sounds frightfully butch," Stevie said.

"In that case, you'll adore it," Cecil murmured.

The crowd circled around George's bar but Marcus hung back. Maybe this Carl Standish guy could help him out.

The five letters Marcus stole from Hugo were nestled in his inside jacket pocket. He'd tried his best to translate them himself, but his Spanish was too rudimentary for the task and nobody at the Garden knew enough to do more than order a margarita down at Lucy's El Adobe Café. He wanted to find someone who could translate the letters for him but wouldn't be able to piece together who wrote them. After all, he had no idea what they might reveal. So he'd taken to carting them around in his jacket whenever he went out, just on the off chance he'd meet someone who could help. He knew it was ridiculous, but he couldn't let them go until he knew what they said.

Cecil handed him a Hemingway Daiquiri. The sharp smell of grapefruit and limes wafted up from the glass. William Haines, a boyish-faced ex-MGM movie star and now Beverly Hills' busiest interior decorator, clinked a spoon against his glass. "Here's to our generous host," he said to the group. "May he live long and healthy . . . or at least long enough and healthy enough to survive this marathon now before him. We know that *Gone with the Wind* will be a triumph for you, dear George. Our only hope is that this movie – or Mister David 'Control Absolutely Everyone And Everything' Selznick – doesn't kill you in the process. And while we have our glasses raised, here's to the Long Shot and the Short Shot!"

The conversation returned to the same subject that had been swirling around the Cukor manse all evening: David Selznick had shot two full Technicolor tests for Paulette Goddard and Vivien Leigh. The fact that Selznick ordered them to be done in Technicolor – an expensive option – meant that he'd narrowed his field down to the two actresses that this crowd had dubbed the Long Shot—Leigh, because she was British—and the Short Shot—Goddard, because she'd been in the running all along.

"Come on, Georgie-boy," said Haines, "you must have an inkling about which way Selznick's going to tumble. The fillers have gone. You can talk freely now."

Suddenly a voice boomed over them all, telling them to leave George the hell alone. "His leading lady hasn't even been cast yet. The poor dear needs to pace himself, otherwise he won't make it across the finish line."

Carl Standish turned out to be someone Marcus had seen at a couple of previous soirees but had never been introduced to. He was a pleasantly rotund guy with a fat pink face, circular gold-framed glasses, full lips, and slightly bulging eyes that gave him a rather startled look. He was dressed as stylishly as his Agua Caliente race-goers, in a light tan suit with an apricot tie and a gold tiepin encrusted with emeralds. He apologized for being so late, but "what's a man to do when a *chico bonito* needs assistance so very desperately?"

Marcus hung back while Carl got a drink and made his round of hello kisses, pausing to chat with various men gathered around the bar. When Standish withdrew to hang his jacket in a hall closet, Marcus saw his chance. He introduced himself, pulled the envelope out of his pocket, and explained his dilemma.

"Ah, so you're Marcus!" Carl replied. "George has told me so much about you. I'd be delighted to help you. Let's duck in here."

George's library was paneled chest-high in heavy wood and had dark tartan wallpaper from there to the ceiling. The ceiling itself was overlaid with deeply shellacked mahogany, and two of the walls were mounted with floor-to-ceiling bookshelves packed solid. There was a pair of matching reading chairs lit softly by a Tiffany lamp.

Marcus closed the door behind them and they sat on the reading chairs. Marcus downed the rest of his daiquiri and gripped the arms of his chair as though an earthquake were about to hit. He held his breath as Carl pulled the first letter from its envelope and held it under the lamp. It was the sort that gave off a gentle light, atmosphere over practicality.

"So, let's see what we have here." After a few mmms and uh-huhs, he said, "Whoever's written this letter to Hugo compliments him on his written Spanish, saying that he would think that Hugo was a native speaker. He says it was a pleasure to meet him at Allah's garden the other day. Then he gives details of his tailor, as Hugo requested. Actually, I know that tailor. He made a tuxedo for me; he's very good." Carl read the rest of the letter. "And then it ends with an invitation to an evening of Spanish movies at his home, three weeks hence."

Marcus breathed a little more easily. Nothing incriminating one way or the other.

Carl pulled out the next letter. "In this one he's talking about two Spanish-language movies and how impressed he is with Hugo's grasp of the subtleties of the screenplay. He supposes that Hugo must be a fine addition to the studio's writing department." He turned to the second page. "Now he's saying how nice it was to have an appreciative dinner guest last night. Not everybody can stand such spicy food. And what excellent taste Hugo has in wine."

"Is there anything there that suggests he stayed the night?"

Carl raised an eyebrow and returned to the letter. "No, nothing like that. But they do mention someone else."

"Who?"

"It's more of a nickname. It's a Spanish thing. Kind of like 'Little White Boy.' Kind of disparaging, the way this guy has written it. A little condescending."

Marcus thought of the name Ramon had called him more than once: Marcusito. Ramon had translated it as sort of meaning "Little Marcus," but in an endearing way. At least, that's what he'd said at the time. He was lost in his thoughts for a few moments until Carl said, "The party in the other room has gone awfully quiet, don't you think?"

Marcus listened; Carl was right. The group – normally vocal, but especially so after a few drinks – was unusually quiet.

"What does the next letter say?" Marcus forced a dry swallow.

Carl opened the third envelope. "This is a letter of apology. Apparently he – the writer – got very, very drunk and doesn't remember the second half of the evening, and he hopes he didn't do anything ungentlemanly or anything that embarrassed Hugolita."

"Hugolita? It actually says that?"

Carl nodded. "He says that he'll bring him back something special from Europe."

The next letter appeared to be much later than the previous one, written from some little town outside of London. Ramon was very excited that a series of concerts he'd given had been a huge success, and he was the toast of the town. People were throwing him parties and dinners and it was like the old days.

"He goes on to describe some of the people he's met and the things he's seen. There's a rumor that he's going to be presented to the royal family, which he is very excited about. He says that he can't believe that a little boy from Durango could be presented to royalty, and how he can't wait to tell his father, who will be so proud of him."

Carl opened the last envelope and had only just started to read it when a roar erupted from the living room. It was a mixture of "Finally!" "I don't believe it!" "That'll be twenty bucks, bucko," and "I just *knew* it!"

Carl pointed a thumb toward the door. "Do you think we ought to – ?"

The study door whipped open and Stevie rushed in. "There you are! Selznick just called. We have a Scarlett!"

"Who did he decide on?" Marcus pictured Gwendolyn, so downhearted when she returned from her catastrophic screen test. Wouldn't the world be a glorious place if the next two words out of the costumer's lips were *Gwendolyn Brick*?

"You'll never believe it," Stevie exclaimed. "He chose the goddamned limey."

"He gave it to Vivien Leigh?" Marcus had his money on Paulette Goddard, as did pretty much everybody in Hollywood.

"There goes my twenty bucks," Carl said.

"BUT we are absolutely sworn, sworn, *sworn* to secrecy," Stevie said. "This news cannot leave this house. But come on, whatever you two are doing in here, it can't be more important than this. Come back to the party!" He bounded back out to the living room to rejoin the hubbub.

Marcus turned back to Carl to suggest they rejoin the party, but found Carl sitting on the edge of his chair reading the last letter.

"Sure," Carl replied, his eyes still on the page, "but before we do, you may want to hear this."

CHAPTER 41

Kathryn reached up and pulled Gwendolyn's fist away from Marcus' door. "Perhaps we ought to give him another hour."

"It's after eleven," Gwendolyn replied. "Nobody should still be in bed after eleven on Christmas morning." She rapped three times.

Marcus' door squeaked open and a pale, scruffy face peered into the light like a nocturnal marsupial.

"MERRY CHRISTMAS!" Kathryn and Gwendolyn chimed, perhaps a little too brightly and a little too loudly, given the look on Marcus' face.

"I didn't know they made hangovers this strong," he said. He gazed down at the bottle of champagne in Kathryn's hand and swung open the door to let the girls in. Through the doorway Kathryn saw the debris of last night's clothing strewn from one side of the room to the other. "What time did you get in last night?"

"Didn't look at the clock." He let himself flop onto his bed.

Kathryn pulled up the blind on Marcus' sole window. It didn't contribute much light to the room, but it was better than nothing. She glanced out at the pool and spotted Frances Hackett bent over her husband's ankle. For once, the Garden's Christmas party had been a quiet affair—relatively speaking—but Albert had still gotten drunk enough to slip on some errant gin and twist his ankle. She watched Frances wrap a bandage around his ankle and wondered how Roy was doing.

His bandages had come off the day before—nearly a month since a burning *King Kong* gate collapsed and fell across his back. Fortunately, the Los Angeles Fire Department was close by and doused him with water. The burns were only first- and second-degree and would probably heal without scarring, but not without swelling and pain. She wished she could have been there for him when the bandages were removed, but that was the place for a wife, not a mistress.

Not that she and Roy had done anything yet.

But even wrapped as he was in enough bandages to make an Egyptian mummy jealous, the look in his eye was unmistakable. She knew in her gut it was only a matter of time.

She poured the champagne into flutes. "Here's to a merry Christmas!" she declared. Look at him, she thought. Marcus can barely keep his eyes open. They clinked glasses. "Would you prefer we leave?"

Marcus forced his eyes open. "No. I need to feel human again."

"Big night at Casa del Cukor?"

Marcus downed some champagne and lit a cigarette with shaky hands. "Didn't start out that way, but things started kicking in about midnight."

"Is that when all the boring fillers left?"

Marcus gave Kathryn a withering look. She knew he regretted revealing that in-joke to her, because it meant that she was a filler, too. He'd tried to backtrack, saying that fillers only referred to boring guests and that certainly didn't include her. But it didn't bother her too much: it put her in the same company as Katharine Hepburn, Aldous Huxley, Edith Head, William Faulkner, Carole Lombard, and Sinclair Lewis, all of whom she'd met at one Cukor party or another.

Marcus let his head fall back against his headboard and breathed out a long plume of grey-blue cigarette smoke.

"So we're not witnessing the only hangover in town, then?" Gwendolyn asked.

"This is nothing like what Vivien Leigh's must be like this morning."

Kathryn looked at Gwendolyn and frowned. Vivien Leigh? The British actress she saw that night at the burning of Atlanta shoot? Why would she have a hang—*Oh my goodness!*

"Marcus James Adler," Kathryn said, "is there some news you'd care to share with us?"

"Not that I know of."

The hell there wasn't. "Has Selznick made his decision?"

Marcus gasped and snapped his head off the board so fast it must have felt like a mule kick. "I have no comment to make at this time."

"It's Vivien Leigh, isn't it?" Kathryn pressed.

Marcus closed his eyes again. "I refuse to answer on the grounds of excessive alcohol consumption."

Kathryn refilled Marcus' glass. "If the next thing you do is take another sip of champagne, then we'll take it to mean that Vivien Leigh has Scarlett. If the next thing you do is light a fresh cigarette, then it's gone to Paulette. You haven't said a thing, breathed nary a word, broken no confidences, and you can sleep tonight with a conscience bright and clear."

Marcus looked from Kathryn to Gwendolyn and reached for his cigarettes and Kathryn's lighter. He went to light up, but when Gwendolyn gasped, he put down the cigarette and lighter, then picked up his glass and emptied its entire contents into his mouth.

"The Brit!" Kathryn exclaimed. "I don't believe it."

"I was there at George's when the call came through." He turned to Gwendolyn and held her hands in his. "Gwennie, darling, I'm sorry, but they're not giving you the role."

"Oh, Marcus, that dream burned to the ground when I set fire to Selznick Studios."

Kathryn stared into her champagne.

The scoop of the year has just fallen into my lap.

It was even bigger than the last time she outscooped Louella. The role of the decade had been cast—with a Brit! It was a double scoop. Louella would have a field day.

She noticed the look on Marcus' face. "What?" she asked.

Marcus leaned forward. "George made us all promise on our mothers' graves that we wouldn't divulge this to anyone. If you run this, George will skin us both alive. And Selznick will help. I wouldn't blame them; it'd be justifiable homicide."

"You can relax," Kathryn said. "My next publishing deadline is days away, so it's all a moot point. I'll be reading about this in Louella's column with the rest of you."

A smirk surfaced on Marcus' lips. "But it's killing you, isn't it?"

CHAPTER 42

Gwendolyn handed the telegram to the guard at the front gates of Selznick International Studios.

The guard, a tall, gaunt guy who looked like he'd be more comfortable in rodeo duds than a guard's uniform—which probably meant he wore them in silent movies—took the telegram and read it. "Yuh-huh," he said. "I have you down on my list. Let me give you directions—"

"That's okay," Gwendolyn cut in. "I know where casting is."

The guard frowned at her. "You're listed for the art department."

She took her telegram back and pointed to the name of the sender. "This person isn't in casting?"

"No, miss. She's the head of the art department."

By the time the telegram arrived a few days after Christmas, Gwendolyn had resigned herself to the fact that her dream was kaput. Her every waking moment had been focused on becoming the silver screen's Scarlett O'Hara, and Marcus' slip had crushed her. It had been an effort to get into the spirit at Robert Benchley's Christmas dinner that afternoon. He'd put on a fine spread—Dottie even contributed a delicious figgy pudding—but she was relieved when it was all over and she could slide into bed and let go with a good cry.

But then a telegram arrived and she jumped to the conclusion—a little hastily, it now appeared—that with Scarlett having been cast, they were working their way down the list of lesser roles. Perhaps they'd been magnanimous enough to overlook her catching on fire to think of her for one of Scarlett's sisters, Suellen or Carreen.

"What does the art department do?" Gwendolyn asked the guard.

"Decorate sets and paint backdrops."

"What on earth would they want with me?"

* * *

The first person Gwendolyn encountered inside the cavernous warehouse was a slim woman with greying hair pulled back in a ponytail and a dress that looked like a white painter's smock mottled with dabs and dribs of paint in all colors. She was working on an enormous painting, taller than herself; a portrait of a woman in a sapphire-blue dress draped in a shawl of white lace. The face was only sketched in.

"I wish to God they'd cast Scarlett so I can finish this damn thing," she said. "What do you think of this col—for the love of Mike!" she exclaimed. "You came!" The woman put down her paintbrush and wiped her hands on her smock. "When I sent you that telegram, I really wasn't sure. Alistair can be so ambiguous, can't he?" She stuck out her hand. "Pleased to meet you. I'm Linda Morgan."

Gwendolyn shook the woman's hand. "Are you talking about Alistair Dunne?"

"I most certainly am." The woman winked at her in an almost conspiratorial way.

"You know Alistair?"

"He worked here at the studio. He was a superb painter of backdrops."

Fronting up for a regular job painting backdrops for a movie studio was the last thing Gwendolyn could picture Alistair doing. But what did she know? Irene Selznick had been quite right. Since that morning under the pier, Alistair had mutated into a whole different person. All that light and joy that had once beamed out of him like a summer's day soured and darkened. Their meetings at his loft tapered off, along with the heat their lovemaking generated. It became mechanical and half-hearted; a far cry from the sweaty sessions that had lasted all afternoon and left them satisfied and yet hungry for more.

The last time she saw him was more than a year ago—just before that Christmas morning stunt of hers outside Selznick's house. He'd barely even said goodbye, and she was left with the feeling that she might never see him again. She'd replayed that moment in her head over and over, giving them a fond fare-thee-well scene together; she would've given just about anything to see him one more time.

Gwendolyn followed Linda through an obstacle course of paint cans, enormous swathes of canvas, easels, and brushes of every imaginable size. "He was as surprised as you are to learn he had a knack for all this," Linda said. "In fact, I'd say he excelled at it, but I knew he wasn't happy, so when he left—"

"How long did he work here?"

"Wasn't even a year. We were all sad to see him go, but not surprised." They reached the back wall of the studio, where an office was partitioned off with makeshift walls of cheap wood and glass windows. Once inside, the woman reached behind the door for a canvas covered with a picnic blanket and set it up on a chair. "But even I wasn't prepared for this." She pulled the blanket away.

The shock of seeing her portrait again sent a loud "OH!" shooting from Gwendolyn's mouth.

"Remarkable, isn't it?" Linda said. "And now that I've met you, the resemblance is even more striking. Alistair should be the one painting Scarlett O'Hara out there, not me." She shook her head from side to side. "I'm starting to wish I'd just taken this portrait home with me. But when I saw that screen test—"

"You saw it? My screen test?"

"I've seen pretty much everybody's. Mr. Selznick wants to gauge a wide variety of reactions to the people he's testing. You weren't badly burned, I hope."

"You saw my dress catch fire?"

"It must have given you a terrible fright."

Gwendolyn wanted to ask if Linda thought she was any good, but decided she preferred not to know. She didn't get invited back, she didn't get the role; all she got was embarrassed. She turned back to the portrait. "But I watched him take a match to this."

"I guess he must have done it over."

Gwendolyn studied the painting more closely. The color of her dress wasn't quite as she remembered it. It was brighter somehow, richer, deeper. And he'd caught the angles of her face more accurately, too. It'd been ages since he'd seen her, and still he'd been able to pull off a work like this. Gwendolyn pressed a hand to the heaviness weighing down her heart.

"At any rate," Linda continued, "I found it the other day behind a stack of test sketches for some *Gone with the Wind* backdrops we've been working on, so my guess is that he painted this one on his own time. He used the studio's resources, so technically it's ours, but the portrait is yours if you want it."

"Really?" Gwendolyn gasped. "Are you sure?"

"If you don't want it, I've got a perfect place in my music room just begging for something like this."

"No, no! I'll take it." She wondered how Kathryn would feel about a life-sized portrait of her in their living room. "But how did you know how to contact me?"

"Look on the back of the portrait."

Gwendolyn flipped the portrait over. An envelope taped into the bottom right-hand corner was labeled *GWENDOLYN BRICK – GARDEN OF ALLAH HOTEL, SUNSET BLVD.*

She pulled the envelope off the canvas and took out a single sheet of paper.

My darling angel, after seeing that screen test, I realized that I need to take more chances. To be brave and fearless like Gwendolyn! To go after what I really want, just like you do. Repainting your portrait showed me that I have strayed from my path. I am ready to live my life undistracted. I want to paint and paint until my fingers drop off. You will always be my muse. With everlasting love and admiration, Alistair.

A sheen of tears blurred Gwendolyn's vision.

"Bad news?" Linda asked.

"He told me that I'll always be his muse."

"Not a bad way to be remembered," Linda said, "all things considered."

Gwendolyn smiled to herself. Alistair could say "Thanks for everything and see you later" so much better with a paintbrush than he ever could with words. She gazed up at the painting, drinking in each hypnotizing detail, then turned to the woman beside her. "My screen test. How was I? Any good?"

Linda smiled an odd, puzzled sort of smile. "You were certainly memorable."

"Getting set on fire wasn't exactly the sort of impression I was shooting for."

"I was thinking about what happened after you fell over and your hoop skirt flipped up."

Gwendolyn looked at her blankly.

Linda laid a gentle hand on her arm. "They kept the cameras rolling. They caught everything. Or, more to the point, they caught *nothing*, if you catch my drift."

Linda's meaning hit Gwendolyn like a wet towel. She gripped the portrait's frame and watched her knuckles blanch. "Oh my stars! How many people saw my screen test?"

"There were probably a couple dozen of us—"

"A couple dozen? Have seen my . . . seen me? Oh, Lord no!"

"Oh, that's not the way to look at it at all," Linda told her. "As a movie actress trying to get your big break, the hardest thing in the world is to get noticed. Everyone in Hollywood is dying to see anything connected to *Gone with the Wind*. That screen test is being seen by every bigwig in Hollywood."

"It's *what* . . . ?" Gwendolyn's horror deepened.

"You should be thankful for the opportunity to be a part of Hattie McDaniel's screen test. Everyone who's seen it is in full agreement: Selznick has to give the role of Mammy to her. She's perfect. Well, you were there, you would know better than any of us."

"Hattie's screen test?" Gwendolyn lifted her face to Linda. "That was *my* screen test. Hattie was just reading the part of Mammy for me to play against."

Linda offered her a sympathetic smile. "I don't know what they told you that day, but I can tell you that the clapperboard said *Selznick Studios*, then the date, and then *Screen test of Miss Hattie McDaniel for the role of Mammy.*"

CHAPTER 43

Time was running out for Marcus. January twenty-sixth, 1939, was fast approaching, and if he was going to get in to see George Cukor, it had to be before that day. It seemed like all of Hollywood was holding its breath for principal photography on *Gone with the Wind* to commence. Marcus knew that if he didn't see George before the twenty-sixth, he wouldn't see him until after the premiere – a whole year away.

Since the night the Vivien Leigh news came in, Carl's translation of the last of Hugo's letters from Ramon had preoccupied Marcus to the point of obsession. Time he should have spent trying to secure a new studio job was wasted on staring at Ramon's fifth letter while Carl's translation rolled around and around in his head.

I nearly died when Cukor walked in on us at Errol Flynn's party! The room was dark – but was it dark enough? Cukor has a lot of class and knows all about discretion – plus he is a member of the family – so I do not think he will say anything to anyone, even if he saw what we were doing.

It was hard not to pole-vault to the obvious, but if the obvious turned out to be the truth, Marcus was going to have to confront Hugo over it. Planting that poisonous blind item in the *Lion's Roar* was bad enough, but this was worse. But he wanted to be sure of his facts, and the only way of doing that was to ask George directly. He didn't want to do it over the telephone, but *Gone with the Wind*'s start date loomed like the Hindenburg.

"Don't be ridiculous," George had said when Marcus called. "If you need to ask me something face to face, then that's what you deserve. I abhor the telephone in that respect."

"Tonight, perhaps?"

"Oh, heavens no! Vivien's gotten herself all worked up over conquering the Southern accent so I've started to work privately at night with her. Now that she's got the role, she's keen to exceed all expectations. She's terrified there'll be a hundred million Americans booing at her to leave the country when they learn it's her. It hasn't helped her confidence that she got the role largely because Paulette landed on that list with Clark."

At the start of the month, *Photoplay* magazine published an article titled "Hollywood's Unmarried Husbands and Wives." It exposed a number of leading movie star couples who were living "without the benefit of matrimony." Over impromptu Manhattans in the Sahara Room at the Garden of Allah, Scott Fitzgerald confided to Marcus that Sheilah wrote it under a pseudonym for a huge sum of money. The article caused the biggest flap Hollywood had seen since the advent of talkies, and unfortunately for Selznick, his two leads – Clark Gable and Paulette Goddard – both appeared on the list. Unwed movie stars all over Hollywood were sent scurrying for churches. Mayer ordered Clark Gable to divorce his wife Ria and marry Carole Lombard at the first opportunity. Marcus hadn't heard any rumors about Paulette rushing to the altar with Charlie Chaplin yet.

"Perhaps we can catch a sandwich after Clark's costume fitting," George offered. "Can you be at Selznick Studios tomorrow? We should be done by one."

Gable's reluctance to join the picture was well-known and negotiations had dragged on for the best part of a year. In the end, Selznick dangled a $50,000 carrot in front of the only actor the public would accept as Rhett Butler. Gable caved, America rejoiced, and Selznick breathed a sigh of relief. But George didn't. He now had a disgruntled leading man on his hands.

When Marcus arrived at Selznick International's ramshackle costume department, he found George and Gable fussing around with the jacket planned for Rhett's first on-screen appearance. *Gone with the Wind* was to be Gable's first color picture: a big moment for any actor. The tension on his face was etched into the creases around his eyes and mouth.

Marcus didn't venture beyond the fitting room door. George looked at him and rolled his eyes. Gable was focused on his reflection in the large mirror in front of him. He pulled at the cuffs of an expensive velvet jacket that looked softer than Christobel, the Adler family's Persian ball of fluff back home. But it struck Marcus that the color—a yellow-orange cross—seemed all wrong. The Rhett Butler Marcus saw in his mind wasn't the type to parade around a society barbeque in a jacket the shade of a sunburned carrot.

Gable hunched his shoulders and stretched his arms. He spotted Marcus standing just inside the doorway and turned to face him. "What do *you* think?"

Marcus gingerly stepped forward.

"Clark," George said, "I want you to meet a good friend of mine, Marcus Adler. Marcus, this is Clark Gable."

Gable shot out his hand for Marcus to shake. It was a vigorous, manly shake, like his father used to insist upon. "So, this jacket, what's your take on it?"

Marcus glanced at George, who shot him back a pleading look. Marcus couldn't tell if George was pleading with him to say it looked fine or to propose a solution.

"If you ask me, it's the wrong color," he ventured.

Gable and George both turned back to the enormous mirror. "What color do you think would be better?" Gable asked.

"I'd be going with a black jacket."

George's eyes bulged in horror.

Gable laughed. "Moviegoers finally see me in color, and what am I wearing? A black jacket? I don't think so, Adler."

"You want to hear my reasoning?" Marcus asked, more to George than to Gable.

"Shoot."

"As I recall, Scarlett sees Rhett for the first time at Twelve Oaks and asks a friend who he is. The friend tells Scarlett it's Rhett Butler, who got thrown out of West Point and is no longer received by any of the good families in the area. He's the black sheep of the family."

"Go on," Gable said.

Marcus pointed at the jacket. "This reeks of someone saying, 'This is Gable's first color movie. We need to put him in color.' But I assume that Walter Plunkett's team is busily sewing together dozens of huge, frilly hoopskirts in blues and greens and yellows and pinks. Nobody else on camera will be dressed in black except the black-hearted blaggard, Captain Rhett Butler."

Marcus held his breath. Nobody said anything for a few moments, but the seamstress appeared as if on cue with a bolt of black velvet. George grabbed it from her and stretched a length of it over Gable's shoulder and down his side. It perfectly matched the black of his hair.

"Hang me high and dry, Adler, you're exactly right. That color made me look like fried shit. I think we are done here."

As Gable stepped behind the curtained screen to change out of his costume, George mouthed a "Thank You."

"You working on this picture, Adler?" Gable asked from behind the curtain.

"No," Marcus replied. "I owe George a meal, so I thought I'd get in before nobody sees him for the next year."

"You're going for a bite to eat?" Gable asked. "Mind if I join you?"

Marcus felt his heart sink. George looked at him. *What can I do? It's Gable.*

"We were just going to go to the commissary," George said.

"Terrific! Carole tells me they do a great chicken pot pie."

* * *

Marcus had been to his fair share of parties with stars known coast-to-coast, but this was the first time he'd sat down for a meal in public with someone of Gable's stature. Ginger Rogers remarked to him once during a break in a tennis tournament at the Garden that it's the human equivalent of eating in a fishbowl at the zoo with all the lights pointed at you—so for God's sake, don't spill your soup. As they made their way through the commissary, a wave of whispers and stares followed them.

They were shown to a table in the far corner of the wood-paneled room and Gable took the chair facing the wall. With his back to the room, the sight of his famous face wouldn't be considered an open invitation to stop by. They ordered three chicken pot pies and a jug of beer. Marcus had never been much of a beer drinker, nor had George as far as he knew, but it was clear from the way he ordered that when you're with Gable, you eat as Gable eats and you drink as Gable drinks.

After the waitress withdrew, Gable turned to Marcus. "So, Adler, what's your game?"

"My game?"

"You know, what do you do for a living? You a costumer?"

"Marcus here is a first-rate writer," George put in.

"Oh, yeah? Which studio?" But before Marcus could deliver his standard response in which he avoided admitting that he hadn't worked for a studio in more than a year, Gable clicked his fingers. "Say! Adler? Marcus Adler? I know that name."

And here we go, Marcus thought. We're going to have the Hearst Castle Fiasco conversation yet again. Yes, I'm that Marcus Adler. Yes, I actually said *rosebud*. Yes, I really did say it to Hearst's face.

"*The Star-Spangled Banner*, right? You're the guy who helped Scott Fitzgerald through his first screenplay."

A wave of relief washed over Marcus. It was the very first time he felt like he might finally be able to put his infamous reputation behind him. But then he thought about that *Lion's Roar* item. Had he just substituted one infamous reputation for another? Marcus nodded. "I'm impressed that you know about that."

"Carole and I had Scott and Sheilah over for dinner a few weeks ago." Marcus wondered if they'd have been quite so hospitable if they knew it was Sheilah who'd written the unmarried husbands and wives article. "Scott was giving his all to the *Wind* script and—hey, I'll admit it—I wanted him to beef up Rhett's part. I'm determined to make sure Rhett doesn't run around the whole picture being Scarlett's shadow. At any rate, he ended up admitting that he hasn't turned out a decent script since *The Star-Spangled Banner*, and that was largely because of a neighbor of his who helped him through it. You guys all live at the Garden of Allah, right? Oh boy, did he ever sing your praises. Said MGM were nuts to let you slip through their fingers."

Marcus had never been much of a Gable fan—he was always more of a Tyrone Power boy, or perhaps Randolph Scott, in a pinch—but there was a certain ease about Gable that was hard to resist. Sitting with him like this, sharing a jug of beer (barely drinkable, but not altogether noxious) and digging into something as simple as chicken pot pie, Marcus took in the disarming smile, the large manly hands, the deep, ironic voice, and he started to see Gable's appeal in a whole new light. He couldn't help but think of his father. Clark Gable was a man's man, and even though his father wasn't much of a fan of the movies, Marcus could imagine him admitting he enjoyed the odd Gable picture.

What would you say now, Father, if you knew that your good-for-nothing son was having lunch with the one movie star you probably approve of?

They were well into their pies when a shrill voice cut through the commissary. "Mr. Cukor!" it screeched, "I demand that we speak!"

"Holy hell," George muttered.

Louella Parsons marched toward them, clutching something to her matronly bosom as though it were the secret to life itself.

"Don't look now," Marcus said, "but I think she's got a copy of *Photoplay* in her claws."

Clark Gable snorted like a racehorse but didn't move.

Louella slapped the magazine onto the table and flipped it open to Sheilah's article. "Can I assume you've seen this?"

"I'm not much of a magazine man, myself," George replied.

"I have been trying to see Mr. Selznick all day, but he's clearly avoiding me. I'm telling you, Mr. Cukor, the public won't stand for it. They simply won't."

"Stand for what, Louella?" George asked.

"Clark Gable and Carole Lombard top this list of living-in-sinners, and not far below it are Paulette Goddard and Charlie Chaplin. It is bad enough that Gable is playing the lead in the biggest motion picture of the decade, but if Mr. Selznick casts Paulette Goddard in the role of Scarlett O'Hara as well, then he can look forward to the Catholic Legion of Decency leading the charge to boycott the entire movie. Someone needs to take a stand, so let it start with me."

Marcus watched George's face deepen to a paprika red. It had been Marcus' experience that George Cukor didn't get angry very often, but when he did, it was best to lean back. He looked at Gable. The guy wasn't moving a muscle. Marcus could feel every pair of eyeballs in the room trained in their direction.

George crossed his arms. "So, Louella, exactly what is it you expect me to do?"

"I want you to convey a message to your boss. It is bad enough that he has handed Clark the most romantic lead since they invented the talkies, but if—"

The sound of Gable's chair scraping against the tiles cut Louella off. He lurched to his feet and towered over her, yelling, "You got something to say about me, Louella? Why don't you say it to my face?"

Louella's jaw dropped. The color in her face began to drain, but it quickly reappeared as she regained her composure. "I most certainly will. It is outrageous that you are living in sin with Carole. You are a very public, very admired figure. What type of role model do you expect to be when that's the sort of example you set for ordinary Americans who look up to you? Why, they think of you as a god."

"I ain't the slightest bit interested in being a role model for anyone. And I certainly don't have any desire to be seen as some sort of tin god. I just want to spend the rest of my life loving Carole Lombard, and I don't need anyone's approval to do that. Least of all yours!"

He stomped away from the table. Louella turned back to George with thin lips and squinting eyes. She opened her mouth, but George cut her off.

"You were saying something about wanting me to be your message boy?"

Louella glared at George and let out a raspy *humph*. She glanced at Marcus and turned back to George for half a second before she swung back to Marcus with her mouth pulled into a sour grimace. "YOU!" she yelped.

Marcus had never been formally introduced to Louella Parsons, so he was surprised she knew what he looked like.

I guess my infamous reputation isn't so far behind me after all, he thought.

Louella turned back to George. "I believe you understand the message I wish conveyed to Mr. Selznick." She snatched up the *Photoplay*. "The sooner the better." She gallumphed away through the crowded commissary like a rhinoceros.

Marcus could hear George's forced breaths, in—out—in—out, and was almost reluctant to look at him. George's hands shuddered with rage.

"Just when I had Clark where I wanted him," he whispered hoarsely. "You should have seen him when he arrived this morning. So standoffish, so defensive. He found fault with everything. It was written all over him that he regretted signing on to this movie. It wasn't until you came along that he about-faced. But that's all just flown out the window. Damn that interfering old cow." He watched

Louella push open the commissary doors and sweep out of view. After a couple moments' thought, he said to Marcus, "You're still friends with Kathryn Massey, aren't you?"

"Yes. Why?"

"There've been some last-minute hitches in settling Vivien's contract, but that was all settled this morning. We planned to tell Louella on Wednesday." George paused. "But after that little performance, I think she just blew it."

"What are you saying, George?"

"I want Kathryn to have the scoop."

Marcus inhaled suddenly. "Kathryn will love you forever, but do you think that's wise? You should at least run this past Selznick first, don't you think?"

"Screw it."

Marcus leaned in close. "Selznick will *explode* if you give an announcement like that to anyone but Louella. Your appointment as director was one thing; Vivien Leigh is a whole different stratosphere. I get that you're real upset right now, and I get why, but I don't need to remind you that this is one deafening bell you will not be able to unring."

"Truth be told, I'm surprised you didn't tell Kathryn already."

Marcus stared at his friend. "Truth be told, I did."

George looked at Marcus, shock mixed with knowing. "Then why haven't I seen it splashed on every newspaper between here and the moon?"

"She knew the damage she'd cause by leaking something like that."

"Louella wouldn't have hesitated."

"I like to think that's the difference between Louella and Kathryn."

George smiled. "Louella Parsons be damned. Now, what did you want to see me about, face to face?"

CHAPTER 44

Kathryn clasped her hands together to stop them from trembling. "Are you sure?"

"Yes."

"Is George sure?"

"Yes."

"Are *you* sure he's sure? And is *he* sure he's sure?" She laid a hand on her telephone. "Because once I pick this up..."

"He fully understands what he's doing."

"Louella will never forgive me. Not ever."

"And quite possibly anyone connected to her, including your mother and William Randolph Hearst." Marcus winced. "The question is, can you live with that?"

The question, Kathryn thought, is should I tempt fate a second time? The first time she scooped Louella, it put her on the map. This time around, it could put her right at the center of the map—or blow her all the way off it.

* * *

When Marcus left her villa, Kathryn looked at her watch. It was close to seven o'clock—the filing deadline for all West Coast stories was ten. She dialed her boss' number. "Earl, it's Kathryn Massey here. I wouldn't call you if I didn't think we need to stop the presses."

"Shoot."

"I know who's been cast in the role of Scarlett O'Hara." Kathryn pressed her hand against her pounding heart.

There was a long pause at the other end of the line. "Meet me at the office in fifteen minutes."

During the cab ride, she composed her article.

The news that America has anticipated for two long years can now be told: British actress Miss Vivien Leigh has been handed the plum role of Scarlett O'Hara in the much-anticipated movie version of Gone with the Wind.

By the time the taxi pulled up in front of *Life*'s offices, she had virtually the whole thing written in her head. A single light bulb glowed through the frosted glass at the corner of the reporters' room. Kathryn burst into Earl's office. "I just need ten minutes to type it up."

Earl looked up from his desk, grim-faced. "We're not running the story."

Kathryn's heart somersaulted inside her chest. "Hear me out," she said. "You've told me a thousand times the goal of *Life* magazine is to reflect the issues and stories of modern life being lived. *Gone with the Wind* is central to our culture right now. Shouldn't our magazine reflect the country's current obsession with this story?"

Earl held up his hands to stop her. "I agree with you, Kathryn. I know I haven't in the past, but I do now. However, I've spoken to Henry Luce. This is his magazine, and if next week's layout is to be done over, the order has to come from him."

Kathryn closed her eyes and felt the throbbing in her temples.

"He said that *Life* isn't in the business of breaking news or creating news. It's about covering news. If we can get a photograph of Vivien Lowe—"

"Vivien *Leigh*!"

"Whoever. If you can get a photo of her first day on the set or signing her contract, then we'll rush to publish it. But information like this is better left to people like Louella Parsons."

"Translation: The great Henry Luce is too scared to death of Louella Parsons to take her on."

"No. Translation: If Kathryn Massey wants to make a reputation for breaking entertainment news, she needs to find herself another job."

* * *

The taxicab pulled up at 6715 Sunset Boulevard and Kathryn took the elevator to the third floor. She wouldn't have asked the driver to stop, but the lights were still on in the corner office, so she took a chance.

The elevator opened with a quiet *ting*. She made her way down the center passageway and through the last door. She could hear papers rustling in the inner office.

Kathryn's last encounter with Billy Wilkerson—that midnight drunken telephone call—had been so loud and so bitter that she hadn't thought she'd ever want to see him again. But now she wished she hadn't let so much time go past without mending this fence. It felt good to be back in the *Hollywood Reporter* offices; it felt like home.

She stood in the doorway of Wilkerson's office and watched her old boss shift papers around his desk. She cleared her throat.

He looked up and peered through his glasses. "And why would I want to see you?"

Kathryn felt like only an hour had passed since she'd stormed out. "Because I—hey! What the hell's wrong with you? I came here to—"

"I don't care why you came here," he cut her off. "I'll be damned if—"

"Save the speech and screw you!"

She marched out of his office, down the long corridor toward the elevator. "Son of a goddamned bitch." She pressed the elevator button a dozen times. When the elevator didn't appear, she headed toward the stairs. "I come in here to land the goddamned scoop of the goddamned decade in his goddamned lap." But then she found herself standing on cold, dark Sunset Boulevard with the wind biting at her face.

"Don't be a fool, Massey," she said out loud. "This news is bigger than the both of you. It's a win-win."

When she stepped through the doorway of Wilkerson's office for the second time, she waved the white lace handkerchief she knew Vera always kept in the bottom drawer of her desk.

Wilkerson looked up and let out a soft groan. She made her way around to his side of the desk and parked her rear end on its edge. His skin was pale and dull, his eyes glassy and his face unshaved. "You look like hell," she told him gently.

"You'd look like hell too if you lost the contracts for the huge ad campaign MGM is planning for the new Garbo movie."

"Garbo, huh? So you and MGM are chums again?"

He grunted like a wounded boar. "This week."

Kathryn spotted a couple of pages on the floor past Wilkerson's chair and picked them up. "Garbo's new movie is called *Ninotchka*, right?" She handed him the papers. "I never meant to hurt you like that."

"And I had no right to force you to assassinate a perfectly decent movie because of my squabbles. *The Pistol from Pittsburgh* was a damn fine picture."

"And what about that Melody Hope? Talk about a knockout."

The picture had been a huge hit for MGM and made Melody one of the hottest new stars of 1938. The only paper not talking about it was the *Hollywood Reporter*, which made them look out of touch.

They looked at each other with quiet grins. After a few moments, he asked, "You going to tell me what the blazes you're doing here?"

If she opened her mouth now, there was no going back. But Gwendolyn was right: fortune favors the bold.

"I've come into possession of news that will outscoop everyone from here to Timbuktu."

"Outscooping can be a very dangerous pastime."

"I've got the stomach for it if you do."

"If it's worth it."

"I know who's got Scarlett."

Kathryn watched the light in Wilkerson's eyes flicker as he processed the opportunity she was presenting him.

"Same salary. Not a penny more," he said.

"It's not the salary that concerns me."

Wilkerson nodded slowly. "Fair enough."

Kathryn fixed her boss with a heated stare. "Selznick has orchestrated the most brilliant P.R. campaign Hollywood has ever seen. The entire country is holding its breath for this news. If we run with this, we'll be quoted coast to coast. But there will be fallout. Parsons, Hearst, probably Selznick, and Lord knows who else. No matter where the chips fall, I need to know that you have my back."

"You will."

"I'm dead serious, mister. I need your guarantee: no backpedaling. And none of your lousy mea culpas. Not this time."

"I know! All right! I get it! I promise—you have my full support, regardless of what happens from here on out. If we go down, we go down together."

CHAPTER 45

The last time Louella Parsons found herself outscooped by Kathryn Massey, she'd exacted her revenge through a campaign of stealth and inference that made Kathryn feel like every square mile of Hollywood was booby-trapped with land mines.

But this time around, Louella was too angry for subtle measures, too ropeable for stealth. Within hours of the *Hollywood Reporter* hitting the newsstand, the alarm was sounded.

A nameless P.R. flunky at RKO abruptly canceled Kathryn's interview with Fred Astaire and Ginger Rogers on the set of their next musical, *The Story of Vernon and Irene Castle*. But Kathryn and Ginger simply did the interview on the tennis court at Garden of Allah, where Ginger played every other Sunday.

The very next day, an appointment Kathryn had with Myrna Loy to talk about MGM's next Thin Man movie—*Another Thin Man*—similarly evaporated. But Louella didn't realize the movie was written by Francis and Albert Hackett; Kathryn conducted the interview by shuttling written questions to and from the set via her neighbors.

However, Kathryn felt the noose tighten when nobody connected with British director Alfred Hitchcock's first U.S. movie, *Rebecca,* would even so much as return her phone calls. It came as no surprise, though: *Rebecca* was being filmed at Selznick International. In an extensive interview in the Hearst-owned *Los Angeles Examiner*, David Selznick went out of his way to praise Parsons' support for *Gone with the*

Wind and cited the *Hollywood Reporter* as being an untrustworthy purveyor of unsubstantiated half-truths.

To his credit and Kathryn's relief, Wilkerson didn't back down from the barrage of negative publicity shot-putted from the Hearst press. He'd promised Kathryn there would be no mea culpas this time, and he stuck by it, mentioning her often in his daily editorial. In one of them, he even acknowledged that Selznick had every right to be livid that his big news was scooped out from under his expensive Italian loafers. Selznick couldn't afford to have the likes of Parsons fight him every step of the arduous process of making a movie as gargantuan as *Gone with the Wind*'s.

What Wilkerson didn't know, however, was that Kathryn heard through Marcus that the scoop was partially responsible for a further estrangement—not grave, but noticeable—of relations between Selznick and Cukor. George told Marcus to tell Kathryn not to feel that she was to blame, as he'd given her the go-ahead. Selznick couldn't know for sure that George was the leak, but very few people were privy to the information, so Selznick's suspicions had come to rest on George's thinning head.

Kathryn could feel the trenches being dug. Nobody was genuinely on Louella's side, but an awful lot of people had much to lose if their names appeared on her hate list, including all the women in her Association of Hollywood Mothers. Kathryn decided it would be time well spent if she shored up relations, and invited Francine to a long lunch.

* * *

A dainty Strauss violin sonata greeted Kathryn and her mother as they entered the Bullock Wilshire's Tea Room. Two-thirds of the tables were occupied by carefully coiffed, meticulously dressed ladies who'd made a career out of meeting for luncheon.

"This is delightful," Francine said as they waited to be seated. "Do you come here often?"

"I've never been here before. It was Gwendolyn who recommended it."

"The cigarette girl? Eats *here*?"

Kathryn ignored the haughtiness in her mother's voice, even though she couldn't imagine the place held pleasant memories for her roommate. She'd been shocked when Gwendolyn recommended it.

After they ordered potato-leek soup and chicken fricassee, a model floated by in a gorgeous gown of lavender organza. She made a lap around their table before drifting away. They watched her depart, then Kathryn turned to her mother. "So, you heard about my Vivien Leigh scoop?"

Francine made a huffing sound. "I don't live on the moon. What I don't understand is why you go out of your way to make enemies, especially with—well, you know who."

The soup arrived in cherry-blossom pink ceramic bowls. Kathryn busied herself with a mouthful so she wouldn't come across as too preachy. "No one single person should have all that power," she said as evenly as she could muster. "Look at that Hitler guy. They're now saying his ultimate aim is to hold all the power in Europe. How much good do you see coming from a situation like that?"

"Really, Kathryn, if you spent any time really getting to know her, you wouldn't make such comparisons. She's decent and moral, and she's an upright, solid citizen—"

"What are you, her pinochle partner?"

"I'm allowed to choose my friends, thank you very much."

Kathryn wished they could start over. "Nobody said you weren't." She went to put her hand on her mother's arm, but Francine shifted it out of reach.

Well, that was nice while it lasted, Kathryn thought. What is it about this woman that makes me so damn mad so damn fast? A couple of sentences and I'm clenching my fists. And we've had such a nice summer.

"Oh, Mother, of course you're free to choose your friends." Kathryn folded her linen napkin and put it down on her bread plate. "I was simply making the point that—"

"Goodness gracious," Francine cut in. "We're living in Los Angeles, not in the middle of *The Cradle Will Rock*."

"*The Cradle Will Rock*?"

"It's a musical play about corruption and greed—"

"I know what *The Cradle Will Rock* is, Mother." It was a Federal Theater Project show that had a notorious opening in New York a couple of years back. It was so controversial that it ended up being banned and the cast locked out of the theater. "I just don't get how we went from playing pinochle with Parsons to a show about a worker standing up against his greedy boss."

"Let's skip it, then, shall we?"

Kathryn had always assumed her mother's reading didn't veer further than the latest Daphne du Maurier or James Hilton. "No, Mother, I really am keen to know."

"It's just a joke we've been kicking around at work lately, that's all."

Kathryn found it hard to picture the poker-faced staff at the oh-so-proper Chateau Marmont kidding over a leftist musical about unions. "Really?" she asked. "At your work?"

"Nobody knows it yet, but he's going to be stay—" Francine stopped and cast her eyes down to her soup bowl.

"He who?" Kathryn persisted. "Is going to be what?"

"Can we please just drop the whole thing? This is a lovely lunch—Oh, look!" She dropped to a discreet whisper. "Isn't that Louis B. Mayer's secretary?"

When Kathryn looked around the dining room, her eyes connected with Ida's. Kathryn smiled but Ida looked away.

Kathryn wiped her mouth and said, "I'm sorry, Mother, but I need to speak with Ida. If you'll excuse me, this shouldn't take long."

Ida was dining with two other women at a four-top; the fourth chair was piled with striped hatboxes. Ida greeted Kathryn with a pinched and harsh expression. When Ida introduced her to her companions, one of them brightened up at Kathryn's name.

"Kathryn Massey? From the *Hollywood Reporter*?"

When Kathryn nodded, the other one pulled a face and said, "I assumed you'd have headed for the hills by now. Louella's been howling for your scalp."

"Louella can howl all she likes." Kathryn turned to Ida and smiled. "I haven't seen you in such a long time, Ida."

"We all lead busy lives."

The other women got up from the table to go powder their noses. Ida and Kathryn watched them retreat arm in arm, their heads pressed together like a couple of schoolgirls.

Kathryn took one of the empty seats. "You don't hold your cats parties anymore?"

"Can I be frank?" Ida asked, leaning forward.

"Of course."

"I like you, Kathryn. Really I do, so what I'm about to say is nothing personal. We—and by 'we,' I mean most of Hollywood—we needed someone with the capability to upend Louella Parsons, and we decided you'd be perfect."

"I thought that whole Melody Hope thing resolved itself to everyone's satisfaction."

"Oh, it did. I don't know how you squared things with Joan, but you managed that whole tricky situation awfully well."

"And my Vivien Leigh scoop. Surely—"

Ida raised her hand to shush her. "And had you stayed with the *Hollywood Reporter*, we would have continued to support you. But you left to work for *Life*. *Life* is not a daily, so we saw all our plans go up in smoke. Louella's power cannot be broken by someone who works for a weekly. It must be someone with a daily column who can fight battles as soon as news breaks."

"But I'm back at the *Hollywood Reporter* now."

Ida cast a patronizing gaze in Kathryn's direction. "Have you heard of someone called Hedda Hopper?"

"No, I don't think so."

"She has a new movie gossip column; it starts in the *L.A. Times* next week. We've known each other for years; she used to be an actress. If you're on her good side, she's quite a love. But look out if she turns on you. She can be a witch, and plans on giving Louella a run for her money."

Kathryn felt the yoke of reality pressing against her shoulders. "So she's my replacement?"

Ida's companions returned to the table, so Kathryn took her leave and headed back to her mother. Her assumption that she had the support of Ida's cats gave her, in part, the nerve to take the Scarlett scoop to Wilkerson. But they'd moved on without her. The day after the Vivien Leigh news came out, she felt like a lioness—claws extended, ready for anything and everyone. Now she felt like a paper tiger. "Damnit," she muttered to herself, "you've been such a fool, Massey."

It wasn't until she was almost at her table that she realized Louella Parsons herself was chatting with her mother. Parsons was still in her hat, coat, and gloves. They saw each other at the same moment and Louella's mouth unhinged like a cartoon clown's.

"Louella." Kathryn presented her with a wafer-thin smile.

"Kathryn," Louella replied. "Good to be back at the *Hollywood Reporter*?"

"It's wonderful, thank you."

"I was just saying to your mother that you must be an excellent bridge player."

Kathryn saw Francine stiffen. "And why is that?"

"Bridge is all about strategy. Clearly, you're very good at that. You must get that from your mother. It's one of the things I admire her for."

Francine was now noticeably paler than when Kathryn had left her.

"Are you a good strategist, Mother?"

Louella gave Francine a playful slap across the wrist. "Don't be shy, Frannie, you know very well that you're one of my best bridge players."

Kathryn clenched the back of her chair and realized for the first time how very little she knew about her own mother. Any expectations that Francine would side with her over a fight with Louella Parsons sputtered out like a used-up candle.

A trio of soft chimes—bong! bong! bong!—floated over their heads. "Ladies," a smoothed-out woman's voice announced over the P.A., "our exquisite models making their way around the restaurant today are wearing selections from the new Elsa Schiaparelli *Collectionne Parisienne*."

Kathryn felt awkward that she was still standing. She took her seat at the table and a model wafted toward them in an ugly dress the color of bruised avocadoes mixed with mud from a backwoods swamp. As the model swanned past, Louella said, "Kathryn, I can see you in something like that. What would you call that color, Francine?"

"It's not really my taste, Louella," Kathryn said evenly. "A bit too old-fashioned."

"Oh, yes," Louella said, "you're more about flouting the rules than abiding by them, aren't you?"

Another model sailed by in a black dress with a wide white collar and matching belt, but Kathryn could barely see it. "That's not it at all." She leaned forward slightly. "I just think that some rules are long past their usefulness and need to be broken."

"You know what happens when we break things, don't you, Kathryn? We're liable to cut ourselves. And those deep cuts can make a person bleed something awful."

"Oh, cut out the baloney, Louella," Kathryn said in a hoarse whisper. "Why even bother pretending you're not mad about Vivien Leigh?"

"Who said anything about my being angry? Have I written anything in any of my many publications? Really, Kathryn, you do jump to such conclusions."

"You've had a good run keeping all the studios twisted around your finger, but the sun is setting on those days. If they weren't, then I never could have gotten a tip like Selznick casting Vivien Leigh."

Louella's eyes narrowed and she blinked rapidly.

"And then there's Hedda Hopper," Kathryn added.

"Hedda and I go way back." Louella gave a dismissive sniff. "All the way to the start of her actress days, such as they were."

"Did you know she just got a column in the *L.A. Times*?" Kathryn asked. Louella pressed her lips together primly. "Now that I'm back at the *Reporter* and Hedda's in the *Times*—"

"Taking over Hollywood?" Louella retorted. "Is that your strategy? A couple of good scoops and a bitchy column or two and you think you're the new queen bee? You think the studios' P.R. hacks will be lining up to hand you all their exclusives? Is that the plan of attack that you and Hedda have hatched? Really, what is it with all you failed actresses? You're a flop at something as easy as acting, so you think journalism will be a convenient fallback plan."

"Your days are numbered, Louella."

"Don't you count on it!"

Louella shot to her feet at the same moment that the waitress arrived with their chicken fricassee. Louella grabbed one the plates off the waitress' tray, and it took a moment for Kathryn to realize what she intended to do with it. She thought of the look on Gwendolyn's face in the ladies' room at Chasen's, stricken with shock and pale with defeat.

I'll be damned if I go down like that, she thought.

But it was too late. Louella lifted the plate above her head and flung its contents at Kathryn.

The smell of onion filled Kathryn's nose. She looked down to see hot slops of chicken pieces and cream sauce dripping down the brand-new blue crêpe de chine she'd bought especially for today.

Nobody said a word as she grabbed her linen napkin and tried to swipe away the fricassee. It only pressed the sauce deeper into the material.

"And that's just for starters," Louella hissed.

Kathryn got to her feet and picked up Francine's tomato juice. She was moments from throwing it right into Louella's puss when she saw the battle-ax's eyes flare briefly. She paused; she hadn't expected to see fear.

A food fight? Right here in front of your mother, Ida Koverman, and probably the wives of half the studio executives in Hollywood?

She put the glass of tomato juice down and picked up her handbag. "Mother, this wasn't the luncheon I had in mind. Perhaps another time." She would have leaned over to kiss Francine on the cheek, but she didn't want to drip stew all over mother's fox fur collar. Instead, she offered her mother a tight smile and turned on her heel.

With every pair of eyes in the place focused on the plateful of slop still oozing down her dress, Kathryn Massey strode out of the Bullock's Wilshire Tea Room as gracefully as she knew how. She was halfway down the stairs to the jewelry department before the tears burst.

CHAPTER 46

Marcus had neither the skills nor the stomach to pull off a successful break-and-enter, but he could recognize an opportunity when he saw one. When he found out that Hugo Marr had succumbed to a particularly virulent strain of the flu, Marcus saw the chance he was looking for to return the letters.

He stood at Hugo's front door armed with chicken soup and a fly-by-the-seat-of-his-pants plan. He knocked.

"Door's open, come on in. I'm in bed."

Marcus opened the door and poked his head inside. He could see Hugo through the bedroom doorway, sprawled out in a bed of jumbled sheets.

"You always leave your front door unlocked?"

"A pal from my tennis club said he was going to drop by, but I guess he never showed. What time is it now?"

"Nearly six thirty."

Hugo yawned. "Must have dropped off." His face was the color of lard, gleaming with cold sweat. Blotches bloomed down his neck like fresh bruises. The stink of milk of magnesia and vomit lingered in the air.

Marcus eyed the closed closet door. "I ran into Donnie Stewart in the Sahara Bar and he told me you've got the flu. I brought over some beef broth from Gotham Deli. You up for it?"

"You thoughtful angel. My favorite."

"Maybe you'll feel better if you wash your face," Marcus suggested. "Why don't you do that and I'll heat up the soup?"

Hugo shuffled into the bathroom in his bare feet and turned on the faucet. "So what's new with you?"

"I just placed a story with *Collier's,*" Marcus lied. He'd sent one off but it'd been over a month with no word. His real news was that the Garden's management had just bumped his rent up to eighty dollars a month, but he hadn't shared that with anyone.

"*Collier's,* huh?"

"It's about a midget who gets a job as a telephone page boy at a classy hotel but gets mistaken for the grandson of the hotel's dowager resident. Midgets are big now, with all those munchkins they've hired for *Wizard of Oz.*"

With the water in the bathroom still running, Marcus took his chance and opened the closet door. The box holding the letters was no longer there. Jam, scram, and double damn.

"Looking for something?"

"Slippers," Marcus replied without looking around. "You shouldn't be traipsing around barefoot with the flu."

"Oh, pish," Hugo said, but went to his dresser and pulled out a pair of thick grey socks. He sat down on the bed to put them on and Marcus headed for the kitchen. Hugo appeared in the doorway. "Thanks for doing this," he said. He took a seat in the breakfast nook.

For the very first time, Marcus noticed the rather dainty way Hugo held his soup spoon, and how he dabbed at his mouth after every other mouthful. Maybe Hugo was a fairy, after all. How ironic, now that he knew what had happened between Hugo and Ramon. George had caught them in a private moment at Cecil B. DeMille's house, yes, but they'd been sharing a hand mirror striped with cocaine, not a furtive grope in the dark.

He caught Hugo staring at him with hesitant eyes, as though they'd met ten seconds ago, not ten years, and Hugo was still figuring out what to make of him. Then Hugo's face turned even paler and he started to breathe rapidly. "Oh, dear," he said, and let the spoon clatter onto the table. He pressed a hand against his mouth and rushed toward the bathroom.

As Hugo retched into the toilet, Marcus raced back to the closet and rummaged through it, but the damned shoe box was nowhere in sight. He crossed over to the dresser on the other side of the bedroom and pulled out each drawer one by one, but found nothing.

The gagging in the bathroom subsided. "You'd better stay in there." Marcus looked around for other likely places. "Get it all out."

"There can't be much left," Hugo replied, weaker now. "I haven't been able to keep anything down since Wednesday."

Marcus spotted a seaman's chest of weathered wood at the foot of Hugo's bed. "Better safe than sorry." Marcus raised the lid, lifted a layer of fresh bedsheets, and spotted the shoe box. Thank Christ for that.

"What're you looking for now?" Hugo leaned against the bathroom doorway, panting with his eyes half closed.

Marcus lifted off the shoe box's lid and kept his eyes on Hugo. "I'm going to change your sheets, you miserable wretch."

"Thanks, but really, don't bother." Hugo let out a gurgling belch. "What I really need is a change of stomachs."

Marcus' hands were shielded from Hugo's view by the lid of the chest as he pulled the letters out of his jacket pocket.

"There's a Spanish book in there which might interest you." Hugo headed for his bed. "I've been meaning to give it to you."

Marcus looked down and pretended to search through the chest as he stashed the letters in the shoe box. He spotted *Learn Spanish Without Even Trying* and held it up. "You mean this?"

Hugo nodded. "Very useful, unless you already speak Spanish."

Marcus closed the chest and thumbed through the book. "I don't."

"I'm surprised. You've always struck me as being the type to go for Latins." He leaned back into the pillows.

Marcus pressed his lips together and wondered where Hugo was going with this. He caught Hugo looking at him the same way he had in the kitchen: hesitant, undecided.

Hugo closed his eyes and waved a limp hand in the air. "I'm mad for Latins!" he declared. "I used to be all about the Nordic types: Germans, Scandinavians, blonds with deep blue eyes. But then I encountered an Argentinean at one of Carmen Miranda's parties and I did a complete turnaround. Argentineans get *so* worked up."

Marcus remained silent. Nobody had ever asked him what his preferences were. In the back alleys and public toilets he stuck to, conversation was generally frowned upon, preferences never asked about, names never offered. The constant threat of entrapment and arrest by the brutal LAPD was too real, the repercussions too disastrous.

"When Ramon Novarro offered to help me practice my Spanish," Hugo said, "it made conversations with my handsome Argentinean *muy caliente!*"

Marcus kept his eyes fixed on the book as his mind reeled. Hugo had just acknowledged he was queer. "My Spanish is virtually nonexistent," he said.

"Take it, then. In fact, keep it. It's all yours. I've learned all I need to out of that book. Maybe now you and Ramon can start communicating with each other more effectively."

Marcus looked up into Hugo's grey-green eyes. They were glowing like shrewd beacons out of his pale face. Marcus crossed the floor and sat on the edge of the bed.

Hugo pulled the bedclothes over him. "Thank you for playing caring Florence Nightingale to my lonesome Camille."

"What, you haven't had anyone come visit you?" Marcus asked. "Not even your dad? With your mom gone now, it's just the two of—"

Hugo let out a loud "PAH!" and groaned. "A guy would expire waiting for his father to come see how he's doing."

"Your dad hasn't even called you?"

Hugo grunted. "You're lucky *your* father is two thousand miles away. Mine is never satisfied, either, but I have to hear about it in person."

Hugo's father, Edwin Marr, had been a hugely successful director during the days of silent pictures but had failed to manage a successful transition to the talkies. For the very first time in the ten years Marcus and Hugo had known each other, it occurred to Marcus that the two of them had that in common: disapproving fathers.

"I'm sure he's not as bad as all that," Marcus said.

Hugo closed his eyes again. "Marcus, you never talk about your family back East, so I assume your departure for Hollywood wasn't exactly celebrated with marching bands and streamers. Your father doesn't know what you're doing; you have no idea how fortunate that makes you."

Marcus studied his friend's face as he felt his breath seep out of him like the air out of a punctured balloon, and he realized that of all the recriminations that had filled his ears over the years, all those bitter retorts and reprimands through all his blunders and fumbled opportunities – none had actually come from his father. Every single one had been Marcus' own imagination. Roland Adler, McKeesport's chief of police, who ran his son out of town the night he caught him pants down with another guy, had no idea Marcus had been invited to William Randolph Hearst's country estate. He wasn't the slightest bit aware that he'd saved Greta Garbo's life. He didn't know he'd worked with F. Scott Fitzgerald or kissed Ben-Hur.

Tears varnished his eyes. No wonder your career and your love life have stalled over and over, he thought. You've been running around Hollywood doing all the wrong things for all the wrong reasons. "I'm such a fool," he muttered.

"Why?" Hugo asked. "Because you keep letting Ramon Novarro slide through your fingers?" He let out a sigh heavy with fatigue and grabbed a damp cloth from his bedside table to wipe his clammy forehead. "My old pop hasn't taught me much, but he has imparted this one gem:

You have to go after whatever you want in life, and you have to do it before it's too late."

Marcus watched Hugo let out a long, deep sigh. "So, if you won't let me change your sheets, and you can't stomach my soup, what can I do for you?"

"Take that no man's land off my hands," Hugo said, waving towards a script on his nightstand. "I can't fix it, and it's due soon."

A no man's land was a script nobody could make work but the studio had spent a pile of dough buying rights for and was determined to produce. Marcus picked it up.

"What is it?"

"The front office wants it to be Gable's first movie after he's done with *Gone with the Wind.* Convicts escaping from Devil's Island and coming under the influence of a strange Christlike figure. Doesn't sound like a Gable picture to me, but Gable said yes, as long as it doesn't get too preachy. Taggert gave it to Anita Loos, who, according to Taggert, saved an upcoming Crawford picture, *Susan and God*, from the same fate."

Marcus started to leaf through the script as Hugo continued. "She only had it a week and declared it was a lost cause. It got handed around the writers' department and landed on my desk just before I took ill. Anita's right—it's impossible. The only ones who'll love it are with the Catholic Legion of Decency. But if *you* can make that script work, it'll make 'em more grateful than a hooker at dawn."

Marcus thought about the pineapple item in *The Lion's Roar* and realized he no longer cared if Hugo was behind it. These things are going to happen, Marcus told himself. Your successes will be celebrated by your friends and envied by your enemies. He watched Hugo drift off into a light doze. Goddamnit, he realized, I want to write for MGM.

Out on the sidewalk, he stared up at the light in Hugo's living room window. He rolled the *Strange Cargo* script in his hands until it was a white baton that glowed in the moonlight. He started for the nearest streetcar stop and wondered if it was too much to splurge for a taxicab. He wanted to get home to the Garden of Allah just as soon as he possibly could. It was time he got back to work.

CHAPTER 47

Gwendolyn knew it was daytime outside, but what time of day it was, she couldn't tell. And she didn't particularly care. All she knew was she'd been crying for at least a full twenty-four hours. Now that she was all cried out, she just felt drained. Every inch of her innards had been emptied into her pillow.

When she got home from the Selznick studios that day, she leaned her portrait against the living room wall and told Marcus and Kathryn what she'd learned from Linda Morgan, their faces had creased with worry. But she assured them she was fine with the whole thing. Sure, it was awful. So embarrassing. An utter fiasco. But what was done was done, and there was nothing she could do to fix it, so best they all forget about it and look forward to the day when they could have a frightfully good laugh about the whole thing.

Two weeks later, in the middle of a Garden of Allah cribbage tournament-slash-champagne party-slash-jitterbug contest, Gwendolyn played a game-winning fifteen-point hand and Francis Goodrich said, "I don't know if they had cribbage back in the Civil War days, but Gwendolyn, my dear, Scarlett O'Hara herself couldn't play a braver game!"

That's when the tears burst forth with such force that she was caught completely unprepared. Kathryn and Marcus bundled her off to her villa and let her cry her eyes out for the rest of the night, the following day, and the night that followed that. But by the next day, they were both by her bedside again. She felt a sudden draft of cool air against her skin and looked up to find Marcus had whipped off her bed linen. "It's get out of bed time."

"You don't understand." She made a grab for her sheet but he yanked it farther out of her reach. "I've humiliated myself in front of everybody in Hollywood."

"You're right," Kathryn said. "We certainly can't understand that, because the two of us? We're complete strangers to disappointment. Aren't we, Marcus?"

Gwendolyn rolled over to face the wall and pressed her face into the pillow. "This town has disappointed you, but it hasn't humiliated you."

"Gwennie, my darling," Marcus said, "I only have one word to say to that: Rosebud."

* * *

It felt good to feel the warmth of the sun on her skin again and the cold water lapping at her legs. Still, her eyes must look a fright. She hadn't dared look in the mirror before following Kathryn and Marcus out to the pool, so she sought refuge behind her darkest sunglasses.

Across the pool, Scott Fitzgerald and Donnie Stewart—still riding high on their *Marie Antoinette* hit—were playing chess. Although with two large martinis by their side, Gwendolyn wondered how they planned on thinking clearly. Dottie and Benchley were watching them from lounge chairs next to Francis Goodrich and Albert Hackett and Dottie's husband, Alan, who were not so much watching as looking up from their magazines every now and then and exclaiming, "Good move! He's got you now, Fitzy!"

Sheilah Graham appeared from inside Scott's villa. Even today, she was beautifully turned out in silk chiffon in flowery browns, greens, and yellows that matched her neat blonde bob. Her announcement that she had burned the chicken but saved the Peach Melba received a hearty cheer.

Gwendolyn smiled to herself. It was comforting to be reminded that life at the Garden of Allah had gone on without her and her gloom.

Kathryn handed her a Coca-Cola.

"Thanks for pulling me out of my misery," Gwendolyn told her.

"You had every right to be miserable."

"But not forever, sweetcheeks," Marcus added. He was treading water, looking up at her with his cheeky smile. He was looking so much healthier these days. His blue eyes were clearer and his skin glowed. She was glad he'd cut back on the booze. She gulped at her Coke, feeling more refreshed than she had in ages. "I'm glad you're feeling better," he said, "because I think you've got a visitor."

Gwendolyn's first thought was of Alistair. She raked her fingernails through her hair and looked up to see Alla Nazimova approaching.

Madame had aged somewhat since Gwendolyn had last seen her. She'd had a run of terrific stage successes taking her to all corners of the country, but that too had petered out and she was back in villa twenty-four. Madame had to be nearing sixty now. It showed on her face, but in a good way, Gwendolyn decided. The deepening lines and sagging skin gave her the sort of character casting directors liked in older actresses. Maybe all I have to do is wait thirty years, she thought.

"Hello, dear, how are you?" Alla asked.

Gwendolyn pulled her feet out of the pool and hugged Madame. "I've had better weeks."

"I'm sorry to hear that," Alla said. "I have something to ask you. May we sit?" She led Gwendolyn to some sun-bleached wooden patio furniture and took Gwendolyn by the hand. "You can say no if you want to, but when my friend asked me if I knew of anyone suitable, I thought of you."

"Suitable for what?"

"My friend Mercedes. You have heard me speak of her, yes? She throws the elegant parties with the delicious food and the imported wine for her sophisticated friends. Her caterer always has a girl to pass out the food, but the last one," Madame paused to crinkle up her nose, "she stole Mercedes' best jewels during the Christmas party. The police found them in a pawnshop in San Diego and the girl is in jail now, but Mercedes desperately needs someone this Saturday. She asked me to recommend someone and I thought of you."

"Thank you for thinking of me, Madame," Gwendolyn said, "but I don't think so. I'm not really up for—"

"You'd be needed from five to midnight, but she always shows a movie in her screening room, so you'll have a long break in the middle. Not bad for thirty dollars cash."

Thirty dollars was an awful lot to knock back, and she'd lost three days of pay and tips from hibernating like an troll with a toothache. Still, she decided, I really don't feel like it. "It's very nice of you to think of me, but—"

"You'd be doing me a favor. Please, Gwendolyn."

* * *

The woman who answered the front door of the sprawling house in Nichols Canyon possessed an unruly mass of dark brown hair, pale skin and striking hazel eyes, but her smile was warm. She spent a few moments studying Gwendolyn closely, almost the way men did. It left Gwendolyn a little unnerved, but not enough to make excuses and leave.

"You may call me Mercedes," the woman said. Her American accent surprised Gwendolyn, who had imagined she was from some exotic Eastern European country like Romania or Bulgaria. "Unfortunately, I am completely disorganized and nowhere near prepared for twenty guests."

The woman commanded Gwendolyn to follow her into a screening room. It was as long as it was wide, and split into three levels of rows of cinema seats arranged in an arc around a screen at the far end. Bottles of champagne, half-filled glasses, and overfilled ashtrays were scattered from one end of the room to the other. A silk stocking hung from a painting of three pale naked women. Underneath it, a woman's shoe in burgundy suede lay on its side; its partner was nowhere in sight.

"We had a bit of a party here last night," Mercedes explained. "Wasn't planning to, but these just tend to happen, don't they? Impulsive, impromptu actions, even rash ones, can be far more exciting—don't you think, Gwendolyn?" She curved her lips into a half smile. "That name does suit you."

She left Gwendolyn with instructions to clean up the room. "Oh, and be sure to open the windows to set loose the remnants of last night's soiree into the world at large. I'm taking a shower now, so I shall not be able to hear you. If you need me, come to my boudoir at the end of this corridor. The black lacquered door is never closed. Closed doors have such negative energy about them, don't you feel, Gwen-do-lyn? Mmm . . . such a pretty name."

By the time Gwendolyn returned the screening room to some semblance of civilized order, Mercedes had reappeared in the doorway. She was fully made up now, and wore a gorgeous flowing gown in gunmetal grey with purple swirls. The strand of black pearls looped around her neck reached down to her navel and matched her earrings.

"Presentable, am I?"

Gwendolyn had never seen fabric so sheer and translucent. "May I ask what your dress is made of?"

"Japanese silk, from virgin silkworms. Although how a person can tell that a silkworm is a virgin is beyond me. All I know is that when I put it on, there must be nothing between my skin and my virgins." She held out a panel toward Gwendolyn. "Would you care to feel it?"

Gwendolyn slid the fabric between her fingers. "It's like holding moonbeams in your hand."

Mercedes laughed. "That's a perfect description. You make your own clothes, don't you?"

Gwendolyn nodded, her eyes still on the fabric, thinking, Where on earth can I get some of this?

"Only seamstresses and Europeans appreciate fine fabric. Edith found this and designed this dress. I'm sure she'd be delighted to talk to you about it tonight. That is, if she can drag herself away from the studio. She practically *lives* at Paramount."

"Edith Head? Is coming here—tonight?" Miss Head was far and away Gwendolyn's favorite costume designer. She made a full-length gown for Claudette Colbert in *Zazu* with beading so beautiful it made Gwendolyn weep. The chance to meet her sent Gwendolyn into a haze. She looked down at her plain black dress. How could she possibly meet her idol wearing that horrible thing?

* * *

The guests started arriving at six o'clock. The caterer, a stern woman with the sort of haircut rarely seen outside military bases, kept Gwendolyn busy arranging hors d'oeuvres and passing around champagne flutes.

About an hour into the evening, it dawned on Gwendolyn that all the guests were women. Was this one of those cat parties that Kathryn used to go to?

Gwendolyn was so proud of Kathryn. Taking on the likes of Parsons and Hearst took guts, and her name was being mentioned from coast to coast. What a shame she didn't seem to be enjoying it. After that awful fricassee incident, Kathryn had become less chatty and less inclined to laugh, more guarded and cynical with anyone outside the Garden.

Gwendolyn found herself wondering what she'd say to Edith Head if the opportunity arose. The woman was famous for wearing the blue-tinted glasses that helped costumers get a sense of how a particular color would photograph in black and white. That could make a good opener—but would she wear them to a party?

Gwendolyn picked up a plate of anchovy cheese balls and approached a woman sitting off to the side a little, not talking with anyone. It was Greta Garbo, dressed in a mannish suit of brown-green gabardine that was the opposite in every way of Mercedes' gorgeous gown. She had her hair pulled back and wore no makeup at all. Maybe that's how the biggest star in the country had managed to slip into the party without Gwendolyn noticing.

"I know you from the Garden of Allah, don't I?" Garbo said, taking an hors d'oeuvre.

I don't much care for your taste in clothes, Gwendolyn thought, but even without makeup you're lit from within. Gwendolyn smiled at her and was about to nod when a heavy woman with a round, broad face burst into the room and announced, "I've arrived, and I've got the loot!"

She held up a small can of film. Gwendolyn squinted to make out the two words printed by hand on the label at the center: *Hattie McDaniel.*

Gwendolyn felt her underarms go clammy.

The gathering applauded. A couple of women wolf-whistled. All Gwendolyn could do was stare at the can in the large woman's hands. Did Alla know about this? Was that why she'd asked Gwendolyn to work at this party? She felt a hand grip her elbow.

The caterer pulled her back into the kitchen and pointed to several loaded trays. "The caviar and smoked salmon are ready. This crowd loves this stuff, so keep it circulating. Trust me, girlie, you don't want to be around them when they are not satisfied."

When Gwendolyn returned to the living room, a woman with a deep, throaty voice called out, "Hey, girls, Edith's here! And who has she bought with her? Bless my Aunt Patty's ass! It's Alla!"

Alla spotted Gwendolyn and threaded her way through the crowd. "Hello, my dear." She wore a Chinese black silk and a colorful gypsy shawl with long tassels that hung down past her waist. "Mercedes treating you well?

Gwendolyn stared at Madame. *What did I ever do to you?*

Mercedes strode into the living room and clapped her hands. "I have an announcement, ladies. Tonight we've got Missie's new picture *Union Pacific* to show you. But, as you're all now aware, Marcia has somehow gotten ahold of Hattie McDaniel's screen test for *Gone with the Wind.* So my question is, which one do you want to see first?" The gathering let loose a round of catcalls and trooped en masse toward the screening room.

The women were already applauding when Gwendolyn snuck inside the doorway. The projector started up and a clapper board appeared on the screen: *Selznick Studios, December 18, 1937, Screen test of Miss Hattie McDaniel for the role of Mammy.*

Gwendolyn felt a little bit of her heart break. The final smidge of hope that perhaps Linda Morgan was wrong dissolved.

The camera focused in on Hattie and Gwendolyn and the audience let out a collective "WHOOP!" Gwendolyn barely had time to take in her image on the screen before the camera scanned past her and onto Hattie, who paused for a moment before she launched into the scene.

At about the two-thirds mark, it pulled back to show both Hattie and Gwendolyn. It was the point where Mammy gave Scarlett what for about not eating before a barbeque. Some of the girls in the audience were starting to give out long, low whistles. Someone called out to the screen, "Show us what you got, honey lamb!"

Gwendolyn felt herself redden. Did she really want to see this? She brought her hands to her face. That awful moment came up quicker that she expected. Through the cracks between her fingers Gwendolyn watched Hattie look downwards and her eyes bug out. "Oh, my! My! My oh my! Goodness! This girl is on *fire*!"

"Is she ever!" one of the women shrieked toward the screen.

Gwendolyn caught sight of someone turning around to look at her. It was Alla, wide-eyed with realization. She pointed to the screen with her thumb and mouthed the words *Is that YOU?*

"Here it comes! Here it comes!" the same woman yelled.

Gwendolyn could hardly bear to watch herself stumble backwards into the backdrop, lose her wig, and cause her hoop skirt to fly up over her head. Linda was right: her hoo-ha had been caught on film for all Hollywood to see. She leaned against the doorframe for support.

The room erupted—foot stomping, whooping, clapping and whistling. Gwendolyn looked over at Alla, who shook her head sadly, mouthing, *I'm so, so sorry. Please forgive me.*

Garbo was sitting next to Alla, and turned around to see who Alla was talking to. With her insides crumbling, Gwendolyn could see the comprehension dawning on Garbo's face and her eyes widening. On the screen, Hattie yelled, "Get a blanket on that child!" A blanket was thrown across Gwendolyn and patted down. She sat up just as the camera focused in on her face.

"Rewind! Rewind!" someone called out. "Play that last bit again? Can we stop the film at a particular frame—and you know the frame I'm talking about!"

"Now wait just one goddamn cotton-pickin'," someone else in the audience said. "Isn't that the girl—bring up the lights, somebody!"

The lights in the screening room came up and a broad-shouldered woman with slicked-back hair turned around and looked at Gwendolyn. Gwendolyn backed away. Her face burned and her eyes blurred with tears. The woman jabbed a thumb toward the screen. "Ain't that you?"

Several of the women got to their feet. "Hey, Jonni's right," one of them said. "Ho, ho, HOOO! Mercedes, honey, you've outdone yourself!"

Gwendolyn let out an involuntary cry and charged blindly down the dimly lit hallway, across the foyer, and outside. The street to her left wound up into the shadowy folds of the canyon so she turned right and started down the slope. When she had to stop to pull off her too-high heels, she heard feet running toward her. Without turning to see who it was, she took off again.

A voice called out her name. It wasn't Alla, but Gwendolyn stopped anyway and turned around to find Greta Garbo running easily toward her on muscles toned by her famous regimen of swimming, tennis, and hiking.

"Thank you for stopping," Garbo said. She wasn't even out of breath.

"Please don't," Gwendolyn cut in. "Whatever you have to say, thank you for wanting to say it—" She could feel a fresh wall of tears welling up behind her eyes. "But I'd just as soon get away from . . . from everything."

"My dear girl." Garbo took Gwendolyn's hands in hers. "You're a friend of Marcus Adler, are you not? I can only imagine how you must feel at this moment." Gwendolyn felt her tears spill over onto her cheeks and leave a hot trail to her chin. "This misfortune, you must not let it defeat you." Garbo squeezed her hands more tightly.

"You saw what happened!" The words flew from Gwendolyn like shrapnel. She yanked her hands away. "Whatever teeny, tiny reputation I had in this town is ruined. There's no bouncing back from something like this. That—" she pointed back to Mercedes' house, "was—was—"

She was going to say *pornography* but couldn't bring herself to say it. Garbo's perfect face blurred and slithered.

"Nonsense."

"What?"

Garbo reached up and wiped away Gwendolyn's tears with her thumb. "What would it take to restore your confidence? And to show you that your career is not in the trash? What about a part in a movie?"

"A part . . . ?"

"A new picture is being prepared at MGM; it is called *The Women*. It will feature a cast of all females. No men in the entire picture. An inspired idea, yes? My good friend George Cukor should be directing it, but he is, of course, very busy working on *Gone with the Wind*. I am told there is to be a fashion sequence in this picture for which they will need stunning models."

Gwendolyn held her breath.

Garbo smiled her enigmatic smile. "A word from me to George, and a word from George to Hunt Stromberg, and . . ." She waved a hand as if to say, *It is a fait accompli*.

"You would do that?" Gwendolyn gasped. "For me? But why?"

The smile faded from Garbo's face. "Have you ever heard of something called karma?" she asked. "Your friend Marcus, he did a giant favor for me once. He also did one for George and I know you had a hand in coming to his rescue. I tried to repay the favor by helping Marcus, but things did not work out. I'd like to think that if I can do this—if perhaps George and I can do this for you—then a favor is repaid and balance is restored."

"But ordering a producer like Hunt Stromberg to put me in a movie—is that something you can do?"

"It had better be." The actress tried to suppress a smirk. "Otherwise, what's the point of being the Great Garbo?"

Gwendolyn searched Garbo's flawless face for deception and hidden agendas while the words *karma* and *rescue* and *women* fluttered around her mind like petals in a windstorm. She found nothing but candor and concern from this woman who was so famously detached.

She reached for Garbo's hand. "Thank you," she said.

Garbo smiled and gazed up at the moon. "No need for thanks."

"Yes," Gwendolyn insisted and pulled at the woman's hand to make her look at her again. "You've just given me the gift of hope."

CHAPTER 48

"Marcus!"

"George?"

"Are you alone?"

Marcus looked up at the magnificent portrait of Gwendolyn hanging in the deserted foyer of the Garden of Allah as he talked on the hotel's public telephone. "Yes. Why? What's going on? You sound upset."

"I got you a job. Extra work on *Gone with the Wind.*"

Marcus hadn't confessed his increasingly dire financial straits to many people. Scott Fitzgerald had warned him that it diminished one's bargaining power if potential employers knew how desperate you were for a job. But George Cukor had the ability to pick up on clues like nobody Marcus had never met. "Sounds good."

"It's for tomorrow. They're filming the Atlanta railway station scene. Hundreds of extras. It'll be good pay, because they'll need you all day." George's voice was thick with tension.

"What do you mean *they* are filming? That railway scene's got to be one of the biggest in the movie. Won't you be there?"

"Marcus, something's happened."

"George, what's going on?"

A drawn-out pause. "I've been fired."

Marcus slumped forward. "You've *what?*"

"Selznick fired me this morning. I'm no longer directing *Gone with the Wind.*"

"You can't be—*fired* you? Can he do that?"

"He's the sole producer; he can do anything he wants."

"But don't you have a contract?"

"Contract schmontract. I can't compete with Clark Gable."

"What's Gable got to do with it?" There was no response at the other end of the line for the longest time. "George? Are you there?"

"This is just my theory, but from day one, Gable hasn't been happy about being directed by a fairy. He thinks the movie – which he never wanted to do in the first place – will be thrown to the leading lady, relegating him to play second fiddle. Which is absurd, because whatever decisions I make, I make for the good of the picture. However, I strongly suspect there's been some campaigning and threatening behind my back. And I'm sure it didn't help that Selznick still holds me responsible for Kathryn's scoop. Whatever the reason, it doesn't matter – I'm out and Victor Fleming is in."

"George, this is outrageous! You can't take this lying down. Aren't you going to fight it? Aren't you mad as all hell?"

"Trust me, Marcus, there's no point." George's voice had started to wobble. "It's done and over with. Besides, if I were to be reinstated, it would make working with Gable even harder, and frankly, who needs that hassle on top of the enormous logistics of directing a movie like that? I was stomping mad when I got off the phone with Selznick, but now that I've had time to think about it, I'm more relieved than I am angry."

If Marcus hadn't been hearing this from George himself, he wouldn't have believed it. "What a rat!"

"But keep all this under your hat when you go on set – "

"George! I can't take that job. I'd feel like I was betraying you."

George chuckled – probably his first all day. "Oh, you sweet man. Please don't knock this job back on my account. If they keep you there more than eight hours – which they probably will – you'll walk away with a tidy sum. Plus, you'd be doing me a favor. I'm awfully worried about Ling-Ling."

"Who?"

"Vivien has this nickname among her intimates: Vivling. I started to call her that too, but she insisted we have our own nicknames for just the two of us. So she became Ling-Ling."

"And what are you?"

"I'm Koo-Koo Cukor. Koo-Koo and Ling-Ling, that's us! But I really am cuckoo about her. She's going to be extraordinary as Scarlett, but she's rather a fragile English rose. We spent the afternoon together going over her big train station scene that we're—that *they're* filming tomorrow—but it didn't go well. She's nervous about it and my being fired has made her terribly distraught. Nobody's answering the phone over at her place, and I have an important message for her. I need someone to pass it on. Will you do that for me?"

***

The railway station was a long building made of fake red bricks, with half a roof and a big sign painted in green and gold that said *ATLANTA*. When Marcus arrived at the set, dozens of actors in tattered uniforms were already lounging on the grass, but there was no sign of Vivien Leigh. He approached one of the extras, a grizzly man in his fifties with hair that looked like it hadn't been washed in a month. He pointed to a long grey tent three hundred yards north of them. "That's where they'll rough you up."

Half an hour later, Marcus emerged in a moth-eaten Confederate overcoat of weathered blue and chipped gold buttons. He was directed to the Blooding Tent, in which two assistants splashed, daubed, and flicked fake blood into strategic tears and holes in his uniform. At the far end of the tent, a woman handed him a card that read *B9*.

"That's your position in the grid," she explained. "But for now, just show your card at that table down yonder," she pointed to three long lines of trestle tables loaded with brown cardboard boxes, "and you'll get your boxed lunch.

We want you to have your lunch early so you're in position by noon."

His lunch was a turkey on rye with an apple and a small bottle of lukewarm juice that tasted like nothing in particular. Halfway though his sandwich, he heard someone call his name. He looked around and saw Hoppy, from the writing department at MGM, motioning for him to come join him. Hoppy was decked out in a brown soldier's jacket in even shoddier condition than Marcus'.

"I'm surprised to see you here," Marcus said. "Aren't you still writing at MGM?"

"Sure I am." Hoppy lifted his half leg and beamed. "But I'm perfect for a job like this." His stump had been bandaged and bloodied up so expertly that Marcus wondered if that was how it looked when Hoppy lost his leg for real that day in Verdun. "They're paying me double on account of my injury, but I figured it was a good way to be a part of the biggest movie of the year. Did you get your position card?" Hoppy held up his: F4. "They've put me in a prime position because I look like the real deal. Vivien is going to be walking straight past me. And that means you'll see me in the movie. You're B9? Hmm, let's see what we can do about that."

* * *

Marcus slipped the leather cuffs onto his wrists. "That's right," Hoppy said. "Now pull your hands closer to your sides. See?"

The piano wires attached to the cuffs around Marcus' wrists and ankles were connected to the limbs of the department store mannequins that lay on either side of him. The props department had dressed them in dusty tatters and rigged them so when he moved his own limbs, he'd move theirs as well. In this way, they could hire six hundred living men and get a thousand moving bodies.

Extras lay on the reddish dirt around Marcus a dozen rows deep, extending almost as far as he could see. The sun was already warm, guaranteed to bake them like cookies. He watched as the cameraman, overhead in his crane, rehearsed angles for the scene they were about to film.

Marcus let his head rest in the dirt. He was getting hot, swathed as he was in a heavy wool suit that smelled of mold and somebody else's sweat. He closed his eyes and pictured the *Strange Cargo* script lying next to the typewriter on his desk.

No wonder the thing was in no man's land. It was a tricky son of a bitch to pull off. A bunch of cutthroat prison escapees meet up with a mysterious man by the name of Cambreau—the script referred to him as Christlike—who appears out of nowhere and, one by one, helps relieve each convict of his inner torment.

The script Hugo gave him was in such bad shape that Marcus had taken it apart. He literally undid the binding and spread each sheet across the floor of his tiny room. Then he proceeded to write and rewrite, type and retype, take out characters, reset scenes, add new ones, take out unnecessary ones, add backstory, beef up the romance, and cut out repetitions.

But he still hadn't tamed it. A movie script was like a wild mustang: it must be controlled and made to submit. It had to yield to the requirements of good storytelling, the actors' public images, the studio's needs, and the demands of both the Production Code censorship board and the Catholic League of Decency. That's a lot of jockeys in the saddle. Delivering the script of the first movie Clark Gable would make after *Gone with the Wind* was something Marcus couldn't afford to fail at, but he was damned if he could conjure up the solution.

"Psssst!"

Marcus opened an eye toward Hoppy.

"Here she comes!" he whispered.

Hoppy's eyes were on a slim, dark-haired figure wearing a long, heavy dress of faded burgundy stenciled with circles and puffed at the sleeves. A dense line of dark buttons from her waist to her bust kept everything cinched into place. Her large straw hat was fastened under her chin with a green velvet strap. Walking alongside her was a grey-haired man in a tan houndstooth jacket, a collar and tie. He must be roasting in that getup, Marcus thought. The guy looked deep in thought as he fell in step beside her.

"Who's that with Vivien?" Marcus asked.

"Oh, him." Hoppy's voice dropped. "You heard what happened to Cukor? Yeah, well, that's his replacement."

Marcus watched a fellow with a camera lens hung around his neck pull Fleming aside. Vivien hesitated at first, then continued on alone. Marcus had told George he doubted he could get close to the star of the picture—and here she was walking toward him. It was now or never. When she reached the throng of extras, Marcus got to his feet.

"Ling-Ling!"

Vivien spun around. She spotted him and frowned.

"Hey, you!" someone called out behind Marcus. "Get on the ground. We're about to start shooting."

Vivien picked her way through the extras until she was standing in front of him. It looked like an effort for her to haul herself around in the heavy dress. Her face was thin and pale, but her eyes were a magnificent shade of green. The only ones that could compare, Marcus thought, were Gwendolyn's.

"Did you say what I think you said?" she asked in her Southern accent.

"It is Ling-Ling, isn't it?"

"Miss Leigh!" Fleming scolded from the sidelines.

Vivien waved at him but didn't turn around. "You could only have heard that name from one person," she said.

"Koo-Koo sent me."

Vivien's mouth dropped open and her eyes glazed over. "I miss my Koo-Koo so very much." She jutted the back of her head in Fleming's direction. "That one is as opposite to George as a man could possibly be."

"That bad, huh?"

"MISS LEIGH! WHEN YOU ARE READY?"

She dropped out of the drawl into her own clipped British accent. "The problem with Mr. Fleming is that he's Lucifer incarnate, but thinks he's God."

"I have a message from Koo-Koo."

"You do?"

"It's about your reaction as you leave the railway station. He wants you to think about your time in India. Think about how you'd feel if you got off the ship and all that grinding, overwhelming poverty slapped you in the face for the first time."

Her eyes widened in relief. "Oh my goodness, yes, that's absolutely it. I was having a devil of a time with that yesterday. Thank you so very, very much—May I ask your name?"

Marcus introduced himself and she broke into a smile and grabbed him by the hand. Even with her unkempt hair and disheveled costume, the woman was gorgeous.

Vivien still had her back to Fleming, so she didn't know he'd sent a hairdresser over to fetch her. "You'd better get going," Marcus told her. "God beckons."

She found her mark on the edge of the sea of wounded soldiers while Fleming took a seat on the camera platform. A fifty-foot crane attached to a truck the size of a military tank lifted him high above the crowd.

"Look at him up there," Hoppy sneered. "Thinks he's God."

"That's what Vivien said."

"You know her?"

"No. I was just asked to pass on a message."

Hoppy looked back at Fleming. "It ticks me off that Selznick would fire Cukor like that."

Marcus wondered if George was really okay with getting fired or if he was just putting up a front. It must have left a bruise on his ego the size of a punching bag.

The squad of assistant directors fanned out among the extras, shouting that they were ready for a take and to please pay attention to Mr. Fleming when he got on the P.A. system.

The speakers spaced out around the field crackled to life when Fleming's voice boomed out across the crowd, deep and authoritative as a Hemingway character. "Gentlemen. You are badly wounded, desperately hungry, writhing in pain, and most of you are about to die. You are desperate for help from wherever you can find it. Those of you close to where Miss Leigh is about to walk, I want you to call out to her, reach up and get her to notice you. You need water, food, something to dull the pain. You need a doctor, a nurse, a blanket, medicine. Or perhaps just some comfort before you kick the bucket."

The tank roared to life and inched its way toward Vivien, stopping when Fleming's camera platform was a dozen feet away from her. The crane hovered above Marcus like a steel cloud.

Marcus looked up. The sun hung over Fleming's shoulder, lighting him from behind. He'd taken off his jacket and rolled up the sleeves of his white shirt. With his intense concentration, he looked like something Raphael might paint if he was around. "You really do look like God," Marcus said to himself.

"And . . . action!"

The extras started to squirm and moan as Vivien looked around and stepped toward the first line of men in the dirt; they reached up to her, pleading for water and help. She passed two men hauling a soldier in a stretcher and asked, "Have you seen the doctor?" She strode past them, calling, "Doctor? Doctor?"

Fleming's camera platform slowly pulled back, lifting him higher and higher to slowly take in the horrific scene of human carnage until he was a hundred feet in the air.

When she reached the other side, Fleming's voice came over the P.A. system. "Cut!"

Marcus sat up and looked at him again. The sun was on him now, drenching him in hazy California afternoon light.

"That's it!" Marcus cried out loud. "He really is Christ!"

His mind started racing. In *Strange Cargo*, Cambreau was described as highly spiritual—Christlike—but, Marcus realized in a surge of inspiration, the story wasn't working because the character was undefined. None of the screenwriters were clear on who Cambreau was, so the audience wasn't either.

I've done it! I've cracked it! He slapped the dirt, and the two dummies attached to him did the same. Little brown clouds of dust puffed up around him.

Hoppy sat up and looked from Fleming to Marcus. "Are you nuts?" he said. "You must have sunstroke."

"No, not Fleming," Marcus said. "I'm working on a—"

But he caught himself.

Oh, no, no, no, he told himself. Not this time. This is where you start to play it smart.

CHAPTER 49

"There you are!"

Kathryn broke away from the crowd that was milling around inside MGM's enormous soundstage and held her arms out to embrace her friends. "Look at you two! Both fresh from signing your MGM contracts!" She released them and made gimme-gimme motions with her hands. "Come on. Show me!"

Marcus pulled a half dozen papers out of his jacket pocket. They were neatly stapled together and topped with a cover letter embossed with MGM's fancy lion.

Kathryn scanned the letter confirming Marcus' new contract. She gasped when she got to the fourth paragraph. "They offered you a three-picture deal?"

Marcus nodded. "Keep reading."

She looked at his contract again. "They're paying you three hundred and fifty a week to write *Strange Cargo*?"

Marcus was still nodding.

She pulled him into a hug and squeezed him hard as she could. "I'm so happy for you I could cry."

"Beat you to it," he whispered back.

"And you," she said, turning to Gwendolyn. "Show me yours."

Gwendolyn smiled and shook her head. "Tain't nothing compared to Marcus' big deal. It's just two sheets of legalese, and I'll probably be on-screen for maybe a whole minute if I'm lucky."

"Get a load of Miss Casual," Marcus said. "Tain't nothin'. The hell it is. You'll be on-screen! And about time, too."

"That part is exciting, sure, but my piddling little contract's nothing to get excited about."

Kathryn laid out her hand. "This is a big step for you – for both of you – and we want to see the contract that makes it possible."

There was something odd about the way Gwendolyn pulled the contract out of her handbag. She handed it over to Kathryn. "Have they started serving the drinks yet? I'm parched beyond endurance."

"Gwennie," Kathryn said, "it says here that your agent is Eldon Laird."

Gwendolyn continued to scan the vast soundstage. "Uh-huh."

"Did you tell MGM he's your agent?" Marcus asked. "These contracts are legally binding, honey. If anything goes wrong, they can charge you with fraud."

"I wasn't lying," Gwendolyn admitted, somewhat sheepishly.

"What aren't you telling us?"

"Well, okay then. I wasn't going to tell you both because it's no big deal – "

"After what he did to you?"

"Let me explain! He came up to me at work last week. He was all contrite and repentant over what happened."

"Oh, I'll just bet he was."

"No, really, he was. Anyway, we got to talking and he said that if he could ever make it up to me, he would love the chance to do it. Especially, he said, movie studio contracts. You don't want to mess around with those on your own. So I said, as a matter of fact, I'm about to sign one. He seemed very pleased for me. No, really, he did. I told him it was hardly worth his while, it's just a glorified walk-on, but he insisted. So I sent it to him and he ended up getting me double the pay MGM were offering."

Marcus shook his head. "I hope you didn't agree to anything—"

"*And* I get to keep the outfit. He did me a favor," Gwendolyn insisted. "And that was all he did. He actually seemed ashamed of himself. Haven't you guys ever heard of karma? He did me a wrong and now he's done me a right. Balance has been restored, and no, he didn't ask for and I didn't agree to anything more. Can we please now change the subject?"

She's right, Kathryn decided. You need to let Gwennie manage her career whichever way she sees fit and focus on reviving your own.

She looked down at the bright yellow path beneath their feet. "What is this?"

"It's the Yellow Brick Road," Marcus replied.

"It's the road Dorothy takes to go see the Wizard of Oz," Gwendolyn said. "Surely you read the book?"

Kathryn shook her head. Her childhood reading had consisted largely of passages from plays her mother deemed suitable for auditions. There was no time—or money—for "silly kids' books" like *The Wizard of Oz*. Since then she'd tried to make up for it, but there were some books that had simply passed her by.

"You missed out on a good one," Gwendolyn exclaimed. "I can't wait to see this!"

"After I signed my contract, Taggert took me over to the commissary for a late celebratory lunch," Marcus said. "They were playing some of the music over the loudspeakers, and there's this one ballad, *Over the Rainbow*, that Judy Garland sings. Apparently, the front office wants it taken out, but I hope they don't. It's a lovely tune and Judy sings the heck out of it. Look, there she is!"

A small figure in a blue-and-white-checked pinafore over a short-sleeved cream blouse appeared on the far side of the set. Her chocolate-brown hair was braided around her ears and allowed to flop in front of her shoulders in loose curls. She was chatting with a tall older woman whose green face paint was starting to wear off in patches. They were holding each other's hands and laughing over something that made Judy double over. A tall, greying gentleman joined them. Kathryn glanced over at Marcus in time to see his face darken.

"That's Victor Fleming," Marcus said, his voice thick and low.

Victor Fleming was the whole reason they were there. He'd been directing *The Wizard of Oz*—and doing a fine job, by all reports, protecting Judy and giving her room to bloom into her character. But he'd been drafted when things came to a head over at *Gone with the Wind*. Although it was a couple of weeks after the fact, tonight's on-set party was to officially farewell Fleming and welcome the picture's new director, King Vidor.

Kathryn nudged Marcus. "Don't be like that," she scolded him. "You told me yourself, George seems fine. I'm sure he appreciates your devotion, but what's done is done." That was one of the things Kathryn loved so much about her dear friend: his leonine loyalty. But sometimes, like all extreme emotions, it could be misplaced. "And besides," she added, "you owe him your inspiration for solving *Strange Cargo*."

She turned her attention to the set. A village of round wooden huts slathered in white stucco and topped with a thatched roof of brown sticks stood in a wide semicircle around them. The huts themselves seemed extraordinarily small; they couldn't have been more than ten feet across. She pointed to a cluster of them among a forest of paper and cellophane sunflowers. "What are these things? Playhouses?"

"Good God," Marcus laughed, "you really don't know this story, do you? This is the Munchkin village, where the twister sets Dorothy's house down." He pointed to a rickety, weathered house dumped onto the far left of the set. "MGM's imported just about every midget performer in the country to play them. Taggert tells me their costumes are wild!"

It was nice to see Marcus smile. If her own fortunes could turn around the way his had, she'd be smiling, too. She'd been able to find ways around Louella's blackballing at first, but as time dragged on, her contacts had either dried up or were scared off and she'd found herself in Siberia, where interviews and insider tips grew sparsely. When she'd received an invitation to this party, she wondered if some P.R. flunky hadn't been told that she was on the no-no list. Then she received a huge basket of flowers from Joan Crawford with a puzzling card: *Payback can make such strange cargo.*

Kathryn and Joan had become friendly after Kathryn managed to talk Mayer into securing her a screen test for Scarlett. Everyone knew she wasn't right for it, but it was a prestige thing that yielded scads of publicity for all concerned.

When Kathryn heard the name of Marcus' movie and that Joan was being considered for the female lead, the card's inscription made sense. This was a first step out of Siberia, and Kathryn was grateful for it. With Marcus back at MGM and Gwendolyn getting her break, it looked like President Roosevelt was right—happy days were here again. There was only one other person Kathryn wished could be here: Roy.

They hadn't slept together until after his burns had healed, but seven hospital visits in four weeks was more than enough to rekindle the spark. Their romance flourished hesitantly at first, from one meeting a week to two, then escalating to three if the opportunity permitted. She knew she shouldn't—he probably did, too—but it was so awfully cold in Siberia and, she liked to remind herself, a girl needs to know she's not alone.

Her mind returned to a post-coital smoke they shared last week. From out of nowhere he'd said, "You could have retaliated by throwing that tomato juice all over Louella, but you didn't. You refused to be pulled down to her level. Isn't it possible your mother would be proud of that?"

Kathryn wasn't sure how to broach the subject of that appalling scene at Bullock's—how on earth could she ever show her face in that place again?—and so she hadn't spoken to her mother at all since then. She assumed that Francine sided with her bridge-playing best friend and blamed Kathryn for the whole unfortunate episode. The fact that Roy would think the opposite told Kathryn that getting involved with him again was a good thing, and Mr. Roy Quinn was a good guy—even if he was married.

A loud click shot through the soundstage. "Could I have everyone's attention, please?"

A tall chap with a receding hairline and a megaphone was standing on a crate next to a long wooden table. "We have something very special that we would love to share with all of you." Kathryn and Marcus moved closer and saw an enormous cake on the table. It was at least two feet wide and had six-inch-tall frosting replicas of Dorothy Gale and Scarlett O'Hara in their trademark costumes: a blue pinafore and a huge white hoop skirt. "If you'll gather around, I promise the speech will be short and the cake will be sweet."

Word was leaking out that Vivien Leigh was doing a marvelous job, so Kathryn was forced to face the fact that she was only as good as her last story. Without a supply of stories from Ida Koverman and the cats, she was only going to lose ground if she didn't come up with something new and exciting . . . and soon.

As the crowd started to gather, she looked around.

"Where did Gwendolyn get to?" she asked Marcus.

"She went to powder her nose," he said, "but knowing her, she's probably already halfway to the costume department."

"Hello, everybody," the guy with the megaphone said. "My name is Al Shenberg and I'm the assistant director on *Wizard of Oz*." You're also Louis B. Mayer's nephew, Kathryn thought. Maybe I could corner you for an inside scoop on what else MGM has bubbling away for Judy. "As you're no doubt aware, this party is well overdue, but better late than never. It is my reluctant duty to officially say goodbye to our good friend Victor Fleming . . ."

As the guy rambled on about Fleming's virtues, Kathryn surveyed the crowd. It had been her experience that leads popped up from the unlikeliest sources.

She spotted a slightly batty-looking woman in her early fifties picking her way through the crowd toward her. She had that too-much-makeup look of a carefully preserved actress and was wearing the most ridiculous hat Kathryn had ever seen. It was black straw, and sported a huge brim and enormous gobs of white and grey feathers piled up at least six or seven inches. A clump of orange feathers stuck out the back like a rudder.

Kathryn was still watching the hat when its wearer drew alongside her and turned to face her, ignoring Mayer's nephew altogether. "Do you think it's too much?" she asked. "Frankly, I've never met a hat I didn't like. I've got dozens of them. This is my newest one, but do you think it's apropos for a daytime party?"

It looks like a dyspeptic dodo bird crapped on your head, Kathryn thought. "I can't honestly say it's anything I'd wear."

The woman laughed. "It's not about taste, my dear. It's about being noticed and remembered, and creating a lasting impression." She thrust her hand toward Kathryn. "I'm Hedda Hopper, with the *Los Angeles Times*." Kathryn was deliberately slow to take the woman's hand. She shook it lightly and wondered if Hedda knew she was Kathryn's replacement. "You're Kathryn Massey, aren't you?"

"Yes, I am."

"I've long wanted to meet you. Louella and I used to be quite good chums. Back when I was a working actress, she'd mention me in her column from time to time. But things have a habit of changing, don't they?"

Kathryn looked around for Marcus and Gwendolyn. They were huddled together by the dilapidated house at the end of the set with plates of cake in their hands. She tried to catch their eye and signal she needed help. The last thing she wanted was to be stuck with this vituperative bitch. Good taste and decorum rarely made an appearance in Hedda's columns, which was why they were required daily reading by every last man and his valet in Hollywood. But neither Marcus nor Gwendolyn was looking in her direction.

"You know, I was thinking the same thing just this morning," Kathryn said.

"The same thing as what?"

"About things changing."

Hedda let out a hollow laugh. "That's part of the excitement of this town, I've always thought. The sons of janitors and the daughters of laundresses can become idols overnight. They go from earning twelve dollars a month to five hundred a week just because they've got the right look."

Kathryn pulled her patent leather handbag off her arm and made a show of rifling through it. "Oh, shoot!" she said. "I've done it again." Without giving Hedda a chance to respond, she continued, "I have such an awful habit of leaving lipsticks behind. Max Factor just sent one to me, signed a note himself asking me what I thought of it. Did you know he's opening a salon on Highland? Right around the corner from Grauman's." She could see her lipstick in her bag; it wasn't Max Factor at all. She wasn't even sure Max Factor made lipstick. "I've probably left it in the ladies' room." Hedda's mouth flattened. She went to say something but Kathryn parried. "I'm so glad you introduced yourself. We should have met long before now. No doubt we'll be bumping into each other. Bye, now!"

Kathryn propelled herself toward Marcus and Gwendolyn, who were still laughing at something.

"Who was that in the God-awful sombrero?" Gwendolyn asked.

Kathryn rolled her eyes. "Hedda Hopper, and she's every bit as dreadful as her columns. Say, what have you two been laughing at?"

"You'll think we're idiots," Marcus said, "but we've been killing ourselves trying to think of the name of the guy who did that radio play."

Gwendolyn said, "You know, the one that gave me the willies so bad I ran out into the Garden and right into Scott Fitzgerald."

"You mean Orson Welles?"

Marcus and Gwendolyn looked at each other with eyes wide as buttons. "That's it," Gwendolyn said.

"Why are you talking about him?"

"I just overheard a couple of women in the bathroom. One of them has a sister in casting over at RKO, and she said Orson Welles is coming to Hollywood and RKO is going to offer him carte blanche."

Marcus scoffed. "Nobody gets carte blanche. Especially someone who's never made a picture before. RKO would be out of their minds. That can't be right."

"I'm just telling you what I heard."

"I'll believe *that* when it starts raining frogs on Melrose."

"Orson Welles is practically King Midas," Kathryn countered. "If he does as well with his first movie as he did when he put *Macbeth* on stage and *War of the Worlds* on the radio, he'll probably change Hollywood."

"I don't know," Marcus said. "Wasn't he the one behind *The Cradle Will Rock,* where they got locked out of the theater and Welles moved it and got the cast to perform it from the audience because the government had threatened to arrest any performer who appeared onstage?" Marcus shook his head. "That one wasn't such a huge success."

Kathryn grabbed Marcus by the arm. "That was *The Cradle Will Rock*? Orson Welles directed that?"

Kathryn snapped shut her gaping mouth. *The Cradle Will Rock* . . . Francine brought that up at Bullock's Wilshire before Louella arrived and started throwing food around like an epileptic dervish. But what was it Francine had said?

"Ladies and gentlemen!" The assistant director was back on his wooden box with his megaphone again. "We have a real treat for you. Our darling Judy has agreed to give us an impromptu rendition of 'Ding-Dong! The Witch Is Dead.' Won't you please gather around? This song is a humdinger!"

Parties like these were a studio's chance to impress people like Kathryn with their next big thing. The P.R. department was already going all out promoting this movie, and it was clear they were grooming Judy for stardom. Even though she was sixteen and floating vaguely around the early teens for this movie, she was growing into a major talent and the studio knew it.

Judy replaced the assistant director on his upturned wooden box. "This is unrehearsed and a cappella," she said with a chuckle in her voice, "so bear with me."

As the crowd gathered closer around Judy, Kathryn hung back to think about her mother's comment.

"Ding, dong, the witch is dead!" Judy sang in a clear, melodic voice. It was a lively tune, and instantly memorable. Kathryn could imagine how full it would sound backed by MGM's orchestra and piped through those huge speakers at Grauman's Chinese.

Wicked witch? *Wicked witch!*

Kathryn and her mother had been talking about Louella, a wicked witch if she'd ever seen one, when Francine mentioned that she and her coworkers had been joking about *The Cradle Will Rock*. When Kathryn questioned her, she'd started to say something, then cut herself off.

Nobody knows it yet but he's going to be staying –

The rush of realization made Kathryn's body quiver.

Nobody knows it yet but he's going to be staying with us. Orson Welles would be staying at the Marmont and no one else had the slightest clue. Kathryn Massey of the *Hollywood Reporter* had just found her yellow brick road.

A thunderous round of applause brought her back to the present and she found Marcus and Gwendolyn staring at her.

"What's up with you?" Marcus asked. "You look like Lady Godiva about to open her closet."

Kathryn couldn't help the smile that slithered onto her face. "How's that cake? Any good?"

"Yes," Marcus said, "it's real good. You want some?"

Kathryn looked at her earnest, persistent Marcus and her brave, ambitious Gwendolyn.

Do I want some? she thought.

No, I want it all.

THE END

Coming soon . . .

Book Three of the *Garden of Allah* novels

Citizen Hollywood

It's 1939 – Orson Welles, the *enfant terrible* of New York, is coming to Hollywood to make his first movie. Tinsel City is agog! Can he even direct a movie? What will it be about? Will he scandalize the West Coast the way he's shocked the East Coast? And, more importantly, who will he bed first and does he kiss-and-tell?

ACKNOWLEDGMENTS

Heartfelt thanks to the following, who helped shape this book:

My editor, Meghan Pinson, for her dedication, perseverance, guidance, and—above all—humor.

My cover designer, Dan Yeager at Nu-Image Design who thinks in images the way I think in words.

My advance readers, Bob Molinari, Jaye Manus, Philip Mershon, Vince Hans and Gene Strange for their invaluable time, insight, feedback, and advice in shaping this novel.

www.MartinTurnbull.com

Facebook: GardenOfAllahNovels
Twitter: @TurnbullMartin
Blog: martinturnbull.wordpress.com

CPSIA information can be obtained at www.ICGtesting.com
Printed in the USA
LVOW08s1546230813

349370LV00002B/155/P

9 781480 044777